BOOKS BY WILL MURRAY

Doc Savage: Skull Island
Tarzan: Return to Pal-ul-don
King Kong vs. Tarzan
The Spider: The Doom Legion
Wordslingers: an Epitaph for the Western
Forever After: An Inspired Story

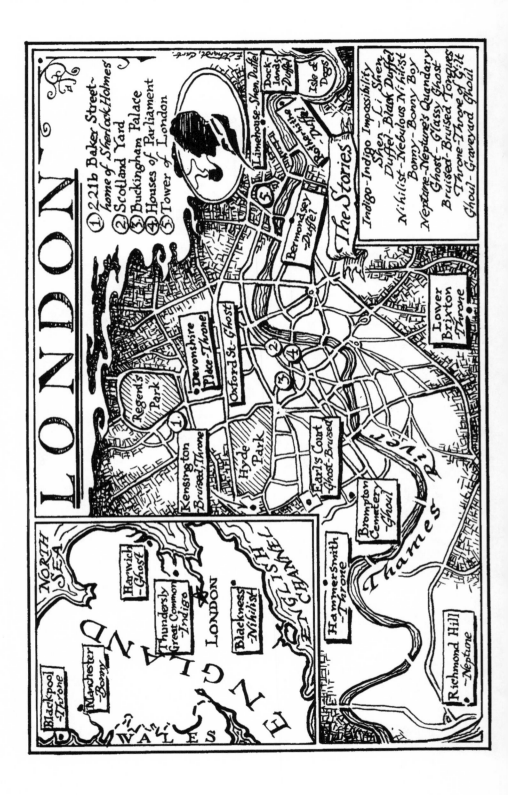

LONDON

① 221b Baker Street-
   home of Sherlock Holmes
② Scotland Yard
③ Buckingham Palace
④ Houses of Parliament
⑤ Tower of London

The Stories

Indigo – Indigo Impossibility
Shen – Li Shen
Duffel – Blank Duffel
Nihilist – Nebulous Nihilist
Bonny – Bonny Boy
Neptune – Neptune's Quandary
Ghost – Glassy Ghost
Bruised – Bruised Torques
Throne – Throne of Silt
Ghoul – Graveyard Ghoul

Bermondsey – Duffel

Devonshire Place – Throne

Oxford St. – Ghost

Regent's Park

Kensington – Bruised Throne

Hyde Park

Earl's Court – Ghost-Bruised

Brompton Cemetery – Ghoul

Limehouse – Shen, Duffel

Ratcliff Highway – Duffel

Dock-lands – Duffel

Isle of Dogs

Lower Brixton – Throne

Thames River

NORTH SEA

ENGLAND

WALES

Blackpool – Throne

Manchester – Bonny

Harwich – Ghost

Thunderley Great Common – Indigo

Blackness – Nihilist

LONDON

ENGLISH CHANNEL

Hammersmith – Throne

Richmond Hill – Neptune

THE **WILD ADVENTURES** OF

SHERLOCK HOLMES

WILL MURRAY

VOLUME **ONE**

Cover by **Joe DeVito**

ALTUS PRESS ○ 2020

THANKS TO
Brian Belanger, Derrick Belanger, Gary Buckingham,
Dafydd Neal Dyer, Joe Gentile, David Marcum, and Matthew Moring.

Series Editor: Ray Riethmeier

PUBLISHING HISTORY
All stories previously published in MX Sherlock Holmes anthologies, with
the exception of "The Adventure of the Nebulous Nihilist" and "The Enigma
of Neptune's Quandary," which appeared in *Sherlock Holmes: The Crossover
Casebook* and *The Irregular Adventures of Sherlock Holmes*, respectively.

DESIGNED BY
Matthew Moring

MAP OF ENGLAND BY
Jason C. Eckhardt

First edition—June 2020

Like us on Facebook: "The Wild Adventures of Sherlock Holmes"

www.adventuresinbronze.com

For Sir Arthur Conan Doyle,

without whom mystery fiction would be
so different as to be unrecognizable...

TABLE OF CONTENTS

INTRODUCTION

A S SOMEONE BEST known for writing revival stories featuring vintage pulp magazine heroes such as Doc Savage, The Shadow, the Spider, Tarzan of the Apes, etc., Sherlock Holmes is a little out of my preferred métier. This despite the fact that many of those classic characters were directly inspired by the great detective.

I first read Arthur Conan Doyle in high school, or perhaps a little before. The stories I recall, such as "Silver Blaze," came from *The Memoirs of Sherlock Holmes*. But I don't recall now if I read that book, or simply selected stories from an anthology.

In the early 1970s, I purchased a box set of the Berkeley Books paperback editions with the wonderful and evocative covers by William Teason. They sat high on a bookshelf, untouched and unread until 2010, when Moonstone Books asked me to contribute to their *Sherlock Holmes: The Crossovers Casebook* volume. The idea was to team Doyle's immortal sleuth with other famous characters from Victorian literature.

That was when I finally plunged into the exploits of Sherlock Holmes in earnest. For my story, "The Adventure of the Nebulous Nihilist," I opted not to utilize a fictitious character, but instead employed Colonel Richard Henry Savage, the 19th century inspiration for both Doc Savage and Richard Henry Benson, The Avenger. I would have much preferred to write a straight Sherlock Holmes story, but this was the assignment. Resorting to a historic person was my workaround.

I was happy with the story. But I made a bonehead mistake, setting the tale during the Great Hiatus. Oh well, Doyle had made the same error once. I've corrected the date for this appearance, and modified the title, which I fear communicated too much in advance of the story's solution.

At this point, I began reading my way through the Holmes Canon, rather randomly, I must confess. I would pick up a volume and begin a story whose title intrigued me. If it grabbed my interest, I kept reading. If not, invariably I found one that did. Eventually, I read every short story and most of the longer tales. I've never read a Sherlock Holmes adventure that did not repay the modest effort. I enjoyed them all.

Three years later, Christopher Sequeira invited me to contribute to *Sherlock Holmes and Doctor Was Not,* yet another crossover compilation, this time replacing John H. Watson with *other* doctors. I chose H.P. Lovecraft's morbid Dr. Herbert West for my tale, "The Adventure of the Reckless Resurrectionist." I enjoyed writing it and believe it to be one of my best Holmes efforts, but once again I lamented the fact that I wasn't writing a traditional tale of Holmes and Watson.

It took a great many years until this book was published, and by that time David Marcum had reached out to me to contribute to the MX Sherlock Holmes anthologies. At long last, I was able to write a straight Sherlock Holmes story.

"The Adventure of the Glassy Ghost" was my contribution. A few months later, David asked me to do another. I jumped on the opportunity. It quickly became a habit as more anthologies appeared and my imaginative skills were challenged.

Over the course of 2017 through 2020, I produced a steady stream of nearly twenty Sherlock Holmes stories. Most of these appeared in expensive anthologies, so I thought collecting several of them would allow my readers to enjoy them in one volume.

As I pen these words, I have another seven or eight Sherlock

Holmes stories awaiting publication. If readers like this volume, I will assemble the rest in a second volume.

And the way things are going, by that time I may have written sufficient additional stories for a *third* volume of the Wild Adventures of Sherlock Holmes.

—Will Murray

THE WILD ADVENTURE OF
THE INDIGO IMPOSSIBILITY

I T WA S A beastly night in London.
A driving rain lashed the city, smothering the gas-lamps and hammering the roofs of home and hotel alike.

The ride from Paddington Station to 221b Baker Street was an exercise in misery. Raindrops pummeled me as I sat alone in the hansom cab as it jounced through the nearly deserted streets, for the hour was late and sensible people had long before claimed their beds.

I shivered in my waterproof and wondered how the cabman could stave off a cold, riding about in such inclement weather.

Presently, with a scraping of wheels against curbing, we drew up to the apartments of Sherlock Holmes and myself. I steeled myself before alighting and rushed to the front door, clutching my Gladstone bag.

I had been on holiday in Northumberland, but now I was home. It was the third of May in the year 1886.

After he deposited my luggage at the doorstep, I paid the driver and used my house key to enter, immediately doffing my soaked waterproof. It lacked but a quarter-hour to midnight.

The mellow light coming from the first-floor window was a surprise, so I was not taken aback when I found Sherlock Holmes seated in his most comfortable chair, puffing on a briar and staring off into space. He might have been a wizard attempting to divine the swirls of tobacco smoke that climbed to the plaster ceiling. Certainly his eyes were dreamy, and his aquiline face possessed an ascetic cast.

Despite my having trooped loudly up the stairs, Holmes took no notice of me when I entered the sitting room.

"Well, good evening, Holmes," I said by way of greeting.

My friend snapped out of his dreamy reverie, and his sharp eyes came into focus in his hawk-like face. Rather than welcoming me home, Holmes asked, "Have you been reading about the sensation in Essex County?"

"I have not."

"In Thundersley. They are calling it 'The Indigo Impossibility.'"

"And what may I inquire is meant by *it?*"

"Why, the Impossibility, of course. It is really rather extraordinary, Watson. Had I not expected you tonight, I already would have arrived in Thundersley to investigate the matter."

Dropping wearily into a chair opposite Holmes, I sighed. "Having come all this way in a beastly rain, I fear I have no appetite for immediate trouble."

"The morning will do," Holmes said thinly.

"You presume to assume that I am free to follow you into the heart of this impossibility."

"The Impossibility is not an event, but a thing. And I presume nothing, my dear Watson. I invite you to accompany me—if you are so inclined," he added in a voice as thin as the smoke emerging with it.

"What is this impossibility?" I asked wearily, for I had no energy for my friend's investigative enthusiasms on this rain-soaked evening. I would have sought my bed forthwith, but common courtesy forebode such rudeness.

"It is a hitherto-unknown creature that should not exist, yet it does. Worse for the rustic inhabitants of Thundersley, Watson, it slays. And in the most savage manner."

"I fear I still do not comprehend the nature of this impossibility," I admitted.

"Nor do I," returned Holmes. "And that is the intriguing aspect of the matter. All that is known is that the creature is a deep indigo color and that it walks upon two legs, leaving foot tracks like great horned talons, of which it possesses three in number."

"A creature, is it? That *is* intriguing."

"A creature undiscovered by modern naturalists, it seems. One sufficiently formidable to disembowel a man with a single stroke of its claws."

Now I feared that I would never get my proper rest, for Holmes had captured my complete interest.

"I should like to read these newspaper accounts."

Gesturing with his pipe stem to a stack of London newspapers, Holmes murmured, "Help yourself, my good fellow."

Naturally, I selected *The Times* to begin with.

Surprisingly, the account was sensational in its details, if staid in the telling. Over several days, a creature standing almost as tall as the average man had been spied in a grove that in pagan times had been dedicated to the thunder god, Thunor, whom we today call Thor. This was in Thundersley, specifically at a place called Thundersley Great Common. The unknown creature stood upright and was never clearly seen, except that its hide was an amazing indigo hue, unknown in any animal dwelling in the British Isles.

On the third day after it was first encountered, a man named Andrew Carrick had been discovered in the vicinity of this village, disemboweled in the most grisly manner. Leading away from the corpse were the bloody tracks of a creature possessing three sharp talons. It was evident that one of the massive talons had raked the man's stomach open with a slash that disgorged its organic contents.

"I have ranged from London to Afghanistan," I remarked as I put down the paper. "I have never heard of such a creature."

"Surely not."

"I beg your pardon?"

"Have you never read of the dinosaurs?"

"You full well know that I have," I snapped with a bit of impatience that I could barely control. "But such creatures are believed to be long extinct."

"Yet something like a dinosaur eviscerated Andrew Carrick. And the manner in which he was slain fits up with no creature known in the present day."

"Are you stating boldly that a dinosaur is loose in Essex?"

"It is difficult to imagine such a thing," admitted Holmes. "For if there is one dinosaur, there must be others. Biological organisms do not exist in isolation. For there to be one, there must have been at least two others, a male and female parent, and these perforce, should have had their own antecedents, if not other offspring of their own."

"Now you stretch my credulity to the breaking point, Holmes. I cannot imagine such a large and distinctly garish creature to be populating a wood so close to London."

"Nor can I," Holmes allowed. "Neither can the authorities. That is why the newspapers have dubbed it an Impossibility."

"Have you been called into the matter?"

"Not as yet. No doubt this eventually will be the case. But I choose not to await the inevitable call. I propose to train to Thundersley in the morning in order to take the measure of this monster, as it were. If you care to accompany me, I would be pleased to have you. But if you cannot, I understand. Fully."

"I had planned to resume my medical duties after a day of recuperation from my trip."

"You can recuperate in Thundersley as well as in London."

"If that is your way of insisting that I accompany you, I will consider it."

"Tut-tut, Watson. I insist upon nothing. I am merely offering you an intriguing opportunity. I might add that your medical skills and insight would be useful."

"A veterinarian might be more suitable to your needs," I retorted abruptly, for my eyes were growing intolerably heavy of lid, and a warm comforter appealed to me more than strong food and drink at this late hour.

"I will sleep upon it," I said, standing up.

"I will wake you at six in the a.m., then," said Holmes dryly.

"By Jove! That allows me only five hours of sleep. I do not think that I can do it."

"Would seven suit you, then?"

"If I am awake at that hour," I said firmly, "I will so inform you. Now if you will be good enough to excuse me, I am late to bed."

"Until tomorrow," said Holmes, tilting his head back and resuming his study of the swirling smoke that his briar produced. The focus went out of his eyes and his face became a mask, like a study of an American Indian communing with his wiser ancestors.

As I sought much-needed sleep, I reflected that Sherlock Holmes did not have to worry about awakening in time to catch a morning train. I did not expect him to do anything other than sit in the chair and apply his tremendous mental powers to the problem of the impossible indigo creature that had seized his vibrant imagination.

I DO NOT clearly recall the morning train ride to Thundersley, for I slept through much of it.

Upon our arrival, I awoke with a start, peered about and was momentarily taken aback to find myself aboard a moving train.

"Did you sleep well?" asked Holmes.

"My word!" I muttered. "I don't clearly recall leaving my bed."

"You were rather logy at the time," observed Holmes. "In fact, you commenced drowsing directly upon our departing Fenchurch Street Station."

"Ah, yes. It is coming back to me. But I feel as if I am in a foggy dream."

"Here is Benfleet Station. Come, come. Let us hope that we aren't disembarking upon a nightmare," suggested Holmes ominously.

We exited the car and sought a hansom cab among the few loitering at the station.

As we stepped aboard a waiting cab, the driver took Holmes's bag and remarked, "What ho! This is rather heavy."

"Mind that you do not drop it, driver," Holmes told the man. Addressing me, he added, "I have come fully prepared. I also took the liberty of dropping your old service revolver into your bag. We may need both before our tour is over."

"Given the frightful descriptions of this Indigo Impossibility," I returned, "I would more describe our day's calendar as in the manner of the hunt."

"Yes, I suppose that it is. But a hunt for what?"

The driver urged his steed onward, and we were soon clicking along the hilly vista and up the slope of Bread and Cheese Hill towards the village center. The cool air was sweet with the scent of heather, which grew profusely hereabouts. A pungent sea breeze drifted in from the estuary to the south.

Apparently feeling deprived of suitable companionship over my slumberous disposition, Sherlock Holmes opened up a lively conversation.

"Watson, tell me: What do you know of the taxonomic order of *Dinosauria?*"

"The term means 'great lizard,' of course. But I believe that you are the expert here, Holmes. I would rather you discourse upon the subject, my brain being in a bit of a morning fog."

"The term was first proposed by the anatomist Sir Richard Owen in 1841," he said. "You may remember that the discovery of the earliest fossil bones was the occasion of great controversy, which raged for years. Prior to Owen, unusual bones that could not be classified were often mistaken for things that they were not. Back in 1802, certain curious fossil tracks unearthed in South Hadley, Massachusetts, were thought to be the remnants of a gigantic raven dating back to the time of Noah's ark, and possibly the very same one released from that improbable vessel of legend, which, as you will recall, friend Watson, never returned. It was not, of course. The Arabian Roc was another mythical creature believed to have deposited their dry bones here and there. In central China, the natives grind up what they believe to be dragon bones into medicinal powders. They are mistaken, of course. All were fossil ossifications of various dinosaurs."

"As I recall," I asserted, "some years elapsed before these mysterious bones were recognized as those of lizards of tremendous size and unimaginable configuration."

"You are very nearly correct. But it was Sir Richard who determined that they were neither avian nor saurian, but belonged to an entirely new group of animals he dubbed *Dinosauria*. Despite his sound determinations, there are those still who dispute his findings."

As we rattled along, I hugged my ulster closer to me. Mercifully, it wasn't raining, but the morning was coolish. I didn't mind this very much, remembering the inclement night before. I glanced warily towards the clouds, and they didn't promise rain, but neither did they deny the possibility.

Turning to Holmes, I inquired, "What species of dinosaur do you suppose this Indigo Impossibility to be?"

"I haven't arrived at any preliminary determination. Perhaps, once I discover its foot marks or other spoor, I will have sufficient data to posit possibilities. For the moment, I prefer not to jump to conclusions, sound or otherwise."

"A wise course of action, no doubt."

"I will point out that among the dinosaurs known to have lived in the British Isles in prehistoric times, the meager descriptions of the Indigo Impossibility fit none of them."

"Yet you don't refuse outright to accept the possibility of a survival from an older age abroad in Thundersley?" I pressed.

"For many reasons, I think it improbable."

"The dinosaur theory is therefore all but ruled out, then?"

"I rule nothing out!" snapped Holmes. "We stand barely on the threshold of our investigation. Our minds must remain open and unbounded by such second-hand facts that come our way."

We soon arrived at Thundersley, where we sought the local constable, a bluff fellow named Hume. We caught him as he was stepping out of his official preserves, presumably to make his morning rounds.

Directly, Holmes stepped up and introduced us.

"Welcome to our little hamlet, Mr. Sherlock Holmes," greeted the constable. "I imagine scientific curiosity brings you to our modest village, but you are welcome to contribute to the hunt."

"A hunt, is it?"

"Yes. Some of our more substantial citizens have been combing the heathland with their shotguns without result. We are about to embark upon another day's search. To a man we are determined to bag the beast."

"I see," mused Holmes. "As to why I am here, this Indigo Impossibility of yours presents a tantalizing mystery, and, as you may have read in your local newspaper, I can scarcely resist investigating such a phenomenon."

"Understandable. And your admirable skills may be of some use. Did you bring a pistol of some sort?"

Setting down his Gladstone, Holmes opened it up and produced a remarkable sight, a four-barreled pistol resembling a top-break shotgun, but of abbreviated barrel length.

"Good Lord!" Constable Hume expostulated. "I have never seen the like of it!"

"But I have," I interjected. "It is a howdah pistol. In India, it is employed to hunt tigers from the backs of elephants, the hunter riding in the howdah basket. Hence the unusual nomenclature."

"This particular weapon is formally known as a Lancaster pistol," supplied Holmes, breaking it open and inserting four .410-calibre shotgun shells. He snapped the breech shut with a satisfactory sound, locking it in place.

Hume laughed out loud. "The very thing to bring down this blue beast of horror, as I call it. Well, come along now. We must begin our business."

A group of local men had gathered. Stern of expression, each one brandished a shotgun of his own. No other weapon was in evidence.

"All expected are present?" asked Hume, searching their serious faces. "Hubbard? Smith? Very good. We shall set out for the heathland."

Off we went. It was not a long walk through the cool morning air along Common Lane, west to the Great Common. Sherlock Holmes and I were introduced as curious Londoners, and the stolid citizens questioned us no further. Holmes thought that his announced presence would be a distraction to the work at hand, and Hume had agreed.

During the march, Sherlock Holmes pressed the man on many particulars.

"I am given to understand that the victim was eviscerated."

"Virtually disemboweled. The creature that attacked him had ripped Carrick from sternum down to his groin, and in such a way as to spill the bloody contents of his guts."

"You are a plain-speaking man, I see."

"No use beating about the bush. It was a savage attack. And nothing that has ever been known to live in Essex could have done it."

"What has been seen of the creature?"

"Quite little. A flash of blue here and there. The thing runs like a streak of lightning. There is some scarlet to it, apparently about its long neck. The eyes are said to be staring and hideous. Russet is their color. A dark-brown comb or crest sits upon the crown of its skull. Understand that this devil has been seen only by moonlight. Where it lairs during the day has not yet been ascertained, but we believe it sleeps at night. It is our hope to ambush it successfully."

"Do you imagine it to be a dinosaur in truth?" asked Holmes.

"I cannot imagine it to be otherwise," returned the man gruffly. "As I said, nothing like it has been seen in Essex before."

"From whence do you suppose it has come?"

"I care not to know. I am only concerned with where I am going to send it. And that is to its lasting demise."

"Has no thought been given to its capture?" pressed Holmes. "If it were truly a living dinosaur, I daresay it would be worth a pretty penny to the London Zoo, or a scientific institute such as the British Museum."

Hume shook his heavy head. "No quantity of coin would tempt a Thundersley man to risk his life against such a terror. You haven't seen the body of Andrew Carrick. It was a grisly thing to behold. A maddened bull could not have gored a man so thoroughly. It was necessary for the county coroner to pack young Carrick's innards back into his stomach cavity and sew up the lot prior to burial."

"I am sorry that I missed the sight," murmured Holmes laconically.

"Be grateful that you were spared it. I wish I could wipe it from my brain, but no such cloth has ever been woven that would accomplish that merciful miracle."

"I'm no connoisseur of morbidity, Constable," Holmes hastened to add. "I venture to say that I might have gleaned a great deal from an examination of the fatal wound."

"It's too late for that. Andrew Carrick lies under the clay, God rest him."

We soon came to the heathland. It was a fairy land, a natural wonder, a heather expanse quite unexpected, given the marshy nature of Essex County. Oak predominated, but I spied birch, aspen, and other sturdy trees.

"I have read up on your heath," remarked Holmes as we

paused to survey our wild surroundings. "It is unusual in Essex, is it not?"

"This has always been a wild and untamed spot, going back to the earliest days of Thundersley, when pagan rites to the Norse god, Thor, were practiced in these parts."

We examined our weapons. Setting ourselves, we plunged in, tramping through bracken and bramble.

Holmes looked about with his keen eye. "I see plants that are not common to Essex County, the lesser spearwort among them."

"Oh, true enough," said Hume. "But they have always been present here."

The farther we marched, the more varied the terrain became. It was a heathery glory. The ground beneath our feet was composed of dry peat. Bronze dragonflies flitted about. We came to a pleasant dell and paused to survey our immediate environment.

Roots of gorse and heather lay about the ground in pleasant islands. I spied fire weal, peewit, and the purple-flowered milkwort. I imagine during warmer days, the area would be humming with wild bees. A solitary Heath Fritillary butterfly flitted by.

The luxury of unchecked growth surrounding us caused me to remark, "I can almost imagine that much of England looked like this back in the days before mankind arrived."

Holmes laughed. "Watson, it was nothing like this. Far, far wilder than you can imagine were the plants and trees of those ancient days. These sedges and heather are tame by comparison."

We pushed on, towards the still waters of a pond.

I enjoyed the fresh smell of heather honey, but I confess that my nerves were becoming as tight as springs.

As we marched along, Holmes abruptly stopped and cast his glance downward.

"Hmm. What is this?" he muttered.

Clutching his shotgun more resolutely, Hume demanded, "Have you come across one of its foul tracks?"

"Alas, no," replied Holmes, stooping to pluck a flower. He lifted it up in order to examine the plant. "But I confess that I did not immediately recognize it."

"What is it?" I asked.

"Trillium—extraordinarily rare in these parts."

Constable Hume grunted, "If you pause to study every unusual plant encountered along the way, I fear that we will make slow progress—if any progress at all."

Dropping the specimen into his Gladstone, Holmes took up his impressive howdah pistol once more and we continued on, soon coming to a marshy spot of high grasses and sedges.

We had scarcely reached the edge of a still pool when we heard a tramping through the brush, and every man swung his shotgun barrel in that direction.

At first, we could only spy a disturbance amid the brush. Dragonflies fled the area, as if stampeded. We grew keenly expectant.

"Steady, men," warned Hume. "Do not fire until you know that the beast stands where your shot will fly."

Holmes inserted, "I would advise forbearance. For those noises suggest the tramp of a man."

It was fortunate that Holmes offered that possibility, for quite quickly the dense thicket parted and out stepped a burly man attired for shooting game. He wore an old hunting coat, cords, Hessian boots, his square head topped by a green cap. He toted a double-barreled fowling piece of vintage manufacture.

Doubtless the blundering fellow would have been riddled with shot had Holmes not cautioned the agitated hunting party to hold their fire.

"What is this?" shouted Hume. "Is that you, Carrick?"

"Who do ye think it is?" demanded Carrick, all but snarling his words. His accent was Scottish. An Aberdeen man, I should judge.

"Step out and let us see you in full," called Hume.

The individual crashed into view and soon joined us. I am known for my nut-brown coloring, acquired in my military adventures, but this man was several shades darker than I could ever aspire to achieve. His eyes held a rather severe squint.

"Are you hunting the blue beast as well?" Hume asked.

"Why would I do otherwise?" the other flung back hotly. "Did it not destroy my only son?"

"No offense to you, Angus Carrick," Hume said firmly. "But if I had lost a son, I would not risk making my wife a widow hunting this blue beast all by yourself. Come join our hunting party."

"I prefer to do my own dirty work."

"And I would prefer not to witness another autopsy such as I did the other day. Do not be stubborn. There is safety in numbers."

Scarcely mollified, the burly fellow changed the subject. "I thought that I spied a flash of blue to the northwest. And towards the northwest I am bound. You may accompany me if you care to. But mistake me not. This is my hunt."

With that, he stormed off.

With a curt gesture of his chin, Constable Hume invited us to follow.

Holmes hurried up to the burly man and engaged him in conversation. I joined them.

"Mr. Carrick. My condolences on the untimely passing of your son, Andrew. My name is Sherlock Holmes. You have perhaps heard of me?"

"I have. What is your business here?"

"It is my pleasure to solve unusual mysteries. This is only the latest in a long string of them. May I ask you some questions?"

"If ye do so intelligently."

If Holmes was stung by this gruff barb, he didn't display it in any outward manner. Calmly, he asked, "Have you lived around here all your life?"

"Much of it. What is that to you?"

"You have a quite outdoorsy look about you. The way your eyes squint reminds me of outdoorsmen encountered all around the world."

"I have tramped the globe, if that is what you are getting at."

"Have you ever been to South America?"

"No."

"North America then?"

"Many times. As well as Asia and Australia. What of it?"

"I do not take you for a seaman."

"By profession, I am nothing of the kind."

"Might I inquire what it is you do for a living?"

"I am a promoter. The circus is my game. Presently, I am between connections."

"A circus man! How marvelous! I must hear more."

"Another time, Mr. Holmes. Your questions are tiring my patience. I am intent upon one thing and one thing only. Revenge."

"Understandable," returned Holmes. "You have a very determined air about you."

"Aye."

"One last question, Carrick. Have you any thoughts as to the nature of this blue beast?"

"Only the most murderous of thoughts, Mr. Holmes. Only the most murderous of thoughts."

"I see," murmured Holmes. With that, we fell back and rejoined the others.

I could tell by the alteration of his expression, and by the curtain of thought that fell over the mask that was his face, that he had gleaned more than what his conversation would reveal to an ordinary ear.

I was tempted to pry into his innermost thoughts, but I knew that it would do little good. Something was stirring in his agile brain, and I knew that if I left it alone, it would soon hatch into something extraordinary, so I bit my tongue for the nonce.

Presently I heard an odd sound emanating from the near distance. Low, intermittent, it reminded me of the grunting of a pig, but there was also a snorting equine quality that baffled me.

Abruptly, Mr. Angus Carrick broke into a dead run, trampling the gorse as he ran.

"He has spied something!" exclaimed Holmes, picking up his own pace.

For all his burly bulk, Angus Carrick ran like a demon and was soon smashing through the piney woods and was lost from sight.

All of us raced after him. Our fingers close to our triggers. We were a resolute lot, and I was amazed at the absence of exclamations or curses as we charged ahead. This was earnest business.

Out of the range of our sight, Carrick blundered about, and then one after the other we heard him discharge the barrels of his shotgun.

"Damn ye!" he cried. "Damn ye to the everlasting regions beneath my feet!"

When we caught up with him, Carrick was breaking his shotgun open and attempting to insert fresh cartridges into the smoking breach.

"What did you see, Carrick?" demanded Holmes.

"The blue beastie himself," said the man hotly. "I think I winged him, but I'm not certain. He tore into the brush like a locomotive."

Snapping his weapon back into proper order, Carrick resumed his charge.

There came the sound of a splash. We raced towards it.

Breaking through the brush and into a clearing, we came upon another pond. But its surface was not still. Something was swimming across it, towards the opposite side. Its color was striking. A deep indigo. I could see slashes of scarlet edging its long, sinuous neck. But other than that, I could make out quite little of the creature, which appeared to be emitting noises reminiscent of a very large bullfrog.

Emerging on the other side, it plunged into the close-lying brush, vanishing from our view.

We stood there, at the edge of the pond, watching the underbrush twitch and squirm as the azure fugitive worked its way through. The speed of the creature was astonishing. A horse couldn't gallop so swiftly. A locomotive alone would exceed its speedy progress.

Before we could get ourselves organized to resume our chase, the underbrush ceased its uncanny animation, and the trail appeared to have gone momentarily cold.

Turning to Holmes, I demanded, "What do you make of it? Surely with your fund of natural knowledge, you recognized the creature."

"It was all but submerged. The back of the head told me nothing. Nor did the shape of its hunched back. It lacked scale or feather, and its smooth hide suggested nothing in my present understanding."

"But the color, man. Surely, the color of its skin meant something to you!"

Holmes shook his head. "Alas, Watson, I know of no living creature possessing a hide of deep blue."

I was staggered by this frank confession, which suggested that we were hunting a survivor from the dawn of time.

"Shall we resume our hunt, gentlemen?" asked Constable Hume, coming up behind us.

We did so wordlessly. Breaking into two groups, we made opposite circles of the pond whose troubled surface was only now returning to its customary placidity.

Once more, Angus Carrick pushed ahead of us as if determined to be the one to rout the beast.

I regret to say that our investigations led us nowhere. We discovered a trace of blood here and there. Other than the fact it was quite red and soon petered out, our progress was disappointing.

Holmes made a special study of the creature's foot marks. Since it had been moving rapidly, they were not distinct, merely choppy gouges in the peat. A few were bloody, but not excessively so.

Constable Hume observed them also and, after examining several specimens, he said, "I can only say that I imagine a dragon might leave such tracks."

He looked to Sherlock Holmes.

"I would not disagree with you, Constable," replied Holmes. "These are remarkable tracks. In size, as well is in configuration. It is plain that the thing has three large talons, and these natural daggers were what opened up the belly of poor Andrew Carrick."

We continued to hunt for many hours, but all efforts were fruitless.

The setting of the sun—combined with a lack of proper nourishment—eventually forced us to reconsider our increasingly precarious position.

"Presently it will become dark," advised Constable Hume. "This is no place to be after the sun goes down. We must return to our hearths. Tomorrow is another day. Perhaps it will be a brighter one."

Sherlock Holmes didn't contradict the man. Tucking his howdah pistol into his Gladstone, he closed it up.

Hume turned to the burly Scot. "What of you, Mr. Carrick? Will you call it a night?"

"I will call it what I will. But only when I am done. There is yet some wee light left."

"True. But is a long and labored walk back to town. And much of it will be in utter darkness."

"I know these woods like the back of my hand. Do not lecture me. If ye see me again, I will have the head of the beastie clutched in my fist. Having wounded it, I am of no mind to leave it to recover its strength."

Hume said, "I will not make you return against your will, Angus Carrick. But I beg you to consider your poor grieving wife above all other considerations."

"It is for the sake of my poor grieving wife that I intend to destroy the creature," Carrick said gruffly. "A good night to you all."

This last was uttered with such poor grace that no one cared to argue further.

As one, we turned about and started the tiresome trek back to Thundersley parish.

It was dark when we reached the little hamlet. Parting from Hume and the others, we sought the comfort of supper in the town's lodging house, where Holmes and I ate in studied silence.

During our rustic but satisfying meal, Holmes's grey eyes were reflective. He didn't avail himself of his old briar pipe, but I could tell that his mind was fixed upon the problem at hand. So deep in thought was he that I might as well have been dining alone in the next town adjacent.

Only once did Holmes break his silence. And that was to remark, as if to himself, "Angus Carrick is a very troubled fellow."

This point was so obvious that I didn't undertake to add any observation of my own. I went on with my eating, and Holmes did the same. We concluded our meal in a silence that was without strain, for I understood my dear friend's eccentricities. When his brain was awhirl like a great cogitation machine, there was no point in disturbing its recondite mental machinations.

Ultimately, he broke his reverie.

"The so-called 'Indigo Impossibility,'" Holmes pronounced with clipped conviction, "is not native to these parts. Of that, I am now convinced."

"Pray tell me your reasoning," I invited.

"If the creature were native to the great heathland, there would have been other encounters down through the years.

Other examples of a supporting population. Bodies of expired specimens. Weird bones. Mysterious disappearances. We have had none of these events. Therefore, the creature is not native to Essex. Indeed, not native to England. Ergo, it was transported from some other land to this remote spot."

"But from where?"

" 'For what purpose' rings more important to my ear. For if we understand that point, we shall understand all."

That was as far as Holmes would take the matter.

We retired early, the day having been long and full of exertion. I slept soundly, but I cannot speak for Holmes. I've known the great detective to expend all of his physical energy by day and remain awake the entire night, his ever-active brain refusing the siren call to rest.

AFTER A CHARMING breakfast, I knocked on Holmes's door to no avail, only to learn from the innkeeper that he had departed earlier to seek Constable Hume.

I found the two men on the green and joined them there.

Turning at my approach, Holmes said, "Just in the nick, Watson! We are going to visit Mr. Angus Carrick at his home."

"Has there been news of his success?"

"None of which I am aware," replied Holmes. "But I am keen to speak with him."

We walked. There was a morning mist but it was burning off. The day promised to be sunny, a prospect that filled me with relief. I had had quite enough of rain.

"Mr. Holmes," remarked Constable Hume. "I am eager to see you go about your work. Your methods fascinate me."

"They are but the disciplined power of observation. The ordinary man isn't very observant, and much eludes him."

"I fancy I notice more than most," said the constable cheerily.

"Then this will be a test of your ability," remarked Holmes.

"But not a contest, for I fear I would be the loser."

"I am confident of it," I chimed in. "My friend is nothing short of a miracle man."

The domicile of Angus Carrick was a homey little cottage a little bit away from the general run of dwellings. We walked through an overgrown patch in order to reach it.

Speaking to the constable, Holmes asked abruptly, "Did you notice it?"

"Notice what?"

"I thought not," said Holmes. But he declined to further illuminate the man's curiosity.

We came at last to the front door, and Holmes stepped aside while the constable did the honors of rapping with the worn brass knocker.

I noticed several chicken coops on either side of the cottage, and it was evident that the Carricks raised poultry and no doubt enjoyed a plentiful supply of eggs year round. There was a large shed for tools, and a great deal of litter of the natural sort. A barrel brimming with rubbish stood off a bit, out of which protruded what I took to be a discarded bed pillow.

Presently a careworn woman of about forty-five years in age opened the door and smiled with great difficulty.

"Good morning, Constable Hume," she said. "If you're after Mr. Carrick, he came home quite late, slept fitfully, and departed with the dawn."

"Back to the heathland?"

"No. Angus told me that he had followed the blue beast of such horror out of the Great Common. Its foot tracks led east to the greater fastness of West Wood, he said."

"I see. Mrs. Carrick, may I present the esteemed Mr. Sherlock Holmes of London, and his associate, Dr. John Watson. May we come in to further discuss the present emergency?"

There was a moment's hesitation, but at last the woman threw open the door and stepped aside that we might enter.

The interior was presentable enough, I suppose. It was also rather eccentric. I noticed that upon the walls were bills bally-

hooing various circuses with which Mr. Carrick had been
attached. I wouldn't have them on an interior wall of my house,
but each man to his own tastes.

Sherlock Holmes addressed the woman in a tone of voice
that was deeply respectful.

"First of all, Mrs. Carrick, may I express my condolences upon
the death of your late son, Andrew? I can only imagine the grief
that now sits upon your shoulders."

"You are very kind, Mr. Holmes. But my grief is compounded
by my fear that my headstrong husband will follow my son to
his sad fate."

"Rest assured that it is my firm intention that nothing of the
sort will transpire," said Holmes. "I had hoped to speak with
your husband, but in his absence, a word with you will suffice."

"I have nothing to tell you that Constable Hume couldn't
have already divulged," the woman said rather quickly.

"One never knows about these things," Holmes said gently. "I
noticed, Mrs. Carrick, that a good deal of trillium grows around
this property."

"I am surprised that you can name the flower, Mr. Holmes.
My husband brought them back from the Carolinas. He likes
to plant exotic blooms. Speaking for myself, good English blos-
soms are more appealing."

"Thank you for confirming my suspicions."

The woman's hand rose to her breast with a start. "Suspicions?"

"Yes, for I also noticed trillium plants growing wild in the
Common. Recognizing that they were not native to England,
I wondered how they could have come to take root here. You
have satisfied my curiosity. You see, I count botany among my
many and varied interests."

The tense-fingered hand fell to her apron and Mrs. Carrick
looked visibly relieved.

"Oh, I see. Of course. No doubt some of the seeds have trav-
eled, for we have had these plants for several years now."

Holmes resumed speaking, "I have had the pleasure of meeting Mr. Angus Carrick on the hunt, as it were. He tells me that he is a promoter connected to the circus business."

"Yes. That is true, as far as it goes."

"Oh? Does it go any further than that?"

"Mr. Carrick is more than a promoter. He is fond of securing 'exotics,' he calls them, for the circus. He is especially interested in stage magic, for he has grown tired of tripping about the world and bringing back the exotic and the unusual. He fancies himself a magician in the style of the late Robert-Houdin."

"I see. Where was he last, insofar as his global endeavors took him?"

"I see no harm in telling you, Mr. Holmes. He has been to Australia and New Guinea and such places. Of course, I did not accompany him. I had young Andrew to raise. Now, I fear that I have been relieved of that pleasant duty."

"Regrettably so," murmured Holmes.

There was a moment in which Mrs. Carrick used her apron to dab fresh tears from the corners of her tired eyes. We observed this in respectful silence.

During this interview, both Holmes and Constable Hume were casting their glances about the sitting room. I had noticed that Mrs. Carrick hadn't invited us to sit down. This permitted Holmes to shift about, under what I took to be the pretense of reading the various circus bills.

His crafty gaze went to an adjacent room, which I perceived to be a modest study. From it came the twittering of a bird.

"I see you have a caged bird."

"Several of them. More of Mr. Carrick's exotics. These came from the United States."

"I do not immediately recognize the specimen. May I study them at close range?"

Here, Mrs. Carrick seemed to grow pale. I couldn't imagine why. It was an innocent enough request.

Gathering herself together, she nodded dutifully and then added, "Of course. I regret that I cannot name the species, only that it is American in origin. These specimens were captured in the Carolinas."

"Thank you, Mrs. Carrick."

Holmes strode into the room, and if he glanced at anything else, I didn't perceive it. He went directly to the caged birds and studied them from several angles.

They were tiny, twittering things, hopping around from perch to perch, with the usual nervousness of the avian species. Some were brown, but the majority was a deep blue. The cage was quite large, of wicker construction, and altogether its inhabitants numbered seven.

In the doorway behind me, Constable Hume exclaimed, "My word!"

"What is it?" I demanded.

Turning, Holmes laid one finger over his thin lips and said, "I agree that these are remarkable specimens. I shall have to look up their classification when we return to London."

Gesturing for us to return to the sitting room, Sherlock Holmes addressed Mrs. Carrick: "I imagine that Mr. Carrick hasn't been sleeping well of late."

"He has not, nor have I. We toss and turn endlessly, so much so that Mr. Carrick asked me to dispose of our feather pillows, which I directly did. He presented me with a fresh pair. But they haven't aided our slumber. Nor did I expect that they would."

"Could you tell me how young Andrew met his untimely demise?"

"Angus and Andrew had gone hunting, during which time they became separated. The terrible thing transpired during that regrettable interval. My husband has been beside himself since that awful day."

"As one naturally would," mused Holmes.

His gaze shot to the bedroom door, but it was shut. I could tell by the look upon his firm features that if he could, he would have investigated that room too. I couldn't imagine why it held any fascination for him.

Once more addressing Mrs. Carrick, he said, "Again, please accept our sincere condolences, but we must be going. Give Mr. Carrick our sincere compliments and let him know we will look forward to speaking with him at his earliest opportunity."

"Oh, I do not think it wise, Mr. Holmes, for Angus is in a foul temper and it will not pass until he has avenged our son. You must understand that even at his best, Angus can be difficult. His uncertain occupation in the ever-changing tastes of the general public forces him to struggle to keep up with the times."

"I can well imagine," said Holmes. "But please convey our sentiments to him. Thank you, and good day."

The door closed behind us and Holmes murmured in an undertone, "Do not speak until we are out of earshot."

We passed the grassy patch where the trillium grew wild and free, its reddish flowers surrounded by broad green leaves. Not until the patch was behind us did anyone speak.

"I was on the point of bursting!" cried Constable Hume when he felt it safe to do so. "Did you notice the color of that bird?"

"I could hardly fail to do so," said Holmes dryly.

"It was indigo," I stated, only then understanding the significance of it all.

"Oh, yes!" Hume gasped. "Virtually the same shade as the Impossibility! I know that it must mean something. But I cannot imagine what."

Holmes did not enlighten us on that point. Instead, he said, "I would have liked to examine the bed pillows that were discarded."

"For what reason?" I asked, thinking it an irrelevant point.

"To determine their color," supplied Holmes.

"What would that mean?" I asked.

"If they prove as black as a raven's wing, it would explain why indigo buntings were kept in the Carrick family birdcage."

"Buntings, you say?" said Hume.

"Yes, a bird of the cardinal family whose range stretches from Canada to South America, although Asia boasts certain species. Like the trillium, one would never find a wild specimen in Britain. The male bunting boasts indigo feathers, while the female is brown. Taken altogether, I believe I have a clear understanding of recent events, as bizarre as they might have seemed until the present moment."

Turning to Constable Hume, he added, "What would you say to an excursion into the wilds of West Wood?"

"To find the Impossibility?"

"Or Angus Carrick. In order to test my little theory, either would suffice."

"Your theory baffles me, Mr. Holmes. I do not connect any of it, except for the coincidence of the indigo bunting and the Indigo Impossibility."

"I think the word 'coincidence' is misused, Constable. It is nothing of the sort. But let us locate Carrick."

We didn't have to go far to find Angus Carrick. He had returned from the wood, but not of his own volition.

A horse-drawn dray cart rattled into the little village, and it became the occasion of a great uproar.

For there in the back of the cart lay Carrick, bleeding profusely.

We rushed over to the spot where the farmer pulled up, calling out to the constable.

"It's Carrick!" he showed hoarsely. "The Impossibility got him."

"He is dead?" demanded Holmes.

"He may wish that he were, but he still breathes."

We reached the back of the dray, and Holmes thrust aside the flannel blanket that covered Angus Carrick.

A gory mess was uncovered. It was fortunate that the great claws had raked across only Carrick's chest and not his belly.

The wound was not mortally deep. Only glimpses of ribs were disclosed. The blow must have been a glancing one.

Hume cursed and called for the village doctor. I replaced the blanket and attempted to compress the worst wound, but I feared that it did little good.

Directing his attention upon the man's face, Holmes asked, "Carrick, do you understand my words?"

Without lifting his head, the fellow managed to nod.

"What befell you?"

With pained expression, Angus Carrick spoke. His words were thick and halting.

"The beastie hopped six feet in the air from behind bushes and came down on me…. Managed to discharge both barrels. Do not know if I hit it … only that it tore off into the bracken. I crawled for my very life until I came to a farm house…."

The effort appeared to be too much for Angus Carrick. His eyes rolled up in his head and he turned his face to the side of the cart.

I placed a hand over the man's heart. I could feel it pounding. His wrist pulses were thready, however.

"Not dead. But rather far gone," I stated. Lacking my medical bag, there was little that I could do for the poor fellow— otherwise I would have administered a sedative. Carrick's torn clothes were ill-suited for use as makeshift bandages, being dirty and unsanitary.

The village physician soon arrived. Inasmuch as he had the advantage over me with his little black bag, I stepped aside to permit him to make an examination, offering professional observations illuminated by my days as an army surgeon in India and Afghanistan, which he found helpful.

"We will take the poor fellow to my office where I will do what I can for him," he swiftly decided. "But no promises can I make."

"I will be happy to assist you," I offered. "I am Dr. John Watson of London."

"And I am Dr. Drake. Your assistance would be very welcome."

We left Holmes and Constable Hume and drove the man to the surgery, where we did what we could for him. This took the better part of the morning.

Alas, Carrick did not speak again. It was necessary to sedate him before sewing up his hideous wounds.

Freed of my immediate medical responsibilities, I found Holmes and the constable just as they were concluding a shared luncheon.

"Carrick may live, or he may not," I informed them. "Has Mrs. Carrick been notified?"

"Belatedly," replied Hume. "No doubt she is now on her way to see him."

Holmes spoke up. "With your kind permission and official indulgence, Constable Hume, I would like to take advantage of Mrs. Carrick's absence and search the Carrick premises. Let me assure you that this will be for the sole purpose of solving the mystery."

Hume hesitated only briefly. "This must be done under my supervision."

"That is satisfactory. I welcome your company. Watson, I'm going to ask you to remain here, since the emergency is far from passed."

"Agreed."

And so they departed. I should like to have accompanied them, but I assumed that I would be of no value whatsoever, and three intruders would be one too many.

I took a late lunch at the lodging house. When I returned to my room, I discovered that Holmes had reclaimed his quarters, for the door was ajar.

"What is that?" I asked, poking my head in.

"This is a feather pillow I have borrowed from the Carrick residence."

"Heavens, Holmes! You have stolen the grieving woman's pillow from her very bed?"

"No, Watson. Please shut the door. I left it open because I was expecting you. This is one of the two pillows that were lately disposed of. I found it among the trash that hadn't yet been burned, having spied it earlier. Two perfectly good pillows lying amid the household rubbish appeared to be out of the ordinary for such a frugal family."

With a pocket knife, Holmes commenced cutting the pillow-case open. It appeared to be a handmade affair, such as if Mrs. Carrick had sewn the casing herself, which I imagined she had.

Taking hold of the parted seam, Holmes ripped it open with his strong fingers.

Out spilled the most amazing profusion of long black bristly quills I ever could have imagined. Holmes took one up and passed it to me. Then he availed himself of another.

"Just as I thought, just as I thought," he murmured.

I examined the plume in my hand. It was exceedingly long. I couldn't imagine what manner of creature had produced it. But it was very black, and quite coarse to the touch.

"Do you recognize this feather?" I asked of Holmes.

"Not from direct experience. But it has confirmed my growing suspicions."

"It has flummoxed my own expectations. What is this dreadful affair all about?"

"Humbug, Watson. It is all about a clever sort of humbug."

"This feather feels quite solid between my fingers."

Standing up, Sherlock Holmes said, "Fetch your pistol, and I will bring my howdah gun. We are going to eradicate the blue beast, and finally put an end to these outrages."

"If you insist," I returned. "But I still cannot imagine what manner of creature can jump six feet into the air, swim across a pond, and slash open two grown men with such savage ferocity."

"I admit that this is beyond my personal experience. Let us see if we cannot run the beast to earth and prove conclusively what I now believe to be the identity of the Indigo Impossibility."

WE REACHED WEST Wood by hiring a hansom cab. At the verge of the ancient woodland, Holmes dismissed the driver with these woods, "Kindly inform Constable Hume that Dr. Watson and I have gone into these words to hunt the Indigo Impossibility. If we do not return by evening, he must undertake a search for our bodies."

The cab man gasped. "Are you quite sure of this, sir?"

"I do not intend to fail," replied Holmes, removing the cumbersome howdah gun from his Gladstone bag.

As the cab rattled off, he turned to me and asked, "Are you quite prepared, Watson?"

"Since I do not know what it is that I am hunting, I do not know how to answer that question. But I'm game to follow you into this mystery."

Holmes uttered a pleased laugh.

"Watson, you are as true as steel. Come, let us seek the phantasm."

We entered gingerly, walking close together, our weapons in hand. As we penetrated the wild wood with its hornbeam and hawthorn trees shading bluebells and yellow cow-wheat, Holmes began explaining himself, a thing contrary to his usual habit. I imagine the possibility of falling victim to the creature we hunted compelled my friend to reveal his thinking prematurely.

"I must confess, my dear Watson, that I was almost entirely without substantial clues in the beginning. You may recall that I was a trifle short with you at one point."

"I didn't take it personally," I assured him.

"I couldn't dismiss the theory of a dinosaur as entirely impossible. That is to say, that an extinct creature might conceivably survive in our modern era. But neither did it seem very plausible for reasons that I've previously stated. If there is one survival, there must be others. There were none that I could discern. Thundersley doesn't have a history of savage animal attacks or mysterious disappearances of men or livestock. Therefore, this couldn't be a native creature."

He paused to study the ground, evidently for foot tracks. None were visible to me.

We pressed on. The light was good, but as we moved into the density of the forest, the intertwining boughs and leaves began to cut into the streaming sunlight, creating a dim shade.

I noticed many interesting plants, but nothing that I hadn't seen before. Bluebell and wood spurge appeared to be plentiful. Still, this was an ancient wood and there was no telling what might be found in its deeper regions.

"Mrs. Carrick had spoken of her husband visiting the Carolinas, Australia, and New Guinea," resumed Holmes. "These seemingly unconnected places, combined with the indigo buntings kept in a cage, created in my mind a sudden and surprising web of associations. Until that point, I confess that I was groping rather blindly for clarity of thought."

"So you suspect Angus Carrick of something?"

"Surely you noticed that Mrs. Carrick was excessively nervous during our discussion."

"She was overwrought. Understandably so."

"Oh, true, Watson. But the guilty often betray themselves in their attempts to conceal the truth. No doubt you are familiar with the stage magician's art of misdirection?"

"I am."

"The clever magician points to his closed fist with his opposite hand so you do not see what the pointing hand is doing. That is the art. Both hands are inside. Your attention is directed towards only one. Thus you miss the cunning pass of the pointing hand, which palms or produces minor wonders."

"Is Mrs. Carrick guilty of something nefarious?"

"Only of having knowledge she wishes to conceal for the sake of her family," responded Holmes. "For Angus Carrick is the truly culpable one."

"Of what, pray tell?"

"Of causing the death of his only son, Andrew," replied Holmes. "Investigation may or may not show that he imported something into this country that he should not have. That remains to be seen. As you are doubtless aware, we are not far from the Thames estuary, where cargo may be unloaded and brought by dray cart into Thundersley."

Holmes paused, searching the demi-shadows between the trees. He was listening, but if he heard something, I failed to achieve his keenness of ear.

He continued on. A rudimentary footpath wound through the woods and we remained on it, where we would not break twigs or crush underbrush noisily beneath our feet. Here and there stood the stools of felled trees.

"The vivid blue of the indigo bunting," Holmes resumed, "struck me like a flash of illumination. My thoughts had been stuck on the curious blue hide, like a gullible man staring at the magician's closed fist, and what sort of animal it might be. Suddenly, what was obscure became plainly obvious."

"Speaking for myself, it does not."

"No, Watson, but to one possessing my fund of knowledge, I found myself staring at the point on the map where longitude met latitude. For whilst observation is of supreme importance, without underlying knowledge, the obvious remains obscure."

We crept along. Holmes fell back into his thoughtful silence. At length, he broke it.

"Do you remember Sir Richard Owen's remarkable fossil discovery, which he called *Dinornis robustus?*"

"Yes. It was an extinct bird also known as the 'Giant Moa,' native to New Zealand. A flightless creature that stands, or should I say, stood seven feet tall before it was hunted to extinction by Maori tribesmen. My word, Holmes!" I exclaimed suddenly, "are we hunting a living moa?"

Holmes's clipped reply surprised me. "No, we are not. I merely remind you of this creature so you are not unduly astonished when we locate the Indigo Impossibility, for we will need our full wits to defeat it."

Holmes fell silent again. I confess that I remained baffled. I didn't know where my friend was attempting to lead me, either mentally or physically.

Holmes stopped dead still and was listening. My own ears told me something was moving some distance to the west.

"I think we are drawing close to the thing," said Holmes in a hush.

"And what thing is that?"

"The creature that Carrick imported from New Guinea, or possibly Australia, which he kept in a cage large enough to encompass its size. I suspect the cage was concealed in the shed that stood some distance from the Carrick cottage. No doubt it was difficult to manage due to its size and natural ferocity. Somehow it escaped and, lacking its natural coating of black feathers, became even more agitated due to the cold and inclement weather, foraging for food as best as it could. But after having crossed the Indian Ocean, it was in no temper to be recaptured. Thus when Angus Carrick and his son went hunting it, tragedy struck."

I felt as if my brain were being placed on a carousel while shown a kaleidoscope of images that came too fast for me to make sense of them in their totality.

"Holmes," I said in exasperation, "I am bedazzled by a mental procession of indigo birds, large black feathers, and misplaced trillium. Kindly enlighten me."

"I suspect the trillium was something that it liked to eat. But that is only surmise."

Sherlock Holmes seemed at the point of clarifying matters when he raised his free hand for me to come to a halt. He had stopped in his tracks, his grey gaze penetrating into the deeper recesses of the ancient forest.

I could hear the thing moving. A succession of measured footsteps like nothing I had ever before heard. This was not the racing sound of the Indigo Impossibility as we encountered it in the Common. This creature was stalking, walking with caution, and, I feared, quite aware of our presence. A low sound came. I could barely hear it. But it suggested a brutish animal with a hoarse voice, akin to a bullfrog.

"Watson," whispered Holmes carefully. "Kindly turn about and keep a watch on our southwestern approach. I will study the northwest prospect."

I obliged. The noise of peculiar footfalls continued to be heard, a fearfully disquieting sound. I felt as if I were the prey to something I could not see, only hear. Glancing back at my friend, I noted that Holmes stood in an attitude of great nervous tension. He swung the impressive howdah gun about, prepared to unleash a fiery blast at whatever was so carefully circling us.

Turning my attention back to the southwest, I caught a momentary streak of blue moving through the greenery, along with a glimpse of a single russet orb. I did not hesitate. Lifting my Adams service revolver, I fired at the flash of color.

A scream was heard, or perhaps I should term it a screech. And out of the brush lunged an ungainly thing that ran towards me like a raucous banshee, grunting and huffing with rage.

It neared five feet tall, the greater part of it indigo. Fierce russet eyes glared hatefully as it came on, head lowered, its high crest thrusting forward in the manner of a ram. My eyes went to its feet. Terrible talons churned up clods of dirt as it closed with us.

That was all I saw. I felt myself being knocked aside, and I wondered if the thing had leapt atop me with such blinding speed that I did not perceive it.

But no, it was Sherlock Holmes. Thrusting me out of the way, he brought up his howdah gun and fired three barrels in rapid succession.

The sound was deafening. The thing's horrid screaming died

when the momentum of its leap was foiled by the cloud of shot riddling its oblate body, causing it to crash backwards and slide several feet before piling up to a stop.

Gathering my wits, I struggled to my feet.

Sherlock Holmes had already raced to the side of the creature, evidently dead, although the powerful claws still twitched in their death throes. Its neck had been severed, with the result that the staring head lay separated from the body. Reddish wattles clung to the long neck, which was mottled by its brilliant life fluid. The beaked mouth was short and bird-like.

In general, it reminded me of an ostrich, but without a coat of feathers. The indigo hide was smooth and hairless, the talons grey and distressingly massive. There was a dark crest of horn running lengthwise over its scalp. One glassy orb glared upward in death-stilled rage. I judged that the pathetic shredded remains would weigh nearly nine stone in life.

"What is it?" I demanded in a hushed voice.

"You will recall the Giant Moa," stated Holmes. "This is another example of a *ratite,* a large flightless bird native to Australasia. In this case, unlike the moa, this beast is not extinct. Naturalists consider this bizarre blue beast among the most dangerous birds living. It is known as a *cassowary.*"

"I have never heard of such a creature."

"But I have," said Holmes, nudging the head with the tip of his shoe tip. "And that is why my observation of the indigo bunting proved illuminating. Recall Mrs. Carrick stating that her husband had begun to show an interest in stage magic. To her, this was an idle comment, intended to steer the conversation away from the truth. But to my ear, it was tantamount to a revelation."

Moving about the wretched tangle of the cruelly-perforated body, Holmes felt and grasped one of the scaly feet. The creature was three-toed. Its outer claws were formidable, their span as large as a man's shirt front. What lay between them was staggering.

"Here you see what accounted for the grievous wounds inflicted upon two men," he said grimly.

"I see it clearly," I said. For the center claw was longer and sharper in appearance than its mates, a fearsome dagger of a nail. Dried blood had darkened it.

STANDING UP, HOLMES continued, "I don't know the precise timing of events, but I would imagine that Mr. Carrick had brought home a number of indigo buntings from the Carolinas in previous years. They naturally reproduced in captivity, sustaining their tiny population through the ensuing years. On his most recent excursion to New Guinea, Carrick happened upon the cassowary, a large flightless bird possessing a striking indigo hide under its bristling black feathers. Thinking with the imagination of a magician, Carrick was struck by a novel idea. What if he could create an illusion for an audience where it seemed as if he could transform a tiny indigo bunting into a ferocious cassowary? What a sensation that would be to a jaded audience! Or perhaps he contemplated the reverse— transforming a fierce caged cassowary into a harmless little bunting. It does not matter. During the course of his practicing for the stage, Carrick lost control of his rare specimen. Tragedy resulted. The rest you know."

"Why, it sounds preposterous!"

"I will not gainsay your good opinion, Watson. But all the pieces appear to fit. Carrick plucked the black feathers from his prize, and not wishing to squander the rare plumes, had his wife sew them into two pillowcases. After the loss of poor Andrew Carrick, sleeping on them became intolerable. Therefore, they were hastily discarded. You see how the unlikely strands fit together. Improbable as they are, a clear pattern is apparent."

Holmes stood, frowning. I imagined that he was contemplating the tragedy of the Carrick family. But he surprised me by saying, "I should have thought to bring a rabbit pouch. I would like to show Constable Hume the head. Well, he will just have to take our word for it, won't he?"

"I imagine that Hume will be relieved, immensely so."

"No doubt he will, Watson. No doubt he will."

Our business done, we reversed course for Thundersley proper. As we walked along, serenaded by the drumming of the elusive great spotted woodpecker, Holmes turned to me and asked, "Watson, I'm surprised that you have never heard of the terrible cassowary bird."

"Why should I?"

"Did you not spend a measure of your younger years in Australia?"

"True."

"Yet you never heard of *Casuarius casuarius,* which is native to that distant continent?"

"I was rather young, and I have only pleasant memories of Australia. That frightful fowl is not among them."

"A pity. But for your lack of experience, you might well have identified the Indigo Impossibility before I did."

"While conceivable, I doubt that I could have solved the mystery in its totality. Only you are capable of such mercurial reasoning."

Sherlock Holmes smiled in his usual restrained manner. "On that point, my dear Watson, we are in perfect accord."

THE MYSTERY OF
THE ELUSIVE LI SHEN

OVER THE COURSE of laying before the public selected cases involving my good friend, Mr. Sherlock Holmes, I have of necessity devised certain rules which I invariably observe as I chronicle his singular exploits. Chief of these is that I recount these tales in strict chronological order. That is to say, I relate each individual case in the precise way that I experienced it, since I've had the good fortune to be present for most of Holmes's adventures.

It should go without saying that one must start a story at the beginning. This I have invariably done. It is also true that one is equally obliged to withhold certain facts from the reader until revealing them during the climax of the matter at hand. For it would do no good, and in fact undermine the narrative value of these records, to begin a tale with the name of the thief or murderer, as it were, announced to the public at large on the first page.

Otherwise, I go to great pains to withhold all salient facts until it is necessary to divulge them.

With this particular account, I fear that I must withhold one significant detail. My reasons for doing so will become apparent at the end of this narrative, but I feel compelled to mention this undisclosed element at the beginning, neither to absolve myself nor unnecessarily confound the public, but to prepare the reader for the unexpected while preserving my cherished role as an honest raconteur.

That duty out of the way, I will begin my story from the point at which Sherlock Holmes received an unexpected letter dated 3rd August, 1890.

It came in the afternoon post, accompanied by the usual trifles.

I was absorbed in *The Times's* agony column as Holmes slipped it open and perused the contents. He soon proffered this to me, asking, "What do you make of this, Watson?"

Upon reading it, I replied, "I make no more of it than what is written in plain English. No doubt you have some penetrating insight, dear fellow."

"This letter was written by an earnest but rather dull chap. Somewhat like yourself, I would imagine."

I started. "What brings you to that questionable conclusion?"

"Nothing specific. Just a general sense based upon the man's selection of words and the fact that he chooses to remain anonymous when there doesn't seem to be any compelling reason to do so."

"As you know, a great many individuals write anonymous letters to *The Times* and other newspapers."

"A great many cranks do as well," Holmes said diffidently.

I couldn't contain my skepticism. "Do you jump to the conclusion that this fellow is a crank?"

"Not at all," replied my friend. "I was merely observing that, among the ranks of anonymous public letter writers, the crank is a significant participant in that rather peculiar game. Read it again, Watson, I beg of you. Tell me if in your opinion the writer is a crank."

Here I made my first mistake. "I don't need to read it again. The person who wrote that letter appears to me to be of sound mind, perhaps merely one who simply values his privacy."

"You detect no ulterior motive?"

"There are many Londoners who would style themselves as concerned citizens. I see nothing out of the ordinary about that.

As for the subject of the letter, it remains to be seen if there is such a person as the one named."

"I have never heard of anyone going by that fanciful name," mused Holmes. "On the other hand, I'm not on intimate acquaintance with the Chinese element currently inhabiting Limehouse. Oh, I have of course certain acquaintances, and even spies, in that sometimes-disreputable quarter, but by no means am I widely known there, nor welcome beyond certain of its exotic portals."

"You refer, of course, to the infamous opium dens."

"Which I have visited in my younger days—purely for the experience and the knowledge to be gained therefrom. All that is behind me though, along with my solution of cocaine."

"And if I may dare say so, Holmes, you are the better man for all that."

"Hmm. That remains to be seen. Not that I doubt your professional opinion. Only that it remains unproven, and I suspect always will be."

Taking up the letter again, Holmes read the missive aloud. I didn't understand why he did so. At least, not at that time. His prior habit was to read something twice to commit it to memory. But now he spoke every word from salutation to signature, pronouncing the words slowly and carefully, as if somehow tasting them with his mental tongue.

> *My Dear Holmes,* (he began)
> *I am penning this letter as a concerned citizen.*
> *There is a mysterious criminal operating in Limehouse who goes by the name of Li Shen, or some similar spelling. This bounder is importing and distributing opium in large quantities, which is flooding the distressed neighborhood. As time goes by, his foul merchandize will contaminate Greater London itself. Li Shen must be stopped before that occurs.*
> *Find Li Shen and see that he is tried and convicted of his crimes, which result will no doubt end this spreading scourge.*
> *Respectfully Yours,*
> *A.C. Citizen*

"Yes," said Holmes, reverting to his normal speaking voice. "The author of this note is an ordinary man of sound, if unimaginative, mind. I would stake my reputation upon it. That being the case, I think that we'll investigate this mysterious individual going by the name of Li Shen."

"Where do you propose we begin?" I inquired.

"I wish that our correspondent had provided a sounder starting point than a mere name and a general location. But if one wishes to locate a specific spot on a map, all that is required are the two imaginary lines known as longitude and latitude. Thus, Li Shen and Limehouse must serve as our substitutes."

Before dusk was quite upon us, we were ensconced in a hansom cab, wheeling in the direction of Limehouse Reach.

"What do you make of the name, 'Li Shen?'" I asked as we bumped along the cobblestones.

"Very little. Li is a common last name among the Chinese people, who as you know place the paternal name before the Christian one, as it were. And Shen is no more distinctive. I imagine that there are hundreds, if not thousands, of individuals so named in faraway China. In Limehouse proper, there may be only seven or eight."

"In other words," I observed, "we are searching for the proverbial needle in the haystack."

"Or a phantom, Watson. For I am not yet convinced that there is any such a personage."

"Yet you're willing to undertake such a search?"

"I'm convinced that the writer of the letter is as substantial as are you."

"I'm beginning to suspect that you are correct in your deduction, if it is in fact that."

SHERLOCK HOLMES AND I were soon walking along Limehouse Causeway, overwhelmed by the gaudy sights and sounds of the dockside district. Odors of frying fish predominated amid the noisome conglomeration of smells,

which also included the River Thames at low tide and the aroma
of tea and sundries from distant China and India as they were
being unloaded by the grimy stevedores.

I couldn't imagine what Holmes expected to discover by such
a casual investigation, but I was more than happy to accompany
him. Often, I only learned of his more strenuous activities after
the fact.

It was a pleasant summer evening, with the heat of the day
already abating. As we strolled along the Chinese quarter, past
the quaint shops with their slashing and cryptic window signs,
I noted the increasing number of foreign faces among the local
dock laborers and wherrymen. Owing to its convenient proximity to the bustling wharves, Limehouse was a marvel of cosmo-
politan citizenry. Chinese made up the greater numbers of its
inhabitants, most but not all of them distinguished by their
skullcaps and long pigtails.

"With more arriving every week," Holmes murmured, as if
reading my thoughts.

Here and there, I recognized the odd Malay or Arab, as well
as the occasional lascar from India. Most had the look of seafar-
ing men, for Limehouse was a sailor's town of long standing.
There were almost no women going about.

"I imagine virtually every Asian nation is now represented in
these confines," I remarked.

"I haven't yet seen a Pacific Islander, nor any of the recent
arrivals from Siam, Annam, and Tonkin, who are fleeing French
oppression," Holmes noted.

"I wouldn't know a man from Siam if I encountered him."

Spying up ahead a thick-bearded man wearing a white
turban, I recognized him as a Sikh, a growing sight in a city
where Hindu turbans might be observed in increasing numbers.
I didn't obtain a closer look at the tall fellow, for he disappeared
down one of the byways until he was lost from my sight, yet
another of the cast of characters comprising this peculiar Asiatic
quarter of greater London.

"Most of these Chinese hail from Shanghai," remarked Holmes, "but others call Canton and various South China ports home. I shall not bore you with the details which enable me to distinguish one from another, but their exotic dress and ornamentation tell me much."

"Would that Dickens were still among the living," I remarked. "He would be enthralled."

"I do not doubt it," murmured my friend.

"What do you expect to see during our promenade?" I pressed.

"Oh, I don't expect to see anything in particular. I merely observe. I have spoken to you about the power of observation many times. Observation by itself enables one to glean many things. For example, the man approaching us is a habitual user of opium. I can see this in his dreamy, rather vacant countenance. As I'm sure you can as well, Watson."

"I'm familiar with the slack expression, clinically speaking."

"He appears to be smoking a new variety of *chandu* that I haven't before encountered."

I knew that *"chandu"* was a term used by some Asiatics to describe opium, but I couldn't imagine how Holmes could determine from the man's face what variety he was addicted to, so I put it to him.

"How the devil can you tell that?"

"By the stains upon his fingertips. The discoloration is commonly seen among opium addicts who burn beads of opium paste over a spirit lamp before rolling it by hand and loading it into their smoking pipes. The golden hue I spy is slightly different from the usual Chinese stuff. No doubt this man is a client—if I may employ so noble a term—of the individual we are seeking."

"Do you mean to follow him?"

"Discreetly, Watson, discreetly."

We did so. The vacant fellow walked along the Causeway, turned corners, and strolled up Pekin Street in the direction of

Pennyfields. There, he entered a storefront which posted a sign in two languages, the English version reading: *Asiatic Aid Society*.

I frowned. "We can hardly follow him in without arousing suspicion."

"Agreed. So we will mark this establishment for a future visit. Let us continue on our way, for I've already learned something of interest, possibly vitally so."

"There you have the better of me."

"And not for the first time," replied my friend in a jocular manner.

I took no offense. Sherlock Holmes's superior mind always appeared to be a jump ahead of me, whose brain didn't tend towards jumps, but steady plodding in commonplace directions. I wasn't sure how Holmes could have gotten anything new from observing the man, but I left the point alone, confident that it would come out in due course.

Walking along, we found ourselves in the heart of Penny-fields. Here the sights were vastly more impressive than along the docks, although that might have been the result of being outnumbered by Oriental passersby. No doubt many were law abiding citizens, but the strangeness of the cast of their faces and the oddness of their costumes, combined with their difficult language, made us feel like outsiders in this remote part of London.

"What ho!" Holmes said suddenly.

"Tell me, for I don't see what you are perceiving."

"Nothing new there, eh, Watson? If you direct your attention beyond that quaint inn marked by a yellow lantern, you will see our good friend Lestrade attempting to be inconspicuous, and failing rather magnificently."

Holmes declined to point the man out, not wishing to draw attention to himself, or to Lestrade. So it took me a moment to pick him out of the crowd.

Lestrade was dressed in a rather slovenly manner, one ill-befitting his position in life. He wore a bowler hat that was rather battered and which resided upon his head at a disreputable angle, inclined truculently forward as if the narrow brim could somehow enshadow his features.

As a disguise, it was a monumental failure to anyone who knew the inspector, but among the inhabitants of this maritime district, he might pass for a common Londoner with no particular occupation or direction in life.

Holmes crossed the street, and I followed. We were soon walking close behind Lestrade.

Overtaking him, Holmes whispered, "A word with you, Lestrade. If you will."

The inspector smothered his impulse to start and took advantage of the first alley he came upon to stop and light a cigarette. He made a pretense of not being able to strike his match alight, so Holmes drew close and did him the kindness of producing a match from his own pocket.

I joined them. Our conversation was pitched low.

"What are you doing here, Mr. Holmes?"

"Possibly seeking the same man as you, Inspector."

"Name the fellow."

"Li Shen."

Lestrade started. "Then we *are* on the same scent. What makes this your business?"

"We received a letter from a concerned citizen, inviting me to take up the chase. We haven't been at it for long."

"I wish that I could say the same, for this is my third week seeking the rather elusive gentleman, and I'm beginning to wonder if I could ever pick him out."

"Have you any leads?" asked Holmes.

"I followed a man that I thought was the suspect one evening last week. I couldn't see his face from behind, and he entered a curio shop, then disappeared into the back. Rushing past the proprietor who didn't seem to speak English, I sought him out. In the poor light, I caught only a glimpse of his furtive face, and that briefly. I daresay that I could pick him out in a crowd, for his facial configurations possessed a rare distinction."

"And what is that?"

"He appeared to have no nose."

"None at all?"

"Only a black void where his nose should have been."

"No nostrils?"

"None that I could see."

"And how did he elude your clutches?"

"The suspect dodged out the back way before I could reach him, and when I emerged into the gaslight, he was nowhere to be found. I searched high and low, Mr. Holmes, but he might as well have vanished."

"Curious," mused Holmes. "A man with no nose."

"The proprietor claimed through a translator not to know the man, but they all say that, the whole lot of them. It is as if they have their own rules and ways, and the police are an inconvenience. Except, of course, when they need our assistance—which they rarely do."

"The Azure Phoenix Tong keeps the peace in Chinatown, I understand."

Lestrade glowered in annoyance. "I wish that were still true. They keep the peace between the Chinese, but not necessarily among their rivals. As you know, there is a fresh wave of immigrants from Cochin-China and nearby countries. They have their own ways, and these newcomers are encroaching upon Chinese territory. There have been running battles, hatchet men, and all that rot. I fear that these troubles will escalate. And at the heart of it all is this human enigma, Li Shen. He is bringing in his own brand of opium, and stealing business from the Chinese. They are out to get him. And so am I."

"As am I," responded Holmes. "Now that I have been apprised of the situation."

I spoke up at this point, remarking, "It seems to me that a man with no nose would be quite conspicuous."

"He would," admitted Lestrade, "if he had the decency to walk the streets in broad daylight, but some of these criminals sleep during the day and come out of their warrens and garrets only in the dark of night. And even that, rarely."

"Well, Lestrade," Holmes offered, "I wish you good fortune in your search, and I trust that you cheerfully return the sentiment."

"After three weeks of fruitless trudging," the inspector replied glumly, "I would be happy if you dragged Li Shen, wherever he came from, bodily into Scotland Yard without our help. Of course, I would prefer to capture him myself."

"You believe the man to hail from other than China proper?"

"It is my suspicion, given what my narks tell me," Lestrade stated. "The growing unrest between the Chinese and these interlopers into their way of life points to the new immigrants. Since they come from many spots, I cannot say for certain who this Li Shen is. His name sounds Chinese, which confuses matters."

"It may be an alias."

"Quite possibly. If so, he is taking an alias that is the equivalent to 'John Smith,' for there are many men in Limehouse named Li Shen. And, so far, I have discovered none who lacks a nose."

"Good hunting to you, Inspector," said Holmes abruptly.

"The same to you, gentlemen."

We left Lestrade smoking in the alley, which he seemed loathe to abandon—at least as long as his cigarette continued to burn.

As we walked along, Holmes grew ruminative. "This is an interesting development," he said after a period of silence.

"Lestrade's unexpected appearance?"

"No, I would have expected it, given the spreading scourge of opium. But a man with no visible nose is a man who would be known to many, if not all, of those who inhabit such a narrow confine as Limehouse and its immediate environs. I think that a check of the immigration office might be in order, as well as the Asiatic Aid Society. I believe that we'll start there, Watson."

Retracing our steps to Pennyfields, we came to the place and entered.

It was staffed by a Chinese man owning a very round face and a pleasant if expressionless countenance. I took an immediate liking to him. While his smile of welcome was tentative, he grew quite warm as we spoke.

"I am Sherlock Holmes. Conceivably you have heard of me."

"Yes, yes," said the man. "Very pleased to make your acquaintance, Mr. Holmes. I am called Wing Fu. How might I help?"

"I have a client who would prefer that his name not to be known," replied Holmes. "He has asked me to locate an Oriental man who lives in Limehouse and may be a recent arrival. This man is remarkable because he appears to have no nose."

The Chinese man's rather smooth features acquired a troubled look.

"I know of no such man, not of recent arrival. Certainly not in the last seven years, which is as long as I have held this position."

"The name he goes by is Li Shen."

"Ah. I know many men named Li Shen. Five, perhaps six in all. They all possess perfectly good noses."

"Perhaps this man has lost his nose since you encountered him last."

"Tidings in Chinatown travel on whispering wings. I hear much. I would have heard of such a man who had lost his nose." He shook his head resolutely. "I do not think there is such a man. I may be mistaken. It is always possible. But I do not think such a man exists."

"Is Li Shen a Chinese name?"

"Yes, of course."

"It is thought that this man might be from another country, such as Siam or Cochin-China."

"Men from those countries are not so called. Li Shen is Chinese name. There is no mistake in this."

"I'm given to understand that this Li Shen is the source of much trouble among the sons of the Flowery Kingdom."

"I hear the same," Wing Fu said cautiously, lowering his voice to a whisper. "But the men of the tong will settle him. Or so I understand. I can say no more."

"I thank you for your time," said Sherlock Holmes graciously. "It may be that you are correct in all of your statements."

The fellow's round face beamed. "I am pleased to have been of service to the illustrious Sherlock Holmes. Do not hesitate to ask if you have other questions, the answers to which I might truthfully know."

We stepped out into the gathering dusk. As Sherlock Holmes led the way back towards Limehouse Causeway, he remarked, "Wing Fu strikes me as an honest soul. I do believe he was telling us the truth, at least as he comprehended it."

"But I don't see how a man with no nose can escape notice in Limehouse," I commented, "his nationality notwithstanding."

"Perhaps it's because the man with no nose in fact owns a proper nose."

"Lestrade doesn't seem to think so."

"Lestrade doesn't know what I know. But I now have several facts in hand which, when combined, point me in the direction of a sound solution to the mystery."

"Now you outpace me, Holmes. If your quarry does in fact possess a nose, then you have nothing more to go on other than that he is an Oriental, might or might not be Chinese, and may or may not be named Li Shen."

"And yet out of this confusion, a picture forms in my mind. Let us see if we can ferret out this figure of mystery."

"How do you propose to do that?"

"First, by sending you back to the comforts of your home while I prowl the byways and alleyways of Limehouse by myself.

Unless, Watson, you would be interested in visiting an opium den?"

"I would not!" I said sharply. "And I strongly advise you not to do the same."

Holmes smiled pleasantly. "Do not fear for old habits creeping back and seizing my spirit. I am an old hand at navigating dens of inequity. I will do what is necessary, but no more. Good night to you. I am sure you can find your way home from here."

That I did, but as I jounced along in a cab, I feared for Sherlock Holmes. Of all the precincts of London, only Limehouse made me fret for his safety, since no disguise could conceal his British nature.

THE NEXT MORNING'S paper bought word of a calamity in Limehouse. From Limehouse Causeway to Shadwell and places in between, there had been an astounding succession of murders. Pistols were not employed. Knives and hatchets were the weapons of choice.

Scotland Yard was beside itself. There had been seven casualties, all told. The newspapers spoke of a war between the Azure Phoenix Tong and unknown rivals who were presumed not to be of Chinese extraction.

The incidents were centered around two competing opium dens, one in New Court, Victoria Street, and the other in the heart of Limehouse, above a gambling den on Narrow Street. The Chinese establishment had been burned to the ground in the first skirmish. Thereupon, the other establishment was assaulted, the attackers beaten off handily.

Among the casualties, one report had it, was a man without a nose.

I immediately rang up Holmes, but Mrs. Hudson answered, saying that he hadn't returned last evening.

"Good heavens!" I exclaimed. "I must see Lestrade at once."

I rang him as well, but the inspector wasn't available to come to the telephone. I hurried down to Scotland Yard in search of him, for I naturally feared for Holmes's life, as he might well have been caught up in the conflagration.

To my utter astonishment, I found Holmes conferring with Lestrade in the latter's office, to which they had repaired.

"Holmes!" I cried out. "I had feared the worst."

"And I have lived through the worst, as I was just explaining to Lestrade. No doubt you've read the morning news reports."

"I have. And I feared that you had perished in the New Court fire."

"Not at all, not at all. I was oblivious to that event whilst it was transpiring. I was safely ensconced in a rookery in a rival establishment, which was soon overrun by angry Chinese. I've never before made a mental connection between the Red Indian of America and the yellow warriors of China, but both seem to have a preference for employing hatchets to settle their differences. I, however, escaped in the course of events—but not without a prize."

"I hope it was worthy of the risk involved," I said more calmly.

Lestrade offered, "Mr. Holmes may have found our man."

Holmes countered, "I rather doubt it. But he should represent a lead of sorts."

"See here, Mr. Holmes," snapped Lestrade. "We have been seeking a man without a nose. Can you or can you not produce a man without a nose?"

"Yes, I can, but this man appears to have lost his nose last night, and your supposed noseless man was without proboscis a week ago. A man cannot lose his nose twice over."

At times I've been accused by Holmes of being slow of wit, but immediately I perceived my friend's point and couldn't understand Lestrade's failure to do so.

The inspector said in exasperation, "Then why did you bring this man in?"

"Because he was a victim of the mêlée, and I believe that once the hospital surgeon is done with him, he will have a tale to tell us."

"We've captured many Orientals who have tales to tell."

"The mere fact that this worthy has been deprived of his nose makes me think that his tale will stand out from the rest."

Lestrade frowned. "Go on."

Holmes obliged, "Last night, I was placidly listening from my curtained smoking compartment to all that I could hear, and it was an interesting way to pass the evening, for I learned much."

"I didn't know that you understood the Chinese tongue so well," I noted. "Will wonders never cease?"

"They may or may not cease, Watson, but they do not begin with me. The language I heard while eavesdropping was not Chinese, but *French*."

"French!" exploded Lestrade.

"Yes, the language spoken by many in the French colony of Cochin-China. Of course, they have their own tongue, but I'm no more a master of it than I am of Chinese. In any event, I was absorbing all that I could, and learning much, when the noisome establishment was invaded by pigtailed men brandishing hatchets, along with the disposition to do as much harm as possible. I didn't understand what it was all about, but I didn't need to. Seeking to escape injury, I witnessed a remarkable sight, a man being deprived of his nose by the crude instrument of a tong hatchet. He was about to have his head split open when I trained my revolver on the hatchet wielder, who promptly fled for his life. Taking the injured man outside, I blew on my police whistle—not that it was necessary, for constables were swarming, summoned by the screams and the screeches of the combatants milling all about us.

"I admit that I contributed to the quelling of the riot by firing shots into the air, followed by a judicious bullet into one intractable soul, one whose hatchet arm is quite useless at present. But my aim was accomplished, and I regret nothing. I took the noseless man in a cab to the nearest hospital, where I stood watch over him until Lestrade could be summoned to fetch him. That is why I am here, Inspector. To fetch you."

"My word!" I exclaimed. "Holmes, you got more than you bargained for!"

"More than I bargained for, yet also as much as I dared to accomplish. I think that a visit to the noseless man is in order, for by now he should be awakened to the day."

We all three went around to the hospital and paid a visit to the unfortunate individual.

The man lay in a bed, the remnant root of his nose bandaged, breathing through his mouth. He was a pitiful sight, pale of visage and crusty of eye. His English proved to be broken, but it was sufficient for a preliminary interrogation.

Lestrade opened this up.

"What is your name?"

"Wong."

"What were you doing at the opium shop last night?"

"Defending my brother."

"And who is your brother?"

The man was reluctant to respond and gave a mixture of English and Chinese, apparently calculated to confuse us. Lestrade pressed him and got from him only that he was part of the attacking party who were avenging a wrong done to them. What "wrong" wasn't made explicit.

Lestrade said to us, "This man is obviously a member of the Azure Phoenix Tong. The attack was doubtless meant to avenge the burning of the Chinese-owned opium den."

Holmes interjected, "With your permission, Lestrade, I have a few questions."

"See what you can do with him," he said huffily.

"Mr. Wong, I am Sherlock Holmes. It doesn't matter if you know my name or not. I witnessed the attack upon you. Your assailant was not Chinese. He made an absolute point of removing your nose. Why is that?"

"Wong not say. Private matter. Matter of honor."

"I preserved your life from a second blow, one calculated to split open your skull. A man intent upon cold-blooded murder by that means doesn't bother with removing a nose prior to slaying his victim. There was significance to the removal of your nose. I would like to know what it is."

Wong remained reluctant to speak. Holmes's penetrating gaze did not leave his bandaged face. It bored into him.

At length, the man relented. Reluctance threaded his voice. "We came for the other man's nose."

"Whose nose?"

"He goes by many names. We call him Gou. Enemies call him Cho."

"Does he also go by the name of Li Shen?'

"Li Shen is another name he uses. But that is not his name. No one knows his true name. But we call him Gou."

"This man is from Tonkin?"

"Yes. From Hanoi. But no one knows his name. Few have seen his face. He has smuggled in his own *chandu* to compete with Chinese. Takes away customers. Angers the Azure Phoenix Tong. Tong seek revenge."

"But why remove Gou's nose?" pressed Holmes.

"I will not say. Private matter. Private matter between Li Shen and Azure Phoenix Tong. To be settled by them and no other."

"He is a stubborn one," remarked Lestrade. "I'm surprised you got that much out of him."

"It is sufficient."

Lestrade raised an eyebrow in Holmes's direction and his mouth fell open. I don't think he knew what to say to that, so I asked the obvious question in his stead.

"Holmes, I don't see how you have advanced your investigation in the least. This business of noses makes no sense to me. If we're looking for a man without a nose, what is this business about other people losing *their* noses?"

Instead of replying directly to my question, Holmes addressed the inspector. "Lestrade, I imagine that your gaols are full of suspects collected during the course of the evening's activities."

"We have over twenty-five Asiatics in custody. We have them packed two and three to a cell. I understand that there have been a number of scuffles, since my men haven't the skill to separate the Chinese from some of the other nationalities, some of whom are apparently their rivals."

"I believe that an examination of these prisoners is in order. Allow me to propose an identity parade."

"If you think that it would accomplish anything useful."

"It's possible that our quarry is among this group. That is, if your men were thorough in apprehending the combatants— particularly those defending the opium den where French is spoken. If not, we should learn additional facts that would enable us to run to earth at last the man at the heart of all the trouble."

"Insofar as I am apprised of the situation," muttered Lestrade, "my men picked up no suspects possessing facial deformities of any kind. I particularly instructed them to look for absent noses."

Holmes smiled diffidently. "Humor me, Inspector. I promise that you will not regret it one jot."

BACK TO SCOTLAND YARD we went. There, Lestrade ordered the Oriental prisoners brought out before us.

There was a spacious hall used for this purpose, and the men were assembled as if upon the theater stage. Guards were posted at the doors and all around the stage. When all was at last in order, we entered.

These fellows made a forlorn picture. They stood elbow to elbow, cheek to jowl, crammed onto the stage, often two abreast, with those more guilty loitering in the rear of the line. Some had long queues, while others sported close-shaven polls. Many bore facial contusions and other marks of the night's battles. All were attired in the shirtings and cotton trousers preferred by the Chinese race.

Holmes paced before the group, which stood in two ragged rows, and scrutinized each man's features as he came to them.

As he conducted his examination, he began a recitation of his tentative conclusions that was as astounding as any I've heard in my capacity as his good friend and confidant.

"Several clues conspired to paint a picture which, while fanciful, seemed inevitable to me, even though I had to strain my imagination to its fullest in order to resolve it in my mind.

"Let's begin with the fact that the names by which we know this man, although apparently aliases, taking together point in a single direction. The Chinese called him *'Gou,'* which in their language means *'Dog.'* Among his own people, the mysterious fellow is known as *'Cho,'* a word that I suspect also has a canine connotation. I'm confident in this last deduction because early on, I received an inkling that the first name by which we became aware of him, Li Shen, was not his real name. Our investigation suggested that he came from French Indochina, which would make him Annamese, not Chinese."

"Chinese also live in French Indochina," Lestrade pointed out.

"Certainly, they do. But for the moment it was simpler to assume that a man from Hanoi would be a native of that country."

Holmes ceased his pacing and directed the guards to move the men standing in the back row forward, many of whom were so short of stature that only the tops of their heads, and perhaps their eyes, could be seen between the heads of those arrayed in the front.

As these individuals were brought into the gaslit glare, Holmes continued. "If the Chinese element were unified against him, it stood to reason that our quarry would not be Chinese. Otherwise, he would be absorbed into the local population. He was not. He stood apart. So when I selected an opium den to frequent last night, I chose one where Chinese was not the dominant language. This proved to be fortunate, because—as I've previously stated—I was able to understand much of what I overheard, since the common language was French."

Additional suspects were hauled forward, some of them reluctantly.

"In our first encounter, Lestrade," Holmes continued, "I was struck by the fact that you pursued a man without a nose. I didn't think that a noseless man would lack nostrils, given that without the nose, the human nasal cavities are rather in the nature of open wounds. I didn't think such gaps could be covered up successfully. Therefore, I considered the possibility that the man was not absent a nose, but that some other physical deformity was present, one that concealed his nose from view in poor light."

Holmes continued studying the new faces that were being thrust forward when there came a commotion, during which a man noisily refused to be brought into the light.

Police guards converged on him. Pulling him by the collar, they manhandled the reluctant one until he stood before us, head bowed, barking and snarling sulphurously in what I assumed was his native tongue.

"Lift his head so that I may see his features," requested Holmes.

A constable seized the man by his dark hair and brought his face into the sputtering gaslight.

Lestrade gasped. I was too shocked to emit such a human sound.

For the Oriental man who snapped so vociferously at us possessed a perfectly whole nose, except that it was flat and as black as a piece of coal. This gave him a peculiarity of countenance, upon which Lestrade remarked excitedly.

"Jove! He looks like a human dog!"

"More like a low cur," remarked Holmes dryly. "Here is your culprit, Lestrade. Li Shen is not a Chinese name. It is not his name at all. Rather, it is a French term, which has been the official language of Tonkin and all of Indochina since the Treaty of Tientsin. His name is actually *'Le Chien,'* otherwise *'The Dog.'* No doubt it was a name that he acquired as a result of his unfortunate birthmark, which appears confined to the vicinity of his rather truncated nose. I imagine the fact that the scoundrel speaks in barks and snaps as he is doing now contributed to the cognomen."

Staring at the fellow, I quickly realized the truth.

"That is a massive liver spot!" I exclaimed. "I have never seen one quite like it!"

A stream of invective erupted from the culprit. I understood none of it.

Lestrade ordered, "Take this man and confine him to a cell of his own."

Snapping and snarling in the Annamese tongue, with occasional outbursts of vituperative French, the elusive Li Shen was dragged away and out of our sight.

Lestrade turned and said graciously, "Mr. Holmes, it is as if you have spun an orderly web out of gossamer moonbeams, with every strand in its proper place. I would never have thought that the disparate threads you unearthed could lead to such a sound conclusion."

"I have already admitted, Lestrade, that imagination played a larger role in my deductions than is usually the case. But a man either owns a nose or he does not. When I considered that fact, as well as the sound of the name *Li Shen,* it all came together in my mind. The rest was, if you will pardon the expression, dogged determination."

"And some luck as well? Had you chosen a different opium den, you might have burned up in that hellish conflagration."

"The clues I had already accumulated led me to the correct den of inequity, Lestrade. No luck was involved. Only sound brain work."

"No matter how the pudding was prepared, we are in your debt again."

"Consider it my contribution as a concerned citizen," remarked Holmes, looking towards me for some obscure reason.

SOMETIME LATER, HOLMES and I were discussing a newspaper account that was as unexpected as it was grisly.

"It seems that our opium dealer of many aliases had an unfortunate encounter with one of his rivals while in prison," my friend related dryly. "An altercation led to the abrupt removal of the man's dark and distinctive nose."

"How was this accomplished under such well-guarded circumstances?" I demanded.

"The Chinese perpetrator employed his natural teeth to effect the amputation."

"How poetic—in a ghastly way," I remarked.

"It seems that Li Shen's unusual physiognomy marked him among other recent non-Chinese arrivals to Limehouse, and it inspired from the start a desire to remove his nose as a way of teaching him a lesson. Perhaps threats were made on that order. Hence the vicious and calculated maiming of the tong man who lost his nose, who remained reluctant to give us the full story, owing to the vows of his secret society. Now Mr. Wong's tragic disfigurement has been avenged and Li Shen has been traded, if reluctantly, one facial deformity for another."

"But how did he escape notice all that time?"

"A man cannot conceal the fact that he lacks a nose, which was another consideration in my thinking at the time. And a black-hued nose is almost equally problematic. But Asian women have their own brand of facial powder. A man could easily avail himself of a supply and powder his nose in such a way that it might pass inspection by night, if not scrutinized too closely."

"So we might have passed him on the street, never noticing his powdered proboscis?"

"Precisely."

"Well, that wraps up the matter rather tidily, even if the details make one pale."

"Not quite, Watson. There still remains the mystery of the man who wrote the intriguing letter signed, *'A. C. Citizen.'*"

"In the scheme of things," I said dismissively, "I consider that to be a trifle, unworthy of further consideration."

"On the contrary. I think it highly significant. And I formed a theory at the first, which I will now share with you."

I confess that I blanched at this point. But I held my tongue. My expression was all that Sherlock Holmes needed to read.

His gaze transfixing me, Holmes stated, "I propose that the author of that letter is no less than the distinguished Dr. John H. Watson of London, otherwise 'A Concerned Citizen,' for it takes no especial skill to divine the meaning of that unimaginative pseudonym."

"This is the limit, Holmes," I returned hotly. "The absolute limit!"

"You deny it?"

"What would be the point?" I said in exasperation. "But however did you deduce this?"

"You have certain cadences in your speech, my dear Watson, which are reproduced in your written work. I recited the letter aloud, if you will recall, which further cemented my first impression. And since you're in the habit of writing me letters from time to time, I've always noted your stubborn insistence upon capitalizing the word *'Yours'* in your customary closing, *'Faithfully Yours.'* While you possessed sufficient guile to replace this with *'Respectfully Yours,'* you repeated the error, rather like a schoolchild carrying over a mistake in mathematical computation."

"You have me. I do not deny it."

"Then pray explain what motivated you to take such a roundabout method to arouse my interest in the matter?"

"That much is simple," I explained. "This new type of opium has been leaking out of Limehouse and into the West End and the general population. I have had no less than three patients who appealed to me for succor. This is unheard-of in my long practice. Questioning my patients, I learned rumors of this *Li Shen*—or should I say, *Le Chien.* I contrived to bring the matter to your attention, but knowing well your ever-changing moods, feared that you might reject it as having insufficient mysterious elements to attract your interest. So I fell upon the ruse of writing you an anonymous letter."

"And I'm very glad that you did, for not only did you hand me an ingenious riddle to unravel, one the nature of which you did not at the time suspect, but I had the distinct pleasure of a secondary mystery, which proved to be the easiest to resolve."

"I don't know what to say. I composed that letter quite carefully, limiting my words, thinking you would never suspect the truth."

"I suspect everything, Watson. You should know that by now."

"I have learned my lesson. You cannot be beaten."

"Kindly refrain from including that erroneous point in one of your stories about me. I have been beaten. More than once, in fact. And I imagine that I'll be beaten yet again one day. But today, I sit triumphant and quite satisfied with the results of my efforts."

"As am I," I admitted reluctantly. "For I have had no recent opium addicts coming to my practice in need of weaning from the poppy's tyranny. And for that I am very grateful to you, my good friend."

THE ADVENTURE OF

OLD BLACK DUFFEL

"**I**T IS AN ever-changing world, is it not, my dear Watson?"

We were strolling along the Strand when my friend Sherlock Holmes chanced to make that remark. I didn't think it apropos of anything in particular. We had been taking the air after sharing a substantial meal in a new restaurant, the Aviary. As is often the case, we rambled along in silence, Holmes mentally ruminating on I know not what. Thus I observed a respectful silence.

More than once, my friend has vouchsafed that comfort with his silent companionship was one of my most endearing traits. I don't think that anyone else I could possibly encounter would share that opinion, but as it happened, many years of being on intimate terms with Holmes had inured me to his prolonged spells of introspection.

This conversation—if I may call something so one-sided— took place in the late autumn of the year 1894. The trees were almost bare. Winter was creeping close. I wore a muffler against its chill advance.

"I suppose that it is," I replied.

"London grows old, yet she renews herself in perpetuity. This is not the Londinium of our distant ancestors. Parts of it aren't even the London of our grandparents. Yet other quarters would be quite familiar to them. Consider the new Tower Bridge. Is it not a wonder? Some future generation may know of it only through photographs and the recollections of the aged.

A newer Tower Bridge may stand in its place, greater than the proud structure we presently admire. For one imagines that, a few centuries hence, it must be pulled down to make room for its inevitable successor."

"The Thames is quite different now than it was in our youth."

"How well I recall. It was filthy, an abomination."

Holmes lapsed into a period of silence, which I didn't trouble. I noticed that he seemed to pay scant attention to those passing by, and yet I suspected that he missed nothing. Many times he has upbraided me—if I may employ so strong a term—at the failures of my powers of observation. His were superlative. If I believed in such things, I would catalog them as supernatural.

Had I dared to use such a preposterous term to describe Holmes's rare abilities, he would have heaped such scorn upon me that I would have been ashamed to call him my friend—at least until such a time as his justifiable ire had subsided.

"That poor woman," he muttered at one point.

"The one with the towering auburn hair?"

"The very same," replied Holmes.

"She doesn't seem to my eye to be poor. I would class her as comfortably well off."

"I am not referring to the obvious, Watson. Not to her dress, nor her shoes. Nor the way her hair is arranged. I was referring to her eyes."

"I didn't note their color."

"A charming russet hue. Rather, the irises were. The whites of her eyes held the faintest traces of green. A very distressing thing to see in a young woman still in her prime."

"My word! I didn't see."

"But I did. I don't have to tell you that the green coloration of the eyeball is a symptom of advancing kidney disease."

"Kidney failure. Quite sad. I doubt that woman will live to be a matron."

"Nor do I. The green was quite pronounced."

Such were the powers of observation possessed by Holmes that I, despite my line of work, failed to diagnose the condition in a passerby. But he spotted it easily, no doubt at a glance. Another man might have admired the woman's figure, the color of her hair, and other feminine attributes. Like a hawk, Holmes's gaze went directly to the most salient feature.

We continued our stroll. Once or twice, Holmes made remarks after glancing at this person or that, deducing their occupation, and at one point, announcing a passing man's home address.

"How the devil could you deduce such a specific thing?" I demanded.

"A letter poking out of his coat. It displayed a street number of considerable digits, along with the initial of the street. Few London streets boast such a number, and the initial completed the revelation."

"I did perceive that he had an envelope sticking out of his coat pocket," I pointed out.

"Hardly a revelatory fact," said Holmes.

He wasn't smoking his pipe. His brow wasn't furrowed. And I hadn't heard from him any mention of a case all week. Yet he didn't seem to be bored. When Sherlock Holmes didn't have a mystery to solve, he often lapsed into boredom. This didn't appear to be the case.

"I imagine that since you are between mysteries, practicing your observational skills keeps them sharp."

"I don't practice them," he retorted. "They are ever-active. I don't even think of using them or not using them. Observing to me is second nature. It would be more difficult to ignore the data my senses pick out than otherwise." Rounding a turn, he added, "And I am not in fact between mysteries. I am at the very beginning of a new undertaking."

"Oh?"

"Have you not heard of the resourceful footpad who has become the scourge of the East End?"

"I have read in *The Evening Standard* that there has been an increase in assaults and robberies. No doubt the onset of winter compels the criminal class to take advantage of the plentitude of pedestrians before the first snowfall."

"I don't think it is that, although I don't doubt that your theory might not carry some weight. I think there is another reason for the increase. Nor do I believe that most of these outrages are the work of various individuals. More than once, the perpetrator has been described as wearing a duffel coat with the hood pulled up."

"Since the Royal Navy issues such coats, and any number of them are discarded each year," I observed, "this doesn't strike me as a very individual item of attire."

"In principle, I agree with you. But this duffel coat is unique in one respect: It has been dyed black as a raven's wing. The naval issue is, as you know, camel-colored."

"I see," said I. "That *does* alter matters. Do you think this footpad is a Royal Navy man?"

"I will not rule it out. But I am inclined to think that a British tar would have more respect for his convoy coat than would someone who plucked one off a trash heap where it had been discarded."

"I gather you have no suspects."

"On the contrary. I have scores of them. Too many to winnow them down to any two or three known police characters. That is the rub, Watson. The crimes are finite, but growing every week. Of suspects, I am blessed with an abundance."

"Have you made any progress?"

"Physically, no. Mentally, some. An insufficient amount, but I'm at liberty to label it as progress. 'Old Black Duffel,' as Scotland Yard has dubbed him, has twice escaped across the Thames, from one section of the city to another. On two occasions, he has disappeared up Kidney Stairs and onto Narrow Street in Limehouse."

"Suggesting that he dwells there."

"Possibly. Between the foreign element and the generally disreputable environment, Limehouse is an excellent section in which to become lost. But it's a place to begin. I don't have a high expectation of success based upon this one line of inquiry—but a start is a start."

"I quite agree. How will you proceed?"

"Old Black Duffel has already provided me with a glimmer of the patterns governing his brain-box. He prefers to commit his crimes on the southern side of the Thames and escape to the opposite bank, traversing the reaches between facing watermen's stairs which lie in a straight line from one another. If I seek him out on the northern bank, perhaps he will pick me out of the throng as a tempting target and attempt to make off with my wallet."

"My word, do you mean to *bait* him?"

"Once it is practical to do so. But first I must get the lay of the land—reconnoiter his haunts, as it were. You will wish me luck, Watson."

"Of course I do. Do you mean to start tonight?"

Coming to the Charing Cross Station, Holmes paused and said, "You have it exactly. We must part here, for where I am bound, a decent and well-dressed fellow such as yourself shouldn't venture, even in the company of a capable person such as myself. I will be in touch."

With that, Holmes disappeared from my sight, leaving me to walk back to Baker Street myself.

I didn't fear for his safety. I knew him too well to doubt his ability to handle himself under difficult circumstances. And yet I couldn't but feel a sense of unease. Holmes didn't normally go about armed, but he did have his single-stick. I hoped that it would prove sufficiently stout.

As I walked back to our common quarters, I made a greater effort to observe those whom I passed on the street. My observations produced only the most meager and routine conclusions, most of which lacked conviction. However, I did observe a fellow who showed signs of emphysema, or some other lung condition. His fingernails displayed a tell-tale blush tinge. Of course, this was precisely in my line. Understanding its medical significance, I resolved to mention it to Holmes at the next opportunity. I didn't think it would impress him, but hope does spring eternal.

I DID NOT see Sherlock Holmes again for several days

He failed to return to Baker Street to sleep, nor did he post any letters that would keep me apprised of his progress, if any.

I began to fear for his well-being. I followed the newspapers closely in that difficult interim, learning that Old Black Duffel had struck again, in Wapping this time, and again in Southwark. In neither case was anyone seriously injured. But still I fretted for his life.

Late one evening, my friend returned to Baker Street and resumed his armchair by the fireplace. I had already gone to bed. But the fragrance of his tobacco smoke wafted to my nostrils, awakening my senses. I threw off the bed covers, donned a dressing gown, and found him puffing away in his usual ruminative manner.

"My word, Holmes!" I exclaimed. "Where on earth have you been all this time?"

"Good evening, Watson. Sorry to rouse you from your rest. As to your question, I have been plying the Thames day and night. For I have taken to toiling as an unlicensed waterman. By day, I've fallen in with the members of that rather downtrodden class. By night, I prowled in search of Old Black Duffel, but without success. He is quite an elusive fellow. If I was in Southwark, he struck in Wapping. When I went to Wapping, he materialized in Southwark. It was as if he anticipated my movements."

"Have you learned nothing of this phantom?"

"I learned that the lot of a waterman isn't as jolly as the song of a century-gone-by would have it. The steamboats and the trains have stolen much of their commerce. They loiter about the crumbling old watermen's stairs along the embankments, virtually idle, ferrying the flotsam-and-jetsam of life that fortune brings to them. Where once they didn't lack customers, now they wait half the day for a farthing fare."

"But nothing of your quarry, I take it?"

"You take it perfectly. I had hoped to ingratiate myself into the watermen's trade, but there were so many of them that I haven't yet encountered any who have seen Old Black Duffel closely enough to describe his features."

"But surely some of these men have."

Holmes puffed away for a moment. Then he said, "Certainly. Between the licensed fellows of the Company of Watermen and Lightermen and his unlicensed rival, I have made many acquaintants. But their sheer numbers far exceed my energy, as well as my patience."

By this time, I had settled into my customary seat, facing Holmes.

"You aren't giving up? That doesn't sound like you."

"No, my dear Watson. Although I am weary, I'm not inclined to give up. But I must contrive a fresh line of inquiry if I'm to get anywhere. Old Black Duffel has continued his depredations, eluding Scotland Yard and, for the moment, confounding me."

"This is rather novel. I had half-expected you to return with the matter entirely resolved."

"I, too, harbored higher hopes than the meager fruits that I lay before you. I'm coming to think that Old Black Duffel is a clever chap. But how clever, I cannot say. His methods are simple. He strikes on one side of the town, seeks out the nearest river stairs where he accosts a waiting waterman, of which there is an ample supply, day or night, and allows himself to be sculled across to the river stairs opposite the scene of his crime. Afterward, he disappears into the night."

"One would think a waterman would report him to the nearest constable."

"A licensed waterman surely would. But an unlicensed one might not, for they are a wretched group, poaching upon guild men, and caring nothing for society at large. I'm inclined to believe Old Black Duffel prefers the unlicensed variety to any other."

"This is regrettable," I said. "You appear to have nothing beyond that with which you started—namely, a description of a coat."

"I have no more nor any less than what Scotland Yard currently possesses. Reports of a skulking black duffel coat, occupant unknown."

"What will you do next?"

Instead of replying directly, Holmes offered, "Let me suggest that you seek restful slumber, Watson. By the time I finish my pipe, I intend to do the same, for I'm at a dead end. I don't deny it. But I will allow my black shag to lull me into a frame of mind in which my brain will cease turning its gears and permit sleep. Tomorrow is a new day. I intend to make use of it, but at the moment I sit before you, unqualifiedly flummoxed."

With a sympathetic good night, I sought out my bed, and was soon fast asleep.

HOLMES WASN'T TO be found at breakfast. Nor did I see him the rest of the morning. His bed was neat, and appeared not to have been slept in. I didn't know what to make of that. And since it was a splendid day, I strolled about the city for several hours, enjoying the fresh air.

Only then did I remember that I neglected to inform Holmes of my observation of the man with the bluish fingernails. No doubt the opportunity would arise soon enough.

I next laid eyes upon Holmes at the supper hour. He came trudging up the steps without his usual spritely spring. From the deathly sound of his tread, I inferred that he had made little or no progress.

"Good evening," I said in greeting. "I was just about to go out for a bite to eat. Would you care to join me?"

"I would not," said Holmes in a disagreeable tone, doffing his raglan overcoat.

"No progress, I gather?"

"If you gathered this from my tone of voice, you are correct," he snapped.

"In truth, I concluded this fact from the sound of your foot-steps trudging up the stairs. They struck my ears as disconsolate. When you are on the hunt, your step is more lively."

Holmes sank into his familiar armchair. "It would appear that my ways are rubbing off on you. My congratulations."

"Since my appetite isn't yet at its peak, I'm prepared to join you as you consider matters."

Holmes reached for his pipe, and then took the Persian slip-per, into which was stuffed a supply of shag tobacco. "Let me not dissuade you from your supper. Such progress as I have made is the progress of the man approaching a fork in the road, only to discover even more forks beyond the one he must select."

"The problem multiplies?"

"The problem splinters like broken glass. I have more data than I possessed one day ago, but like a stained glass window that has fallen to the floor, I no longer hold a recognizable picture in hand, but instead the profoundly shattered remnants of one."

I sat down, knowing that when Holmes stood at an impasse such as this one, only two things were helpful. One was the silence of his own thoughts, and the other a stirring of his deduc-tive powers through conversation. I don't give myself very much credit for assisting my good friend in solving any of the unusual crimes that interest him, but as Holmes himself has said many times, I am something akin to a sounding board whose own observations and insights allow him to turn over a problem in his mind so that he eventually perceives all facets of it, much in the manner of a jeweler rotating a gem he is cutting so that all surfaces present themselves to his attention.

"The problem with observation, Watson, is that so few prac-tice it in a scientific manner. People observe what they happen to observe, nothing more and often less. Yet when impressed, they will expand upon their observations after the fact, filling in the glaring gaps with imagination and premature conclusions. I have been to Scotland Yard. I spent the better part of the day conferring with Inspector Lestrade. He has gotten nowhere. And he has led me to the identical empty destination."

"Surely the unwitting watermen and unfortunate victims provided some useful data," I offered.

"Pah! Useful if it weren't so contradictory. One victim claims that Old Black Duffel has dirty white hair, another says he is grey-haired. Yet another insists it is merely greying."

"In the dark, such distinctions are mere tricks of light and shadow."

"Unquestionably. The bounder hasn't been clearly seen. He no doubt contrived that this be so. He walks about hunched, with his lower face buried in the collar of his duffel coat. During each foray, he keeps his hood pulled over his head, yet is observed to wear different hats, all as black as roosting ravens. Once it was a gambler's hat. On another occasion, it was a so-called pocket cap, which can be crushed and pocketed or discarded. Between the hood and the hats, his visible hair makes little impression."

"Odd that he would wear the same coat, but change hats so frequently."

"Old Black Duffel hasn't worn the same hat whilst committing the robberies he has perpetrated. Lestrade informs me that on each occasion, he has discarded his hat on the side of the river to which he fled. Unfortunately, the hat size is meaningless, since it is invariably worn over the hood. No doubt it is at least a half-size larger than what the phantom would wear in broad daylight, and hence of no further use to him."

"Peculiar, that. His coat is the most distinctive item of his apparel, and therefore the most incriminating."

"Inasmuch as duffel coats are rarely dyed black, this particular coat has been made so for professional reasons. It is conceivable that the thief doesn't wish to abandon his most useful item of apparel."

"I quite concur."

"According to Lestrade," continued Holmes, "every victim agrees on a few points. The thief is an aged man of middling height and weight. He wears a unique black duffel coat. Some report that he has flaring nostrils, while others say they are merely distended from the exertion of his deeds. No one can speak authoritatively as to his eye color, for none have seen his eyes clearly."

"The only certainties appear to be that he is over sixty and lives on the northern bank of the Thames," I remarked.

Holmes made a sound deep inside his throat of derision. It now occurred to him to begin filling his pipe.

"Perhaps, perhaps not. I don't draw any strong conclusion from his method of operation. This is what is so baffling to me. I have handfuls of observational data from the victims and witnesses, but I cannot sort them into anything sensible. I don't know which I can safely discard and what I may retain as factual. Without a stronger foundation of facts, I cannot reason this out. Therefore, action is necessary. The brain has its uses. Reason is a tool. But sometimes men must use their more primitive skills to achieve their objectives."

"What do you propose?"

Holmes filled his pipe. He was looking at it as if not sure what to make of it. I have rarely seen him so distracted.

"I propose that we find ourselves a hospitable restaurant and dine well. After which I'm going to the East Side, where I will stride about and present myself as a potential victim."

"Do you think this wise?"

"Hardly, but I'm a desperate man. I've beaten my brains out against this riddle for nearly a week now. It is time for action. If you have a mind to, you may assist me. You will be my shadow, walking a block or two before or behind me. If he strikes, I will strike back. But if I fail, you will follow him as best you can. Between us, we might capture the bloke."

"It's chancy, but he hasn't committed violence as yet."

"Keep your revolver in readiness, Watson."

"Should you not have it?"

"I carry my own pocket piece, but I prefer to use my stick. The revolver is a tool of last resort. You will be our first resort, as well as my last, should I fall victim, my own weapon unfired."

"I wouldn't mind reversing our roles, as it were," I suggested.

"Not for a minute, Watson! This is my affair, and I prefer to act the central part in it."

"Since your mind appears to be made up, I won't attempt to dissuade you further."

Laying his pipe aside unlit, Holmes stood up and said, "Let us go about our business then."

We departed Baker Street and found a restaurant that we both agreed was substantial as well as economical. We ate our separate repasts, Holmes driving through his meal like a coach-man taking a late-night fare homeward. I was more leisurely, for I understood the value of proper eating in regard to sound digestion.

While we dined, I thought to remark on one puzzling point. "This is a lot of bother to go through, since you appear to have no client, and remuneration is therefore lacking."

"I consider keeping London safe to be in my own personal interest, my dear Watson," Holmes stated. "Inasmuch as I dwell within its confines, I'm not disinclined to contribute to its upkeep in my own way. Civic duty and all that."

"Well stated, Holmes."

When we were done, we made our way to Bermondsey, where we separated, Holmes walking ahead of me while I loitered for a few minutes before falling behind. Over dinner he had explained his reasoning for this choice.

Old Black Duffel appeared to be a creature of the London Docks, and Limehouse in particular. He had struck across the river at Southwark Park and Grand Surrey Docks, retreating to Shadwell and London Docks. Scotland Yard was lying in wait for him. Undercover men were about, watching the watermen's stairs. But the footpad had yet to do any robbing in Bermondsey, across the river from Wapping. This, deduced Holmes, was his likeliest hunting ground if he stayed true to form and wished to elude the police, who were being pressed by newspaper clamor.

The gas-lamps were illuminated by the time Holmes struck out for the congeries of tenement-choked streets that made up Bermondsey in the shadow of Tower Bridge. The leather trade was quite active here, so the parish was usually awash with tanners, leather-dressers, fellmongers, and the like. Longshore laborers, coal porters, bricklayers, costermongers and others added to the ever-shifting human tide. But as the hour was growing late, these examples were little in evidence.

I did my best to keep my friend within view as he wended his way through the darkened byways. The usual nocturnal inhabitants swirled around us—mudlarks, mariners, and stevedores. I kept a watchful eye as I moved from each oasis of gaslight to the intervening pools of shadow.

I observed that Holmes rambled about in approximate circles, keeping close to the river bank—for I understood that Old Black Duffel never struck except where a set of watermen's stairs were convenient for a quick escape.

Holmes turned onto Marygold Street and was briefly lost to view until I hurried up to the corner and made my turn.

When I caught up with him, I saw a remarkable thing. Although he had dressed modestly, he made no effort to disguise himself. Yet the more he walked along, the more subtly he altered his gait, decreasing the swing of his arms as he moved. He appeared to have lost a few inches in height, and his shoulders became slumped, his head hanging forward as if heavy with workaday fatigue.

Up until that point, I hadn't noticed what he had been doing. Having momentarily lost sight of him, upon catching up I would have mistaken him for another fellow, had it not been for the severe cut of his coat.

It has been said that the world lost a great actor when Holmes bent his considerable talents to detection.

As I was marveling over this artful transformation, which was still taking place before my eyes, albeit slowly, from out of a cobbled alley directly ahead, a shadowy figure stepped.

This figure was short and squat, and he came up from behind Holmes on mincing steps. I didn't see the blackthorn cane in his hand until it lifted. With a start, I realized that Holmes was about to be struck a cruel and cowardly blow upon the head.

"Watch out!" I shouted.

It was unnecessary, for Holmes was already turning, his own stick lifting. And for a moment two stout canes banged and clashed against one another as Holmes fought to beat off his attacker.

In the dark, I made out the fact that the man wore a bulky black duffel coat, the hood raised. A hat of some sort sat atop his hunched head.

I rushed ahead. Out of my coat pocket came my revolver.

The battle raged on. Not a word was spoken. Old Black Duffel—for this assailant could only be he—was giving a good account of himself. But he was soon overmastered by the towering strength of Sherlock Holmes.

The hat was knocked off the assailant's head. With his return sweep, Holmes struck the cane from his hand.

At this point, he broke and ran. I lifted my revolver into the air and fired a single shot. I don't know if, in his terror, Old Black Duffel simply didn't hear it, or if he didn't care. Escape was all that was on his maddened mind.

Holmes and I raced after him, I shouting for the blackguard to halt, and Holmes blowing on his police whistle.

These actions only impelled the man to pump his legs more strenuously.

We were in the vicinity of Fountain Stairs. Down them he plunged.

The bulky fellow reached the bottom before we could gain the top. A heated exchange of voices came from below. I could make nothing sensible of it.

When I reached the top step, I could spy Old Black Duffel hunched in a skiff being rowed away by a waterman, his head down, chin tucked into his coat collar, the greater portion of his head enveloped by the bucket hood of his bulky black coat.

His voice rose up in warning. "If you dare to follow, I will shoot this man! Do not tempt me."

The waterman, an elderly fellow with sparse hair, cried out, "Please, sir! He is armed. It is my life if you disobey."

We watched as the oarsman rowed strenuously, with Old Black Duffel keeping his eye on us both.

I demanded, "Holmes, dare we follow?"

Holmes shook his head gravely. "I wouldn't risk it. This is a stalemate. We must respect the danger to the poor waterman."

While we stood at the top of Fountain Stairs, waiting for a constable to arrive, we watched pensively as the poor waterman conveyed his unwanted passenger across the turbid waters of the Outer Pool to the muddy foreshore of Wapping.

There, he was let off. The devil scuttled up Wapping Old Stairs and was quickly lost from sight.

A policeman finally arrived, demanding, "What's the row?"

When Holmes identified himself, he was given all due respect accorded to the greatest consulting detective in London.

"We nearly bagged Old Black Duffel. He got away in that skiff."

The constable didn't have to hear all of it. His whistle skirled, and he shouted for the bewildered waterman to return for us.

This took some minutes, during which Holmes went back to the street and returned with Old Black Duffel's hat.

It was a gambler's hat, black and made of leather. A stylish thing in its extreme way, yet no proper gentleman would be found wearing one on the West Side.

Holmes was examining it as I was relating the events of the evening to the constable.

"A pity you didn't shoot him," the man said. "But it is understandable."

When the skiff bumped the bottom of Fountain Stairs, we were there to meet it and quickly climbed aboard.

"Take us across," the constable instructed.

"And give us your story as you row," added Holmes.

"Well, sir, you saw the whole thing, I take it. I was mindin' my lawful business, waitin' for a fare and the bloke descended upon me. He presented a derringer. An ugly little thing, black as if carved from coal. He showed me both barrels, and I didn't fancy either of them discharging into my entrails, so naturally I did as demanded. I have been on the river all of my adult life, and I wasn't ready to surrender it just yet."

"What does the fellow look like?" demanded the constable.

Holmes gave the answer to that question. "Round faced, not much above the age of sixty. Hair very grey. Clipped salt-and-pepper mustache. The eyes were pale blue. I will be happy to draw you a picture, Constable, when opportunity affords."

Addressing the waterman, the constable asked, "Can you add anything to that description?"

"I would say that the eyes were light grey, not blue."

"I disagree," said Holmes. "But that is the problem with individual powers of observation. No two persons see the same thing in the same way. And there are individuals who possess irises which appear grey or blue, depending on how the light strikes them."

There wasn't much more to the story than that.

We reached the opposite river stairs, bounded up to the top step, and looked about.

No sign of Old Black Duffel could be seen among the throng of dockers, street boys, and other river inhabitants.

"Vanished!" muttered the policeman.

"Not exactly," returned Holmes. "Observe where I point."

Up the way, peeping out from an ashcan was one sleeve of

the black duffel coat. We hurried up to it. Holmes lifted the lid, and the constable removed the threadbare item, now smeared with greyish coal ash.

"It appears that we harried him into abandoning his prized garment," I proclaimed.

"There can be no doubt that this is the same coat," said the constable.

Holmes inspected the garment. "None whatever. Observe the lining. Tartan. Royal Navy coats are lined plainly. This is a common coat, not a convoy coat which has been dyed black. Our man has no connection to the British Navy. We will turn the coat and the hat over to Inspector Lestrade. Perhaps he can make something more of it."

The constable availed himself of his whistle, and before long two of his fellows showed up. Once apprised of the situation, the trio dispersed in three directions, seeking the coatless man, armed only with the most vague of descriptions and his approximate hat size.

We went here and there, Holmes having observed where the police hadn't that in disposing of his coat, the rogue had disturbed some of the ash and stepped unawares in the residue that had leaked onto the cobblestones. We followed the trail of flaky ash for almost a block when at last all trace petered out.

An hour had almost elapsed. All concerned reluctantly concluded that there was nothing more to be discovered. Old Black Duffel had disappeared into whatever disreputable warren had welcomed him.

"This is Wapping," murmured one constable. "There are many gambling houses, spirit cellars, and other such unsavory establishments that would welcome such a man. We've looked about, but wherever he has gone, the edifice has swallowed him entirely."

Holmes said, "Very well. Give Inspector Lestrade my regards. Perhaps we will have better hunting tomorrow." He walked back to the river stairs and we descended to the bottom step, where

the gurgling Thames lapped against the stone. A different waterman was standing on the little jetty, his punt tied up there.

"Take us across," Holmes directed.

"Of course, sir."

We got in and the fellow began pulling at his oars. Engaging him in conversation, Holmes asked, "How is your business,
fellow?"

"Mighty poor. If you're workin' below the bridge, a bloke is
lucky to make ten shillings. But when winter comes it will be
far worse. I don't speak just for myself, but for my brothers on
the river. The steamships and the railways, as well as changin'
times, have all but done us in. When I was younger, this was a
good trade to apprentice in. No more. It would've been better
to become a scavenger or a mummer."

"I hear the same from others of your guild. I imagine it is
harder on a man of your years."

"Neither harder nor softer, sir. Us old 'uns have been puttin'
their pennies aside for many years yet. It is the young 'uns just
startin' out that struggle most. They never had the good times.
If you saved, you can press onward. If you didn't, I imagine your
future is bleak."

"Are you licensed, my good man?"

"I am, sir. But many aren't. They steal from us who are. But
what is a man to do? All one needs to be an able waterman is a
boat and a brace of oars. In my youthful days, I wore the dark
blue jacket and white ducks of my trade, as well as pumps so
polished they turned fair heads, they did. I cannot afford such
things anymore, for I have children to feed."

He pointed to his checked shirt and the black silk neckerchief
tied in a sailor's knot about his throat. "This is all the uniform I
can afford now. Most scullers don't bother with even that much.
It's rare to see the round glazed hat of old. But these are the
times we swim in."

When we reached the southern bank, Holmes paid the man

and asked, almost as an afterthought, "Do you know the other watermen who ply this reach?"

"Most, but not all."

"The man who took us across in the last hour might be familiar to you."

Holmes gave an accurate description of the fellow, but after scratching his head, the waterman said, "I don't know the bloke. I doubt if he has a license. I know all the licensed scullers by face and by name. I know their boats as well as I know my shoes. He must be in the way of a scalawag. Do you understand?"

"I do," said replied Holmes. "Good evening, and thank you."

Holmes strode about the neighborhood, looking in the alley out of which Old Black Duffel had emerged, but found nothing of interest.

Standing in this ill-lit court, I remarked, "Apparently we have struck a dead end as blind as this very cul-de-sac."

"Not entirely, for I have seen the bounder's face. And tonight I'll make a sketch of it and see that Lestrade has it by morning. Although we haven't captured the phantom, we have made the first progress that I can measure."

"No doubt he will lie low for a period of time."

"I would expect so."

"And when he resurfaces, if he does, he'll be wearing a different coat."

"But the same face, Watson. The same face."

OVER BREAKFAST THE next morning, Holmes wasn't in a talkative mood. Evidently he had slept, albeit fitfully. More than once, I had heard pacing in the sitting room. The odor of his tobacco smoke was fresh in the air when I awoke.

I permitted a certain interval of silence to pass while we consumed our eggs, scones, and tea. Then I ventured to remark, "Have you finished your drawing?"

"I have, but it doesn't satisfy me."

From the pocket of his dressing gown he removed a folded sheet of paper and laid it down on the table.

Sketched in sure-handed detail was the face of a man. His hair was concealed by a black hood, but his features were executed with the distinctness of an etching. The clipped mustache was rendered so that it was unmistakably of the salt-and-pepper variety.

"I didn't see the man's features as well as you did," I remarked, "but I would say that it is a credible likeness."

"It is the spitting image. Make no mistake about that—the spitting image. Yet for reasons I cannot fully articulate, it doesn't satisfy me."

"I wouldn't be so hard on yourself. A pen-and-ink sketch isn't the same as a camera study."

Holmes didn't reply. He continued eating.

The morning paper was at hand, and I opened it, seeking respite from Holmes's rather fuming silence.

"Good heavens!" I exclaimed.

"What is it?"

"Old Black Duffel struck again last night. Or should I say, quite early this morning. In Southwark, this time. A waterman carried him across the river to Queen's Stairs at Tower Wharf, where he made his escape."

"Would you hand me that?"

I did so. Holmes took the paper and read the account.

"According to this," he mused, "he's still up to his familiar tricks. He accosted a docker who was coming home drunk from a public house, relieving him of his wallet. Remarkable!"

"He isn't easily dissuaded from his self-appointed rounds." I remarked. "I wonder where he acquired another duffel coat dyed black so quickly?"

"It would be nearly impossible for him to do so, it seems to me. Therefore, one can only conclude that the old boy owns more than one such coat."

"The hat he wore this time was a derby. It was found on the other side of the river after he made his escape."

"Strange that he should change hats, but retain the same style of coat. What it offers in the way of concealment would seem to be a hindrance, insofar as his breathless escapes are concerned."

"Yet he has made them each time," mused Holmes, "effortlessly and apparently flawlessly."

"Except that you have clearly seen his face."

"Yes, I knocked his hat off his head at my first opportunity."

Holmes dwindled again into a sullen silence.

After I resumed my breakfast, I remembered something. "Do you recall the passing woman with the greenish eyes?"

"I do."

"After we parted that very night, I happened to notice a man striding along and, applying your own edict of observing closely, chanced to see that his fingernails were unusually blue."

Holmes frowned. "No doubt he suffers from some affliction of the lungs, or possibly the heart."

"Exactly. Oxygen isn't getting to his fingertips as it should. I passed by him rather quickly. But not so quickly that I failed to see that one telling thing."

Holmes's frown increased slightly. A notch formed between his bushy eyebrows.

"Tell me, Watson," he said dryly, "what was the color of his hair?"

"I didn't take note of that. He wore a top hat."

"I see. Did you happen to glance at his face? Did his eyes reveal their color?"

"In those brief moments, I had only time to study his hands. I couldn't tell you anything about his face or features."

"What type of coat did he wear? Surely, you spotted that?"

Feeling deflated, I allowed, "I confess that I didn't. Nor do I clearly recall."

"Therefore, Watson, you are deficient in the art of observation. You observed one thing closely and it so captivated your attention that you failed to apprehend any other details, other than the subject was a man who is well dressed."

"As a doctor, I would naturally observe things that are in my line."

"True enough. But as an observer, one must perceive as many things as possible, commit them to memory, and draw as many conclusions as possible from the data acquired. The eye must be quick. The mind even quicker. One must see and one must catalog, and most importantly one must retain all that one perceives. For what good is observation if the memory is faulty?"

"I fear that despite your example, my dear Holmes, I am still a mere amateur in the game of observation. With practice, I may improve."

"No doubt you will, no doubt you will." His voice was distracted, and I could tell that his mind was on the matter of Old Black Duffel even as his attention was struggling to get through his breakfast. When baffled, Holmes's appetite was thin. I imagine that he anticipated a long day ahead of him, or he would have skipped it altogether.

"As a medical man," I said with a trace of defensiveness, "I would naturally pay more attention to the morbid than the fashionable. One can hardly diagnose a man's condition from the cut of his coat, any more than one can tell very much from the duffel coat discarded so urgently."

"On the contrary. One can tell a great many things from a coat. A man's height. Conceivably his weight. Certainly his sense of fashion is evident in what he wears, from which one can readily deduce his station in life."

"Not in this instance, Holmes. Surely the man has affected the dark duffel coat in order to skulk about, and for no other reason."

Something appeared to click in Holmes's brain. I didn't think he had heard my last remark, but evidently he did. For I saw a sharp light spring into his keen eyes.

"Watson, you are a godsend. I have the key!"

"I beg your pardon?"

He stood up abruptly, his breakfast forgotten. He folded the sketch of Old Black Duffel and placed it into his dressing gown.

"I must be off and hasten to share my theory with Inspector Lestrade."

"Do you have a theory?"

"When you noticed the man's fingers but failed to observe his coat, you were demonstrating a principal known to all who practice the arcane art of stage magic."

I struggled to respond.

"Misdirection, Watson! Misdirection is the key!"

And with no more explanation than that cryptic refrain, Holmes dashed to his room, dressed for the day, and left for Scotland Yard, leaving me in a most profound quandary.

I couldn't imagine what he was talking about.

TWILIGHT WAS UPON the city as I was walking homeward for the day. Turning towards Baker Street, I was startled by a hansom cab pulling up to the curbstone. Out of it stepped Sherlock Holmes.

"Watson! Ask no questions. Join me."

I did as my friend requested, climbing in ahead of him. The driver was soon off and running.

"May I inquire where we are bound?"

"I have had an interesting afternoon with Lestrade. I believe that I've worked out a great many things that were previously obscured."

"This is good news. Congratulations!"

"It may be some time yet before true congratulations can be accepted, but we're once more on the scent-trail."

"Jolly good. Knowing the blighter's face should make the battle so much easier."

"I wish that were true, but it is only partially true. Perhaps half-true. Perhaps only a third true."

"I don't follow these strange constructions of yours."

"If we're successful, all will be revealed. And the shadowy footpad will be ours."

We were let off in Rotherhithe at Cockold's Point, where Inspector Lestrade appeared to be waiting for us. Dusk was gathering. Evening would soon be upon us.

"Good evening to you both," Lestrade greeted. "Dr. Watson, are you ready?"

"As ready as I imagine I will ever be. But Holmes hasn't explained precisely what I should be ready for."

"All around us, constables are strolling about in disguise. Mr. Holmes will select a path, and I understand that you will select another."

"If you're willing," said Holmes. "Previously, the bait was sparse. Now it will be plentiful."

"I see. I suppose that I shouldn't refuse. But I don't have my pistol."

"You may not need it, for I don't intend to stray very far from your path. You see, having been waylaid once, I expect that I will be avoided henceforth."

At this point we separated, Holmes admonishing me to keep near to Pageant Stairs and Horse Ferry Stairs.

Knowing that my friend was close at hand, I set out on my way. I walked at a slower pace than is my wont, circling about as if I had lost my way, a gentleman from the West Side slumming through this East Side labyrinth.

Holmes was a canny man. He left little to chance. On this evening, his plan appeared to be sound—but that didn't mean that it was foolproof.

As I traversed Rotherhithe Street, I approached Pageant Stairs. Below its steep incline, watermen and lightermen were pushing their boats about the slate river. Darkness lay upon the Thames like a blanket of sable.

It was ebb tide. The mudlarks and scavengers were out, digging away at the exposed mud of the shore in search of dropped coins and other minor salvage. I paid them no heed. They were as eternal as the ravens at The Tower of London.

Looking out at the sluggishly flowing river, I saw a small punt approach—a waterman with his fare.

In the dark, I could make nothing of them, but one sat hunched in the bow of the boat, swathed in shadow. He held his head down, as if it was raining. Perhaps it was the chill that caused him to do so.

As the waterman feathered his oars to bring his boat alongside the bottom of the stairs without undo jarring, the passenger stepped off without a word or even to pay his fare.

Up the steps he came, his spring purposeful.

As he walked, he took a hat out from a commodious coat pocket and, blocking the crown properly, placed it up on his head. It was a gamblers hat. His coat was a black, bulky affair and the hood was up.

That was when I realized the truth.

Mounting the steps came Old Black Duffel himself!

I stepped away, feigning nonchalance.

As the fellow reached the top step, I said to him, "Good evening." I kept my voice level.

"It will be a good evening if all goes well," the fellow said thinly.

"All seldom goes well, especially in this part of the city at this hour."

The man halted, and he stared at me. The brim of his hat threw his features into deep shadow.

"Queer thing to say."

"But truthful," I returned.

"Do I know you?"

"I doubt it. I'm rarely in Rotherhithe."

Curiosity caused his head to cock like that of a dog as he approached me.

"Slumming, are you?"

I stared at him closely, expecting to behold the features sketched by Holmes from memory. But to my surprise and relief, this old fellow bore no resemblance to the man so sought by Holmes and Scotland Yard. His upper lip was cleanly shaven. The clipped mustache of the other night was wholly absent. Of course, mustaches are easily shorn.

My failure to reply caused him concern.

"Do you know me?" he demanded.

"I scarcely think so," I said curtly. "Good night to you. Have a pleasant evening."

With that, I turned on my heel and began to walk briskly. I didn't care for the man's tone of voice. Nor was I any longer certain that I had correctly identified him.

With a scuffling of leather heels, he caught up with me and blocked my way.

"I will trouble you for your wallet, sir."

Ordinarily, I would resist. But I knew that Holmes was nearby.

"This is rather rough, sir!"

"I'm a rough sort of fellow. Now your billfold. Hand it over."

Reaching into my coat, I produced the item and tendered it to the fellow.

He was quick off the mark, I'll give him that. Down the river stairs he raced and into the boat bobbing below he jumped.

I heard him shout, "Haste! I'm returning to Limehouse."

I couldn't see if Old Black Duffel produced his pocket pistol, but the waterman didn't give an argument. He dropped upon his bench and took up his oars. Soon, he was pushing across the sluggish currents of Limehouse Reach.

"Holmes!" I cried out. "Holmes!"

He came out of the shadows from a direction I didn't expect.

"He has my wallet!" I told him, pointing down the stairs.

"I know. I saw it all, Watson. You did well."

Holmes raced down the stairs. Upon reaching the bottom, he called to the waterman to turn around.

Back came the piteous reply. "I cannot, sir! That would mean my end."

"It will mean jail for you if you don't return after you have dropped off your passenger," warned Holmes.

"I understand, sir."

In the darkness, Old Black Duffel was hectoring the poor waterman to pull harder, ever harder.

By this time, I had joined my friend at the bottom of the river stairs.

"If there were only another waterman about," I said. "We could give chase."

"Chase may not be necessary. All has been thought out well in advance."

Soon, the boat was all but lost to our view. But across the dark current, we could hear its bow grate against Kidney Stairs.

Hearing that sound, Holmes lifted his pistol and fired two shots into the air.

"A signal?" I cried.

"Yes, Watson. A signal to our allies."

Before long, the waterman returned and bumped his craft into the bottom of the stairs at our feet.

We leapt aboard with Holmes exhorting the man to return to the opposite bank. "That was him. Did you see his features clearly?"

"I did, sir. He was round of face and with red cheeks. His nose cut exceedingly narrow. Like the back fin of a shark, it was. I would know him anywhere."

I said nothing. The bounder who accosted me didn't lay claim to either description, but in the darkness, such mistakes were commonly made by the unobservant, as Holmes would no doubt remind me.

The waterman got us across in excellent time.

Down Kidney Stairs came Inspector Lestrade, saying, "My men are following him. He shall not get away this time."

"Excellent!" said Holmes. "This waterman got a good look at him."

Inspector Lestrade addressed the fellow. "You must come with us as a witness. Strictly a matter of form, you understand."

"If I must," the man said hesitantly.

He stood up in his boat, then stepped off.

We four pounded up Kidney Stairs. When we reached the top, I saw the waterman's face clearly in the gaslight.

"Upon my word!"

"What is it?" the waterman demanded, startled by my outburst.

Holmes interrupted. "Time enough for conversation later. Let us see what the constables have accomplished."

We strolled up gaslit Narrow Street with its Georgian terraced houses and dust-heaps. A uniformed constable came to meet us, the black gamblers hat in hand.

"An undercover man is right behind the blighter. He'll blow his whistle at the appropriate moment."

The waterman quavered, "Sirs, is there danger for me here?"

"I imagine so," admitted Holmes. "But as a good citizen I trust that you'll put aside all considerations of personal risk, for we are on the trail of Old Black Duffel, the scourge of the Thames."

"I don't feel comfortable, sir, for I'm up in years. I don't wish to squander any of my remaining time on earth."

"Buck up!" encouraged Holmes. "This is Inspector Lestrade of Scotland Yard, and I'm Sherlock Holmes. This is Doctor Watson. Together, we'll see that no harm comes to you. But it's essential that you aid us in identifying the man who stole the doctor's wallet."

"Can *he* not identify him?"

Lestrade said, "Two witnesses are more material than one. Especially under these circumstances."

We walked along. It wasn't many blocks farther when a police whistle resounded. We picked up our pace and hurried in its direction.

The undercover man waved to us and pointed to a plain door that led to a basement of a decrepit building.

"He went down there, sir. It is a gambling den of known disrepute."

"Sound your whistle again, constable."

The piercing whistle brought additional reinforcements. One constable was deputed to hold the frightened waterman in safety while the rest of us went down the creaking and rickety stairs into such a foul den of perdition as I had never before seen.

As we descended, I whispered to Holmes, "That waterman looked familiar to me."

"Thank you, Watson," Holmes returned.

I didn't immediately understand his reply.

Three constables surged into the smoky gambling den and announced themselves to the shiftless Chinese, English bully boys, and polyglot harridans who congregated there.

"We seek a wanted man. Once we have him in hand, we will trouble you no more."

Holmes raised his drawing for all to see, adding, "This is the man in question. If he is on the premises, he should present himself and submit to arrest forthwith."

Holmes went among the riffraff, displaying the drawing and receiving muttering responses to the effect that no one present had ever laid eyes upon such an individual.

"He is Old Black Duffel himself," Lestrade announced. "He was seen entering this establishment. Once we have him, our business here will be concluded."

The constables failed to find their man, but they did locate a black duffel coat. It was hanging from a hook amid a flock of others, conspicuously buried between varied items of apparel.

"Who is the owner of this?" demanded Inspector Lestrade.

No one claimed the coat.

Drawing close to me, Holmes made his voice very low. "Watson, point out the man who accosted you."

I confessed to being quite puzzled. But I did as my friend requested. I went among the group, and soon found him.

Out from a pocket of the red-faced bounder's waistcoat came a small black derringer.

"I'm not afraid to use this!" he cried out.

Lestrade was firm and without fear. "You have two bullets to expend. And we are many."

Producing his own revolver, Holmes pointed out, "There are six shells in my cylinder. I don't believe the numbers are in your favor tonight."

Old Black Duffel was having none of it. "Nevertheless, you will let me go free, or some of you will die. Now make a path. I'm a desperate man. Do not underestimate me."

The crowd in the gambler's den didn't seem very agitated by the sight of the small black derringer. No one made any outcry. Nor did anyone drop to the floor in fear.

I took a step back from the man and bumped into the edge of a round table. Reaching back, I found a stout mug of beer. This I grasped.

The man's eyes were on the door leading up and out, and he directed the blunt barrels of his derringer on the uniformed men. He was quite intent upon escape.

Hence, as he moved past me, it didn't register on him that I was swinging the mug downward, knocking the derringer from his fist, and incidentally but fortuitously stinging his eyes with a flying wave of beer.

His empty hands clapped over his eyes in blinkered surprise.

"Well done, Watson! Well done!" cried Holmes as the constables descended upon the shocked man.

"I will trouble you for my wallet when you are no longer engaged in resisting arrest," I said casually.

Handcuffs in place, the man was hauled to his feet and stood before Lestrade and Holmes.

"If you don't need my wallet as evidence," I said firmly, "I would like it back."

Lestrade's questing hand found the wallet and surrendered it to me.

"But I don't understand," I said, studying the man. "This isn't the robber you drew."

"Let's take our prisoner out into the fresh air, Lestrade," suggested Holmes. "We'll sort things out under cleaner light."

The prisoner was taken to the sidewalk, and his vociferations were coarse and repugnant.

Turning to me, Holmes asked, "Watson, did you not say something about the waterman being familiar to you?"

"In a vague way, yes."

"Perhaps this will assist your memory."

Holmes held up the drawing of the man who had accosted him previously. Except for the absence of a recently-removed clipped mustache, the likeness was sound.

"There is your answer."

Lestrade said, "Consider yourself to be under arrest." Handcuffs were placed on the waterman's wrists. He made no resistance. Shock made his face pale and his expression momentarily vacant, slackening his lean jaw.

"What is this?" he managed. "Am I not a witness?"

Holmes asserted, "I believe the correct term is *accomplice*."

The prisoners were taken away forthwith. Lestrade addressed Holmes, saying, "Your theory was correct, Mr. Holmes. Congratulations. You have done it again."

"Thank you, Inspector. It was quite a chase, but in the end the hounds won the day, whilst the foxes now stand to pay the penalty for being the wretched curs that they truly are."

ON THE RIDE back to Baker Street, Holmes divulged the remaining pieces of the puzzle.

"You see," he was saying, "Misdirection was the key to everything. I had thought that the differing descriptions could be laid at the failure of ordinary persons to note and recall items of description faithfully. While this is demonstrably true, it wasn't necessarily the answer. When you mentioned your failure to recall the coat worn by the man with the blue fingernails, it was as if my brain was a photographic darkroom that had been illuminated by a candle.

"Heretofore, we had assumed that our footpad wore a black duffel coat to assist in his nocturnal operations. That he was an aged man seemed beyond question. But it dawned on me that when Old Black Duffel disposed of his coat, yet reappeared within hours wearing another, I knew that there were two coats, not one. Two coats suggested two rogues. The uncommon black duffel coat had to be replaced, because it was the key to their misdirection. In reality, it proved to be their undoing."

"I see now. One man rowed the other to the scene of the crime and then brought him back to his safe harbor in Limehouse, or some waterside stretch convenient to it. But Holmes, the waterman of the other night is neither of these criminals."

"And here I came to another conclusion: If there were two rogues playing the part of Old Black Duffel, why not three, or four, or more?"

"It is a ring of thieves!" I cried.

"More correctly, it is a clutch of starving watermen who banded together in a joint scheme. Unable to make a living by day, they turned the disadvantages of their dying profession into the illicit advantages of a common cause. All were older, and most were destitute and unlicensed. Virtually anonymous, they were able to operate with impunity, wearing different hats, but the same jacket. In all reports, the bucket hood was raised, concealing much of the guilty party's head even after the hat was abandoned."

"No doubt the idle watermen plying the river served as spies, frustrating the police investigation."

"As well as my own. In gaining the confidence of certain scull-ers, I inadvertently betrayed the fact that I was on their scent. Small wonder Old Black Duffel never struck where I toiled. He was advised of my whereabouts."

"But what about the others? There are thousands of unli-censed watermen plying the Thames. We have no idea how many number this ring."

"Small matter. I will draw another sketch for Scotland Yard. The waterman who slipped away the other evening will be picked up before long. I imagine Lestrade and his men will extract much useful information from their prisoners. That is work best suited for them. We have achieved our goal, Watson. The ring is smashed. Their ways are known. No more will they glide across the mighty Thames in search of meager fares and greater plunder."

"Well done," I said heartily. "But I remain unclear on one point: How did you know to come to Rotherhithe on this very night?"

"Even though he was not a single individual, Old Black Duffel showed that he was a creature of habit. Invariably, he came 'round to Limehouse. I imagined that meant that one of the footpads who took on the dark mantle lived there."

"I see. Each man retreated to his own personal stamping ground at the conclusion of a foray."

"Precisely. It was only a matter of time before the inhabit-ant of Limehouse took his turn. If it didn't occur tonight, the man's turn would soon arrive. I was prepared to stalk Rother-hithe until it did."

"Ah, so patience won this day, as much as did scientific obser-vation."

"The salient lesson here, Watson, is that observation without discernment is only a half-measure. One can recognize a shil-ling at a distance, but if the distance is too great, it is difficult to impossible to tell whether one is looking at the face of the coin, or its reverse."

"Remarkable what alterations the passing years bring about," I mused. "A group of aging idlers down on their luck banded together to make an unsavory living. Desperation motivated them. Once they were jolly young watermen in their polished pumps, white ducks, and black hats. And now—"

"And now they are bound for prison...."

THE ADVENTURE OF
THE NEBULOUS NIHILIST

ONE OF THE most remarkable experiences in all of my dealings with the illustrious Mr. Sherlock Holmes began with the simple act of opening a door.

It was half-past three in the afternoon of April 28, 1895, when the brass clapper gave up a resounding clamor.

Holmes was deep in the study of a pamphlet on something or other and looked up to request, "Be good enough to answer that, would you, Watson?"

"Are you expecting a client?" I inquired.

"I daresay I am always *half*-expecting a client. But this afternoon, no."

I threw open the door and took in a sharp inward breath of surprise.

The man standing at the stoop was of military bearing. He stood no less than six feet tall in height, and his black eyes snapped under a shock of dark hair shot with glints of grey. But these details were not what flummoxed me at first sight, rather it was the vague yet alarming resemblance to Holmes himself. It was in his gaunt face, in the steely look in the man's eyes. The predatory nose, the sharp features. All of it.

I found myself searching this man for other clues, when he said in a brusque American voice, "I should like to see Mr. Sherlock Holmes. If I may."

He presented me with his card. It read:

COLONEL RICHARD HENRY SAVAGE
U.S. Army
Retired

"One moment," I requested.

Taking the card to Holmes, I waited expectedly for some sign of familiarity. There was none.

Instead, Holmes laid his pamphlet to one side and arose.

"Bring him in," Holmes said.

I did as instructed, and when the two men came face to face, they did so as evident strangers.

"Mr. Holmes, I understand that you accept private consultations," said the American colonel. His manner was direct, and admirably to the point. There was an air of brisk, nervous energy about the colonel that reminded me again of Holmes, but in a rather different way.

"If the matter is of sufficient moment to interest me," Holmes allowed. "Pray be seated."

The two men sat down without the preliminary of a handshake.

Holmes appraised the man with his inquisitive eyes. "You are a man of the world, I take it, Colonel Savage."

"I consider myself an old campaigner," Savage replied.

Holmes nodded. "They are much the same thing."

Holmes lit his pipe thoughtfully. I often saw him doing this as a cover for sizing up visitors. He resumed his inquiry. "You are an author, I take it?"

"Yes. You have heard of me?"

"Your novel, *My Official Wife*, received an enthusiastic review from *The Times*. I recall the reviewer wrote that 'It is a wonderful clever *tour de force*, in which improbabilities and impossibilities disappear, under an air of plausibility that is irresistible.'"

"You have a remarkable memory, Mr. Holmes. I believe that those are very nearly the exact words employed."

"They are *precisely* the exact words," said Holmes. "They

impelled me to lay hands on your extravagant novel, which I have read."

The colonel's dark eyes seemed to light up, only to dim as Holmes went on with his characteristic frankness. "I found it to be, in *The Times*' words, 'wildly extravagant.' But I congratulate you upon its success, Colonel Savage. Now what service may I render you?"

"That you have read my little novel greatly reduces the need for explanation, as you will see," said Savage. "I am a world traveler, and have seen many lands."

"Among them, Russia," Holmes suggested.

"Yes. I was present in that vast land when Tsar Alexander II was assassinated a decade ago. You see, the events as described in my story have a basis in actuality."

"Say no more. Watson, have you read the colonel's novel?"

"I confess that I have not," I admitted.

"Simply told," says Holmes, "it is a fanciful account of the colonel gallantly passing off a Russian Nihilist as his wife, as she fled the Russian Secret Police in the wake of the assassination."

"Exactly," said Colonel Savage. "The woman in the matter was no figment of an author's imagination, but a creature of flesh and blood like ourselves. Although I took liberties with the greater portion of the tale, up until our arrival in St. Petersburg, the story is, with only minor embellishments, the truth."

"I see," said Holmes. "And now you seek my aid in determining her fate?"

The colonel gave a short gasp. "How the devil did you deduce that?" he fairly exploded.

"It is quite elementary, my dear colonel. If the woman in question is taken from life and the factual account ceased at Saint Petersburg, therefore her fate must be unknown to you."

The colonel composed himself. "Yes. Allow me to finish. I am in London in response to a secure wire that was signed by a *nom de guerre* known only to me. It is the selfsame *nom de guerre* used by my Nihilistic friend during our brief time together. Naturally, I was astounded to receive such a communication, since I had assumed that the woman in question had been captured by the Royalists and no doubt shot, or quietly strangled for her political activities."

"Go on, Colonel," Holmes urged.

"Arriving in London I went straightaway to her hotel. But the clerk swore up and down that no one of that name, or any name by which I knew her, had taken rooms there. Nor did anyone on staff recognize her description, which I gave most minutely."

"Therefore you suspect a hoax, perhaps some enemy luring you to London for dire and murky motives?"

"I admit that such has crossed my mind. But my chief concern is the woman. Did she survive? Is she now in London? Have agents of the Tsar tracked her down? Has she been—"

"Murdered?" Holmes supplied.

"Yes! You can understand that although I am a married man, and happily married to boot, having assumed this woman long dead, I could not resist the call to find out for myself."

"And you have had some luck in your quest, I take it?"

Savage started. "However did you guess that?"

"I did not. I am a student of human nature. If a man crossed the Atlantic in order to track down a long lost compatriot, one who was presumed dead, only to find an empty hotel room, I daresay he would be depressed. On the contrary, you are ener-vated. You have found more than a blind alley filled with ques-tions."

"It is true," said Savage, "I was reconnoitering the streets of London when I chanced to spy her in the crowd. I called out her name. I ran after her. But she fled. And I lost her in the teeming throng, damn the luck."

"A glimpse of a woman in a crowd is hardly sufficient to ascer-tain identity," Holmes offered.

"This was no ghost. I would swear that it was she!"

"A trifle older, I imagine."

"Not so that I could have been fooled," Savage countered. "She is in London. And I must locate her, Holmes. Will you help?"

"Having read your book," Holmes essayed after a pause, "I confess the mystery intrigues me."

At this point I interjected, "But Holmes. Why would the woman in question wire Colonel Savage to come to a certain address, then disappear into thin air?"

"Ah, Watson. She did not vanish. She was never at the address to begin with. Don't you see? Fearing for her life, she dared not relay her actual lodgings. But they cannot be far. For how else could she monitor the colonel's arrival?"

Colonel Savage leapt to his feet. "Then you will consent to come with me, my dear Holmes?"

"Colonel Savage, I deem it your second chance to entertain my fancy," said Holmes, taking his revolver from a drawer and pocketing it.

AS THE FOUR-WHEELER drew us along London's substantial cobbles, Holmes pressed Colonel Savage for additional details.

"I never knew the woman's true name," the colonel related. "She called herself Helene Marie Vanderbilt-Astor Gaines—a concoction no doubt derived from a close reading of the news of the world mixed, perhaps, with gleanings from tawdry shop girl romances."

"Describe her, please," Holmes prompted.

Colonel Savage painted a portrait in words that any artist might transfer to canvas without difficulty. He was a keen observer, of that there could be no doubt.

"This is a delicate matter for you, is it not, Savage?" Holmes said after absorbing the careful description.

"Indeed. I left my wife at New York, lest there be any misunderstanding."

"No doubt," replied Holmes. "But I was referring to your connection to the Russian Royal family."

"You know of that!" Savage sputtered.

"Tut-tut. You give me overmuch credit. Much publicity attended the publication of your popular novel. It was reported that your daughter is married to the Chamberlain to the throne."

"True. And the survival of the unfortunate Nihilist might lead to political complications with the Russ. For I have done considerable diplomatic work in my time, much of it of a confidential nature."

"Complications that it would be best to avoid," said Holmes.

Savage bowed his head gravely. "Your discretion would be greatly appreciated, Holmes."

"My discretion is at your disposal."

At length, we arrived at our destination.

Alighting, Holmes invited, "Now, Colonel Savage, if you would be so good as to show us the precise spot where you spied the beautiful Nihilist."

"This way, gentlemen."

The colonel went to a street corner where a tobacconist had his little shop. Taking a position, he faced slightly northwest, and lined up his penetrating dark eyes with a far alley.

"There!"

We followed him to the area in question.

"It was much busier than it is now," Colonel Savage explained. "But I am certain that I ran to this very spot, by which time she was no longer there."

Holmes took a position on the designated spot. He turned about in a slow circle, eyeing the view from every possible angle.

"Any number of avenues by which she might have fled," he mused. Then he selected one, by what means of calculation I confess that I do not know. But Holmes strode with the purposefulness of a fox on a scent until he arrived at a certain door.

"The woman you spied," he announced suddenly, "vanished through this door."

"What leads you to that conclusion, Mr. Holmes?" Savage asked without a trace of surprise in his voice. Evidently, he was fast becoming accustomed to Sherlock Holmes's rapid deductions.

"Look about you, Colonel. Do you see any other means by which an adult woman might disappear from sight of a throng of passersby?"

"I do not," Savage admitted. And I could not gainsay him. It was the only door close enough to the spot where the woman was last seen which could be reached in the time it would have taken the colonel to cross the street from the far corner.

That settled, Holmes gave the handle of the door a firm tug.

The door surrendered easily. It proved to open into a kind of cul-de-sac where ash barrels and rude tools were stored. Its confines were small, to be sure.

"I daresay a woman might have loitered here undetected if one did not possess the wit to try the door," Holmes said.

"I am not in the habit of opening strange doors," Colonel Savage said stiffly.

"I meant no offense, Colonel Savage," Holmes said hastily. "I was merely thinking out loud. For two things are now obvious."

"Not to me," said the colonel.

"The first is that the lady in question did not wish to be found by you at the time you came across her. That much is evident by her seeking refuge in such squalor."

"And the second?"

"The second is that she greatly desires a meeting with you, but under circumstances far more to her liking. I would judge that she deliberately showed herself to further that end."

"What makes you say that?"

Holmes pointed to a fragment of lace he had removed from under the rim of an ash barrel's dented lid. He was looking at it in the dim light. With a flourish worthy of a stage conjuror, he turned it about, presenting one face. On the faintly soiled surface a solitary word had been written in ink, apparently in a woman's delicate hand:

Blackness

"Good Lord!" Colonel Savage said hoarsely. "What can that possibly mean?"

"Not possibly," returned Holmes. "Definitely."

NOT A QUARTER hour later, Holmes had guided us to Charing Cross Station and as nightfall smothered the surrounding towns, we were whisking south to some unknown place.

"If I may inquire, Holmes," asked I. "What is our final destination?"

"Blackness," said Holmes gravely. "Nothing more and scarcely less."

Puzzlement was evidently written on my face, for Holmes swiftly dispelled it with a singular sentence.

"Have you never heard of the village of Blackness, near Crowborough, Watson? It lies in Sussex. I know that Colonel Savage is unlikely to be familiar with it, man of the world that he is entirely notwithstanding."

I confessed placid ignorance.

"What type of place would be cursed with such a foul name?" asked Colonel Savage. "Is it the lair of thieves?"

"Actually, it is quite unremarkable," Holmes related. "I daresay we may not find it so prosaic if my suspicions are proved to be true."

"And precisely what are your suspicions?" Savage asked.

"Only that your woman of mystery fears to meet with you in the city, where she might be observed. Beyond that, I am still working on the problem."

"But Holmes," asked I. "How can you be certain that the

village of Blackness was meant by the scrawl on the handkerchief?"

"While I deduced that the message was written by a woman,
based upon the unavoidable fact that a man would scarcely
employ a woman's handkerchief to leave a message, the handwriting itself was sufficiently bold to proclaim the author a
person of some mental fortitude. The choice of message might
have been improvised, or preplanned. But the manner in which
it was conveyed suggests one accustomed to the writing of secret
messages calculated to mean little or nothing at casual inspection, but which are fraught with hidden meaning to the initiated.
In short, the colonel's charming conspirator of old."

"Bully good logic, Holmes!" cried the colonel enthusiastically.
"But by what arcane skill did you ascertain that the village of
Blackness was meant?"

"By a skill no more remarkable than the ability to read the
King's English." From a pocket Holmes produced the handkerchief in question and invited us to examine it anew.

We studied it a moment. The truth became distressingly
clear. Colonel Savage spoke it one jump ahead of my unuttered
thought.

"The B is capitalized," said he.

Holmes nodded sagely. "In the heat of the discovery, this
simple fact was overlooked. It is often thus."

Savage settled back into his cushions. "Now how do you
propose to flush our fugitive quail out of the underbrush?"

"I confess that I have no idea," Holmes admitted, closing his
eyes as if desirous of sleep. "But inasmuch as we will not arrive
at our destination for some time, we have ample time to rumi-
nate on the prospects ahead."

With that, to the colonel's visible disappointment, Sherlock
Holmes dropped off into a deep sleep from which our uninter-
rupted conversation failed to rouse him.

AT CROWBOROUGH STATION, we commandeered a four-wheeler, which took us straightaway to Blackness, which, given the late hour, seemed well named.

"Is there an inn?" asked Holmes of our driver as we approached.

"But the one. The Ruddy Fox."

"Take us to the Ruddy Fox, then."

"WE WOULD LIKE to engage rooms," Holmes told the innkeeper upon our arrival.

"For the night, sir?"

"At least."

"Very good. This way please." As our genial host led us to our rooms, Holmes asked, "Have you given lodging to a woman traveling alone in the last day or so?"

"Why do you ask, sir?" the keeper asked with the studied caution of his breed.

Colonel Savage interjected. "She would be aged about 30, and possessed of marvelous caramel hair."

"A relative of yours?"

"My wife, as it were," Colonel Savage asserted boldly.

"Odd. She did not say to expect you."

"We are…estranged. I believe her to be traveling incognito, as the saying goes. Mrs. Savage has been under much strain these last months."

"Shall I announce you, Mr.—"

"Colonel Richard Henry Savage. United States Army, retired."

The innkeeper's eyes grew wide. "The author, sir?"

"The very same. And since it is so late, and Madame Savage has doubtless retired for the evening, I think any announcement can await the rosy dawn."

"Very good, sir. I will leave that to your discretion."

After the innkeeper left us to our rooms, Sherlock Holmes paid our companion a rare compliment.

"Well played, Savage."

"Thank you. Now what is our itinerary?"

"A stealthy reconnoiter, I should think."

"Why not knock on 'Madame Savage's' door?"

"We do not know for certain the identity of your mystery woman, so I should judge that impudent, if not rash."

"I bow to your superior instincts in these matters," Savage said.

We went out into the gathering evening. There was but a sliver of a moon, yet Holmes refrained from use of his hand-lamp. He seemed preoccupied, and spoke little. I noted the unimportant fact that the fleet-winged swifts of summer had arrived early. Their startled cries as we passed were unmistakable.

After we had thoroughly circumnavigated the vicinity, Colonel Savage asked, "For what are we searching, Holmes?"

"That most illusive and imponderable of earthly stuff."

"Yes?"

"Time," said Holmes.

"We are seeking time?"

"No, we are killing it."

Savage frowned darkly. I confess that my countenance must have resembled his in that wise. For I was as perplexed as the American colonel.

Beyond that cryptic pronouncement, Holmes could be induced to say no more.

Once midnight had come and gone, Holmes abruptly changed course, leading us back to the Ruddy Fox.

"And now?" asked Savage as we reached the door.

"Now," said Holmes. "To bed! And a good night to you both."

He left us standing in our boots, exchanging glances of studied consternation.

THE DAY WAS still assembling itself when Holmes and I and Colonel Savage foregathered in the inn's quaint breakfast room to take tea.

"I fear you must prepare yourself for dire tidings," said Holmes.

Colonel Savage glowered over his morning cup.

"Your faithless 'wife' has fled the inn," explained Holmes.

For a moment, I thought the American would storm out of the room. His predatory features colored angrily. But he soon mastered himself.

"It is as I anticipated," Holmes went on without evident concern. "In fact, I rather hoped that she would do so."

"Hoped!" Savage flared. "Why, I sought your assistance precisely so that she would not escape me a second time!"

"Her escape," said Holmes, "was entirely unavoidable. In truth, you could no more have arrested her flight than you could have apprehended a spirit of the dead."

"I do not entirely take your meaning, Holmes," said Savage, his ire subsiding somewhat.

"All will be explained," Holmes promised. "Come, finish up. We must be off."

We went out into the milky morning, where the horrid screech of the newly-arrived migratory swifts resounded. Holmes led the way, as he had before. He seemed to select a direct course into the Ashdown Forest and followed it unerringly like the proverbial sleuth hound.

"How are your tracking skills, Colonel?" Holmes asked after a time.

"I can read sign. We are following boot tracks."

"Male or female?"

Savage studied the ground as we walked.

"Both, I should say."

"What leads you to that conclusion?" asked Holmes.

"Two heavy sets. One rather light. Suggesting a dainty foot."

"Very good. You will be our guide whilst I scan the higher reaches."

"For what?"

"For whatever may be discovered," said Holmes.

Savage favored me with another doubtful glance, and we could think of nothing better to do than to follow the enigmatic detective.

We pushed far into the forest when Holmes suddenly cried, "Halloa! What have we here!"

Stopping at the foot of a sturdy copper beech tree, Holmes set aside his walking stick and began a climb that would have intrigued a monkey. Reaching a high bough, he sat astride it and seemed preoccupied with what he discovered there.

At length, he called down, "Watson, do you recall the disappearance of one Mary Morgan?"

"How could I not? Her slain body lay in woods very much like these, utterly unfindable owing to decomposition and the actions of animals."

"Indeed. She might never have been found except for the natural habits of an enterprising woodpecker, who in constructing her maternal nest, plucked ginger hairs from the dead scalp, employing them to feather her nest, as it were. By that reckoning alone was the unhappy girl's body unearthed."

Holmes lowered himself out of the tree in careful stages.

"May I present," said he, "proof of the mortal remains of your Helene Marie Vanderbilt-Astor Gaines."

Accepting the clump of hair, Colonel Savage gave a profound gasp. "She is deceased!"

"So it would seem."

I glanced at the hair, and offered, "The color is yet vibrant. No sign of weathering."

"Suggesting that the body is fresh and not far off," Holmes snapped. "Let us continue. The game is afoot."

Still clutching the caramel hair, Colonel Savage followed woodenly. For his part, Holmes picked up his pace. His dilating nostrils resembled those of the hound after the fox.

"If I am not mistaken," said he, "the malefactors are not far ahead of us."

Rousing from his newfound grief, Savage swore, "This outrage will be avenged." He brandished a substantial revolver. "We'll give them Billy Hell!"

"Caution foremost, Colonel Savage," said Holmes. "Vengeance later, perhaps. If you still possess the appetite for it."

Holmes's suggestive words were still ringing in our ears when we happened upon the discarded kidskin glove.

Retrieving it, Holmes unexpectedly took its mate from a coat pocket.

"Wherever did you get that?" I cried.

"From the empty room of the former Miss Gaines," explained Holmes. "I thought it odd that there was only the one."

"The fiends!" Savage exploded. "They are disposing of her personal effects piecemeal."

Holmes seemed unperturbed. We pressed on through the purple heather and yellow gorse that feather the High Weald so charmingly.

We caught up with them in a dell. At sight of us, they startled like so many flushed quail before the advancing sportsman.

One called out, "We told you to come alone!"

A pistol shot rang out. Another. The whistle of bullets through foliage sent us ducking in turn.

Savage coolly returned fire, causing the trio to scatter wildly.

Holmes swung his walking stick, knocking the revolver from his grip.

"Enough!" he cried.

"The murderers fired upon us!" Savage retorted.

"They are deliberately aiming high—and you are the last person on earth they wish to harm."

Savage looked thunderstruck. Holmes snatched the revolver from the ground and ran forward, his own pistol still pocketed, I noticed.

Colonel Savage drew abreast of us. "You are a brave man, Holmes."

"Tut-tut. The only danger is that of misadventure."

"They have killed once already! Return my pistol please. I am not so foolhardy as to blunder into a gun fray unarmed!"

Without delay, Holmes did. Savage took the firearm, neglecting to notice that the cylinder was now empty of shells. I take pride that I spotted the brass cartridges tumbling to the ground after Holmes broke the action open, knocking the weapon sharply against his hip to dislodge them.

We soon surrounded one of the fleeing men. He was of small stature, and utter terror marked his eyes. Unarmed, he wore a cap pulled low over his pale features.

"What have you done with Miss Gaines!" Savage demanded, thrusting the pistol barrel into the man's heaving chest with intimidating force.

When the culprit spoke, his accents betrayed his national origins. "I have done nothing with her. For she is my sister."

"A Russ!" Savage cried. "Tell me, man. Where is she?"

The man gulped air greedily, and it was possible that he was playing for time, hoping for succor from his fellows.

Holmes interjected, "Come now. The game is up. There is nothing to be gained by denying the facts of the matter."

At length, he spoke, his words and accent thick. "You ask where my sister is. I will tell you now: Dead in her grave."

"Scoundrel!" Savage snapped. "You murdered her!"

"Nyet, nyet! For the woman you knew as Helene Marie Vanderbilt-Astor Gaines is long in her grave—although where she lies buried not even I, her only brother, know for certain."

"Holmes, what does this mean?" I cried out.

"This man is lying," Colonel Savage insisted. "I saw Miss Gaines in London, only days ago." He grabbed the small man by the collar and shook him vigorously, as if to shake the living truth from him.

"Lies. All lies!" the culprit sobbed.

"My eyes do not lie, sir!" Savage returned with steel in his voice. He placed his formidable revolver to the man's forehead, cocking it.

"It was all a plot, sir. I swear it."

"Allow me to explain," Holmes interjected. "Colonel, look to this man's boots and pray tell me what you see."

Savage stepped back and regarded the boots with which the captive was shod.

"My God!" he cried. "He is wearing her boots."

"Yes, just as he once wore the kidskin gloves I retrieved. In his haste to flee, he had time only to don such articles as were at hand. For the innkeeper had apprised all concerned of our arrival."

"He promised confidence," Savage said.

"Promises, alas, are often sealed with gold. He was paid to alert his mysterious guests of your coming. The fact that you did not come alone made the conspirators uneasy. They slipped a note under your door, then made their escape during our midnight ramble, as I imagined they would. While you slept, I took the liberty of fetching the note from under your door with my pocket knife. Here it is."

Savage took the envelope and saw that it had been unsealed. Removing the paper within, he read the contents.

"It is a request that I meet Miss Gaines at a clearing two miles northwest of the Ruddy Fox. And to come alone."

"This very dell," said Holmes, "where they waited for you."

"For what fell purpose, Holmes?" I asked, failing to follow the skeins of the scheme.

"An old story, I am afraid," said Holmes. "Blackmail. Extortion."

Consternation enwrapped Colonel Savage's haggard features.

"Nonsense! I am above reproach!"

"Pray let me tell the tale," said Holmes. "In Miss Gaines's

room, I discovered certain articles which led me to suspect, if not conclude, the truth of the imposture. With full knowledge that they awaited you at this spot, I set out, giving the impression that I was following an obscure trail."

I asked, "But why conceal the truth, Holmes?"

"Out of an abundance of caution, I must confess. And owing to a dawning belief that I had erred in an earlier deduction, when I prematurely concluded that the note inscribed on the lady's handkerchief had been written by a woman."

"It *was!*" Savage insisted. "It *must* have been!"

"Logically, yes. But among the articles I unearthed in the abandoned room were a man's straight razor and a woman's wig-stand. Yet the room was occupied by a single party. These items led me to doubt my original assumption."

"I fail to understand the significance of that curious combination," Savage said.

Holmes raised an admonishing finger. "Knowing that this is the height of swift nest-building season," he continued, "and understanding the habits of the redoubtable feathered migrants, I merely kept a weather eye cocked for new bird's nests. Such, I reasoned, would prove more fruitful than a tedious canvas of the forest floor."

"For what?"

"A discarded caramel wig," replied Holmes.

"Wig!" The words left Colonel Savage's lips with the force of an explosion.

"If you will trouble yourself to examine the clump of hair I retrieved from the swift's nest," invited Holmes, "you will discover for yourself an absence of natural roots. In short, you hold strands of Miss Gaines's hairpiece."

"But you implied that she had been killed—"

"No, you inferred such," responded Holmes. "Miss Gaines was in truth dead, as I indicated. But she has suffered from that unfortunate condition for several years now."

"But, Holmes," I interjected. "What of the woman who tantalized Colonel Savage like a some nebulous apparition?"

"She was entirely imaginary," said Holmes. "Yes, she wanted to be seen. But only that. She wished to lure the colonel to Blackness, there to consummate the bold plan."

Colonel Savage spoke up stiffly. "As I have indicated, Holmes, I am not subject to blackmail."

"No? You penned a novel of your exploits in Russia with a woman not your wife and let the world know that the tale was half-true. On that alone, you might be extorted. But the scheme was more clever than that. You were to be presented with a facsimile of your long-lost Nihilist, and appeals were to be made to your generosity. Gallant soldier that you are, no doubt you would have succumbed to an opportunity to aid a woman you thought long dead. For here was a golden opportunity to rescue your charming co-conspirator. If not, blackmail was still a possibility."

Colonel Savage's military bearing took on a crestfallen posture. His revolver wilted in his hand.

"Then who wore the caramel wig?" he asked at last. "Who could possibly have succeeded in passing herself off as Miss Gaines?"

"Who else but the one person on earth who most resembled her?" returned Holmes. "Who but her own brother?"

With that, Sherlock Holmes snatched the rough cap off the head of the man who wore woman's boots. The features thus exposed were fair, the close-shorn hair a hue akin to caramel.

"When the three confederates fled," he explained, "they dared not leave behind the wig, for its distinctive color would doubtless expose the imposture. Nor could they risk being caught with it, if apprehended. I reasoned therefore that they must dispose of it in the forest. No doubt other bits of Miss Gaines's costume will be discovered there."

"*Da,*" said the miserable blackmailer. "We did not foresee the hiring of English detectives."

Colonel Savage exhibited all the symptoms of a man struggling with great emotion. Hoarsely, he asked the conspirator, "She is in truth dead?"

The man nodded. "The fame of your novel reached even imperial Russia. I saw in your fame an opportunity to profit. But now I am lost." He hung his head.

"Let us escort this man back to the Ruddy Fox," Holmes suggested. "There we will alert the local authorities. No doubt it will be a good morning's work to capture the other two. But capture them, I am certain they will."

"Capital!" said Colonel Savage. "Simply capital."

I regarded the American colonel with wonder. "You are in good spirits for a man who has suffered a grievous wrong and an even greater disappointment."

"The contrary. To this very day, I have never been certain of the fate of that improbable but unforgettable woman who was temporarily my wife. Now I know the truth. For that I have you to thank, Mr. Holmes. How can I repay you?"

"You may begin," said Holmes, "by accepting a present of these bullets to replace those which somehow fell from your revolver whilst it was in my possession."

THE MISADVENTURE OF
THE BONNY BOY

T HE PASSENGER LOCOMOTIVE was wheezing through the Cheshire countryside, stirring up clouds of newly-fallen leaves. But I had no eye for their warmly enchanting autumn hues. We were bound north for Manchester, Sherlock Holmes and I. An urgent telegram had summoned us. The yellow flimsy had lacked all but the essential details of the matter.

> *Sherlock Holmes,* (it began)
> *Come to Manchester at once. My bonny boy is alive. You must help recover him safe and sound.*

The message was signed, *Ronald Talbert.*

The name meant nothing to Sherlock Holmes, for he had been out of England until comparatively recently, and mistakenly believed lost to this world.

"What do you make of this?" he asked me upon its receipt.

I glanced at the telegram and gave a start.

"I recognize the name. It was in all the papers during your European *interregnum,* as it were. Ronald Talbert's only son Allister had disappeared after an argument with his father. Something about running away to sea. Ronald Talbert put his foot down and the son rebelled. He went out into the cold night, and was never heard of again. At least, not directly."

"This is news to me," replied Holmes. "Pray continue, Watson."

"Less than a month after all hope had been given up, the parents received a demand letter asking for ransom. A photograph of the boy was enclosed, but it was taken in a room that was dimly lit. Moreover, the picture was blurred by an unsteady hand holding the camera. Nevertheless, the camera study convinced the parents to pay the ransom. This was done. But nothing more was heard of the laddie, nor did the extortionist make any further demand. The case was never resolved."

This was sufficient to pique Sherlock Holmes's interest. Without further consideration, he bustled me out of the sitting room and we were on our way to Euston Station, where Holmes dispatched a telegram to Manchester, promising an early arrival.

During our picturesque journey, my good friend plied me with many questions. I did the best I could, but my memory for details failed me in many respects.

"There were some peculiarities attending the lad's disappearance," I offered. "Mad talk of him having been spirited away by fairies and the like. Circumstantial stuff, amounting to not very much. The particulars have faded from memory."

"No matter," reassured Holmes. "We will soon plunge into the matter."

"Have you any preliminary deductions?" I inquired.

"I would not think the boy was still alive, based on the data you have provided me, Watson. Except for one particular."

"The fact that he threatened to go to sea?"

"Precisely."

"I believe inquiries were made at all the shipping concerns, as well as of the Royal Navy. No boy matching that description had secured passage on any vessel departing Manchester in that December month. All of this was before the Manchester Ship Canal was completed, of course."

Holmes nodded. "This would not preclude a nipper from stowing away and being discovered days after shipping out. I would suggest a clever boy might successfully secrete himself for upward of a week, possibly a week-and-a-half. By which time, there would be no practical way to return him home until the voyage was concluded."

"It was such a sensational case that I rather doubt any ship's master would have failed to deliver the boy at the completion of his round. Then there was the strangeness."

"You alluded to this before, Watson. Kindly elaborate."

"The authorities in Manchester dismissed these reports as the workings of local imaginations heated up by the mysterious disappearance. For several days after the boy disappeared, his cries for help were heard less than a mile from his home."

"I imagine that a thorough search was conducted."

"Quite thorough. Alas, it came to naught. Those who heard those cries, heard them distinctly, yet swore that they issued from the open sky. I believe there were other oddities surrounding the disappearance, but here my memory fails me utterly."

Holmes settled back in his seat, his features relaxing. "No doubt the parents will have better recall of these details than you have retained, Watson."

"I wish it were in my power to more reliably supply you with additional facts, my dear Holmes, the better for you to work your remarkable powers upon the mystery."

Holmes nodded distractedly. "Had I more to go on, I might well arrive at a theory before we arrive at our destination. But without sufficient data, I have threads, but an insufficient quantity with which to weave a skein."

"My apologies."

"Tut-tut, Watson. Three years is a long time. No matter how sensational the case, memory naturally fades. Experience shows that the longer the interval between the time an event is impressed upon the brain and the need to recall it, significant and understandable distortion in the details follows. Indeed, even in the order of the details. But I agree with you upon one point.

"And what is that?"

"My remarkable powers, as you call them, will get to the root of the matter sooner than later."

"Is that a boast, my good fellow?"

"Not at all. Nearly a prediction supported by past successes. This sounds like a simple enough matter, complicated by unusual circumstances."

"Kidnappings are not often complicated crimes," I allowed.

"I am not yet convinced that this is a kidnapping."

"Is it because the child was not returned?"

"No. Kidnappers are rogues of the first water, and rogues cannot be counted on to live up to their promises. Simply because a ransom is paid does not automatically lead to the release of the ransomed party. Especially when the perpetrator is known to the victim. Remember the case of Martha Roberts. Abducted, ransomed, and later found strangled in her own bed, having been placed there by the criminal who lived up to his part of the bargain for her return, but neglected to honor the portion that stipulated a *safe* return. He was caught, of course."

"Were you involved, Holmes?

"Only insofar as I wrote a letter to the authorities in Brighton, pointing out the obvious."

"Which I confess escapes me completely."

"Surely you can puzzle it out, Watson. No? Ask yourself what motive would compel a kidnapper to risk discovery and capture whilst in the brazen act of restoring a strangled woman to her own bed?"

"As I recall, her unfaithful husband did the deed."

"Precisely. Mrs. Roberts had never left her own home. Lured into her attic, she was dispatched there and placed into a steamer trunk. The parents paid the greater part of the ransom, with the husband contributing a mere third. A sum he soon recouped, since he was the ransoming party."

"Which he forfeited upon his arrest, as I recall."

"Mr. Roberts forfeited a price far dearer than that tidy sum,"

Holmes reminded. "I understand they were buried side by side, despite everything."

A slowing of the train, accompanied by blasts of its steam whistle, signified that we were nearing Manchester London Road station. Soon we were within its capacious confines.

"Halloa, we have arrived," remarked Holmes, gathering up his coat.

Disembarking, I took notice of the magnificent iron-and-glass train-shed that distinguished the modern station from all others. The air was more chilly than it had been in London a few hours previous, but the advancing hour no doubt explained the abrupt change in atmosphere.

A man rushed up to greet us, his face red with excitement. "I am Ronald Talbert," he said, clasping Holmes's hand eagerly.

"Good to meet you," said Holmes diffidently. "My esteemed associate, Dr. Watson, has given me as many essentials in the case as his memory would disgorge. But I am lacking many of the fine details. If we could repair to a quiet spot, I would like to hear your story and ask pertinent questions. I am confident that we can get to the bottom of this if we approach the problem systematically."

Mr. Talbert escorted us to a cab stand and we availed ourselves of a handsome four-wheeler. Soon we were rattling along to their modest home not a mile distant.

A fair-haired woman with a care-worn face greeted us at the door. There was no maid in evidence.

"This is my wife, Melissa," said Talbert, closing the door behind us.

The woman wrung her hands strenuously. "Oh, it is so good of you to come, Mr. Holmes, so good." Her pale blue eyes were bright with an eager anticipation.

A cold supper was served, and we addressed it properly while Holmes listened to the couple's tale.

It was much as I remembered it. Allister Talbert was nine years old in the year in which he disappeared. A reader of nautical books, he aspired to go to sea, but his father, an accountant, had other aspirations he considered to be paramount.

"I forbade him from going to sea," the man said firmly. "And I have never regretted it. It was the right way to deal with the laddie, for he was dreamy of mind and awkward of manner. He was not fit for shipboard life—at least not at his tender age."

"Allister was a bonny boy," chimed in Mrs. Talbot. "Fair to look upon, he was, and gentle in his manners. I agreed with my husband. The sea was not for him."

At that juncture, Mrs. Talbert left the table and returned with the framed photograph of the boy. He appeared younger than nine in the photograph, a point on which Sherlock Holmes immediately remarked.

"Taken when he was seven, I should judge," remarked Holmes.

"Quite perceptive, Mr. Holmes," said Ronald Talbert. "He was seven years and three months old at the time of that sitting."

"You can see that he was a bonny boy," added the mother. "A very bonny boy."

"Indeed," said Holmes agreeably, sharp eyes studying the lad's features as if seeking some arcane sign that he yet lived.

After committing the features to memory, Holmes looked up.

"Watson informs me that the boy was heard calling for help some time after his disappearance."

The mother responded instantly. "Yes, he was! I did not personally hear it, but those living around the condemned crematorium in the fairy burying ground said that it was a boy's voice, calling faintly for help. I am certain that it was young Allister."

The father interjected, "We went to the old burying ground and searched endlessly. No sign of Allister did we find. Nor did we hear any calls for aid."

"Were there any open tombs?" asked Holmes.

The mother responded. "None. All were sealed. The burying ground has been shunned for more than a generation, ever since the fairy rings started to sprout." She paused. "Mr. Holmes, they were in full cry then. Rings of mushroom chaps, with the sward all around them dead as if blackened by fire!"

Ronald Talbert noted, "The bricked-up crematorium was forced open by police order and it, too, was searched, but to no avail. It would have been impossible for the lad to have sought shelter within, had he a mind to do so, for the old iron door was padlocked and the windows sealed with brick."

"I see," said Holmes thoughtfully.

"One thing was found, however," added the father. "A crow landed upon a hawthorn branch during the time of our search. In its beak was a fragment of white cloth. Curiously, the bird happened to drop the fragment, and out of curiosity, or perhaps desperation, I fetched it. It was a bit of shirt cuff, and written on it was a single word: *Flew! F-L-E-W,* all in capital letters."

"I will never forget it!" wailed the mother. "For hawthorns are the fairy's favorite trees!"

The father went on in a grave voice. "I could not make oath upon it, Mr. Holmes, but I believe that it was a fragment of Allister's shirt cuff. And the word was inscribed in dried blood, in thick strokes taking up the entire patch."

"My word!" I cried.

The mother looked to Sherlock Holmes with widening eyes.

"Do you think that the fairies carried him off, Mr. Holmes?"

"I do not," returned Holmes in a restrained tone of voice. I had no doubt but that under less delicate circumstances, Sherlock Holmes's response would have been coldly dismissive. But he restrained himself, out of respect for the aggrieved mother of Allister Talbert.

Mrs. Talbert then launched into a teary soliloquy.

"You must understand that, as Allister's mother, I possess a sympathetic bond with my son. During that horrible day of searching, I felt that he was alive, and nearby. In my heart, I still feel it to be so. But with the passing years, it is harder, much harder to hold onto that feeling. Can you understand a mother's heart, Mr. Holmes?"

"I believe, as do you, that Allister was alive at the time of the search. In fact, I have little doubt about it."

The woman's right hand flew to Holmes's coat sleeve and squeezed it mightily.

"Oh, thank you, kind sir! Thank you from the bottom of a mother's broken heart."

Sherlock Holmes looked as uncomfortable as I have ever seen him. Mrs. Talbert withdrew her hand and her handkerchief came out, blotting her moist eyes.

"Now what new evidence convinces you that your son is alive?" Holmes asked suddenly.

The father brought a manila envelope, and from it extracted a candid photograph. It showed a blond shaver about twelve years old, seated before what appeared to be a bedsheet hung behind him in order to disguise the room in which he stood. It was impossible to determine the eye color, of course. Yet Holmes astonished us all by stating, "Your son Allister's eyes were a pale blue, I perceive."

"Very pale," said the mother excitedly. "But however did you know this, Mr. Holmes?"

"I have made a close study of photographs," replied Holmes. "While it is sometimes challenging to do so, sifting out the eye color in black-and-white photographs is a skill in which I take justifiable pride. Your husband is brown-eyed. I see that your eyes are a pale blue and they suggested to me that the eyes of the seven-year-old boy in the studio portrait were much the same."

"Oh, yes, yes," replied the father excitedly. "Allister took after his mother more than he did me."

"He was a very bonny boy," repeated the mother.

"Yet this recent photograph I now hold in my hand," continued Holmes, "shows a boy whose hair is undoubtedly a combed but clumsy wig and whose eyes I would judge to be grey."

"But Holmes!" I exclaimed. "How can you be certain of this fact?"

"The gradation in tone tells me that this young man is grey of eye, not blue of iris."

I observed the parents closely as Holmes spoke in his neutral tone of voice. He was entirely unemotional. The father's shoulders sank, while the mother brought her delicate hands up to her open mouth.

"Moreover," continued Holmes, "the shape of the ears are dissimilar. This recent photo shows the young man with pendulous ear lobes, while your son has rather truncated lobes. There are other configurations which inform to someone who has studied the various configuration of the human ear that the nine-year-old in the older photograph could not have grown to be this twelve-year-old. In short, this photograph is a cruel hoax."

"Oh, and I so wanted it to be my bonny boy!" cried the mother in despair.

Stealing himself against the understandable emotional onrush, Sherlock Holmes asked politely, "Did it come with a note?"

The father produced a sheet from the manila envelope.

Holmes took this and read it silently, and then read it again aloud:

> *To the Talberts:*
> *Your son Allister lives. I am quite done with him. As I find myself to be hard up at present, I am prepared to return him to you if you are able to pay the second half of the ransom you so kindly surrendered all these years ago.*
> *If you agree to this, your Allister will be restored to you. But not before. And certainly not ever, if you fail to complete the payment in full. I need not state the amount in pounds. No doubt the sum is branded into your brains. Kindly surrender an equal amount and there will be no further difficulties, I promise you. Place an advert in* The Manchester Guardian *saying the following:*

"We are grateful to a merciful God for what He has restored to us."
Once I read this in printed form, instructions will be posted to you.
Do not under any circumstances contact the authorities, and all will
shortly be squared away, and Allister will come through with flying
colors, I promise you."

The letter was not signed.

"Do you have in your possession the original ransom note?" asked Holmes, laying aside the sheet of paper.

"No longer," replied the husband. "The authorities took it."

Holmes frowned. "And if I request a look at it, it would arouse police suspicions, and could well cause the culprits to flee."

Holmes studied the letter again and squeezed the bridge of his nose between two fingers. I didn't recognize the gesture, but I knew it signified something. My friend's mannerisms were well-known to me, so I deduced that he was struggling with an unaccustomed emotion.

"As difficult as this is to convey to you, Mr. and Mrs. Talbert," Sherlock Holmes began. "I do not recommend paying any ransom to this rogue, whomever he may be. It will not result in the return of your son, Allister. I would stake my modest fortune upon it."

"That is exactly why we summoned you, Mr. Holmes," Ronald Talbert explained. "We do not possess the required sum, and have no means by which to raise it—certainly not without arousing sharp interest in our financial activities to that end. So we beseech you, how can our son be restored to us under such impossible circumstances?"

Holmes's reply was immediate. It did not show that he gave the question any extended consideration. But when I heard his next words, I knew that he had already formulated a plan.

"You may place the required advertisement in the newspaper. That will do no harm, and may accomplish some good. Place it tonight. We will not worry about raising the required funds until we have our response."

The mother clapped her hands together, tears starting from

the corners of her eyes. Her care-worn face was all but glori-
fied by some inner emotion that was suffused by a rising hope.

"So there is a chance that our bonny boy may be restored to
the bosom of his loving family?"

Sherlock Holmes said solemnly, "If it is within my powers
to do so, rest assured that the fate of your son will no longer
endure as an open wound in your hearts. For all mysteries have
solutions, and I have solved more than my fair share of mysteries in my career."

"Did you hear, Ronald?" cried the mother. "Our son is coming
home. Our bonny boy will belong to us again."

The father had been in charge of his emotions up until this
point. But hearing these words, his shoulders commenced shaking and his face was received by his upraised hands. We did not
see his tears, for his manly pride refused to permit us to behold
them.

Excusing ourselves from the supper table, Sherlock Holmes
and I went out into the night air in order to give the couple
their privacy.

As we walked along, I asked my friend, "Have you true hope
of the restoration of the lad?"

"If he has not gone to sea, I do," Sherlock Holmes said quietly.
Again, he pinched the bridge of his nose between elongated
fingers and his expression was unreadable to me. "But I fear the
worst," he added in a low voice.

Sherlock Holmes and I walked the streets of Manchester as
dusk grew deeper and a freshening wind made the trees rustle
with their dying leaves of autumn, like tiny decaying hands.

Holmes walked with his chin tucked into his chest, his
somber eyes raking the cobbles before him. I knew him to be
in deep thought, so forbore to speak. My friend's powers of
concentration were such that it was as if he were immersed in
another world than the one through which we strolled—a world
of thought in which logic, data, and the myriad connections
thereof substituted for the familiar pathways of Manchester.

I did not think that Holmes's promenade possessed a definite destination, for he seemed to wander, lost in thought. Withal, we found ourselves at the gates of the old burying ground, all but abandoned, according to local legend, due to the fairy rings that came and went with the changing seasons.

The iron gate was ajar and Holmes slipped in without inviting me to follow. Naturally, I did follow.

The ancient burial ground was a dreary spot, the grass more dead than any sward I had ever personally beheld. Necrotic grass, I have heard such dead spots termed. Some of the leaning stones were centuries old, so worn by the elements that they were all but unreadable. Once, we passed a headstone whose surface was pocked by musket balls, no doubt fired into it approximately during the reign of George III. Or so the deceased's date of death suggested.

A brilliant moon illuminated all. It made the waving trees spectral, for night was upon us. It had crept up steadily, but now it had arrived in full force.

The moon substituting for his lantern, Holmes wended his careful way through the grassy paths. Amid the rustle of dead and dying leaves there came an intermittent creaking, as if the rigging of a sailing ship was stirred.

Apparently drawn to that sound, Holmes padded along, his feet strikingly silent in their methodical tread. I knew my friend to be capable of the stealth of an American Indian when necessary, but here his quiet tread seemed inexplicable to me. I did not think it was respect for the long interred, but I could imagine no other reason. Holmes didn't subscribe to the existence of fairy folk.

I wasn't surprised when we arrived at the door of the crematorium, for its leaning chimney stood out strongly in the moonlight, prominent as the mainmast of a sailing ship. It possessed an odd history, for it was not so very old. But it had been condemned and abandoned, according to Mr. Talbert, in 1887, only three years after its erection. Rumors abounded as to why.

Some held that it was haunted, presumably by the restless spirits of those whose mortal remains had been turned to ashes by
its charnel furnaces.

Observing the unsteady structure, his eye going to the weed-
choked foundation, Sherlock Holmes remarked, "I judge this
place to be structurally unsound. Whoever erected it made a
poor choice in choosing this plot of land, or else in hiring his
surveyor. Subsidence of the earth appears to be the main culprit.
Note the roof corners are out of plumb, Watson."

Holmes paused at the door, noted the heavy iron padlock was
firmly in place, and made a circuit of the building. The vertical
windows had been sealed with brick, as reported. The building
was not so old that it appeared to have fallen into disuse from
age, but it showed signs of being unsound. That the structure
was settling was undeniable. Perhaps the foundation was faulty.

Arriving at the rear of the forbidding building, Holmes
stopped and turned his attention to a spreading hawthorn tree
growing several yards distant. It threw out amazingly gnarled
yet sturdy branches, and it was one of these which produced the
creaking sound. The outstretched branch had reached out over
the roof of the crematorium and was rubbing up against the
tilting brick flue, its terminus passing beyond the brick face, as
if a woodsy hand with spindly fingers had attempted to grasp
the chimney, but failed to do so.

This towering chimney appeared unsound to my eyes. Missing and crumbling bricks lent it the semblance of a mouth with
vacant teeth, and the rectangular structure teetered alarmingly.
Here, thought I, was another possible reason why the crematorium was abandoned.

Holmes studied the chimney for some minutes in absorbed
silence. Then to my surprise he doffed his coat and started scal-
ing the hoary hawthorn, causing its dying yellow-green leaves
to tremble.

Reaching the crown with the agility of a monkey, he clambered around and thrust his hands into an orifice that he discov-

ered in the upper reaches of the trunk. Extracting something, he examined it in the moonlight, then placed his discovery in a pocket. I couldn't see what it was.

After that, he climbed higher and studied the roof of the crematorium at great length, paying particular attention to the tottering chimney.

When at last he returned to solid ground, Holmes's expression was an unreadable etching in the stony planes of his countenance.

"Come, Watson," he said glumly. "Let us find lodgings for the night."

"What did you discover?" I inquired.

"I discovered that a mother's sympathy for her son's welfare is unerring. The boy was indeed alive at the time of the search."

But that was all he would say about the matter.

We found a public house that would take us in and retired for the night. I, for one, slept soundly. I cannot speak for Sherlock Holmes. I could hear him rattling about in the adjoining room, a certain indication that he was immersed in the unsettling case before us.

MORNING FOUND US at the bustling and rejuvenated Manchester docks, which threatened to take so much sea-trade from old Liverpool. Cranes were hoisting bails of Alabama cotton, cargoes of Cuban sugar, and what-not from the decks of steamer ships that had worked their way inland along that marvel of Victorian engineering, the stupendous Manchester Ship Canal, and which were fast transforming the formerly landlocked city into one of England's most formidable ports.

Sherlock Holmes led me to Trafford Wharf, his chin low, eyes downcast, countenance doleful, the very picture of the so-called "brown study." He seemed to have no eye for anything we encountered until we were dockside. Then he took special notice of the boys who were naturally congregating about, the day not being a school day, watching the still-novel activity along the quays.

"You aren't searching for the boy among these scruffy ruffi-ans, are you?" I inquired when I perceived the pattern of his attentions.

"I am looking for one boy in particular, Watson," replied he. "I will settle for no substitutes."

That cryptic utterance gave me hope for the life of young Allister Talbert.

The boys congregating about the busy wharves were naturally varied as to their ages, but Holmes didn't seem to discriminate against anyone, regardless of their station of youth.

To my immense disappointment, none seemed to capture his attention beyond the immediate glance. It was clear that he was classifying them, sorting them out in his mind as it were, and casting them aside when they didn't meet his measure.

At a news agency on the Salford side of the canal, he purchased a newspaper and, after glancing at the front page, turned immediately to the advertisements.

"Ah, the advertisement has been published. We may not see any results for some hours yet. I should like to stroll the quays in order to pass the time, if you don't mind, Watson."

"If you think it will advance your cause," I responded heart-ily, "I offer no objections. The day is pleasant, and the westerly breezes invigorating without being excessively bracing. And I do not look forward to treating with the Talberts unless it is with their long-lost son in tow."

"Fear not on that score, my dear Watson. Allister will be restored to his family in the proper order through events that are now unfolding."

I confess that my heart gave a violent leap of hopeful antici-pation upon hearing these electrifying words, but I didn't press Holmes further on the point. I knew that it would do no good and might only evoke an example of the terseness that comes over him when he is engrossed in a case. Sometimes I wonder why I am invited along, since Holmes's mental machinery, as it were, operates best when lubricated by solitude and sustained through silence.

At the same time, I full well understood that even an eccentric fellow such as Sherlock Holmes ofttimes craves companionship—although I sometimes detected a tart tinge of ego suggesting that he enjoyed my expressions of astonishment whenever he produced one of his miracles of ratiocination.

We whiled away the next few hours in absorbed silence, at one juncture mesmerized by the Barton Road swing bridge which revolved majestically in order to permit a steamer to make its way back to the Mersey Estuary and thence to the Irish Sea. I wondered why Holmes took so little notice of the dockers and stevedores bustling about. If Allister had been kidnapped so many years ago, and his abductor had resurfaced once more to claim his pound of flesh, in exchange for the many pounds of Allister Talbert, I would have thought my friend to have gleaned at least an inkling of his nature, if not his identity. I have in the past witnessed feats of deduction that would have passed on the stage as examples of a magician's legerdemain.

Noon had come and gone without result. Holmes laconically suggested lunch. I was more than happy to join him in a meal, my breakfast having been limited to excellent India tea and a single scone.

Instead of turning back to the heart of town, Holmes found a dockside pub that served food. Into this we entered.

Over a simple but satisfying repast, Holmes ruminated at length. To my disappointment, almost all of it was in silence. I understood that I was often a sounding board for his theories, even if my own musings seldom rose to the level of excellence that marked the work of my superlative friend. Yet I was disappointed in the prolonged silence.

When lunch was almost fully consumed, I ventured to break into his unfathomable thoughts.

"Do you suppose that Allister Talbert has returned from the sea?"

Holmes was uncharacteristically slow in replying. "I do not."

"How odd. I had assumed that was the reason for our scouring of these docks."

"Never assume," said Holmes. "Always seek certain knowledge. Assumptions are dangerous. They lead one astray, and down dark alleys and byways that should never be plumbed."

"I do not possess your powers, Holmes. My mind tends to leap to assumptions and conclusions, no matter how I discipline it through your example. As I have said so often, there is only one Sherlock Holmes."

"And there is only one Dr. John H. Watson. Just as there is only one Allister Talbert. Your statement is as vacuous as it is obvious."

I must admit to being slightly stung by my friend's soft yet sharp words. Had we not shared so many adventures, I might have taken offense. And I knew that his moods shifted with his mental tides, from calm to turbulent and back again. Peaceful waters were never far off.

"I apologize for my vacuousness," I replied, keeping the stiffness from my tone.

"It is of no consequence," returned Holmes dismissively. I had seen him sink into gloom before, but this brown study seemed to be of a distinctly darker hue.

"You confuse me, Holmes," I burst out, unable to keep my emotions in check. "On the one hand, you show signs of having solved the case. On the other, you appear to be in a quandary. It is as if no progress has been made whatsoever."

Holmes's eyes were dark and reflective.

"The progress I have made," he said slowly, "manages to be both excellent and entirely unsatisfactory."

"Well, is that not half the battle?"

"It is not the battle that concerns me, for the outcome is all but certain. It is the aftermath."

After that, he would not speak again.

Another hour mingling with the rough denizens of the Salford and Manchester wharves produced no manifest consequence, whether good or bad. Abruptly, Sherlock Holmes spun about and stalked back towards the Talbert residence, head lowered, his outward demeanor that of a man consumed by an accompanying cloud of gloom.

Ronald Talbert greeted us at the door in a state of mingled agitation and anticipation.

"Mr. Holmes! We have received our instructions. This note was found in the jamb of the front door. We do not know who put it there. It was not the postman."

Eagerly, Holmes snatched a sheet of paper from the man's hand. Swiftly, he perused it. Then he handed it to me. It was disappointing in its brevity, and seemed devoid of clues.

> *At first light tomorrow give the one who calls for it the funds. Do not follow him. If you do this, we will all be in the clear, you and I and young Allister.*

"This tells me nothing," said I, returning the ransom note. "Do you glean anything from these few lines, Holmes?"

"No more than I did from the first communication," he snapped. "The writer of that note is a knave and a seaman, for he employs common nautical phrases. Beyond that, the details do not matter. It is the boy who will call for the ransom money who is of interest to me."

"How the devil did you know a boy was involved?" I exclaimed.

"Do not be so dense, Watson. A boy has been involved since the beginning of this affair. Do you not recall the first photograph of the supposed Allister?"

Holmes's tone was so sharp that no doubt the expression on my face betrayed what was in my heart.

Seeing this, Holmes's stiff countenance at once softened. He turned and clapped me on the shoulder, saying, "Buck up, Watson. This is a difficult matter. It has been fretting upon my nerves since last night. I meant you no offense. Please do not take the sharpness of my words to heart, for they have nothing to do with your question, I assure you."

Mrs. Talbert was standing nearby, and commenced wringing her hands once again. "Oh, Mr. Holmes. Do you truly in your heart believe that our Allister will be restored to us very soon?"

Sherlock Holmes did not turn to address her, and in fact studiously avoided her beseeching gaze, but spoke to the room at large. "I have no doubt upon the score, madam. It will be as I have held it to be from the beginning."

Ronald Talbert raised his voice, which quavered with uncontrolled emotions.

"Do you believe the scamp who is coming for the ransom money to be Allister himself?"

"It would be foolish of the villain to send the object of the ransom to call for the ransom, would it not?"

"Yes, I suppose it would. Surely we would recognize our own son."

Holmes's mouth drooped glumly. "No, you might not recognize your own son. The hardships of sea might have changed him significantly. Allister would have aged three years, and grown accordingly."

"Do you now think that, contrary to your previous understanding, Allister has been at sea all these years?"

"At this time, I prefer not to put forth theories when facts are all that matter. Your son will be restored to you, such as he is."

No more could any of us get out of Sherlock Holmes.

Declining the Talberts' kind offer of hospitality, Holmes said that he would return to the docks and continue his search, but that he could be counted upon to return before daybreak and lie in wait for the boy who was expected. "If he isn't discovered before that fateful hour," he concluded.

"You propose to capture the boy?"

"I would prefer to hand him a ransom and follow him to his confederate, but we must make do with the resources available to us. When he knocks upon the door, we will pounce upon him."

THE BOY CAME at the announced hour.

We were crouching amid the privet hedges adjacent to the house, Holmes and I. The morning sun was peeping over the rooftops, and dawn was breaking with its customary autumn clarity. Morning birds were flitting about here and there. All was otherwise quiet.

In the diminishing darkness of the incipient dawn, a young urchin came striding up the street, silent as a mouse, but showing no furtiveness. His clothes were of the sort common about the wharves. I took him to be about twelve years of age. In the dusky dawn, I couldn't discern his features. The color of his hair was concealed by a cloth cap.

He walked up to the front door of the Talbert dwelling, took the iron knocker firmly in hand, and banged it smartly.

At once, Ronald Talbert threw the door open and looked down upon the stripling who had presented himself upon his threshold with the boldness of fearless youth.

"What is it you want?"

"Nothing more than what I have come for," replied the gamin in a breezy tone.

"Well, here it is," snapped the father, surrendering a bulging envelope stuffed fat with paper. Eager fingers clutched the parcel. The loose flap fell open, disgorging only newspaper cuttings.

"Here now! What's this?" the boy exclaimed.

It was at this point that Sherlock Holmes and I sprang out of our concealment and rushed in.

Being fleeter of foot than I, my friend reached the young fellow first, took him by the shoulders, and spun him around.

"The game is up, my fine young imp! Give us your name for a start."

"Why, it's Allister. Allister Talbert."

With that announcement, Mrs. Talbert flew out of the doorway, and confronted the boy.

She searched his face, his unkempt hair and clothing in turn, then took him up in an irresistible embrace, exclaiming, "My bonny boy! My son has come home to us!"

Looking uncomfortable of countenance, Sherlock Holmes said in a strict tone of voice, "That is not your son. His ears are all wrong. His hair is darker than your son's fair locks."

"I know my only son when I behold him, sir!" she cried out. "Yes, his face is older and more bony. His hair has darkened. But these are the clothes Allister was wearing the very day he vanished."

"Nonsense!" retorted Holmes firmly. "Look at his eyes. They are grey."

"It was the fairies! They wrought these strange alterations upon him. But this is Allister! He admits to it. Why would he say such a thing if he were not my own son?"

"Because he is a willing accomplice to the crime of extortion. And he will lead us to his confederate, if I have anything to say about it."

But the mother was adamant. She refused all facts and all logic. "I birthed only one son, and it is he!"

Ronald Talbert had stepped out and was examining the boy's face in the ever-warming light. He yanked off the cloth cap, studying the shock of light brown hair.

"Melissa," he said gently. "I do not believe this is Allister."

"He *is* Allister. He admits it! The rest is the work of the fairies."

Now faith in fairy folk remains common throughout the British Isles, even in this day and age. It was pointless to argue against such closely held beliefs. But the evidence of my senses told me that this was not Allister Talbert.

Then the youth gave himself away. "Where is the ransom money? Quick, if you want to see your son again!" His words were strikingly bold for one of his callow years.

Blue eyes mirroring sudden horror, the mother recoiled from the twisted mouth from which emerged those cutting words.

"Ransom!" she cried. "What need is there for ransom when you have delivered yourself back to our very doorstep, Allister?"

The woman's confusion was pitiful to behold. Clinging to the fading belief that this was her long-lost son, Melissa Talbert was struggling with the boy's cruel words.

"I must take the ransom money back to him," the lad insisted. "He will beat me if I don't. Worse, he will beat Allister. Mark my words. He is a cruel man, cruel and unyielding."

"You are not Allister!" she shrieked.

"I have admitted it," the brat returned in his surly tone.

"But your clothes!"

Sherlock Holmes said gently, "Those could not be Allister's garments. They would hardly fit him after three years of growth."

"Fairies could have worked their will upon him," the distraught woman insisted.

"This is no changeling," Holmes insisted, "but rather the urchin who impersonated your son in the false photograph. The ears match perfectly."

A low moan as if produced by a banshee escaped Melissa Talbert's throat. Climbing in pitch and volume, it became an inconsolable wail. Her lank form seemed to shrink into her simple dress.

"You promised that Allister would be restored to us, Mr. Holmes!" she cried out weepingly. "You gave your word of honor!"

"And I shall keep it, I assure you," Holmes said stiffly.

His own features collapsing in misery, Ronald Talbert took his wife by the shoulders and led her back into the house, her shoulders shaking with her sobs. The truth of Holmes's words, combined with the young man's manner, had crushed her fragile bubble of belief.

Once the front door was shut, Holmes grasped the boy by one arm and squeezed him so hard his entire beardless face winced. My friend's strength was not to be countenanced.

"Name the man behind this outrage!" Holmes demanded. "Is he on shipboard, or dwelling at a sailor's inn?"

"Damn you, I'll not tell!"

Holmes squeezed again and the young man's face clenched like an arthritic fist. The pressure was not gentle.

"Give me his name before I turn you in to the authorities."

"If you do so, young Allister will never be seen again. Mark me!"

In a low voice Holmes said, "I think otherwise. Your words ring hollow as a cracked bell. Now, I will ask you only one more time: Who is your confederate in this foul crime?"

Fingers that were scarred and stained by chemicals squeezed once more, this time with less restraint. The nipper gave a wretched cry, and tears fled his eyes.

"Neil! Neil Nelligan. You'll find him at the Sailors Inn, waiting for me."

"Describe the culprit."

"He's fifty, if he's a day. Thick neck. Weight about thirteen stone. Scraggly hair as grey and dirty as an old mop. You'll know him by his missing ear."

"The right ear," prompted Holmes.

"Yes. However did you know?"

"I spied a sailor by the docks missing his right ear and made a mental note of it. But there was nothing otherwise suspicious about him. Now, your name."

"Alec McGuinnis."

"Very well, young McGuinnis. You must be surrendered to the authorities."

"But Holmes," I interrupted. "What of poor Allister?"

"The fate of Allister Talbert is known to me," murmured Holmes. Taking out a silver whistle, he blew upon it shrilly. Before long a constable came bounding up.

"I am Sherlock Holmes. Take this boy into custody."

"What is the charge?"

"Aiding and abetting an extortion for ransom fraud. I will have more to say about it later today. Allow me the freedom to seek out his confederate, the actual extortionist."

"It is highly irregular."

"Not in London. Ask Inspector Lestrade of Scotland Yard. And if it is good enough for London, it should go in Manchester. Do you not agree?"

The constable took the unresisting boy well in hand, and he scratched his head for a moment before speaking. "I expect I will see you at headquarters before very long, Mr. Holmes."

"You may count on it, Constable. Thank you."

Without further ado, we strolled to the waterfront quays, walking because there were no cabs or carriages about. Holmes appeared to be in no great hurry to reach his destination. Again his chin was sunk upon his chest, and he seemed deep in thought. Once he pinched the thin bridge of his nose, and again I failed to detect the significance of the gesture.

WE ARRIVED AT the docks forthwith. Dawn illuminated the usual bustle of dockside life. Seagulls wheeled about, crying raucously as is their way.

Going straight to the Sailors Inn, we at once spied a sailorly ruffian pacing Trafford Wharf, just short of the graving dock and with view of the Mode Wheel locks beyond. As he promenaded about, it could be perceived that the impatient fellow lacked a right ear. Beneath his woolly cap, a dirty grey mop of hair grew down, concealing whatever orifice remained, but otherwise not hiding the fact that he lacked the aural organ's natural cartilage.

Quickening his pace, Sherlock Holmes strode up to the fellow and accosted him in a manner less artful and more rude than was his normal demeanor.

"Your name is Nelligan, I take it?" he demanded.

The fellow turned, his voice and expression becoming surly. "What if it is? And who the devil are you?"

"Sherlock Holmes. I imagine you have heard of me."

Holmes might have introduced himself as Satan incarnate, for the reaction of Sailor Nelligan was virtually identical.

Spinning about, he attempted to flee.

But my friend was too quick for him. The same steely fingers that had squeezed the truth out of Alec McGuinnis took hold of the man's collar and jerked him almost off his feet.

"The game is undone, sir. Your cabin boy—for that is what I assume him to be—is in police custody."

"I have done nothing!"

"On the contrary," Holmes returned coldly. "You have callously excavated a mother's grief and laid her sorrows bare like a fresh wound. At the same time, your dastardly scheme has brought me to this city, and the truth about Allister Talbert has come out. So I will give you a measure of credit for that result—even though it was largely my doing and certainly not your intention."

"Your talk is nonsense. Unhand me, or I will have a constable on you!"

To my surprise, Sherlock Holmes released the man's collar. Then in an example of pugilistic skill that was breathtaking in its speed and accuracy, his hard right fist came up and struck the point of the unshaven chin, rocking the sailor's head back so sharply I feared the man's thick neck would snap.

To his credit, Sailor Nelligan did not lose his feet. He stepped backwards several paces, his burly arms waving aimlessly. Shaking his head, he struggled to clear his stupefied brain. Seeing Holmes produce the silver police whistle, he turned with every intention of taking blind flight—and plunged into the water.

I imagine he had been intending to mount a gangplank and flee into the bowels of the merchant ship that was docked there, but he was so addled by Holmes's unexpected blow that he missed it entirely.

Nelligan floundered about in the filthy water.

"Is this your ship?" Holmes called down to him.

"What if it is, ye stinkard?"

"Thank you. I will have your captain place you in irons, pending a police inquiry."

"Who the devil are you to think that you can do such a thing to a sailor of Her Majesty's merchant fleet!"

"Have you forgotten? I am Sherlock Holmes."

ONCE MATTERS WERE explained to the captain of the steamer *Finsbury,* the cruel scoundrel was lodged irretrievably in the ship's brig, and after Holmes made his explanations to the police, I found myself once more standing before the old crematorium in the ancient burial ground shunned because of its fairy reputation.

The police were there in numbers, as were several local laborers who had been summoned.

Mr. and Mrs. Talbert were standing by the gate, looking anxious and bewildered.

As the workmen climbed onto the roof and set ladders all around the tottering brick chimney, Holmes recited his conclusions.

"Allister Talbert was never kidnapped. Neil Nelligan and his cabin boy took advantage of newspaper reports of the young boy's disappearance, and knowing that their ship was about to sail, taking them out of reach of the authorities, he endeavored to extort ransom money, which he did successfully."

Climbing their ladders, the workers commenced chipping away at the chimney pot with their steel hammers, knocking it off and going to work on the loose and crumbling mortar.

"In time, Nelligan no doubt squandered that handsome sum in various unsavory ports. Finding himself once again back in the Port of Manchester, he decided to prey upon the grieving couple anew. In both cases, Alec McGuinnis, for that is his true name, posed for the absent Allister. But this time the conspirators took the game too far, Watson. Worse for them, not being content to leave well enough alone, he inadvertently drew me into the affair."

"That much I comprehend." I asserted. "But I fail to understand why we are here, and what became of the poor missing boy."

Precariously balanced workmen were now employing wooden mallets to knock the bricks out and away. They clattered to the roof and slid down to the dead grass surrounding the old crematorium. With each section reduced, they descended another rung or two, continuing their painstakingly destructive toil.

"Surely you have an idea as to Allister's fate by now," murmured my friend in a morose tone.

"I fear that I do," I replied, watching the workmen chip away at the tottering chimney with the single-minded industry of termites at an old tree stump.

"You will recall that Allister vanished on a late December evening. No doubt the weather was inclement, and hostile to sleeping in the rough. Whether Allister intended to run away to sea, or was afraid to return home to his father's wrath is immaterial at this point. He found his way to the cemetery grounds and, seeking shelter, was thwarted by the padlock on the front door of this structure and the fact that the windows are all bricked up. Yet the solidity of this impermissible building promised comfort. So he climbed the old hawthorn tree, and crawled his way across the stout branch that scrapes against the chimney. For someone that young, it was not difficult to scale the last few feet of the chimney and slip down the flue."

"So he did gain entry to the place?"

Holmes shook his head solemnly. "Watson, do you recall the word written in blood upon the young man's torn shirt cuff?"

"Yes. It spelt *'Flew!'* Curious message, if it was a message in truth."

"That it was. It was curious only because it was misspelled. Allister was attempting to communicate that he was stuck in the *chimney flue,* whose base had also been sealed against the elements. His forlorn cries for aid availed him little, for the chimney flue carried them skyward, where they resounded untraceably. Strength flagging, the trapped youth eventually abandoned that tack. Lacking a pencil, he managed to break his skin and trace four letters on his torn shirt cuff in blood and send it skyward. Had he more material to work with, he might have inscribed a more complete message, but by the time desperation had birthed this idea, he was no doubt far gone from thirst and hunger, as well as numbed by the bitter cold."

"But however did he get the fragment of cloth out of the chimney flue?"

"By wrapping it up about a rubber ball carried in his pocket. The weight of this allowed him to throw the ball high enough that it escaped the chimney top and landed on the sloping roof, where it rolled to the ground, apparently becoming dislodged. A canny crow happened to pick up the note and deposit it where the parents could see it. By that time, Allister was far gone. Otherwise, the eerie and untraceable cries for help that had preceded the discovery of the fragmentary note would have been heard."

"How can you be certain of this?"

From a pocket, Holmes drew a small rubber ball. Etched in flaking dried blood onto the surface were the initials *A. T.* Wrapped tightly around this was a faded elastic band, which no doubt had kept the note in place.

"A squirrel happened to pick up this ball and secrete it in his drey, which was a cavity in the hoary hawthorn, where I discovered it. When I recognized the initials, everything fell into place. I made my way to the chimney and peered downward, confirming my suspicions. Wedged in the blocked chimney and unable to climb out again, the unfortunate boy had succumbed to exposure, if not privation."

At that moment, the methodical workmen had successfully reduced the chimney by one-fourth. Visible in the noon daylight was revealed a small immobile head, distinguishable by its faded locks of yellow hair, which breezes stirred to a sad semblance of life.

From the old iron gate, Mrs. Talbert gave out a keening cry. "My boy! My bonny, bonny boy. I have you back!"

"It is as I promised," said Sherlock Holmes solemnly. "Alas, this is not the outcome that I desired."

My friend took the bridge of his nose between finger and thumb, and at last I understood the significance of the gesture. Holmes had put off breaking the unimpartible news as long as he could, and it had pained him to do so to the last.

We took our leave without saying our goodbyes, Sherlock Holmes because a mother's inconsolable grief was something that he could not bear to confront, and I because I had no comfort that I could offer in this terrible hour of desolation.

But I shall never forget to my dying day, the weird timbre of Mrs. Talbert's voice as she repeated, "My bonny boy! My poor, poor bonny boy!"

THE ENIGMA OF
NEPTUNE'S QUANDARY

"**A** MOST PECULIAR VISITOR to see you," announced Mrs. Hudson, the landlady.

I looked up from reading the newspaper. Sherlock Holmes did the same. It is an interesting commentary on our long friendship that we had been thus immersed in complete silence for over an hour, not engaged in conversation but instead silently enjoying one another's company in our shared Baker Street sitting room.

"What is peculiar about him?" I asked.

"He complimented me on the fresh peonies in the window vase."

I confess to being confused by the comment.

"What is so peculiar about that?" I further inquired.

Holmes remarked dryly, "If you were more observant, my dear Watson, you would not need to ask that question."

"Please do not remind me of my deficiencies, Holmes. And the question stands unanswered."

"With a little thought, you could answer it yourself," Holmes continued, putting down his newspaper.

"The window flowers," explained the housekeeper, "are not peonies. They are buttercups."

"So they are!" I remarked. "I had forgotten. The man is obviously abjectly ignorant of botany."

"Or perhaps merely a peculiar fellow," noted Holmes. "Send him up, Mrs. Hudson."

There was very little outwardly peculiar about the man who stepped into the study a moment later. He was well dressed, and had an air of prosperity. Perhaps his expression was not as serious as most of the clients who appealed to the deductive skills of the famed consulting detective, but there was nothing uncouth about it. His mustache was waxed to extreme points. There was a gleam in his eye that struck one as a trifle supercilious. But that was all.

His black wool Inverness cape was of the finest quality, but when he removed his trilby hat and white gloves, it fell open. I was shocked by what was revealed. Both his Windsor scarf and the matching waistcoat were an abominable chartreuse green, which clashed with his otherwise-tasteful ensemble. A golden scarf pin in the shape of a crab stood out against the vivid green of the silk knot.

The man offered Holmes his card, which the great detective glanced at and then tossed to me. It proclaimed him to be Roy Darlington. It showed an address and a telephone number, but nothing else to say what his occupation or station in life might be.

"You have a matter to lay before us?" asked Holmes casually.

"You might put it that way," stated Darlington suavely. "But it is more in the nature of a challenge."

Holmes nodded slightly. "Most of the conundrums that are brought to my attention are of the nature you characterize. Pray take a seat."

Darlington took a comfortable chair and crossed one leg over the opposite knee in a jaunty fashion. Based upon that gesture alone, I took an immediate dislike to him.

"I have a baffling mystery for you, my dear Mr. Holmes, that I daresay will confound your renowned wits."

Holmes regarded the fellow in prolonged silence. I knew that he was taking in every detail of the fellow's appearance and mannerisms, analyzing and cataloguing all evident points like a human tabulating machine.

"I see that you are a man of means, but also of unique tastes."

"I would not disagree with that observation," returned Darlington. "But if that is an example of your deductive skills, it is hardly impressive. My clothes will tell you the former, and possibly the latter."

"It is the ring upon your finger that tells me the latter. It is not a wedding ring, nor a signet ring, but an ornament. Rather on the ostentatious side but unequivocally expensive."

I had not paid attention to the ring. But I studied it now. The gemstone was a pale pink, set in a heavy silver band. I thought it showy if not vulgar, but the workmanship appeared exquisite.

"I fancied this ring the first time I saw it in a Mayfair jewelry shop. The stone is rather rare." Eyes glittering, he added, "Perhaps it is unfamiliar to you?" There was a hint of challenge in his smooth tone.

"A pink Andean opal," said Holmes without hesitation. "It is darker than other specimens of my acquaintance, which makes it all the more rare."

Frowning in silent defeat, our visitor murmured, "I admit that it is an indulgence, but it is hardly my only one."

"You collect fine art as well, do you not?" suggested Holmes.

"Ah! Very good, my fine fellow. And how did you come to that conclusion?"

"By association. A man who would wear such a ring might be expected to surround himself with some of the finer things in life. My mind went immediately to art."

"Now I *am* impressed! For I am a private collector and I rather doubt you would have heard of me. "

"I have not," admitted Holmes. "Now what is the nature of your challenge?"

"I have been following your career for some time, and I am understandably impressed. Particularly with the Baskervilles hound case. But there were others over which Fleet Street dazzled the credulous public. Here, I thought, is a man of penetrating intellect and unsurpassed deductive power. But no one is perfect."

"I hardly make any such claim," allowed Holmes.

"Yet this thought led me to wonder if it were possible to conceive an enigma that even the redoubtable Sherlock Holmes could not unravel."

Taking up his pipe, Holmes remarked, "I have several unsolved mysteries scattered among my papers. Dr. Watson can attest to that. You would not be accomplishing very much if you presented me with something that was beyond the scope of my abilities." He lit his pipe. "But do go on. You intrigue me."

"I have in my possession a problem that I daresay will defeat you, provided you agree to undertake to solve it."

"This is not a police matter."

"Is that a statement or a question?"

I knew that it was, in fact, both. For one of the subtle arts that Sherlock Holmes practiced was to offer a frank statement in such a way that the other party could take it as firm conclusion or respond as if it were a question, each according to his lights. Either way, it inevitably brought a satisfactory result.

Holmes did not reply directly. Instead, he said, "Your casual manner suggests that the matter is not serious, therefore it does not involve the authorities."

"A good point. And soundly reasoned. I salute you, sir."

Holmes was puffing away by now. He then said, "I venture to say that your art collection lies at the center of this matter."

"I did not say that," our visitor said sharply. "Neither did I imply it in anything I have told you to this moment."

"Nevertheless, I assert that it does."

"Which I now freely admit. And by inference alone you have gotten to the heart of the matter. I own a painting which will interest you."

"It interests me already, inasmuch as you bring it up. Pray tell me more."

"There is a mystery about this painting. I wish you to undertake to solve it."

"For a fee?"

Roy Darlington smiled rather insouciantly and said, "I am prepared to pay you one thousand pounds if you can solve this riddle."

"It is a riddle, is it?"

"I imply the expression in its most casual sense," Darlington said hastily. "One might call it an enigma, a puzzle, a stumper. Or all three. I prefer the opaque term, enigma. But I say too much. It is you who must apprehend the clues and then decipher them. Do you agree?"

"Not quite yet. But I gather from your relaxed attitude that the answer to this enigma is already known to you."

"I did not say that!"

"You might as well have, for your manner has disclosed this already."

Darlington stroked the wings of his wilting mustaches, rendering them symmetrical once more. "I will say no more. The problem has been laid before you, and the fee for success stipulated. Do you agree to take up this challenge?"

Holmes puffed in silence. His thin face was lost in thought far longer than I believed necessary. Whatever he was contemplating, he was giving it a thorough going over in his active brain.

At length, he directed, "Take us to this painting of yours."

"Excellent! We will depart at once."

And so we did. I was rather breathless at the speed at which we found ourselves in a four-wheeler carriage, jouncing through the streets of central London and beyond its confines. The driver took us southwest to Richmond Hill rising over the Thames Meadowlands and up to the front door of a house that was not quite a mansion, but was substantial, if a trifle eccentric. In short, it appeared to be the ideal residence of Mr. Roy Darlington of peculiar habits and lively personal adornment.

A rather plain maid greeted us at the door and took our coats.

Darlington informed her, "I have brought visitors, Mary. The famous Sherlock Holmes and his trusted interlocutor, Dr.

Watson. Make us a spot of hot tea whilst I show them my art collection."

"Yes, sir," murmured the maid, withdrawing to the kitchen.

The furnishings of the home were more tasteful than I expected, but Holmes gave them only cursory glances. I noticed daffodils in a vase of cut crystal, and idly wondered if our host thought them to be mums—an unkind thought I forbore to express aloud.

One rather spacious wing of the dwelling was given over to framed artworks. The room was semi-circular and lacked furniture. Not even a comfortable chair. The white-painted walls were hung with an assortment of framed paintings that brought a gasp from my lips.

These were by no means museum-worthy works. They were remarkably uniform in their appeal, both in terms of subject matter and execution. Invariably, they were seascapes or sky studies. The artist or artists had worked with a painfully limited palette. For every canvas was exclusively rendered in cool colors—primarily bold greens and vivid blues with touches of turquoise, chartreuse, ultramarine, and aquamarine blended into the whole. The overall effect managed to be both gaudy and garish, so much so that the flamboyant colors all but repelled the eye.

One framed canvas stood out among the others. Occupying the central position of the curved display wall, this was a large composition depicting an underwater scene, one that might have been taken from Roman mythology. Bearded King Neptune was the central figure. About him cavorted various undifferentiated fish, as well as dolphins, crabs, seahorses, and three immodest mermaids who were smiling upon their becrowned ruler. The canvas was to my mind marred by an excess of air bubbles. That these were semi-transparent was beside the point. There were too many of them. Nor were they all the same hue, some daubed in emerald, some jade and others cobalt, many simply suggested by brushstrokes of color limning their rims. Seen at a remove, the combination of overlapping hues tended to blend into a visual cacophony of green and blue, and the coarseness of the canvas combined with the overdone application of oils brought to mind a distinctly radical experiment in Impressionism. It was as if the artist was ignorant of relative color values, which led to an unfortunate flattening out of the composition, obscuring and confusing many details a more skillful artist would have brought out.

The impression one received upon viewing the image in its totality was of an askew attempt to emulate Lawrence Alma-Tedema's "Roses of Heliogabalus" but in assorted greens and blues. Neither Alma-Tedama nor Frederic Leighton, who so loved the Greek mythological theme, need concern themselves over this emerging rival, whoever he might be. For I spied no signature on the canvas.

"The artist called this work 'Neptune's Quandary,'" remarked Darlington. "I fancy it may become infamous as 'Sherlock Holmes's Waterloo.'" He smiled at his own rather facile humor.

Sherlock Holmes regarded the confusing composition in respectful silence.

Seeing this, our host commented, "It is a bit of a poser, is it not?"

Privately, I considered Darlington himself to be a bit of a poseur, but kept that opinion to myself.

"To my eye, the cavorting mermaids appear to be central to King Neptune's quandary," I remarked. "Perhaps the composition contains a rebus, a message spelled out in pictured objects sounding like the words intended to be conveyed."

"I prefer not to comment, Dr. Watson," retorted Darlington. "This challenge is for Mr. Sherlock Holmes to properly answer."

Holmes broke his reverie. "May I inquire if any restrictions are attached to this unique challenge of yours?"

"Only one. That the work cannot be removed from this house. But I will permit you unlimited and unfettered access to this room for the duration of the challenge."

"That sounds to my ear like a second condition," suggested Holmes.

Darlington stated, "Call it what you like. I give you one week to solve the enigma that is staring you in the face, Holmes. Can you accomplish this in seven days?"

"I imagine it will require less than one day," remarked Holmes without hesitation.

At that, Roy Darlington threw back his head and laughed rather unsettlingly. His off-key mirth smacked of a hen cackling, and I suspected in that moment that the fellow was a trifle off in the head. But the peculiar painting hanging on his wall had already cemented that impression in my mind. It was a debacle in oils, a travesty of art. I imagined that the man's mentality was a similar shambles.

My friend was unaffected by the blatant mockery. When Darlington had regained control of his composure, Sherlock Holmes said, "I have seen enough. Allow us to return tomorrow to conclude our agreement and collect the fee."

Darlington looked nonplussed. That was momentary. His rather crooked smile returned and he said thinly, "Are you confessing to being stumped?"

"Momentarily at a disadvantage, perhaps. But I remain confident of securing the stipulated sum."

The maid stepped in and announced tea. We took this refreshment in the subdued dining room, Holmes with barely concealed reluctance.

As we sipped our beverages, Roy Darlington became inquisitive.

"You appear rather confident, Holmes."

"I *am* confident," returned the detective, his eyes hooded in thought. "Supremely so."

"I suspect that you are bluffing."

"I have been known to bluff from time to time," admitted Holmes, unmoved by the accusation.

Darlington's wretched smile returned.

"But I am not bluffing at present," stated Holmes.

The lobsided smile collapsed, but Darlington struggled to rearrange it. I noticed perspiration made his forehead gleam under the electric lights.

He continued probing.

"I would be interested in hearing your preliminary theories, Holmes."

"I prefer not to expound upon theories in advance of concrete conclusions," said Holmes dismissively.

"But certainly you have a line of inquiry in mind," pressed the connoisseur of the finer things in life. "Have you ever encountered such a puzzler?"

"Never," returned Holmes flatly. "I will admit that it is novel, if trivial. Its novelty is the only element that makes the challenge interesting. Aside from the fee, of course. Fees are always of interest. Especially when they are so easily won."

Holmes took another sip of tea. He seemed to enjoy it. He had an appreciation of fine Indian teas, and this one was an exquisite Darjeeling.

Darlington chuckled again. His laugh was nervous. He could not cover for this. "You truly think that after all the trouble I have gone to in order to create a challenge that you could not meet, that it would be so easy to solve?"

"I do. Especially when you offer me so many clues."

"Name one!" Darlington demanded hotly.

"I had the essential clue before I made your acquaintance."

"Impossible! Explain yourself."

"I would rather reveal that when I reveal all," stated Holmes with unflappable aplomb.

Darlington was now frowning furiously, but he mastered himself. Settling himself back into his chair, he drank his tea contemplatively. I noticed a single bead of perspiration erupt upon our host's right temple to slide down his cheek like an errant tear.

I inserted myself into the silence in order to clarify a point I had begun to suspect.

"Do I gather, Darlington, that you commissioned this outlandish painting for the ultimate purpose of confounding my friend?"

"Precisely. I personally directed every brush stroke."

"Remarkable," I said. I would have employed a less kind word, but for the fact that we were guests in this unique man's home.

"I thought it a worthy challenge for the unsurpassed detective, the inheritor of Dupin, and Scotland Yard's special pet," he added smugly.

If Sherlock Holmes took offense at that last cutting comment, his austere features did not betray him in the least. For my part, I began to comprehend the way of things. Darlington was a rich idler, and his motivation to challenge my friend was impelled by a combination of jealousy and egotism. I imagined Holmes had already arrived at that determination.

Once we had drunk our fill, Holmes stood up and announced, "Shall we say at ten o'clock tomorrow morning?"

"That is agreeable to me."

By this point, Roy Darlington had resumed his good humor and air of sophistication. He essayed a brave smile.

"You really think you can solve it?"

As the maid brought our coats, Sherlock Holmes made an astounding statement with austere coolness.

"Mr. Darlington," he said crisply, "a child could solve this purported enigma."

"Surely you jest!"

"I assure you that I am asserting a sober truth. Tomorrow at ten a.m., then."

With that, our host saw us out, and we walked a short distance until we encountered a hansom cab that would convey us to the railway station in time to catch a late train to central London.

The ride back to the city was one of profound frustration for me.

"Good Heavens! I cannot for the life of me settle in my mind whether you were bluffing that awful fellow, or truly confident in the outcome."

"Watson," Holmes said, taking out his traveling pipe, "I am supremely confident."

"You barely studied the painting."

"It was unnecessary to do so. I learned all I needed to glean in order to act upon my initial conclusions earlier today."

"My word, Holmes, you stagger me at times."

"As I have often remarked," Sherlock Holmes returned, as he charged the pipe bowl with black shag tobacco and applied the soft yellow flame of a match, "you see what is about you, but you observe very little of your surroundings."

"Now I *am* baffled."

"You will recall the window peonies?"

"You mean Mrs. Hudson's arrangement of buttercups?"

"I mean both, my dear Watson. Sleep on the difference between buttercups and peonies. Perhaps my line of reasoning will occur to you by the break of dawn."

"I rather doubt it," I informed my friend. "I will expect to set off at nine sharp tomorrow morning then."

"I expect that we will be joined by another companion."

"Oh? Do I know this individual?"

"I believe that you may possibly be acquainted. If not, formal introductions will be made."

And that was all I could get out of Mr. Sherlock Holmes for the remainder of the train ride home. Having filled his pipe, my companion settled in to enjoy its fiery fumes. I failed to detect any outward indications of his canny mental machinery applying itself to the purported enigma. Truth be told, he appeared to be distracted rather than meditative, as if the mystery were already solved and the matter behind him. I did not see how that could be. Yet all the certain signs were present.

THE NEXT MORNING I found Sherlock Holmes outside of 221b Baker Street, speaking to an urchin of the streets, a scruffy lad of about ten years' standing in the world. Holmes had left our apartment after breakfast and was gone an hour, returning with the young fellow.

When I emerged to join him, my oft-times frustrating friend hailed me with a hearty, "Watson! Have you made the acquaintance of Mr. Weems?"

"I have not, I am sorry to say."

"James Weems is a member in good standing of what you know to be called the Baker Street Irregulars."

Then it dawned upon me. This was one of the legion of street orphans Sherlock Holmes employed from time to time as spies, and for other sometimes unsavory tasks that provided him with important information that he needed to solve his varied cases.

Lifting a hand, Holmes signaled a passing carriage to pull up to the curb. "Mr. Weems will be joining us."

"Oh, he will, will he? In what formal capacity?"

"Resolver of quandaries. For he is one of my most apt pupils. And his capacity must be styled as informal, in keeping with his attire."

As we climbed into the four-wheeler, we took our seats and I examined the young man. He appeared to be intelligent of face but rather slovenly in dress and general hygiene. I did not think him a very prepossessing detective, if that was what he was supposed to be. The vivid color of his shirt reminded me of Mr. Darlington's chartreuse waistcoat, and I noted a similar lack of harmony in his uncouth attire, but I thought no more of it.

"Do you require an apprentice in order to solve this challenge?" I asked Holmes.

Seated across from us, Jimmy Weems ventured a ragged

laugh. It sounded to my ear a trifle saucy. It was as if he was in on some sort of secret joke.

"If our task required a pickpocket or a lock picker, Watson, we would hire a professional."

"Does this enterprising young man pick locks, or pockets?"

"Neither, Watson. Those were merely examples. Mr. Weems' talents are, I dare say, on the unique side of the ledger of human capabilities. Quite probably very few individuals living in London possess his penetrating discernment."

Weems giggled again. I could not imagine where the humor lay in Holmes's assertion. The boy did not appear to be particularly discerning to me.

"I imagine everyone has their own unique gifts," I allowed. I kept my skepticism to myself. I knew better than to doubt Sherlock Holmes.

"Are we not transferring to the Charing Cross Station?" I inquired, noticing that we were departing the city proper.

"Since we are shortly to be the beneficiaries of Mr. Darlington's generous largess," stated Holmes, "we will indulge ourselves in a leisurely journey."

It had not been lost upon me that Darlington had left us to our own devices after seeing us out the night before. Evidently, Holmes took mild offense at that inhospitable lapse, and had decided to spend some of the man's money before he collected it.

Upon our arrival at the Darlington residence, Holmes asked the carriage driver to wait, a request that astonished me in its lavish profligateness as much as it communicated the undeniable fact that my ordinarily thrifty companion did not anticipate a visit of long duration.

The maid met us once more. She took one look at young Weems, and her nose bunched up.

"Is this your son?" she asked of Sherlock Holmes.

"Accomplice might be a more accurate term," offered Holmes.

"Such a disreputable word to describe a young boy," she noted firmly.

"Young master Weems has his disreputable side, but he is also quite useful at times," countered Holmes.

James Weems suppressed a giggle as we were led into the spacious semicircular room where hung the Neptunian portrait that was so inharmoniously rendered and uniformly colored.

Roy Darlington joined us shortly. His selection of shirt and waistcoat were so appalling that I will not describe it here other than to note that the man's sartorial instincts appeared to be defective. At first sight of the young boy, his smiling countenance wavered a trifle.

"And who is this likely young lad?"

"James Weems, sir," spoke up the young fellow. "Pleased to make your acquaintance." He put up his hand, but our fastidious host pretended not to notice the offered fingers.

Darlington looked to Sherlock Holmes and noted, "I fail to comprehend this young man's purpose here today."

Holmes smiled coolly. "You will recall, Darlington, that I ventured to say that a child could solve your impenetrable enigma."

"I took that as a brave joke."

"I know that you did. But it was hardly anything of the sort. For I have produced the specific child in question. And enlisting an accomplice was not barred according to the brief catalog of your stated conditions."

Darlington swallowed so noticeably that the silk knot of his cravat momentarily shifted to one side. "Quite."

"Since we are punctual this morning," continued Holmes, "shall we get on with it?"

"Get on with what exactly?" asked our host suspiciously, glancing towards the boy.

"Mr. Weems will endeavor to scale the towering enigma you believe to be insurmountable and offer up its solution."

Laughing, Roy Darlington said, "Well, he is welcome to do exactly that. And to take as long as he wishes to do so. But really, Holmes, is this not beneath you? Should you not solve the problem yourself?"

Holmes sounded not in the least offended.

"As I informed you last night, Darlington, I solved one portion prior to our first acquaintance. Now with the help of my accomplice—and I use the word pointedly—I will complete the task, collect my fee, and be on my way."

Darlington actually turned pale at this last. Sherlock Holmes had spoken so directly, so firmly, so confidently, that the flummoxed fellow realized he teetered on the edge of utter failure and that the surrender of the fee was imminent.

Nevertheless, he regained his composure and croaked, "Pray proceed."

Holmes took the boy by the shoulders and guided him up to the central painting. There, they fell into low converse as they studied King Neptune and his marine subjects. The boy was pointing to the bubbles that decorated the canvas, indicating with a grimy finger certain ones, all of which were predominately sea green. He whispered to Holmes a few words, then laughed rudely. His laughter was not shared by my good friend.

After several moments of this, Sherlock Holmes turned and addressed Roy Darlington stiffly, "I politely decline your request."

"Sorry." Darlington's voice shook. "What request is that?"

"The unkind request that I bark like a dog."

Hearing those words, Roy Darlington did an entirely unexpected thing. He fainted on the spot. Fortunately, the rich nap of the carpet cushioned him from significant injury to anything other than his dignity. The maid had to be summoned and smelling salts liberally applied. I performed that thankless duty.

When he returned to wakeful consciousness, Darlington had to be helped to a comfortable armchair, where he showed considerable confusion of thought. The points of his waxed mustaches were noticeably askew.

"Have…have I been dreaming?" he mumbled.

Holmes informed him, "If you dreamed that I solved the enigma brushed into your painting, no. It was not a dream. Perhaps for you it is a nightmare. But only you can say for certain what the loss of one thousand pounds means to you."

I had been an intrigued but silent observer up to this point; now I could no longer contain myself.

"Good Heavens, Holmes, could you kindly explain yourself?"

"Certainly, Watson. Mr. Darlington no doubt has an inkling of what I am about to tell you. But perhaps hearing the steps I took in order to arrive at this juncture will be instructive to him.

"You will recall that when he called upon us, Mrs. Hudson informed us that he had complimented her buttercups, but mistook them for peonies. This absurd error told me that Mr. Darlington is color blind. Most sufferers of this affliction confuse red and green. His type of color blindness is of a rather different order. He sees the color yellow as pink. Hence his mistaking yellow buttercups for pink peonies, and his choice of an opal ring whose pink stone fitted into a more comfortable range of the spectrum, as it was visible to him."

"I have read about such a condition," I admitted. "It is quite rare."

Holmes continued. "Darlington's habit of wearing a grotesquely chartreuse scarf and matching waistcoat was another tell-tale symptom of his handicap. Where you and I perceive a garish green, his defective vision communicated to his brain a more subdued teal hue. For he cannot discern any shade of green, except as low-grade variations of blue and grey."

"I see now!" I exclaimed.

"This deduction was confirmed when we were shown his singular art collection. For he had every canvas painted to accommodate his visual quirk. Knowing that the disputed work in question was created for him, I deduced that the mystery lay in the canvas, and not its origin or with the artist himself. Hence there had to be a hidden message in 'Neptune's Quandary,' a message that Darlington directed his artist to brush into the canvas. I quickly dismissed the notion that it had anything to do with the three mermaids, of any such rebus. Since I am not myself color blind, I would have scant hope of deciphering this message, unless I could remove and photograph it, which was barred. A black and white replica might or might not bring out the artfully-concealed message.

"As it happens, Mr. Weems shares the same deficiency of which Mr. Darlington has taken unfair advantage. Having established the foundation of the mystery, it was a simple matter of enlisting the lad in the second and final act of the resolution, there being no necessity for a third act, as it were."

James Weems grinned from ear to ear while rubbing the blunt tip of his nose with pleasure during this recitation.

He spoke up eagerly. "When I looked at the picture, some of the bubbles stood out dull against the blue of it. They spelled out a message: 'If you can decipher this, bark like the famous Baskervilles' hound.'"

"Which I naturally declined to do," noted Holmes dryly, "my innate dignity refusing to acquiesce to so offensive a request." His sharp gaze went to the daze-faced Darlington. "But I imagine that my dignified response does not disqualify me from earning what was promised."

"I will not indulge in any form of welching," snarled our host, his voice becoming hoarse. "I am a man of my word. You shall have your damned fee."

"I was promised five quid for my expert opinion," Weems gloated, obviously enjoying his role in the humbling of Roy Darlington.

"And you shall have it," assured Holmes. Turning to Darlington, he added, "Mr. Weems would like to compliment your anonymous artist. Apparently, if one sees the world as he does, 'Neptune's Quandary' is both tasteful and subdued, although marred by distracting superfluities."

The dispirited man did not appear to appreciate the offhanded compliment.

"Now," concluded Holmes, "if you would be so good as to settle your obligation, we have a carriage waiting." I thought I detected an edge in my friend's tone of voice, an otherwise unexpressed reprimand of the previous evening's discourtesies, and no doubt other insults.

Darlington looked as if he was about to swoon once more. He grabbed at the wings of his armchair to steady himself.

"Of course. I will write out the check at once. I am contrite. I thought I had devised an enigma so ingenious, so devious, that you would not have the first inkling of its true nature."

"What you thought was complicated," said Holmes coldly, "was to me simplicity itself. Once I had the first clue, it was just a matter of reasoning to an accurate outcome. The choice of subject matter for your painting, King Neptune and his under-water realm, made perfect sense once one understood that you would perceive its varied greens as a visual symphony of muted and distorted blues and greys, and that certain uniformly-colored elements would stand out if viewed through the prism of your own affliction, which would otherwise be indiscernible to the more common eye."

"But Holmes," I interjected, "what if you did not have available to you the services of young Weems? Whatever would you have done?"

"While I would admit that this was a happy convenience, if not a freak of fate, if it came to it, I would have advertised in the London newspapers for a person who possessed the same rare form of color blindness that the occasion required. It would have called for some additional effort, but for the substantial fee at stake, well worth it."

"You make it sound so simple," muttered Darlington as he produced his fountain pen and checkbook.

"That is because it *was* simple," returned Holmes dismissively. "It was only in your untutored mind that it was otherwise. Elementary. Entirely elementary. Is that not correct, Mr. Weems?"

The lad laughed lightly. His reply filled me with horror as to the fashion sense of the coming generation.

"With my winnings, I think I will buy a shirt and waistcoat as fine as Mr. Darlington's. I rather fancy the way the colors strike my eye."

THE ADVENTURE OF
THE GLASSY GHOST

I HAVE RARELY BEEN reluctant to join my esteemed friend Sherlock Holmes in one of his fascinating investigations, but the law of averages, not to mention the inexorable wheel of fate, both conspired in an attempt to block me from participating in the tantalizing mystery which I will now relate.

Let me be clear that it was not an absence of curiosity, but rather a surfeit of energy that caused me to all but miss out on one of my dear friend's most baffling intrigues.

I had been away in the country for a week, visiting distant relatives. What had promised in the beginning to be a relaxing period of welcome respite from city life ultimately devolved into a dismal and unnaturally depressive and forced captivity.

The rain had commenced at mid-week. In spite of periodic respites, the elements had whipped themselves into an electrical froth, culminating on the night of 12 October in 1901. A thunderstorm of such ferocity that the house periodically shook as if the earth were being made to convulse by burrowing creatures raged half the day and well into the night. Slumber was impossible. The house lights, which were illuminated by electricity, failed miserably and had not returned. When morning came, it was time for me to take the train back to London.

Fortunately, by that hour the beastly rain had abated. The air smelled clean, as well it should have, having been relentlessly washed by successive downpours. Despite that, hailing a cab at

Victoria Station proved to be an ordeal. The skies were still an ugly slate hue, and the fear of fresh downpours motivated even the most hearty hikers to avail themselves of any cab that rolled up to the station entrance.

Impatience was getting the better of me when finally my turn arrived. The coachman dutifully accepted and stowed my luggage, and I climbed aboard feeling that the clap of the coach door closing upon me was one of the most welcome sounds ever to impinge upon my hearing. For the homey sound signified that quite soon I would be safely ensconced in my own domicile, perfectly dry, and prepared to catch up on my sleep, which I fully expected to restore frazzled nerve strings.

The short ride through London's muddy streets showed that the familiar metropolis had not escaped the fury of the overnight elements. The overcast sky hung low and oppressive, promising more dreary misery.

As the cab pulled up before 221b Baker Street, I alighted. I happened to glance up at the windows overlooking the thoroughfare from the first floor apartment we shared, Mr. Sherlock Holmes and I.

I recognized Holmes, almost cadaverous in his vertical gauntness, looking down upon the muddy prospect, his hawk-like features wearing a predatory if slightly worried cast.

His sharp eyes glanced my way and he threw off his singular immobility. Swiftly, he disappeared from view. In my overwhelming fatigue, I took no special import from his sudden vanishment. Nor did I then imagine that Holmes had been standing sentry, awaiting my return. That I was expected upon this day did not rise to the level of my conscious thinking, for I desired but one thing. That was bed rest. And I was determined to have it as quickly as I could shrug off my garments and fling myself upon my familiar mattress.

As the coachman was unloading my luggage, the door abruptly flew open and Holmes stalked out, displaying the weird nervous energy that characterized him, even when he was in repose.

"Your timing is hardly perfect, Watson," he snapped out, "but it will have to do."

"I beg your pardon, Holmes?" I sputtered.

"No time for idle chat," snapped Holmes. "Have the coachman place your belongings inside. He will convey us to our destination."

I confess that my nerves had been abraded to a rawness that caused me to snap back impatiently, "The only thing I seek at the moment is my bed!"

Holmes appeared momentarily taken aback. "Have you not just returned from a restful week in the country?"

"I have returned from the country, yes," I shot back. "But restful it was not!"

Holmes stepped back, and his keen eyes raked me up and down. Owing to long association with his canny ways, I was not surprised by his next statement.

"No sleep, I take it," he enjoined.

"Not so whatsoever in two nights. Although last night was the worst."

"The thunderstorm, no doubt."

"The very same," I allowed. "Now if you'll excuse me, Holmes, as much as I would normally be pleased to accompany you to your destination, you will have to make your own arrangements with the coachman. I am really exhausted and without interest in anything other than temporary oblivion."

Holmes's expression was fixed and firm. A sparkle was in his eyes, quite deeply held.

"This is regrettable, for I have waited nearly an hour for your expected return. And now you fail me."

"I am doing nothing of the kind. I will be happy to join you after a suitable interval of rest, provided my presence is required.

But I trust you can carry on without my limited insight in the interim."

"I see that I shall have to," murmured Holmes slowly. "But it is a pity. This promises to be one of the most intriguing mysteries to come my way in months."

I nodded. Curiosity did not awaken in me one iota. Instead, I waited for Holmes to carry on and avail himself of the convenient carriage.

But he did not. Instead, he remarked, "You are familiar with the solicitor, Morland?"

"Yes, yes. Of course I know the name."

"It appears that the poor fellow perished last night at the height of the thunderstorm."

"Murder?" I returned dully.

"I have formed no firm convictions on Morland's demise, one way or another. The manner of his death may or may not be explicable. But it is what happened to him after his death that intrigues me."

Now Holmes had me. "Did you say *after?*"

"I did, Watson. For after the man expired, it appears that the window glass of his office on Oxford Street captured his departing soul, and is now displaying it there for all to see."

"Extraordinary, if true," I burst out in spite of myself.

"Extraordinary if *not* true," countered Holmes, "for several persons claim to have seen the dead man's spirit after it had been captured by the window pane."

At these words, my tongue became still. I momentarily lost the power of speech. I stood rooted.

Sherlock Holmes eyed me with his appraising gaze. No doubt he was searching my face to discern if I wavered in my resolve for slumber.

I inquired, "This took place on Oxford Street?"

"It did. Not five minutes away by cab. Surely, you could

accompany me that far. I promise to hold the driver, who will take you back if you are not up to a complete investigation."

Fatigue will do many things to a man's brain. It will dull it, stupefy it, and work other mischief upon its pliable grey matter. In this particular instance, I fear it robbed me of my resolve, if not my better judgment.

"I can spare fifteen minutes, Holmes. Perhaps twenty. But that is my limit." I spoke these words firmly, but I might as well have been a man who was sodden with drink. I had no will of my own before the master of psychology who was Sherlock Holmes.

Before I could change my mind, Holmes urged me back into the cab and the doors were shut, the driver having deposited my luggage in the entryway and closed the outer door firmly.

And so we were off on what promised to be a truly baffling mystery. And so it proved to be. I only wish that I had the clarity of thought necessary to fully participate in its unfolding.

During the brief journey, Holmes recounted what was known of the matter to date.

"Morland happened to be working late last night, and failed to return home at a reasonable hour. It was initially believed that the downpour had stranded him in his office, but when midnight came and went, his wife braved the elements and entered the place. It was dark and the lights were inoperative. Fumbling about the office, she all but tripped over the cold corpse of her late husband. The police were immediately summoned, and under the light of our electric torches, they pronounced the unfortunate solicitor deceased."

I nodded, too fagged to comment.

Holmes resumed his account. "It was in the torchlight that the apparition in the window pane came to light. It was a head, not much more than a silhouette. The wife was still present when torch illumination brought it to light. At the site of the stark image, she let out a hysterical scream and fainted. Upon being revived, she swore that the silhouette was that of her late husband. She particularly remarked that the unruly hair could belong to none other than Sylvester Morland, Esquire. The shape of the head also convinced her, for Morland's skull was quite broad at the crown and tapered to a rather narrow pointed chin. Only one ear could be discerned by its shape. This, too, Mrs. Morland pronounced to be evidential."

This choice of words roused me. "Evidential! Is that not the word spiritists employ to compliment a so-called medium that they consider genuine?"

Holmes nodded. "I believe you are correct, Watson. You are not so sleepy headed as you imagine yourself to be. My use of the term was inadvertent. But it augers for intriguing times ahead, does it not?"

"I should hope so, Holmes," I said, rather dispiritedly, for my thoughts kept careening back to my comfortable pillow, upon which I dearly wished to lay my tired head.

Within minutes, we were dropped off before the Oxford Street offices of the late attorney. They were those of a man of middling achievement, as the shabby-genteel appointments suggested once we entered.

Inspector Lestrade was there to greet us. Our initial conversation was perfunctory and to the point. The body of late Morland had been borne off to the morgue and little remained of the death scene, other than the empty office.

Pleasantries abandoned, Holmes snapped, "Show me the window in question, Lestrade. I am keen to examine it."

"Would that I could, Mr. Holmes," said the police official. "But I fear it has been removed to Scotland Yard for minute examination. A glazier has already set the replacement glass in its place, the apparition understandably attracting a noisy crowd."

"Then my own examination must await official permission. Now then, I understand from the morning newspaper that Mr. Morland was discovered lying upon the floor." Holmes cast his penetrating gaze about the office. He pointed to an inner wall, remarking, "I would say that the corpse was found upon that spot."

"Why, exactly upon that spot," returned Lestrade. "However did you puzzle that out, Holmes?"

"There was no doubt considerable scuffling following the discovery of the deceased, and scuff marks, many of them moist from the recent rain, display that trampling to even the casual eye. One spot, however, appears relatively untrammeled." Holmes strode over to the spot and began surveying the immediate surroundings.

There was nothing of interest there, but his attention became fixed on the electrical switch controlling the ceiling light. This consisted of a black knurled knob. Reaching out, he gave it a turn, producing a click, but no illumination from the light fixture overhead.

"It appears to be due to defective wiring," Holmes pronounced.

"That may be so," said Lestrade. "Perhaps the evening thunderstorm had something to do with it. As you doubtless noticed, lightning lashed the heavens continually for several hours."

"It was quite a performance," agreed Holmes. "One could readily imagine why less sophisticated men in olden times came to believe in thunder gods of various sorts. Tell me, Lestrade, were there any unusual marks upon the body?"

"A bruise on the left temple. That was all."

"I see. No doubt it was occasioned by the dead man's fall."

"There is no reason to suspect the man was dead before he fell," countered Lestrade.

"On the contrary," returned Holmes. "There is no doubt upon the matter."

The inspector's eyes became unnaturally narrow.

Cord wiring ran from the electrical switch to the ceiling fixture, held in space by hasps and staples set into the plaster wall and baseboard. Holmes was examining this closely.

"When will the autopsy be performed?" he asked suddenly.

"There will be no delay. It may have already commenced."

I confess that I heard the proceedings as if through a curtain that smothered my senses. The lively exchange was not without interest, but was insufficient to rouse me from my low state.

Abruptly, my overwhelming sleepiness was shattered—along with the sharp sound of breaking glass.

The spartan desk was suddenly littered with shards of glass, and the cobblestone rebounded off its polished surface, banged off a wall, and came to rest under the desk.

"Hullo?" Holmes expounded. "What have we here?"

A constable had been posted on guard outside, but he had wandered up to the corner. Now he came hurrying back.

Holmes dashed out into the street and it was he who spied the street urchin ducking around a corner. He gave chase, the constable and Lestrade hot behind him.

I was content to step out onto the pavement and await developments. My energy was not up to hot pursuit.

Not long after, Holmes returned, the urchin in tow. The latter was squalling in the most unbelievable manner, and his words were hardly articulate.

Marching the boy up to Inspector Lestrade and the constable, Holmes instructed him firmly, "Repeat now what you have just told me."

"I fear to do so, sirs," sobbed the boy.

Holmes gave him a rough shake. That was all that was needed.

"A fellow I never saw before gave me a silver crown and asked me to do the deed."

"To break a window pane?" demanded Lestrade.

"No, sir, to break a particular window pane. The man was quite particular about the exact one. He wanted nothing broken but that particular pane."

"Did the fellow say why he wanted this done?" demanded Holmes.

"He did, sir. But I fear to relate it to you."

Holmes directed, "Fear not. Simply speak the plain truth."

"This fellow Bob said that a man's spirit has been captured by the window glass and needed to be liberated to complete his journey heavenward. He was so sincere in his words, that I took them to heart. He told me that if I did this, I would be doing the poor unfortunate fellow who had died a great service."

"My word!" I exclaimed.

"Describe the fellow," encouraged Holmes. "It will go better on you if you do a good job."

The distraught lad did the best he could, but his powers of speech were insufficient to the task.

"The man was neither very tall, nor was he short. He did not dress in a gentlemanly fashion, but rather rough, sirs. I did not like his eyes, but it was his hair that was the most arresting thing about him. It was wild and unruly."

"What color, boy?" demanded Lestrade.

"The hair or his eyes, sir?"

"Both, if you would."

"The eyes I should say were a rather sad blue color, verging upon grey. His hair reminded me of a chestnut mare, one that had not been groomed in a fortnight."

Holmes interjected, "I take it he did not introduce himself formally."

"He said his name was Bob. Just plain Bob. I've never seen him before in my life. But the silver crown swept my senses away. After he flashed it, I was his to command."

Lestrade said tightly, "Now you are the law's to command. Constable, take this young scalawag away. The charge will be disorderly conduct and wanton destruction of property."

The officer dragged off the sobbing, unresisting boy. We repaired to the late solicitor's office to consider matters.

Holmes said, "It need not be overemphasized that the boy was importuned to shatter the window upon which the apparition had been inscribed."

Again the choice of words caught my attention. Lestrade also noted this, for he remarked, "Inscribed, did you say? Whatever do you mean, Mr. Holmes?"

"I merely used a convenient word, for I have no inkling as yet as to the truth of the matter. Once I see the window pane, I may have a theory to offer. But first I would like to examine the body while it is still fresh and reasonably intact."

The growler was still standing by the curb, and we three availed ourselves of it after shutting up Mr. Morland's dingy office.

By this time, my interest in the matter was overcome by fatigue, and I went along without resistance. Although I must add without great relish, either. It was not that I was determined to see it through, but rather that I lacked the force of will to remove myself from the rush of events.

We soon found ourselves in the morgue. The body was rolled out of its metal drawer, still clothed. Holmes gave the man's corpse careful scrutiny, then he lifted the hands by their wrists, one at a time, examining the fingernails, the palms, the tips of the fingers, and apparently nothing else.

I noted that the man's features seemed stark and vexed, as if a great fright had been experienced prior to the moment of death. His head of hair was rather full, but very carefully arranged. Death had not greatly disordered it. The smell of pomade, although faint, lingered about him. This made me think that he was more fastidious about his hair than his attire, for the latter was a trifle worn here and there, especially at the cuffs and elbows.

One ear protruded, the left. It did not match its opposite appendage. To my physician's practiced eye, I took this to be a malformation present at birth, and not the result of disfigurement.

"I have seen what I expected to see," announced Holmes, after opening one eyelid to ascertain the color of the hidden orb. "Let us examine the window pane next."

This caused Lestrade's jaw to sag slowly. He regained control of it sufficiently to blurt out, "What did you see that I failed to discern?"

"Time enough for that later. The window glass, if you please."

The specimen had been carefully placed in a wooden box large enough to encase it, and this was brought out and placed upon a work table. The lid was lifted, and Holmes reached in and raised it to a vertical position. He rested the lower edge upon the work table and moved the glass back and forth, peering into it with the steady intensity of a soothsayer staring into a crystal ball.

I joined him in this endeavor.

"I fail to perceive any image, ghostly or otherwise," I admitted frankly.

Inspector Lestrade was gaping openly at the smooth surface. It appeared to be unblemished.

"I examined this window pane while it was still in its casement," he said tightly. "The silhouette was as plain as day. Now I do not see it."

Then Holmes made a remark that utterly baffled me. "That does not mean that it is not there."

Lestrade turned to him. "Whatever do you mean by that, Holmes? It is either there, or it is not there. My eyes inform me it is no longer there."

"My eyes communicate the same information. Perhaps it will return. Perhaps not."

Without another comment, Holmes laid the glass carefully in its wooden receptacle and said, "I should like to examine this more closely."

"If you think it will do any good," allowed the inspector. "But if I had not seen the window glass with my own eyes earlier this morning, I would doubt the testimony of all witnesses, including my own constables."

When the box was carefully sealed, Holmes said, "I wish to speak with the widow next."

EN ROUTE TO the Morland domicile, Inspector Lestrade ruminated, "Whatever could have been the motive for hiring the wayward boy to shatter the replacement window pane?"

I ventured, "Is there someone who cared very much for the late Mr. Morland, and the repose of his spirit? Or, conversely, someone who hated him thoroughly?"

Holmes astonished me with his next remark. "Neither motivation is exclusive of the other."

As the growler rumbled along, Lestrade and I stared at Holmes with undisguised astonishment. But Holmes kept his own counsel. His eyes were exceedingly thoughtful.

Understandably enough, Mrs. Morland had taken to her bed. As the maid showed us in, and I beheld the widow resting comfortably in her soft bed, I felt pangs of envy, but suppressed them.

Inspector Lestrade introduced us. "This is the renowned Mr. Sherlock Holmes, and his friend, Dr. Watson. They would like a word with you if you would, Mrs. Morland."

"I regret that I cannot properly greet you gentlemen, but I am sure you understand my situation."

"It is a grievous one," allowed Holmes. "I have a very few questions. I beg you to pay attention to them closely."

"Proceed, Mr. Holmes," invited the bereaved woman.

"Had Mr. Morland lost any significant cases in recent weeks?"

"Two."

"Did either of his clients quarrel with him, or deny him his fee?"

"There was trouble with both gentlemen. But I do not know the particulars."

The inspector interjected, "No doubt the details can be gleaned from court records."

"No doubt," agreed Holmes. "Mrs. Morland, tell us why you believed the apparition shown in the window pane was that of the late Mr. Morland."

"It was the shape of the head. Sylvester's skull was rather distinct. Broad at the top, it tapered down, rather like a turnip. But it was the hair. The way it stuck out, the wildness of it. That was my husband's hair most mornings upon awakening. You see, he tossed and turned in his sleep. As a result, his hair became as disordered as a rag mop."

"I beg your indulgence for the following indelicacy, Mrs. Morland," said Holmes carefully. "I have just examined Mr. Morland's remains. And his hair was rather well cared for."

"Yes, no doubt it was. Sylvester took great pains to keep it under control. The wildness was something he tamed only through careful grooming and the liberal application of pomade."

"I take it that his hair was in place when you found him?" pressed Holmes.

"It was, sir."

"Then why is it, Mrs. Morland, I beg you to say, do you believe that this was his spirit captured upon the window pane?"

"For the identical reason I told you. That was Sylvester's hair apparent in the glass. Also one ear had stuck out, and was the proper shape. The shape of the head, combined with the formation of the ear, surrounded by the crown of unruly locks, could only be my late husband. Please accept my word upon that."

"I do. Yet I find myself dissatisfied."

"In what way, Mister Holmes?"

"Why would the soul of a man display the wildness of hair when his body lay on the floor correctly coiffed?"

"I do not know. But something in the aspect of the silhouette upon the window suggested sudden fright. Perhaps his spirit was taken aback by his sudden and unfortunate passing and expressed itself by reverting to its natural appearance."

At this point I was forced to interject, "That is an extraordinary statement, Mrs. Morland, if I do say so."

"This is an extraordinary eventuality, Dr. Watson," returned the woman gravely.

"Had Mr. Morland any relatives?"

"A brother. They were estranged. We had not heard from him in years. He lives in Harwich."

"His profession?"

"I believe he is, or was, a chemist. I do not know any other particulars. As I said, they were estranged, a condition that was mature when I first married Sylvester nearly eleven years ago."

"I see," said Holmes. "I am sorry for your misfortune, Mrs. Morland, and I want to assure you that I will do everything in my power to bring the murderer of your husband to justice."

The statement was delivered with such calmness that it nearly escaped my notice. But I beg to remind the reader that I was extremely fatigued. Inspector Lestrade, however, was not. His rejoinder was sudden and sharp.

"Murderer, you say!" he exclaimed. "What brings you to that conclusion, Holmes?"

"The evidence of my senses, Inspector. Nothing more and nothing less. Now we must take leave of you, Mrs. Morland. My condolences to you. You will be hearing from Scotland Yard in due course."

Mrs. Morland said nothing. She had clapped her hands to her face as if her grief had suddenly become overwhelming, and she was no longer able to control herself.

I felt pass over me a great wave of sympathy for the unfortunate woman, and we quitted the room as quietly as practical.

Standing by the waiting cab, Holmes addressed the inspector.

"Watson and I must take leave of you, Lestrade. I imagine you are going to look into court records."

Lestrade nodded vigorously. "No doubt they will prove illuminating."

"No doubt. And I would be eager to hear of your discoveries when you have made them."

"Good day to you, Mr. Holmes," said Lestrade, turning on his heel and departing.

As we piled into the faithful cab, Holmes remarked, "That

will keep Lestrade occupied while we pursue more fruitful lines of inquiry."

"Such as?"

"Such as may be found in my private library. And if not there, in my chemical laboratory."

I imagine that I looked a trifle blank, or perhaps it was sheepish. But I was grateful when we returned to 221b Baker Street and Holmes released me to my bed chamber and an unbroken sleep that lasted nearly twelve blissful hours.

I SAW LITTLE of Sherlock Holmes the remainder of the day and that evening. He was shut up in the sitting room, and I could hear the occasional clinking of glass, as if he were mixing chemicals. To what end, I could not imagine.

Most alarming to me were the flashes of light visible round the edges of the closed door and through the keyhole. It was as if the fellow were brewing a tempest in the chamber.

I knocked once to inquire if he needed anything.

His retort was abrupt. "I require solitude, Watson. Nothing more, nothing less. Thank you."

So I left him to his alchemy, and dined alone.

Inasmuch as I had slept late, I took an evening stroll rather than retire at my usual hour. When I returned from my walk along the Strand, I chanced to look up to see the intermittent flashes so much like indoor lightning coming from the sitting room windows that I could not imagine if he were emulating the Norse thunder god, Thor, or experimenting with electrical apparatus.

I considered the irony that Sylvester Morland had died at the height of a thunderstorm in a chamber whose electricity had been extinguished. These two thoughts I attempted to combine, braiding and unbraiding possibilities, but accomplished nothing for all that mental exertion.

I could only wonder as to my dear friend's line of experimentation, for it was baffling.

Inevitably, the hour came when I needed to retire, and while sleep did not come swiftly, it did finally arrive. It was interrupted once by a low grumble of thunder, and I imagined that Sherlock Holmes, not the elements, was the responsible party.

Fortunately, the noise was not repeated and my slumber resumed, this time without any unwelcome breaks.

Morning found Holmes bustling about the apartment, looking for all the world like a fox hound unable to catch a proper scent.

"Difficulties, Holmes?" I inquired.

"Complications, Watson," Holmes responded shortly. "I have reconstructed pieces of the puzzle, but I do not know yet if they constitute a whole, or merely an unmeasured portion of the entire skein."

The ringing of the doorbell stopped Holmes in his tracks.

"Ah," he announced. "That would be Inspector Lestrade, possibly bearing other parts."

I imagine my expression communicated my surprise. For, noticing it, Holmes remarked, "The inspector employs his thumb to ring the doorbell. He lets it rest there far too long. His calling is as distinctive as a fingerprint. Let us not keep him waiting, Watson. Show him in."

Moments later, I brought Lestrade up to the sitting room and we all settled into comfortable chairs.

"Once again," the inspector began, "I must compliment you, Mr. Holmes. You correctly deduced murder where mere misadventure was what met the casual eye."

Holmes waved the compliment away impatiently. "Please get on with your report, Inspector."

Unruffled, Lestrade produced a small square notebook and began reading from it.

"The bruise to the left temple was determined to precede the fall, and was not caused by it."

Holmes interrupted shortly, "That was obvious. The man fell

on the opposite side, according to the crushed state of his hair. What produced the disabling blow? A hammer?"

"That is the likeliest implement," rejoined Lestrade with no trace of injured pride. "Someone struck Morland, knocking him down, if not out. Whether conscious or not, the man would certainly have been dazed by the blow."

"Rendered helpless, in any event," I remarked.

"What was the pernicious substance injected into his veins?" demanded Holmes.

Astonishment made Lestrade's eyebrows shoot upward. I have no doubt that my own greying brows matched their acrobatics.

Rather impatiently, I thought, Holmes related, "I detected the needle puncture mark visible in the cloth of Morland's coat, but was undecided on the point of the lethal brew injected."

"The autopsy suggests that it was a solution of arsenic."

Holmes frowned. "Too common a substance to point the finger of guilt towards a definite party." His expression darkened. Faint shadows of unreadable thoughts paraded across his sharp features, making his eyes cloudy. At length, he lifted his head and asked, "Have you any suspects among aggrieved clients?"

"Two. Both were recently represented by Morland, who failed to win their cases."

"Their names?"

Lestrade said, "A Mr. Robert Daisley and a Mr. Donald Thorson."

Holmes caused the inspector's eyebrows to perform miracles with his next question.

"Which of the two gentlemen was by profession an electrician?"

Lestrade sat momentarily speechless. Finally he said, "The latter gentleman."

"Then that is the man we must interview," cried Holmes, rising to his feet.

MR. DONALD THORSON lived in a respectable house in the suburb of Earl's Court.

En route to the residence, the lowering skies commenced to grumble and I cast a worried glance upward.

"Rain in the offing," I muttered.

"A downpour for a certainty," answered Holmes flatly.

I shivered inwardly. I had had enough of rain in recent days.

Inspector Lestrade accompanied us, of course. It was he who knocked upon the door of the modest dwelling.

Donald Thorson answered the door himself, and seemed startled by the trio of strangers confronting him. He was a bluff fellow, as wide of face as a bear, with hair and eyes grey as the storm clouds marching over our heads.

"Mr. Donald Thorson?" demanded Lestrade.

"The same," replied the man. "Who is it calling upon me?"

Lestrade identified himself and presented Sherlock Holmes and myself.

"The celebrated sleuthhound himself!" Thorson marveled. "To what do I owe the rare and unexpected pleasure?"

He seemed truly impressed, and not at all concerned by our unannounced arrival on his doorstep.

Lestrade answered officially. "We are investigating the death of Sylvester Morland, with whom you are professionally acquainted. We would like a word with you."

Thorson hesitated only momentarily, and then threw the door wide while stepping back to permit our entry. "Enter at once."

We were seated in his little parlor a moment later.

Holmes regarded the man with his canny grey eyes and remained silent while Lestrade opened the proceedings.

"Well, no doubt you have read of Mr. Morland's untimely passing in the newspapers," the inspector began.

Thorson laughed raggedly, "Strike me, I have. And quite a shock it was, too. I had seen him on the night in question."

Lestrade blinked rapidly, rather like an animal who sights unexpected prey.

"Do you mean upon the night he perished?"

"I do, Inspector. Mr. Morland rang me up, requesting my immediate services. After a bit of haggling, I agreed to come out and restore his electrical service. The blasted storm had knocked it out."

"It is our understanding," said Lestrade, "that you and Mr. Morland had had a falling out over services rendered in a recent legal matter."

"I do not deny it. On the contrary. I had been dawdling on the matter of settling the bill, for I felt that Morland had let me down in his representation of my case. It was a simple matter, and I should have prevailed in court. But I did not. It cost me dearly. The details are neither here nor there."

"So how was this settled between you?" pressed Lestrade.

"Well, as I have said," continued Thorson pleasantly enough, "Morland rang me up and suggested a settlement. Namely, that I restore his electrical service in lieu of paying the outstanding bill. I was hesitant, for I was still nursing a bit of a grudge. But upon reflection, Morland convinced me that this was a reasonable resolution for our impasse. He had previously hinted that he might sue me for the balance due, which was his perfect right, of course. But I did not hold that against him. I hurried out into the storm, found him holding forth in his office—in the dark as it were—and resolved the matter, at the same time concluding our business amicably. That is all there is to it. And that is the last time I beheld poor Morland alive."

During this interview, the intermittent grumble of distant thunder grew into a clamor of increasing detonations. Rain began cascading down, all but drowning out the man's words, which were couched in a forthright but low tone, as befits discussing the recently deceased.

All the while, Holmes simply regarded the man without comment. It was uncharacteristic of him not to probe with questions of his own, and I took this to mean that my friend accepted the electrician's account without qualm.

I was soon to be disabused of this assumption. I should not have been greatly surprised. But I confess that I was.

A streak of lightning slashed the heavens framed in the window behind Thorson's head. He jumped up. His head turned about, and he stared out the window at the jagged electrical bolt. It was like a luminous artery fading from sight.

"My word!" he exclaimed. "From the sound of it, we are in for another beastly round of weather."

Lestrade said, "Pray resume your seat, Mr. Thorson. To return to the matter at hand, have you nothing else to offer?"

Donald Thorson gave the question no great consideration. He answered readily. "Once I had completed my work, I left Mr. Morland to his own toil. I daresay we were both well satisfied with the resolution to our disagreement, but of course I should only speak for myself."

Another bolt hurtled earthward and the entire room lit up with a blue-white discharge that made us all resemble startled ghosts. I know that I felt that way, and Thorson's stark aspect in the searing electrical light gave me that impression.

Again the electrician jumped out of his chair and looked about rather nervously.

Holmes spoke for the first time. "For a man who works with electricity, you appear to be apprehensive when it manifests in its natural state."

Slowly, carefully, Thorson sat down again, but this time his fingers clutched the arms of the overstuffed chair, and he looked as if he were prepared to propel himself to his feet at the slightest excuse. Had it not been for the resounding storm, I would have judged him guilty of something.

"Mr. Holmes," he said carefully, "I work with the Jovian stuff. Who would know better than I of its potentials for destruction?"

"Elegantly stated," agreed Holmes. "Now I have a question

or two, if you do not mind." This was pitched to both Lestrade and Mr. Thorson, both of whom nodded wordlessly.

"When Morland was found deceased upon the floor of his office," said Holmes carefully, "the electrical lights were not functioning. How do you explain that fact if you restored service?"

"You don't say! Let me see, I left around nine-twenty that evening. The storm raged more than half the night. It is possible, in fact it is quite likely, that an errant thunderbolt undid all of my hard work."

"Yes," agreed Holmes. "Both possible and plausible. Let me ask this: Did Mr. Morland give you a receipt for the work done?"

"No, he did not."

Thunder grew louder in the background.

"Did Morland provide documentation that the debt between you was settled?"

"He did not, Mr. Holmes. As professional gentlemen, we simply shook hands on the matter. That sealed it forever."

"At least, it was sealed forever," mused Holmes thoughtfully. "But by death rather than by any human agency."

Thorson batted his eyes several times nervously. From his expression, it was clear that he did not know what to make of that laconic comment. Nor did Sherlock Holmes enlighten him.

An interval of silence came and went. I noted that Thorson's fingers on the arms of his comfortable chair became tenser, as if in expectation of something unpleasant.

Holmes supplied that ingredient with his next words. "You might be wondering why we are so interested in the death of Sylvester Morland."

"It had crossed my mind, yes."

Holmes's next words shocked me. "We are considering the theory, still unproven, that Morland was electrocuted by the very wiring you claim to have restored."

A wild little laugh shook itself out of the electrician's mouth.

His eyes lit up strangely. "What are you gentlemen suggesting—that Morland was done away with deliberately?"

"If you take that implication from my words, you were taking them too far," said Holmes flatly. "My suggestion was merely that Sylvester Morland might have met his fate through faulty electrical work."

Thorson became slightly indignant. "My work is considered to be of impeccable quality. And your accusation a canard. If the electricity went out after I had departed Morland's office, it was through no fault of mine. You might as well blame almighty Zeus as me."

Sherlock Holmes appeared to be leading up to something, but that same deity invoked by Morland seemed to intervene.

Another bright thunderbolt manifested, followed by booming thunder. The house shook noticeably.

This time, Thorson sprang from his chair with the feral look of a tiger. He turned this way and that, then his eyes fixed upon the window pane to his right. They widened, and out of his mouth came a strange scream, trailing off into a wail.

"Look! Look, it's the accusing devil himself!"

At those words, we were all up on our feet, staring in the direction the quaking man had indicated.

I confess in retrospect to experiencing a shock unlike anything I have ever before felt. I am not a believer in the supernatural, but for a moment, my scientific convictions were shaken to the core.

For the lower pane of glass framed a face, a countenance I had beheld once before. But not in life—in death!

In the semidarkness, it appeared to be the face of the late Sylvester Morland!

With a fearfully shrill outcry, Donald Thorson bolted in the direction of the kitchen. Holmes, followed by Inspector Lestrade and myself, rushed in the opposite direction.

We went out the front door, and pounded towards the parlor window on its opposite side.

There was no one lurking there. The pane was perfectly transparent, unblemished by anything other than dripping raindrops.

"Quickly!" yelled Holmes. "Search in all directions. The ghost is abroad."

We three dispersed, inspected bushes, peered around corners, and rushed about in the rain, all the while fearful of another punishing thunderbolt.

Holmes vanished to the rear of the house, after first examining the muddy ground which had accumulated so much rain water that tracks were not easily discerned.

When finally we were forced to conclude that our quarry had either successfully fled, or was not in any way, shape, or form physical, we returned to the welcome shelter of the parlor.

Donald Morland could not be found. He had fled out the back way, apparently in utter terror.

When his absence was firmly established by search, Lestrade turned to Holmes and demanded, "What do you make of it, Mr. Holmes?"

"I make of it murder."

"That fact has already been established—by you."

Holmes waved the statement aside. "I'm not referring to the late Mr. Morland. But to another party."

"Thorson?"

"Perhaps. Perhaps not."

Holmes strode up to the very parlor window through which the apparition had appeared. He gazed into the glass a long time, as if expecting to discern something there. Finally, he turned to address us.

"I found this in the mud," said Holmes. "Dropped, no doubt, by one of the parties who fled."

Out of a pocket he produced a long white envelope, quite wet and soiled. It was addressed to Donald Thorson. There was no stamp or postmark upon the envelope, nor any return address. It was sealed. Holmes took the liberty of opening it.

From within, he took and unfolded a sheet of plain stationery. It bore no salutation or signature. Instead, there was a blob of India ink, in which three smeared words were visible.

I read the running letters aloud: *"Pay your debt!"*

"What does that mean?" demanded Lestrade.

"On the surface, it would suggest that the ghost of Sylvester Morland is continuing to dun Mr. Thorson for an unpaid debt incurred in life," intoned Holmes.

The seriousness of his utterance took me aback. This infuriated Inspector Lestrade, who burst out, "You cannot be serious, Holmes!"

"There is one fact which I consider to be both unassailable and unimpeachable. And that is this: Mr. Morland is demanding that Mr. Thorson pay him."

Neither Inspector Lestrade nor I knew what to say to that.

Without another word, Holmes stalked out into the elements and we were forced to follow.

Huddled in the rain, Sherlock Holmes turned to Lestrade. "Inspector, let me suggest that you muster a number of your constables and search for Donald Thorson. If your men prove swift, they may be able to forestall another murder."

"I will do as you say, Holmes," returned Lestrade, "but I would expect an explanation first."

"There is no time for explanations," snapped Holmes. "If your men can lay hands upon Thorson, you may lawfully arrest him on the charge of murdering Sylvester Morland."

"Really, Holmes!" I interjected. "Thorson seemed perfectly innocent during the course of our conversation, and only became nervous at the approaching thunderstorm. How can you so casually deem him a murderer?"

Holmes did not answer directly, but instead took us around to the back of the house where he had previously sought the missing electrician.

In the rear glowed a small single-pane window. The window was sheltered by overgrown bushes, which Holmes thrust aside.

In the light from the street lamps, we could see the glass. Distinct as if etched there was fixed a frozen face. Its features were shadowy and not discernible, but the unkempt halo of hair and protruding right ear were outlined perfectly. But to my eye it was all but identical to the fearsome silhouette that we had been told was somehow impressed into the glass of Sylvester Morland's office window pane.

Lestrade pushed forward, placed one hand upon the glass, and rubbed it vigorously. The image did not fade or disappear.

"I confess I do not know what to make of this," he said, withdrawing in frustration.

Holmes stated, "Consider that Mr. Thorson is being haunted by his misdeeds, Lestrade. If you will be good enough to mobilize the local constabulary, you may have your man before midnight."

Looking rather bleak, the inspector rushed off to do exactly that.

Holmes turned to me. "Quickly, Watson. We must catch the next train to Harwich."

"Harwich? Whatever for?"

"Because I have no doubt that Donald Thorson has in mind to take that very train."

We found an unoccupied cab, availed ourselves of it, and were rushed to the train station. But, alas, we were too late. The train to Harwich had departed only ten minutes before.

A hasty consultation with the ticket agent brought forth the fact that a rain-soaked individual had boarded the late train to Harwich. "He was a wild-haired sort," the agent averred. "I did not see his face very clearly. But in a rush, he was."

Holmes next described Donald Thorson.

"That fellow also purchased a ticket," the agent offered.

"Thank you," said Holmes.

Taking me aside, he said, "Thorson trailed the revenant and they are on the same train. No doubt the quarry is unaware of his pursuer."

"Do you expect violence to be done?"

"Not upon a moving passenger train, no."

Holmes possessed a remarkable memory. One might call it phenomenal in its retentive powers. Without consulting a time-table, he announced, "The train to Great Yarmouth will be along in twenty minutes. It stops at Ipswich. We will get off there, and hire a cab to take us to Harwich."

I objected slightly. "Do you not think that Lestrade will be put out once he discovers that you have sent him off on a wild goose chase?"

Holmes frowned. "I rather doubt that Lestrade ever arrives at that particular suspicion. Inasmuch as I could not be certain of Thorson's ability to make the Harwich train, it was a reasonable suggestion, circumstances being what they are."

In due course, the train pulled in and we boarded.

As it rattled through the intervening towns, Sherlock Holmes unburdened himself of certain facts.

"Thorson was clever enough," said Holmes. "But he made a number of slips, one of which was to volunteer that he had been with Morland on the night in question. Most of what he related was substantially true, save for certain particulars. I descried no sign of electrical wiring repair in the Morland office, and the lights had not been restored, the electrician's representations notwithstanding. No doubt the solicitor summoned him for the very reasons stated, but Donald Thorson was playing a deeper game. Namely, to revenge himself.

"As proof of his fabrications, we have Thorson's failure to produce written proof of the resolved debt. Watson, have you ever heard of a man of the law failing to draw up a memorandum attesting to the receipt of funds or services rendered?"

"Never!"

"I rest my case," said Holmes. "Furthermore, did you mark the man's swift assumption of a murder accusation when I implied nothing of the sort?"

"I did, but not immediately."

Holmes nodded. "Thorson's failure to bring up the subject of the apparition in Sylvester Morland's office window is also suggestive of guilt."

"How so?"

"Why would he avoid what the newspapers have made a sensation?" asked Holmes.

"Perhaps he puts no stock in ghosts," I ventured.

"Yet he fled in terror from what appeared to be a visitation from the revenant."

"So he did. Puzzling."

"Not puzzling when you comprehend all the skeins in this particular web."

"Holmes, why did you suggest that Morland was murdered by electricity?"

"Why, to make it appear that I was not on the correct track. Thorson was doing a credible job of appearing to be an innocent person. I was encouraging him in the belief of his successful imposture, the better to trap him, you see. Unfortunately, the thunderstorm disrupted the placid snare of my interrogation."

After a pause, Holmes scrutinized me silently for some moments, then inquired, "Why have you not leapt upon the most basic question of all, Watson?"

I managed a blank frown, I suppose.

Holmes smiled thinly. "You failed to ask how I knew that among Morland's dissatisfied clients, one must be an electrician?"

I smiled. "That was elementary, my dear Holmes. Who else would be present at such a late hour under the circumstances?"

Holmes suppressed a dry chuckle. "I'd accuse you of reasoning backwards from subsequent facts, but no matter. That was my thinking."

The train soon arrived. Subsequently, I found myself sitting beside Holmes in a rain-slickened hansom cab, rushing to an address he told the driver. The address meant nothing to me, but it was within sight of the Harwich High Lighthouse.

As we raced along, Holmes broke his silence. "I trust you have your revolver, Watson?"

"I have it."

"Would you lend it to me? That's a good fellow."

Holmes carefully checked the weapon, saw that it was loaded, but that the chamber under the hammer was empty. This was a common precaution against accidental discharge. Only when he was certain that the weapon was safe to pocket, did he conceal it on his person.

As we approached our destination, Holmes asked that we be let off two streets short of the stipulated address.

We walked the remainder of the distance in the rain, which was steady but not extreme. Fortunately, there was no electrical activity present in the clouds massing above our heads.

The home to which Holmes led me proved to be dilapidated and in a state of disrepair, but not distressingly so. It was an ancient cottage and the years had not been kind to it. Evidently, the occupant had given it little attention in recent years.

Holmes approached cautiously, one hand stuffed in the pocket of his coat where the revolver rested.

He stalked up the front walk, whose flagstones were cracked and loose. Holmes appeared to be determined and not at all inhibited in his bold stride.

"I pray that we are in time," he said to me, "but I fear that the interval between trains will prove decisive."

A muffled report coming from the confines of the house stamped a grisly period at the end of Holmes's sentence.

Rushing forward, he assaulted the door. It proved to be unlocked. Holmes thrust himself inside, the revolver in hand.

A strange voice cried out, "Murder! Murder!"

The familiar voice of Donald Thorson screamed in rage, "Not murder, you low blackmailer! Doom! Righteous doom!"

Another shot rang out. It came from the far room.

Heedless of the danger to himself, Sherlock Holmes barged into the room in question, I myself not far behind him.

Sharp shots were traded! One gouged a doorframe perilously close to my head. I heard the ugly sound of a body falling to the floor, followed by another.

When I entered the room, I was greeted by the spectacle of Sherlock Holmes standing over the bodies of two men. One I recognized instantly. It was Donald Thorson. A smoking pistol was clutched in one hand, but the fingers would never again move of their own accord. The fellow was dead.

Kneeling, Holmes removed the pistol and then turned his attention to the other corpse.

The body in question was jittering in its death throes, and soon completed them. The nervous tension in the muscles relaxed, and it was as if the newly dead man was gaining in stature even though he was stretched out upon the floor. A modest lake of blood seeped out from beneath him. The powder marks of two point-blank gunshots showed blackly on the man's shirt front. But my attention did not linger there—they went to the fellow's face.

I knew it. Or thought that I did. For I had seen the identical cadaver stretched out before me in the London morgue. It appeared to be the face of Sylvester Morland!

"There is your ghost, Watson," pronounced Holmes solemnly.

All but tongue-tied, I blurted, "How can a newly-dead man produce a ghost three days in the past?"

"Of course, he cannot," Holmes returned sharply. "Any more than the spirit of a dead man could become trapped in glass. For all is not what it seems to be, despite the seemingly inconvertible certainty of otherwise unfathomable evidence."

I offered nothing, for I had nothing to say. I was utterly baffled. Staggered would not be too strong a word.

"Kindly explain yourself, my dear fellow," I entreated Holmes.

"Do you recall mention that Sylvester Morland had a brother? One who lived in Harwich."

"Well, now that you remind me, I do. Is this his twin, then?"

"Not a fraternal twin, no," said Holmes. "My research revealed, they were but a year apart in age, as you might surmise from this man's general appearance. You will note the wild hair not tamed by pomade, as well as the protruding right ear, which is not precisely the same configuration as the one that I noted in the morgue. That was one of my first clues that the image in the solicitor's window was not that of the dead man himself. The differences were subtle, true, but also undeniable."

"How, then, did the image come to be embedded in the window?" I wondered.

"Come, come, Watson. Surely, now that the supernatural explanation has been discarded, it should not be hard to deduce the obvious."

"Obvious to you, I have no doubt, but I confess that I remain flummoxed."

"You cannot be ignorant of the fact that glass negative plates remain the most common means of capturing images for photographic reproduction."

"Well, yes. Of course I am familiar with glass negatives. Who is not?"

"From the sensation caused by the original glassy image, one might conclude that few were," said Holmes dryly. "The late Mr. Artemis Morland here is—or was—a chemist. And if we investigate his basement, I am sure we will find the inevitable photographer's darkroom, as well as all the necessary ingredients to coat ordinary window glass with the proper emulsion that will make it sensitive to retaining photographic impressions when subjected to bright light."

"By what means were these images imprinted?"

"During the time that you were taking your extended sleep of recovery," said Holmes, "I was exceedingly busy. I had already formed a possibility in my mind, which I verified by consulting a local photographer, as well as going to the Royal Observatory where, as I am sure you will recall, photographs of the stars are captured on glass plates. In our sitting room, I studied the original window pane closely and attempted to duplicate the process by means of flash powder. I would have preferred a lightning bolt, but the elements were uncooperative."

Holmes continued, "All whom I consulted agreed that it was possible for images to be imprinted upon glass by lightning flashes. This has occurred in the past, but it is a rare phenomenon. I might note that similar occurrences have given rise to credible reports of haunted houses. This is what happened on the night Morland was murdered."

I was now even more baffled than before, for Sherlock Holmes appeared to be suggesting a different murderer than the one named previously.

"My thoughts are tangled, Holmes. Your assistance in straightening them out would be greatly appreciated."

"Mr. Artemis Morland was the estranged brother of Sylvester Morland, the solicitor," Holmes related. "The reasons are somewhat obscure, but discreet inquiries revealed that Artemis Morland greatly lamented being excluded from his brother's life. He dearly yearned to alter that circumstance, but the stubborn solicitor rebuffed all fraternal overtures. The younger brother, Artemis, a chemist of modest repute, hit upon a scheme that was as fantastic as it was unlikely to move his obdurate older brother. He had developed an ingenious colloid emulsion that could be applied to the surface of a window in such a way that when illuminated by flash powder, the image of anyone staring in or out of the pane would be imprinted upon it, albeit without impressive clarity or fidelity. It had the regrettable limitation of fading within days, making it commercially of doubtful value.

"It was the younger brother's thinking that by surreptitiously coating his brother's window by night, during a thunderstorm, an interesting effect would be produced. This is surmise, Watson, but I give it great weight. Artemis appears to have hoped that by marking his distinctive countenance upon the window as a perplexing reminder of the unresolved issues existing between them, his brother would weaken and relent in time."

I was moved to say, "That sounds preposterous, to put it mildly."

"Absurd might be equally descriptive, I will grant you," said Holmes. "But this was the scheme, and during the recent stormy night Artemis Morland set out to implement it. As it happened, he arrived at his brother's office at an inopportune moment, and witnessed the cold-blooded murder of his own brother. During that interval, a lightning bolt streaked through the sky in such near proximity that the abrupt flare imprinted a perfect outline of his own head upon the glass. This later was incorrectly assumed to be the image of the dead man, when it was not."

"I see. Obviously, after this Morland fled the scene."

"Obviously," returned Holmes. "What he witnessed was shocking in the extreme, and there was nothing he could do about it. Sensational newspaper accounts published the next morning apprised Artemis of the silhouette created on the window, for the murder prevented him from igniting flash powder in his possession. No doubt he feared being accused as an accessory to the crime—hence the appearance the next day of 'Bob,' who inveigled the poor street urchin into hurling a cobblestone at the incriminating window pane."

"May we assume that Bob was acting upon the orders of Artemis Morland?"

"We assume nothing of the sort," shot back Holmes. "Call to mind the boy's description—unruly hair and blue eyes. Attributes of the dead solicitor, as well as his younger sibling."

"Ah! I see now. Bob was Morland the younger."

"In any event," continued Holmes. "Sylvester Morland's brother hit upon a fresh game. Blackmail. In some way, he discovered the identity of the murderer—I suspect by following him to Earl's Court—and set about to apply his foiled plan to this new endeavor. First, he painted the emulsion on one of

Thorson's windows, imprinting his own face upon it by igniting flash powder when the man was not home. No doubt he was inspired by the newspaper reports of the original haunted window pane. I also do not doubt that at least one letter or note of demand was sent to Thorson—the one I discovered was dropped before being slipped into the electrician's mailbox. As you will recall, it exhorted, *'Pay your debt.'* Here, then, was a demand for blackmail, not an unpaid bill."

"Remarkable," I said.

"If you're referring to my deductions, Watson, I must deflect a great deal of your praise, intended or otherwise. But if you are referring to the schemes of Artemis Morland, I will agree that they are remarkable, although also pathetic and tragic at the same time. All he wished was to reconcile with his brother, and now they are both deceased. This is a tragedy, Watson. And a testament to the folly of bruised feelings and unbending egos."

"You hint that you know more about the estrangement than you let on," I suggested.

"I would let the details be buried with both men. They are no longer important. Now, we must inform Inspector Lestrade of the unfortunate outcome of these proceedings."

As Holmes turned to seek a telephone, I remarked, "There was never a ghost then, Holmes?"

"Or to put it another way," replied my friend, "now there are *three*."

THE PROBLEM OF
THE BRUISED TONGUES

I T IS T H E rarest of occurrences when I enter a mystery before my esteemed friend, Sherlock Holmes, has stepped into the picture. More commonly, I am drawn into his adventures—not entirely against my will, I readily confess.

On the morning of October 31, 1902—mark the date—I was summoned to the home of Nathan Chalmers, who had been discovered in his bed, unresponsive. I hurried over to Chalmer's residence, where I was greeted by a flustered housekeeper, who shakily told me, "When Mr. Chalmers failed to present himself at breakfast, I took the liberty of knocking upon his bedroom door. Receiving no response after numerous vigorous entreaties, I became concerned for his welfare and so took the liberty of entering. The poor man would not wake up. Since you are his physician, Dr. Watson, my first thought was to summon you."

"I am sure that it is well that you did so," I replied hastily as we mounted the stairs to the bed chamber.

The flustered maid stood outside the room while I entered and began an examination. It proved to be quite short indeed. I had only to observe the pallor of my late patient and touch his brow and cheek to determine that he had been deceased for some hours.

Covering his face with the bed quilt, I turned gravely to the woman and enquired, "Had Mr. Chalmers been unwell of late?"

The maid was staring, her thin face stark. She did not appear to be of very high intelligence, but the meaning of my respectful gesture struck her with great force.

Her thick voice was a croak. "Not in the least, Dr. Watson. Not in the least. He—he has departed?"

"Sometime in the night," I told her.

Although I last examined Chalmers three months ago, he had been in exceedingly good health at that time.

Turning her face away while attempting to get hold of her trembling arms, the poor maid replied as she stared up at the ceiling blankly, "Nor had he given me any reason to question his vitality."

"Inasmuch as this is an unattended death, I must summon the coroner before the body can be removed from this house."

Shaking, the poor woman pointed towards the telephone stand in the hallway and withdrew.

The medical examiner arrived within twenty minutes. He threw back the quilt, observing the dead man's set features critically. Chalmers' eyes were shut, his expression composed. His mouth lay open, but not excessively so.

The coroner moved the man's head back-and-forth, evidently to determine if *rigor mortis* had set in and to gauge how long the deceased had been dead.

The head moved easily, but when the open mouth moved towards the morning light streaming through one window, a peculiarity was revealed. Sight of it caused the medical examiner to gasp.

"What is this?" he blurted to himself.

I had only a glimpse of what he had clearly seen, perforce I drew nearer to observe the yawning cavity of the open mouth, for the jaw dropped open under the coroner's manipulations.

The poor man's tongue had protruded as far as his bite, and the tip of it was as blue as if it had been bruised. It was a distinct blue against the dull enamel of his teeth.

Seeing this, I remarked, "I have never heard of a human tongue displaying signs of bruising."

"Nor have I," admitted that medical examiner. "I did not think such a thing to be possible," he added.

"I daresay it is a rare sight," said I.

"Grotesque," snapped the coroner. "Nothing less. And fitting for a Halloween morning."

I produced a tongue depressor from my medical satchel and offered it. The man accepted the tool wordlessly and used it to press down on Chalmers' tongue, while simultaneously prying the jaws open. I assisted insofar as shining the beam of a pocket torch into the dead cavity.

Only the tip of the tongue showed blue. There seemed to be no injury, no laceration, no abrasion. The man had not bitten down on his tongue in a death agony, as sometimes happens. There was absolutely nothing to indicate what had discolored the member.

The medical examiner pried open the lids. The eyes were thus examined. There was nothing remarkable there, just a glassy sheen common in the newly dead.

"Most peculiar," said he. "I have attended many deaths, but this symptom is out of my range of experience."

"It's new to me as well," I confessed. "What do you make of it?"

The coroner was a long time in replying. "I can make nothing at all of it without going more deeply into the matter. But I am wondering if this might be a freak occurrence worthy of your good friend, Holmes."

I was taken aback, admittedly. I blurted out, "Do you suspect foul play?"

The man turned to me and his expression was one of chagrin. "I only suggested that this may be a puzzle worthy of a greater brain than my own."

"Well, if you are so firm in your opinion, I will summon him, if he deems the matter worthy of inquiry."

"Well, tell him I am the most senior man in my field in all of London, and this is beyond my understanding."

I attempted to ring Holmes, but received no answer. Reporting this to the medical examiner, I said there was no telling if Holmes was out for a stroll or off on some fox-and-hounds affair of his own.

"In that case," said the official, "I must have the body removed to the morgue. Let us hope that Holmes returns in time to peer into this man's mysterious mouth."

At that, I took my leave.

IT WAS EVENING before I caught up with Sherlock Holmes.

I found him in his usual preserves, and at first he seemed abstracted to the point of disinterest as he puffed way at his briar pipe, filling the room with the bluish smoke of black tobacco.

Beside him lay a calabash pipe unfamiliar to me, and next to it a small brass dish in which lay a cold bit of dottle, presumably knocked from the bowl of the pipe. The unburnt plug of tobacco was crumbled into the ashy remains of the rest. A scattering of slobber next to a pipe tool suggested that the bowl had been scrupulously scraped clean.

I had barely begun my recounting of the matter when Holmes cut me off and snapped, "Men die in bed every day. The fortunate ones at least. You say this fellow was a patient of yours?"

I nodded patiently. It was a patience that I did not keenly feel. "Nathan Chalmers. Not quite fifty years in age, healthy as the proverbial horse. An unlikely candidate to pass in his sleep."

"And yet he did," said Holmes. "Would that we be so fortunate in our own hopefully distant futures."

Sherlock Holmes's countenance was a severe mask, his austere grey eyes unfocused, as if attempting to peer into another world—the world perhaps of pure and untarnished mental machinery. For I could see that he was focused on another problem than the one I was attempting to lay before him.

Bluntly, I demanded, "Holmes, have you been engaged on another matter?"

He nodded. "One has been brought to my attention. A most puzzling case. I do not yet know what to make of it."

"Perhaps the one I have in mind pales in significance against the one that is already on your plate," I averred. "Perhaps it must wait."

As if half hearing my words, Holmes murmured, "Perhaps, perhaps…."

"It is just that the medical examiner requested that I make clear to you that he had never seen such a thing in all of his professional years."

Holmes waved my statement away with a careless gesture. "There is nothing new under the sun, Watson. Each man rediscovers what those who came before him first uncovered."

"No doubt," I said. "But a bruised tongue seemed to me to rise to the level of a mystery."

My words did not appear to impinge immediately upon Holmes's consciousness, so deeply was he immersed in his own problem. I was in the act of turning to go when his eyes seemed to spring back into clarity, as if taking notice of his surroundings in earnest. His head lifted and his gaze locked into mine.

"Would you repeat that, Watson? I am not certain I heard you properly."

"I merely remarked that the deceased was found to have a protruding tongue whose tip was an unusual blue color."

Those grey eyes were snapping now. His sere features swiftly shook off the fog of a restive night and deep contemplative thought.

I was shocked by the pointedness of his next question, not to mention its essential character. "What color blue?"

"I beg your pardon?" I retorted, somewhat taken aback by Holmes's sudden vehemence.

Impatiently, he said, "Was the blue the color of a robin's egg, or the hue of an unclouded sky? Quickly, Watson! Do not ponder it too long. Give voice to your initial impression. There are many shades of blue, both natural and unnatural. What shade was this?"

It was not something to which I had given any consideration prior to this. I hesitated. "Why, I would judge it to be on the order of an exceedingly pale blue."

Holmes was rising from his chair. An eagerness seized his countenance. It was as if a fox was concentrating all of its being on what lay before it.

"Come, come, Watson. Name the exact shade of blue! Out with it!"

"Why, I would judge it to be in an Egyptian Blue."

"Are you certain?"

"As certain as memory would permit certainty. I was so aghast at the sight I did not attempt to classify the exact coloration. It did not remind me very strongly of a bruise blue, nor did it have any purple or green attributes. It was as though the tip of the tongue had been dipped in dye."

"It was not a Prussian Blue?"

Irritation coming into my own tone, I responded, "I have already asserted that it was closer to an Egyptian Blue. Why do you press this point?"

"Because," replied Holmes calmly, "before you entered this apartment, I was engaged in a problem. The problem had to do with a man named Arthur Chambers. Chambers was found dead late last night. He was at his writing desk slumped over. There was not a mark on him, Watson. Not even a bruise upon the forehead that had forcefully encountered the ink blotter. Yet when he was examined, it was found that the tip of his tongue was exceedingly blue. I have had the opportunity to examine it myself, and I can attest to the exact shade. It was a deep Indigo. Nothing less."

"My word, Holmes, that makes two men found in identical circumstances!"

Holmes shook his head violently. "No, no, certainly not identical at all. One man discovered at his writing desk, the other in his bed the following morning. There is nothing identical about either circumstance, except for the matter of the tongue. And the tongues in question were not identical either. Could there exist two shades of blue farther apart than Indigo and Egyptian Blue?"

"Two dead men found within hours apart with the tips of their tongue discolored blue strikes me as virtually identical," I retorted.

"Similar, I grant you, Watson. But not identical. You know better than to use the word improperly."

I was becoming agitated at my friend's brusque manner. But his next words soothed my rising wrath.

"Watson, as you know, I have sometimes questioned you with asperity, but today you are a godsend. I have been up half the night pondering this question without results."

"I rang you up earlier this morning."

"I seem to recall the telephone ringing, but I was too absorbed in thought to heed it any mind."

"Had you answered," I pointed out, "you might have spared yourself some wasted effort, for only now are you learning that this matter of yours is assuming a greater significance. My only question is, what does it portend?"

Holmes was striding towards the door, where he put on a coat and hat. "It portends, Watson, a visit to the London morgue. Are you up to the rigors of such a visit?"

"I am undeterred by the prospect of dead bodies," I replied coolly.

"Capital. Then be good enough to follow me. We are going to compare tongues."

"I beg your pardon?"

"Of course, I do not mean our own, for Mr. Arthur Chambers is also reposing in the London morgue. No doubt the two men can be found in adjoining compartments."

London's great morgue was not unfamiliar to us. Holmes and I had visited it more than I care to recall. It was a cool, dank, foreboding place. The Chief Medical Examiner, whose name was Curray, welcomed us in his rather dour manner.

His smile was on the grim side, but it was welcoming, even if it was not noticeably warm.

"Ah, Mr. Holmes! I assume you are to here to examine the remains of Mr. Nathan Chalmers."

"And Mr. Arthur Chambers. Would you be so good as to lay them out side by side for us?"

The medical examiner looked momentarily nonplussed.

I intruded by saying, "Evidently, you were not informed that the late Mr. Chalmers was discovered with a discolored tongue."

"I will speak to my associates about the oversight," he replied shortly. "But first I will make the arrangements you request. Be so good as to wait here."

While we waited, I asked Holmes, "Do you imagine that Chalmers and Chambers were acquainted in any way?"

"I imagine nothing of the kind. I prefer to leave such a rash conclusion unjumped upon, as it were."

Holmes appeared irritated. I suspected he had put so much effort into mentally masticating the problem of the first dead blue tongue that when I arrived with a second example, he was having difficulty tearing his mind away from his original train of thought. I had no doubt that I'd brought unwelcome tidings, but Holmes is a man who likes to reason out his own problems by himself in the austere solitude of his brain.

When the two corpses had been arranged on dissection tables side-by-side, we were called in.

Having already familiarized himself with the tongue of the late Arthur Chambers, Holmes went immediately to Mr. Chalmers and used a steel implement to examine the tongue, as well as the interior of the mouth. He was at this some time.

When he straightened, Holmes said, "You are correct, Watson. My apologies for doubting you. This is an Egyptian Blue."

I nodded my head in recognition of the apology.

Then Holmes went to the other dead man and, using a forceps, pulled out the flaccid tongue and showed that it was clearly a richer shade of blue.

"What would you call this hue, Watson?"

"Indigo."

"What does Indigo suggest to you?"

"Various subtropical plants yield Indigo, such as woad and Dyer's Knotweed."

"And Egyptian Blue?"

"Natron, such as the ancient Egyptians employed in the course of their mummification procedures. More commonly called sodium carbonate *decahydrate*. But what do the two distinctly different shades signify to you? Murder? Poison?"

"Without a doubt both, but there is a third element present."

"Yes?"

"Experimentation!"

With that startling word, Sherlock Holmes fell silent. He examined the bodies for marks and other clues, but found nothing. At least, he offered up nothing.

Grim of face, Holmes turned to the medical examiner and said, "Be on the watch for more such tongues."

The man became aghast of expression. "Do you suspect a plague of some sort?"

"A plague, most definitely. But a man-made one. A plague of poison. Exactly what motivates the author of these outrages is at this point obscure. Perhaps an examination of the Chalmers residence will unearth something interesting."

As we left, I asked Holmes, "Had you examined Arthur Chambers's living quarters for traces of poison?"

"Thoroughly," replied Holmes. "Yet I found nothing. Perhaps the Chalmers domicile will yield something more tangible."

"Will you inform Lestrade of your findings?"

"I have no doubt that the medical examiner is doing exactly

that at this moment. I would not be surprised if Inspector Lestrade beats us to the Chalmers house."

It was exactly as predicted. I was not in the least bit surprised. Inspector Lestrade was already questioning the housekeeper when we arrived at the Chalmers modest home in Earl's Court.

The woman in question answered our knock and, by all appearances, was even more flustered than she had been during the difficult morning.

"So it is you again, Dr. Watson?"

"Yes, and I have brought my friend, the esteemed Sherlock Holmes."

From inside the dwelling came Lestrade's sharp tones. "Mr. Holmes! Is that you? Enter, please."

The maid permitted us to go inside, and we made our reacquaintance with Inspector Lestrade of the Yard.

"I have been questioning this woman, but to no special conclusion," he said solemnly.

"Will you permit me to look around the residence?" asked Holmes.

"As you wish, Mr. Holmes."

Sherlock Holmes addressed the flustered housekeeper and directed, "Take me to your late employer's store of tobacco."

The woman blinked. "Why sir, Mr. Chalmers did not take tobacco in any form."

Holmes seemed slightly taken aback by this declaration. "Are you certain?"

"Quite certain, sir," the woman said levelly. "Why, you have only merely to take a turn around his study and have a sniff yourself. It is as fresh as Surrey air."

Not being one to take a statement at face value without investigation, Holmes moved about the first floor, his sharp nose lifted like that of a sleuth hound, finally arriving at the late Chalmers' study.

After sampling the air with twitching nostrils, Holmes examined the man's desk and bookshelves. All seemed in order. It was exceptionally neat and tidy.

Turning to the woman, Holmes demanded, "Did Mr. Chalmers avail himself of his writing desk last night?"

"Yes, he wrote letters before he retired. He directed me to post them in the morning, but owing to his sudden demise, I did not get around to it till this afternoon. Not that that matters a jot now."

"Had he any known enemies?"

"Not known to myself, sir," replied the housekeeper.

Holmes frowned. "It was the same with Chambers. Only Chambers smoked a pipe. I had expected to discover the same with Chalmers. Or at least that he indulged in the odd after-dinner cigar."

Inspector Lestrade spoke up, giving voice to the thoughts rising in my own mind. "Is it your theory that both men were done away with through tainted tobacco?"

"It was one of my theories—now discarded, I admit frankly," replied Holmes.

I spoke next. "It is a sound theory, if I may say so myself. For a man's tongue to be so severely discolored at the time of death suggests that the appendage came into contact with a virulent poison."

Holmes shook his head furiously. "Not so virulent that the victims succumbed immediately after coming into contact with the agent of death. Otherwise, we would discover said agent. Instead, there is nothing." Disgust tinged his last utterance.

I could scarcely believe my ears. "What are you saying, Holmes? That you are utterly baffled?"

"No," said Holmes tersely. "I am stating what I know to be the facts in the matter. Had food or drink been responsible for either man's demise, it would have stood at hand. Were tobacco the cause, the pipe or cigar would be in evidence. It is absolutely clear that Chalmers did not smoke. The fact the Chambers did is no longer of significance."

My good friend was clearly frustrated. I could hear it in the sharp edge in his voice. He had given deep thought to the matter of Arthur Chambers during the day and now that that day was exhausting itself, his lengthy ruminations had proven futile. It was common for Sherlock Holmes to arrive at conclusions before all others. But not upon this unique occasion, it seemed.

"Well, it is back to the beginning for all of us," commented Lestrade.

Holmes began pacing, his eyes searching the titles of the books neatly arrayed upon the shelves. I could not tell if he was reading their spines, or merely seeing past them. He was again deep in thought, and his nervous energy suggested controlled agitation.

At length, he began speaking.

"The nature of the poison can be narrowed down through autopsy. No doubt it will be. But no poison with which I am acquainted—and I am familiar with virtually all of the devilish cornucopia of murder—fits the salutary problem of the blue tongues."

Lestrade interjected, "I, too, am familiar with most poisons employed to do away with innocent persons," he mused. "And I know of none that will turn the tongue a vivid blue."

With a nearly savage ferocity, Holmes turned on Lestrade and barked, "The organ is not blue. Only the tip. This suggests a poison that acts upon contact, not upon ingestion. Hence my initial suspicion that a common tobacco product had been tampered with."

"Sound reasoning," I remarked.

"Not sound enough," snapped Holmes. He resumed his pacing.

Lestrade ventured, "Could a venomous insect have bitten either man?"

Holmes laughed dismissively. "Upon the tongue? In both cases? Surely, Lestrade, you can do better than that. Why, I fancy Watson here can summon up a better theory."

His hooded eyes turned in my direction, and I rose to the challenge as best I could.

"Let me think," I mused. "A man's tongue comes into contact with his food, his drink, and anything else that he dares to put in his mouth—"

"False!"

I started. Holmes's tone was extreme. I stared at him.

"You disappoint me, Watson. Have you forgotten that tongues also protrude?"

"I have not, for I had not completed my catalog," I countered. "Of course tongues protrude from the mouth, but a sane individual is fastidious about what he brings into contact with the organ of taste."

"Some examples?"

"Perhaps sweets," I suggested. "A man may touch his tongue to some form of dessert before eating, if he fears it to be too sweet."

"Few would," returned Holmes dismissively. "If cherry pie is set before him, he will either eat it or not, according to his lights."

"What if the food was unfamiliar to him? Say, a candy confection or an exotic fruit."

"If you are suggesting that either man was poisoned by lychee nuts or some foreign berry, I reject your suggestion out of hand." Catching himself, Holmes added, "But I thank you for that suggestion nevertheless."

With that, he lapsed into silence.

Inspector Lestrade and I exchanged glances, and neither one of us had anything to offer.

Suddenly, Holmes asked, "Do you recall the addresses of those letters you posted earlier today?" His eyes were fixed on the hovering housekeeper.

"I may have glanced at them, sir, but I paid the addresses no special heed. I am not the prying sort. Mr. Chalmers' correspondence was his own affair, not any business of mine. I simply posted them as he asked."

Holmes went to the late occupant's desk, and examined the ink blotter minutely.

"Was it Chalmers' habit to write directly upon his desk?"

"Yes, but not upon the blotter's surface. He preferred to stack papers and write upon the top sheets."

Holmes barked, "Show me that stack—what remains of it."

"I put it away, sir. Let me fetch it."

Forthwith, the housekeeper brought forth a sheaf of stationery from the right-hand top drawer, and set it down upon the ink blotter.

Holmes lifted the top sheet and held it up to the light. Eyes narrowing, he shifted the blank sheet of paper this way and that, as if attempting to divine something written in invisible ink.

"May I borrow this?" he asked the housekeeper.

"You may keep it, sir, if you think it will be of use in your investigation. You are welcome to it."

Very carefully, Holmes bent the sheet without folding it and kept it firmly in hand rather than place it in a pocket.

"I believe we are done here," he announced abruptly.

"I have some further questions of this good woman," Lestrade said.

"Carry on then, Inspector. I will inform you of my findings, if any."

As we departed, we turned up the street in search of a hansom cab, and I asked of Holmes, "Do you see any significance in the similarity between the last names of both individuals?"

Sherlock Holmes was so deep in thought I had to repeat my query.

"I have noticed the similarity, Watson. As to its significance, there may be none. I defer judgment on that score. This is an oddly confounding situation. From my study, I am unable to identify the poison or the means by which it was delivered, not to mention the killer's motives."

"What do you imagine that blank sheet of paper will give up?"

"Impressions of the last piece of correspondence Nathan Chalmers wrote in this world."

"Well, let us hope, then, that it was more significant than a note to the greengrocer."

We failed to find a hansom cab, and Holmes abruptly announced, "I believe, Watson, that I will walk home. I suggest that you do the same."

"Very well. I imagine that you will be working on this matter through the night and wish no company, nor any evening meal."

"You imagine correctly," said Holmes with a trace of coldness that I ascribed to his mood and not any fracture in our friendship.

I went my way, and Sherlock Holmes went his.

"WATSON, I AM an imbecile!"

"I would hardly agree," I replied civilly.

It was the next morning, and I had dropped around to visit with my friend. Curiosity, as much as solicitousness for his state of mind, motivated me.

Holmes was at his briar again. "I have been racking my brain, seeking among the appointments of the victims the source of the poison. In vain. Conceivably because the instrument of murder had been in both cases disposed of in the most clever and, I daresay, elegant manner."

"I fail to follow, Holmes."

"Come, come, the absence of poison should have proclaimed the truth. I was too focused on uncovering the hidden, to consider the absent."

"Now I am thoroughly confused."

"No poison, nor instrument of delivery, was found because it had been disposed of in a unique manner. The killer is no doubt a fiend in human form. But a fiend who devised a method of murder so ingenious that it nearly caused me brain strain."

I held my tongue. Holmes continued.

"By the careful application of emery dust, I brought out the impressions made upon the blank sheet of paper inscribed by the late Nathan Chalmers. I present them to you, Watson, for analysis."

I took the sheet, and studied it carefully. The method by which my friend had brought out the writing was not unique, but it was certainly novel. Certain words were quite clear while others somewhat obscure. I read carefully, but to little profit.

"These appear to be merely scattered, disconnected words," I decided. "I can construct no sense, nor discover any train of thought in these rambling jottings."

"That is because there is none. Mr. Chambers was not writing a letter. But answering questions with unusual brevity."

"I see the word *'yes'* several times. One *'no.'* And another word I might assume to be *'perhaps.'*"

"There are also circles and checkmarks," pointed out Holmes. "What do you make of it?"

"An unknown person or business entity sent Chalmers an unsolicited questionnaire. Chalmers duly obliged by filling it out. More than that we do not know, since we can safely assume that the questionnaire was promptly mailed by the housekeeper."

"So it is a dead end then?"

Holmes responded thoughtfully. "A blind alley, perhaps. For motive remains elusive and the perpetrator unknown."

"And the method of murder as well, I daresay."

Holmes's eyes grew bright. Well did I know that look. It told that he had broken through the impenetrable cobwebs that had hitherto constrained his investigation.

"I fell victim to a simple assumption," he related, "That the tongue is used primarily to taste. But in that I overlooked something so elementary that I hesitate to confess my failure."

"Go on, Holmes," I entreated. "I am eager to hear more."

His bright eyes glanced up and seized my own. "Surely, Watson, you can deduce the truth from the point to which I have led you."

"I confess that I cannot. I remain baffled."

"Well, reason it out, my good man."

"From what point? There are so many."

He puffed at his pipe. "Very well, I will take hold of your restraining intellectual leash and drag you to a conclusion. That it is obvious to me does not necessarily mean that it is obvious. Only that it should be. Consider the questionnaire, Watson. If you had received one from a medical association, what would you do?"

"Why, fill it out, of course."

"Of course, of course," Holmes said impatiently. "Follow the necessary train of actions. What would you do next?"

"Post it, I imagine."

"And in between?"

I hesitated. Holmes's impatience grew apace.

"Visualize it, my dear friend." There was an edge in his voice, but I did not take it personally. "It might assist your efforts if you close your eyes and imagine that you were doing it in fact. Leave out nothing, no matter how routine."

I did exactly as bid. I imagined myself filling out the document, folding it, and inserting it into an envelope, addressing the latter and applying a stamp.

After I had related all of this to Sherlock Holmes, he asked, "Would you lick the stamp?"

"I would have to, unless I applied a moist sponge, which would seem to me to be an excessive tool for such a modest task."

Holmes regarded me in silence.

A sudden thought flared up in my brain. I gave it voice. "Do you mean to say, Holmes, that the stamp was in some manner poisoned?"

"The thought had crossed my mind," he said dryly. "But I dismissed it almost immediately."

"Why is that?"

"Do you realize that you left out a step in your mental reenactment?"

"If I did not know you better, Holmes," I returned. "I would insist that I had not."

"Well said. You know me too well." The briar came into play briefly. "To answer your first question: No, the stamp was not poisoned. Why would it be? There is little doubt that the questionnaire arrived with a folded envelope addressed to the originating party, and doubtless a stamp for convenience already affixed to the envelope."

"I struggle to glean the step you claim I have left out."

Holmes's tone became almost mockingly thin. "You would have had to seal the envelope, Watson."

"A minor trifle," I scoffed.

"Men have lost their lives over trifles," he retorted. Holmes's enunciation turned flat and emotionless. "The envelope flap," he said simply, "was unquestionably poisoned."

When this theory sank in. I fairly shouted, "Upon my word! Why, this has the makings of the perfect crime!"

"And there you have it, Watson. At last you have wrenched a successful conclusion from the morass of facts. The gum in the envelope flap was in some way impregnated with a poison that, when it came into contact with the tip of the tongue, turned the moist tissue blue, and set into motion the onset of death, however long delayed. There was sufficient time for the letter to be posted to the sender, taking with it all clues to the killer's identity, along with the method of murder and instrument of death, which were one. And all for the price of a stamp."

"Then we have no way forward?"

"The fact that two separate shades of blue bloomed upon the tongues of two victims suggests a man experimenting with a poison. Such experimentation further suggests someone with the knowledge of a chemist, if not a chemist by trade."

"A slim enough clue, given the number of chemists in greater London."

"Greater London and beyond," snapped Holmes.

"Have you any notion as to the nature of the poison?"

"Again I feel rather stupid, Watson. The discoloration of the victim's tongues caused me to grope in exotic directions. In fact, I have little doubt that the autopsies will show that the agent of doom was a salt of ferrocyanic and carbonate. But such pharmacological knowledge gets us only a little further along the path to the truth."

"Perhaps the housekeeper who mailed the sheaf of letters might be interviewed again. Her memory might be subject to jarring in the matter of the addresses of the fatal envelope."

"Sorry to disappoint. But I hardly think that would be a profitable endeavor, Watson. Such a clever schemer could hardly be expected to use his true address, in the event that the expected order of events went awry."

"So where did the return envelopes end up?"

To my mild astonishment, Sherlock Holmes seemed not to have followed his thinking to its logical point. He rose from his chair, suddenly innervated.

"In the dead letter office, of course!" he cried. "Let us go there at once."

It was not far, so we walked briskly.

Holmes paid a visit to the postmaster's office, laid out as much of his concerns as practical, and received an encouraging reply.

"Two envelopes have been brought to my attention which are outside the normal range of stray mail. In most cases, an improperly addressed envelope is missing a digit, or two or more numerals are transposed. In this case, neither the address nor the addressee can be found in any directory."

"May I see these letters?" Holmes requested.

The items in question were swiftly produced, and laid out on the postmaster's desk for Holmes to inspect. They were ordinary envelopes, and the addresses had been tapped out on a machine. Holmes's black brows crowded together when he saw that there would be no handwriting to analyze.

The addresses were identical.

Institute of Hermetical Science
55 Greenlawn Way
Brixton

"There is no such institute!" snapped Holmes. "Of that, I am certain."

The postmaster concurred, saying, "We have been unable to locate any such enterprise."

"May I borrow these?" asked Holmes.

"How are they of interest to you?"

"If I am not mistaken," Holmes said gravely, "they are instruments of murder. I would like to analyze one and offer the other to Inspector Lestrade for his good opinion."

The postmaster became shockingly pale of countenance, as would anyone coming into contact with cold-blooded murder. "In that case, Mr. Holmes," he said crisply, "I will dutifully commend them to your good care, asking only a letter of receipt in return."

"And you shall have it," returned Holmes, accepting pen and paper from the postal official.

Once we were out on the street, Holmes remarked, "Let us visit Lestrade and compare notes."

"Do you think the inspector has made progress in the intervening hours?"

"Unlikely," said Holmes. "But it would be more politic to suggest otherwise when we encounter Lestrade."

"I will keep that injunction in mind," I said dryly.

WE WERE FATED never to reach Inspector Lestrade's office.

Upon turning a corner, a hansom cab trundled by and out poked the police official's head. "Mr. Holmes!" he cried. "There has been another!"

It was pointless to ask another what. The inspector urged the cab to a halt and threw open the door. Holmes climbed in, leaving me to call for another.

I was soon bringing up the rear in my own cab.

Both conveyances pulled up before a neat and respectable-seeming house in Kensington. The name of the mailbox was "Gideon Chandler."

Sherlock Holmes and Inspector Lestrade had already entered. I naturally hastened to follow.

The door had been left ajar for me and, when I slipped in, two men were engaging another individual earnestly.

"She seemed perfectly healthy," this man was insisting in an agitated manner. "On awakening, I found her as cold as a stone."

Lestrade asked, "Did she have any complaints in recent days?"

"None, none! Mrs. Chandler was the picture of health."

I took this man to be Mr. Gideon Chandler.

Lestrade continued his interrogation. "Were you aware of the fact that her tongue was discolored prior to the arrival of the family physician?"

"Well, no sir, I was not. In fact, I was not aware of this fact until Dr. Allgood brought it to my attention."

Lestrade asked several other questions which seemed pertinent, and Sherlock Holmes appeared content to observe and take silent note of the answers.

When at last the inspector had exhausted his questioning, Holmes spoke up. His first question brought all eyebrows into highest elevation.

"What, may I ask, was your wife's maiden name?"

The bereaved husband was so taken aback that he was momentarily speechless. In fact, his inability to answer dragged on for more than a minute. Eventually, he got his tongue untangled and operating in correct gear.

"Why do you ask?"

"Why do you hesitate to reply?" countered Holmes. "Certainly you know the answer full well. Do you not?"

The fellow continued to hesitate, but finally he gave forth. "Mrs. Chandler was known as Virginia Dowling when we first met. But I do not see where that fact has any bearing on what has transpired this morning."

"No doubt you are correct, but the query came to mind, so I gave it voice," returned Holmes smoothly. He next asked, "Was your wife recently engaged in answering correspondence?"

At this, Inspector Lestrade's eyes grew baffled. But he held his tongue.

"That is a peculiar question, if I may be so bold as to put it plainly."

"The question stands, sir," said Holmes calmly.

"As is a matter of routine, she invariably attended to any correspondence in the hour before taking to her bed. It was no different last night. I believe there are several letters on the kitchen table that have yet to be posted."

Something in the unfortunate fellow's eyes seemed to catch fire like a bit of coal set to smoldering. It was resentment there. Resentment, and a dash of anger.

With his wife lying dead one floor above, no doubt he was feeling helpless and besieged.

Holmes said, "I would like to see them, as would, I am sure, the inspector." This last was evidently calculated to mollify the widowed man. And it seemed to work to that end. Whereupon, Mr. Chandler immediately launched into the kitchen and came back clutching a sheath of envelopes, his features a sullen brick-red.

Chandler handed them to Inspector Lestrade, who riffled through the lot and remarked, "I see nothing out of the usual here."

"Allow me," interposed Holmes. After accepting the envelopes, he examined them quickly and, without asking permission, he tore one end off a sealed envelope.

"Oh, I say!" thundered Chandler. "Of all the nerve!"

"Mr. Holmes no doubt has his reasons," Lestrade reassured the man.

Shaking out the contents, Holmes unfolded a single sheet of stationery, handing it to Inspector Lestrade after the briefest of perusals.

Lestrade took a full minute to read what was on the sheet. I had already formed an opinion. The inspector announced it for me.

"This is a printed survey of some sort."

Holmes showed the address on the envelope and remarked coolly, "I have already ascertained that the address on this envelope is imaginary. A falsification. There is no such institute, nor any address corresponding to it."

"How the devil did you determine that?" demanded Lestrade.

"The postmaster can vouch for my assertions," said Holmes. "I have in my pocket two envelopes just like it. And if you take them both back to Scotland Yard, your forensic scientists will swiftly confirm that the glue on both flaps are impregnated with a salt of ferrocyanic and carbonate, as well as other substances, including one which reacts with the saliva coating the human tongue to produce vivid colorations."

Inspector Lestrade seemed at a loss for coherent words. "This smacks of black magic, Holmes!" he cried.

"The only black art involved in this grisly matter," corrected Holmes firmly, "is the dark art of cold-blooded murder."

Mr. Chandler intruded at that point. Evidently, his brain had assembled the facts floating about the room into something sensible.

"Are you saying that my wife was murdered? And by a poisoned envelope flap?"

"She was not the first," supplied Holmes.

The man staggered backwards, leaning his back against the fireplace mantel. I thought he might swoon. Certainly, he blanched noticeably.

"But who would do such a dastardly deed? My wife is—was a commonplace but good soul."

"Whoever engineered such perfidy," assured Sherlock Holmes, "will be brought to book in short order."

Lestrade demanded, "If what you say is true, Holmes, and this address is a false one, how may we track backwards to the perpetrator? We do not even have a motive."

"It may be that a madman is at work," said Holmes carefully. "Yet it is my experience in these matters that most premeditated murders have in back of them a cold, logical brain. Something connects the death of this woman with the other two victims. It will be brought to light, one way or the other."

In a stiff voice that was seething with repressed anger, Mr. Chandler said, "I am certain my late wife would find cold comfort in your words, sir."

"No doubt," said Holmes, taking no visible umbrage. "What is your occupation, Mr. Chandler?"

This time there was no hesitation. "I am a chemist by trade."

"Ah, a chemist. Very good. Did you happen to notice the discoloration of your late wife's tongue?"

"Did I not already say so?"

"I believe you did," said Holmes calmly. His grey eyes appraised the man who had stepped back from the mantel and was visibly reasserting his self-control.

"What color was it?"

"Blue. A particularly livid blue."

"Could you be more specific?"

"If I could, I would judge the hue to be Prussian Blue."

"And what substance would produce such a specific shade of blue?"

"I—I am not quite certain, sir. Nor do I see the point of your question. In fact, if I am not mistaken, you have no true standing in a murder investigation, except by leave of Inspector Lestrade.

So if you do not mind, I will entertain any further questions from the lawful authority present and bid you a good day."

Having finished his speech, Mr. Chandler turned his attention to Lestrade. But at the next pronouncement from Sherlock Holmes, his face fell like a brick wall under the wrecking ball.

"Inspector Lestrade, I suggest you arrest that man in the murder of his wife."

"Are you mad, Mr. Holmes? Upon what evidence?"

"Upon no direct evidence, but I point out to you that a common housewife is unlikely to receive a survey from a scientific institution. Nor is she in the same class as the other two victims. Therefore, she was singled out by someone close to her."

"That is rather thin," Lestrade said flatly.

Undaunted, Sherlock Holmes went on. "Consider then that it would be a very poor chemist who did not know that Prussian Blue is produced by the reaction of salts of iron with potassium ferrocyanide. Looking at Mr. Chandler, I judge him to have been in his trade for several years. So elementary a fact could not possibly have escaped him. Therefore, he is temporizing, as well as prevaricating. I have no doubt that if you search this dwelling, you may find certain pernicious poisons. If not here, then in his place of work. Either way, I guarantee his guilt. Place him in handcuffs now, or risk his flight before your investigation is over."

I tore my eyes from Sherlock Holmes and studied the accused.

Various expressions crawled across his wide, meaty face. His features flushed, and his yellowish teeth were bared as if he were a human cur. Fire was in his eyes, but it was not the flame of anger now—instead, it was the red rage of thwarted ambition. The transformation of his countenance was swift and unsettling.

"Sherlock Holmes, is it?" he snarled. No man ever voiced a snarl that was so bestial, so charged with malicious passion. "The consummate sleuth. The master investigator. I do not know how you stumbled upon your facts, sir, but I congratulate you. Yes, I congratulate you—but I would rather rip your throat out with my naked teeth."

"Mr. Chandler!" cried Lestrade. "What has come over you?"

By a visible effort, the man took hold of his nerve and his passion, and heaved a prodigious sigh. Reaching into a vest pocket, he produced a hunter-case pocket watch. Clicking open the cover, he consulted the dial.

"I see that I have been awake less than an hour. Less than one hour of my final day on earth has already elapsed…."

Hearing these ominous words, Sherlock Holmes launched forward—but, alas, too late.

Gideon Chandler brought the timepiece up to his mouth, and swiftly touched his tongue to the concave inner surface of the watch cover. It came away turning a vivid blue.

Holmes wrenched the pocket watch from the man's grasp, spilling the contents upon the floor. It proved to be a pale powder having the semblance of dry snow.

"The tell-tale poison, Lestrade!" he crowed. "There is your definite proof."

As if his legs had turned into water, Mr. Chandler sank to the floor, his broad back to the mantelpiece. His expression was that of a defeated man, and his eyes were dazed.

"It is done," he croaked out. "I am poisoned. In less than six hours, I shall be dead. And no one will know my motives. For they no longer matter in this world. Whether or not they will matter in the next one, I will shortly learn." He gave out a dry little cackle of a laugh. It struck me as a trifle demented. "I daresay you gentlemen will have to await your own passing before you can uncover the truth. For I have interred it rather deeply."

With that, he closed his eyes.

Turning to Lestrade, Sherlock Holmes said, "Summon an ambulance, Inspector, although I doubt the physicians at the hospital can do much good. But perhaps it is worth a try. And while you are at it, kindly alert the postal authorities to be on the lookout for any other letters emanating from the sinister Institute of Hermetical Science."

Hearing this, Mr. Chandler laughed anew. This chortle was ghoulish in a way that made my skin crawl. I shall never forget it, although I would like to.

WE FORTHWITH REPAIRED to Holmes's quarters, where he produced an envelope from his pocket and laid it on a side table.

I could not fail to notice that it was addressed to him in a flourishing hand.

"Wherever the devil did you find that?" I exclaimed.

"It was among the last letters written by the late Mrs. Chandler."

"It was among those found on the kitchen table?"

"Fortunately, no. It arrived only this morning, having been posted the day the deaths of Chalmers and Chambers were reported in the newspapers. The timing is unfortunate," Holmes added dryly.

"Did Mr. Chandler not realize this astonishing fact?"

"Evidently not. No doubt he forebore from rifling through his wife's recent correspondence, lest he leave his own finger marks on any incriminating envelopes."

Holmes produced his oily black clay pipe, filled it with black shag, and applied a match. Soon he was smoking thoughtfully and peering up at the ceiling with an increasingly dream-like expression.

I enquired, "Are you not going to open the letter?"

"No, not at this time," replied Holmes in that distracted tone I knew so well.

"I imagine that it may contain the ultimate solutions to this maddening mystery."

"No doubt you are correct, Watson. But I prefer to apply my own intellect to the remaining skeins of the problem at hand.

To open this envelope now would be to cheat me of one of the most challenging schemes I have ever attempted to unravel."

"Understandable, I suppose. But to open it later would be anticlimactic."

"Perhaps. But if it contains what I suspect it might, any threads that escape me will be tied up neatly. But I prefer to do my own spinning, just as does the lowly spider."

With that, Sherlock Holmes fell into a reverie of intense contemplation. Seeing the direction in which his attention trended, I quietly bid him a good night, promising to return if summoned before then.

"I do not think I will require it, but I thank you for your kind indulgence, Watson."

I left without another word.

HOLMES RANG ME up less than twenty-four hours later. His tone was a trifle disappointed, I thought, as he asked if I would come round to see him.

"I shall be over directly," I promised.

Upon my arrival, I discovered Holmes seated in the identical posture as the day before. His attire was different, although his thin hair was somewhat unkempt. I imagine he had not slept in the interim, but I could never determine the truth of that assumption.

"You appear to be in a less-than-enthusiastic mood," I suggested as I took a chair facing my friend.

"It is all dreadfully dreary," he proclaimed in a subdued voice.

"The fact of murder?"

"The now-tattered cobweb that underlies this particular chain of useless destruction," he returned, offering the now opened letter written by the deceased Mrs. Gideon Chandler.

Before I could read it, Holmes offered, "The key to the whole thing lay in the detestable lie that Mr. Chandler told during our brief association. Namely, that his wife's maiden name was Dowling."

"You suspected otherwise?"

"Only in the sense that I am always on the lookout for deceit, even in the most innocuous statements. It did not take me a very long prowl through official records to determine that Mrs. Chandler had, during infancy, briefly borne the last name of Chalmers."

"Ah! She is related to the first victim then?"

"And the second. It appears that Nathan Chalmers and Arthur Chambers were brothers, who were separated at a very young age, as was Virginia Chalmers, who happened to be an infant at the time. When they were separated, their names were changed, apparently by the parent who surrendered them to the orphanage. Disturbingly, Chandler was the last name assigned to the brother who in time became Gideon Chandler, chemist."

"Peculiar."

"Sordid," corrected Holmes. "Merely sordid. The mother had died of consumption after giving birth to the last of four children, all of whom were scattered to the winds by their father, an importer named Crowninshield, who did not care to raise them alone, nor bestir himself to find a proper wife to carry on in the stead of his first spouse. As is often the custom in these matters, the newly renamed Virginia Chalmers was given the name of her adoptive parents, and grew up never suspecting that her last name was not Dowling."

"Then Chandler did not lie."

"He lied, for he had lately discovered the awful truth— namely, that he had accidentally married his own sister."

"My word!"

"Yes. It is a tragedy from start to finish. But it grew more horrible in the unfolding, for when the recalcitrant father had at last slipped into his dotage, he commenced a search for his abandoned children. Unfortunately for all concerned, he uncovered Gideon Chandler first. Learning of his true origins, Chandler plunged into the dusty records of a certain orphanage and was staggered—and no doubt horrified—to discover that he had wed his unsuspected sister, whom he had not beheld since her infancy. But that was not the worst of it. He and the other three Crowninshield siblings stood to come into a great deal of money once the repentant father rewrote his will accordingly.

"Promising to help locate the other three former foundlings, Mr. Chandler instead formulated a rather diabolical scheme to do away with them all, leaving him the sole Crowninshield heir—and incidentally burying from public discovery his acute marital embarrassment, which, I suspect, was his overriding motivation."

"Ghastly," I gasped out.

"Merely sordid," reminded Holmes. His tone was listless. I imagine he had suspected more exotic motivations underlay the situation, before it had resolved itself.

"But how did the wife uncover the truth?" I enquired.

"It is all in her letter. You may read it for yourself. For myself, I am both sickened and bored by the whole grotesque affair. Would that the criminal mind be as ingenious as I sometimes imagine it to be. In this case, the ingenuity at work is over-whelmed by the banality of the parties involved, as well as by their respective motivations."

"What of the poisons? You can scarcely deny the cleverness with which the poisoner operated."

"Nor do I. The problem was as engaging as any I have ever encountered. That it led to such ugly doings is what I object to. The poison was, as I suspected, a salt of ferrocyanic and carbon-ate. The clever chemist had merely added differently colored dyes to the gum mucilage in order retard the poison's effects long enough for the doomed recipient to post the completed survey. This was where experimentation played a significant role. The choice of blue substances was doubtless intended to create an effect that the villain hoped would confuse the inevitable police investigation."

"He reckoned without Sherlock Holmes," I commented.

"I have learned that Gideon Chandler died without speaking

further. Not that there is any significant loss attending his passing. Now, you may read the letter Watson. If you are so inclined."

I remained captivated and intrigued, so I did exactly that.

It was a tangle, one not worth recapitulating in full.

Mrs. Chandler had been oblivious to her own origins at the start. It happened that her husband belonged to that group of people who are afflicted with nightmares. Once, she was startled to be aroused in the deepest part of night by Chandler's thrashing about wildly, crying out in his sleep, "Sister! I married my own sister!"

She woke him and repeated the blurted outcry, but Chandler professed ignorance, dismissing the words as the product of a bad dream.

Thereafter, she noticed a creeping aloofness in his manner, which gradually shaded into a sullen coldness. In short order, insomnia overtook them. One night, Mrs. Chandler awoke to discover herself alone in the marital bed. Creeping downstairs, she found him pacing his study, muttering over and over, "My own sister—my lawful wife! How could such a queer fate befoul my existence?"

Unnoticed, she crept back to the bed chamber, where she resolved to seek her own origins, in which she had hitherto showed scant interest, having lived up until then a fortunate life.

Virginia Chandler's private investigations concluded just days before Arthur Chambers was found dead. The matter of the blue-tinted tongue suggested to her an exotic poison, and her thoughts inevitably careened in the direction of her chemist spouse. Naturally, she could scarcely credit her theory. Then Nathan Chalmers was done away with. Straight away, she resolved to write Sherlock Holmes and lay all facts before him— but alas, too late. She sensed that she might be the next to turn up with a discolored tongue, and took precautions with her food and drink, but did not imagine that an innocent survey might be the deliverer of her own doom—as it had for the others, her unsuspected brothers.

The rest was merely lamentations and questions. She, too, was aghast at the realization that her husband was in truth her oldest brother. In her despair, she wrote to Holmes, requesting assistance in the queer affair.

Folding the note, I wondered, "Why, on that murderous morning, didn't Chandler post the fatal letter, thus disposing of the murder weapon?"

"Evidently, the wife attended to her correspondence very late, presumably well after her faithless husband's bedtime, for he was a working man who rose at an early hour, and she a late riser. As with all schemers, his brain was filled with mental rehearsals of how he would act upon discovering the cold corpse in the morning. Chandler neglected to consider the possibility that his carefully-executed scheme would have been penetrated in its essential details."

"He expected an opportunity to post the deadly letter after the body was carried off, I take it."

"Goaded by me, in his agitation Chandler handed the evidence over," noted Holmes with satisfaction.

"I suppose that no other fatal letters were intercepted."

A slow, tired sigh carried with it the essence of pipe tobacco. "No, Watson. Presumably, there are none. The circle has been closed."

"What of the repentant father?"

"Mercifully, Mr. Meldrum Crowninshield passed away in his sleep the very night his last surviving son succumbed to his own diabolical poison. I am informed that the tip of Crowninshield's own tongue was also an exquisite Turquoise."

"Remarkable. The circle has indeed been closed. There will be no need for Fleet Street to learn all the dreary details."

"Why add to the common misery?" murmured Holmes. "Especially when so many are so industriously dedicated to multiplying it."

I could think of no suitable rejoinder, and so let my silence speak for me.

THE ADVENTURE OF
THE THRONE OF GILT

I N A L L O F my dealings with Mr. Sherlock Holmes, I never in my wildest imaginings conceived that one day I would have to turn to him, not as friend to friend, but as suppli-cant to consulting detective.

These events occurred not long after my marriage, and after I had again moved out of our shared flat. The year was 1903. It was spring. Edward had not been long on the throne. The world seemed to have been renewed, and only then settling into a new normalcy.

An envelope arrived at my Queen Anne Street home, bear-ing no return address, only a scribbled signature that appeared to say *"Mr. Thursday."*

It was addressed to *Dr. John Watson, M.D.*

I thought immediately that this was the work of an ignorant fellow, inasmuch as the title would normally render the initials superfluous.

When I tore open the envelope, it contained only a single sheet of folded foolscap on which was written the following:

> *Dr. Watson:*
> *You will one day be sat upon the throne of gilt.*

The note was signed in the same crabbed hand, *"Mr. Thurs-day."*

Normally, I might have thrown out such a bit of nonsense, but my long association with Sherlock Holmes inspired me to replace the note into its envelope and pocket it. While it might represent only a minor mystery, I thought it would be entertaining, if not instructive, to show it to my good friend.

Upon bidding my new bride *adieu,* I hied over to 221b Baker Street and paid Holmes a call. A hansom cab was loitering outside my door and the bewhiskered driver looked at me expectantly, but I did not care for the look of the fellow and his profusion of unkempt side-whiskers.

Ignoring the appeal of his glowering gaze, I walked on, for it was a pleasant day and the air was good to breathe.

Holmes greeted me with his usual diffidence as he lounged in his sitting room, wearing a pinched expression that I took to mean boredom. He was between consultations, and it showed upon his sharp countenance.

"What brings you here at the supper hour, Watson?" inquired he.

"That is a peculiar question coming from you, Holmes."

"Please be good enough to make yourself plain," grunted Holmes. He appeared to be in a foul mood. Not disagreeably so, but if I were a prescriber of remedies for moods, I would recommend direct and abundant sunlight.

"You may recall how many times have I or some other caller entered your presence and been subjected to a barrage of penetrating questions leading to definitive conclusions that possibly no other man in the world could arrive at from scant evidence."

My mild rebuke stirred Holmes partially out of his funk. He looked up, his penetrating eyes coming into focus.

They rested upon my shoes first, saw nothing of interest, and his gaze climbed to my throat and then shifted to my hands, making an inventory of details and, apparently, discarding most of them.

Something about the manner of which I held my right hand caused him to remark, "You bring me something, Watson. Something to read." He paused, then went on. "A letter perhaps?"

"Very good, Holmes. It is exactly that. But however did you know?"

"From the way you held your hand, close to your lower right coat pocket, you seemed poised to produce something of interest. It could not be a magazine or newspaper article, because I know you to present such articles whole, and not torn out or cut free. That meant that the article was not very large or thick, and this to me suggested a letter."

"Well done."

I produced the envelope without delay and handed it to my friend.

Holmes regarded the return address and the postmark, and then he lifted the torn flap, drawing out a coarse sheet of paper. He read this several times, despite its brevity. His expression did not alter.

"What do you make of it?" I asked impatiently.

"Well, there is very little to go on. I see that it was posted in Hackney this morning, which tells us precious little, for anyone can mail a letter from any convenient spot."

Before he could inquire further, I volunteered, "I do not know of any Mr. Thursday."

"What about a Mr. *Thorsday?* For that is the correct pronunciation of the signature, as I decipher it."

"It looked like Thursday to me. Are you certain?"

"The way the man shapes his letter *O*'s makes it absolutely conclusive. There is no doubt that the signature is *Thorsday.* And my question yet stands."

I said, "That name, too, is unfamiliar to me. But that is not as puzzling as the message itself. I can make nothing of it, other than my correspondent is a rough and untutored fellow."

"Nor can I, but I agree with your assessment. Furthermore, I imagine it to be a threat of some sort—veiled and obscure, but a threat nevertheless."

"Threat? I take nothing of the sort from the single sentence."

Holmes looked up. "Have you lost any patients in recent weeks?"

"None so far this year."

"But you have lost patients who have succumbed to their maladies, never to recover."

"There is hardly a medical man in all of London, never mind the world, who has not lost patients through no fault of his own. What of it?"

"I know you well enough, Watson, to understand that you are not a man who makes enemies, nor gives slights requiring an avenging rejoinder. Given your profession, I would judge that this letter was written by someone upset over your failure to preserve a life."

"Well, of course I have lost many patients over the years, but none of them named Thorsday *or* Thursday. But heavens, man, are you not making a great pile out of very little wool?"

"I think not," murmured Holmes. "If I were you, I would take precautions."

"Far be it from me to discount the soundness of your conclusions," I returned. "Would you be good enough to suggest how I may go about ascertaining the truth behind this veiled threat?"

Holmes seemed lost in thought, and his attention returned to the sheet of paper, which he examined on both sides.

"I do not think Thorsday is the name of your mysterious correspondent, Watson," he mused. "Nor Thursday. The first is not a name one could find in the London city directory, nor do I think in any city directory. It is entirely made up. Therefore, it must have significance, being the product of the writer's imagination."

"What do you make of the allusion to a 'gilt throne?'"

Holmes frowned reflectively. "Nothing at first blush. I believe this will require a pipe and some good tobacco. Why don't you run along, good fellow, and leave me to my ruminations? I will let you know when I have something of interest to tell you. In the meanwhile, please take all precautions. And kindly let me

know if further communications are received from the mysterious Mr. Thorsday."

With that, Sherlock Holmes seemed to have dismissed me
from all awareness, and I made a graceful exit, not as reassured
as I had expected to be.

NOTHING TRANSPIRED FOR exactly one week.
Then the second letter came, posted from Hammersmith. I did
not open it, but took it forthwith to my friend, of whom I had
heard nothing in the intervening seven days.

After being ushered into his tobacco-fumed presence, I burst
out, "I have received a second letter. I present it to you, Holmes,
unopened."

"Give it here," said Holmes without outward expression of
excitement. "And mark the day of the week."

"Thursday!" I exclaimed. "The same as previously. Do you
think it significant?"

Holmes was employing a letter opener to slit the envelope.

"I do. But of what, I cannot yet say."

The letter fell out into Holmes's waiting palm. Unfolding it,
he read in silence, then handed the sheet to me.

Taking it, I read it aloud.

> *My Dear Watson:*
> *I intend to do away with you in a most novel manner, sir. Await*
> *my pleasure. The gilt throne also awaits. I promise you a hot tyme.*

Looking up, I said, "I do not understand this business of
a gilded throne, which is what this ignorant fellow evidently
means."

"I disagree, Watson. Not about the fellow's ignorance, of
course, but with his meaning."

"I will admit that this talk of a 'gilt throne' is obscure, but what
could he otherwise possibly mean?"

"A throne cannot be fashioned of 'gilt,' Watson. It is an impossibility, for gold leaf by definition is thin. Otherwise, the phrase

would be 'throne of gold.' If it were 'gilded,' Mr. Thorson would have written the words 'gilded throne.'"

"An ignorant man might be unaware of this distinction," I countered. Then: "What did you say his name was?"

"Thorson."

"Are you psychic now, Holmes?"

"No, merely ordinarily observant. I have not divined his true name. Please look at the signature again."

I did so. And there I saw what I had carelessly overlooked before. The signature was *Mr. Thorson,* as was the one on the envelope proper. In my excitement, I had missed this.

I asked, "What do you make of it?"

"I prefer to hurl your question back at you, Watson. Tell me where your thoughts lead you."

"Thorson. Thorsday. It appears clear that the latter name was not Thursday, as you surmised. Yet both letters were posted so as to arrive on a Thursday. Unless that is a coincidence."

"I think not," snapped Holmes. "Pray continue with your train of thought. The workings of a mind less rigorously scientific than mine are of interest to me."

"Thor was the Norse god of lightning and thunder," I mused. "A wielder of a magical hammer that produced earthly storms, according to legend. But I am not aware that he sat upon a throne. Odin, his father, may well have, but Thor was a warrior. Besides, he is entirely mythical. A superstition of a bygone age not our own."

"Yet, Watson, the legend survives into our time," prompted Holmes.

"Yes, in storybooks. But nowhere else. I seriously doubt that worship of Thor continues to the present day. Not in England, at any rate. Perhaps in some backwoods enclave in Norway, or elsewhere in Scandinavia. I must reject the notion that I have incurred the wrath of a modern-day Thor worshipper."

"You are overlooking the obvious, Watson," said Holmes pointedly.

"If I am, it is not obvious to me."

"You previously accused me of futile wool-gathering, as it were," continued Holmes. "Yet you overlook bright yarn laying in plain sight."

I stood there stupefied, thoroughly flummoxed. My brain refused to function. "I am at a loss," I confessed at last.

"I have not been idle these last seven days," remarked Holmes, apparently changing the subject and leaving me to stew in my mental confusion. "In reviewing the facts then at hand, I realized the significance of the day upon which you received the first communication. So I was not entirely surprised when the second arrived on this day. I half expected it, in truth."

No doubt my expression became extreme at that point. I was on the point of asking my astute friend to explain his reasoning, when the connection struck me forcefully.

"By Jove! Thursday is named after Thor!"

Holmes's tone turned dry. "You mix your mythologies, but you are correct, Watson. The present day of the week is a conflation of Thor's Day. From that weak thread, I began surmising that the fellow has a fixation on the mythological Thor. Although I cannot now rule out that his name is Thorson, of which many exist, I think it unlikely. This trend of thought carried me through two pipefuls of tobacco without concrete result. But when I turned my attention to the connection with the day of the week, I found a measure of wool, as it were."

"I am under your spell, Holmes, as always."

"Searching my memory for unusual events that had taken place on Thursdays in recent memory, I found two, and they appeared to belong to the same strange skein. Three weeks ago, on a Thursday evening, a body was found in a field near Coddington. It was that of Mr. Ambrose Dexter."

"The retired tragedian?"

"The very same. It seems that he had been out and about when a sudden electrical storm brewed up. The poor fellow was apparently felled by a lightning bolt."

"Surely not dispatched from Asgard by the red-haired thunder-god himself!"

"Hardly. When the police discovered the body the next morning, the verdict was death by misadventure. The normally intelligent Dexter had been caught in a rainstorm and had the misfortune to attract a thunderbolt. There was no more to it than that, according to the coroner, who had seen such tragedies before."

"If this a coincidence, it is truly bizarre," I ventured.

"It was no coincidence," returned Holmes. "For on the following Thursday, now a fortnight ago, another body was discovered in another field, this one a cricket field in Shoreditch. Again, the victim was electrocuted. Once again, it was during a storm. But a *rainstorm*, Watson. Not a thunderstorm. No clap of thunder nor flash of lightning was reported by any inhabitant of the region. Yet such is the conventionality of the police and the local coroner that death was again attributed to an errant lightning bolt."

"A week apart, you say?"

Holmes nodded sagely. "And a week before the first letter was received by you."

"What do you make of this chain of Thursday happenstances?"

Pausing to puff on his pipe, Holmes replied diffidently, "I decided to visit Shoreditch and made inquiries of the locals. One witness claimed to have seen a hansom cab in the vicinity, and saw the cabman carry something onto the field hours before the body was discovered. "

"The body!"

"No doubt. So I made inquiries of the cab companies. No driver would admit to having been in the vicinity upon that night."

"Of course, the guilty man would offer no such confession," I pointed out.

"The peculiar thing is that the second dead man was himself a hansom cab driver," added Holmes. "Dunn was his name."

"A falling out among co-employees!" I cried.

"Yet accounts of no such argument could be unearthed. I think the truth lies in another direction. I think the man who deposited the body was not the cabman, but a thief. For Mr. Dunn's cab has not been recovered."

"So we are searching for a phantom cab and its gypsy driver."

"Almost certainly."

"But what would be the motive to steal the cab in question?"

"For a quick and unobtrusive escape, I would ordinarily conjecture. But not in this instance, for the cabriolet would have been found by now, abandoned. To store it somewhere would be the same as hanging a sign over a stable or barn, attesting that the owner is a murderer and thief."

"How do you imagine the dead cabman was killed, if the coroner believed him to have been electrocuted?"

"The answer to that, Watson, is so elementary that you should not have posed the question, but produced the answer on your own initiative."

"I cannot fathom it, Holmes. Therefore, I stand on my unanswered question."

"The unfortunate Mr. Dunn, Watson, was obviously and unquestionably electrocuted."

"But surely not by Thor incarnate!"

"Nor by Thorson, nor Thorsday. But by an unknown madman who may even now be prowling the byways of London in a stolen hansom cab in search of an unwary fare."

"I confess that I fail to perceive a recognizable garment amid all this gathered cast-off wool."

"I suggest that we go for a promenade, Watson."

"To what end?"

"To see if we cannot entice your Mr. Thorson into offering you a ride to some unknown destination."

"Such as?"

"Possibly the grave," returned Holmes coolly. "Certainly towards eternity...."

"You propose to use me as bait in a murder snare!"

Holmes appeared unperturbed by my expostulation. "Why wait for your killer to come to you when you can draw him out on terms of our choosing, not his?"

I hesitated. "I had hoped to have supper before the hour grew too late."

Standing up, Holmes proclaimed, "And you will, Watson. It shall be my treat. Now, let us be on our way."

The old fire was back in my friend's eyes as he led me out the door of 221b Baker Street. I confess that I felt more like a lamb being led to slaughter than companion to the greatest sleuth hound in all of London, if not the world....

OUR PROMENADE APPEARED to be aimless. First, we sauntered along Baker Street, and then turned into Paddington Street. From there, Holmes turned south and brought us to Weymouth Street. If he had a definite destination in mind, it escaped me, but we covered much of Marylebone.

After a long interval of silence, Holmes began speaking aloud.

"I would have liked to examine the cadavers of the two electrocuted victims," he mused, "but of course they had been interred by the time the significance of their deaths had been discovered."

"Whatever would you expect to learn from them?"

"Persons struck down by lightning often display certain types of burn marks and striation patterns on their epidermis. Often, these resemble lightning bolts, but with uncountable minute hairs or branches."

"I see."

"No two are alike, but many similar patterns recur," added Holmes. "I spoke at length with the coroners of the two towns where the bodies were found, and both reported localized burn marks that fit no pattern with which I am familiar. But I hasten to add that my study of such burn marks is limited, since murder by lightning is not a phenomenon that has presented itself for inspection up until now."

"How do you imagine such a weird thing might be engineered? By strapping a man down in an electrical storm and planting a lightning rod upon his helpless person?"

"An intriguing thought, Watson. I commend you for a rare flight of imagination. I daresay such a contrivance might succeed, if luck was on the side of the perpetrator and the intended victim was experiencing an utter absence of that metaphysical condition. But no, I believe the instrument of murder to be mechanical in nature."

"It is almost a relief to hear you state it so plainly, Holmes," I offered sincerely. "The thought of a blackguard such as Mr. Thorson being able to call down the elements upon his victims is intolerable to contemplate."

As we walked along, Holmes's sharp gaze went to every passing hansom cab. He studied the drivers' exposed faces in turn, paying no heed to the passengers safely ensconced within.

At one point on our perambulations, a hearty voice called out, "Holmes! I say, good to see you, fellow!"

A man waved from a cab, and flashed his perfect teeth. I thought they were extraordinarily white.

I did not recognize the fellow, and inquired, "Who is that man?"

"That," my dear Watson, "is my esteemed dentist, Dr. Crawford. His passing is fortuitous. I must have a word with him."

Raising his right hand, Holmes attempted to flag down the cabman, but the driver instead gave his whip a sharp crack and the horse leaped ahead.

From the cab, Dr. Crawford began expostulating. The driver seemed not to hear, but instead turned a corner with alacrity, with Holmes following on his heels, as it were. The clink of horseshoes upon cobblestone became a rapid syncopation.

I rushed after my excited friend, panting, "Whatever is the matter, Holmes?"

"I merely wished to inquire for an appointment, but that cabman seems determined to prevent any conversation. It smacks of rank obstruction, Watson."

Reaching the cross street, we were in time to witness the cabriolet round the far corner. The rude driver cast a glowering glance backwards before he disappeared. His face was dark with some emotion I could not decipher, his unkempt side-whiskers bristling like a startled hedgehog. I recognized him only then.

Realizing that he could never hope to catch up with the hurtling cab, Holmes pulled up short.

"Why would that cabman behave in such a disagreeable fashion?" I wondered aloud as I caught my breath.

Holmes pondered this question, or perhaps another that had occurred to him. For suddenly, he was pounding up a parallel street with renewed haste.

Following, I demanded, "What is the matter now? You cannot hope to catch up!"

"But I must! I must, if I am to preserve Dr. Crawford's life."

"What!"

Holmes soon outpaced me and reached the distant corner, vanishing from my sight.

But the strenuous efforts of Sherlock Holmes were futile. No sign of the fleeing hansom cab could be found. It was lost in the choke of wagons, carriages, omnibuses, and other wheeled flotsam of London.

In time, Holmes gave it up as a bad job of work.

I caught up with him as he was hailing a different cab. Motioning for me to join him, he clambered aboard. I did likewise.

Immediately we were off to join the endless stream of traffic.

As we rolled along, Holmes spoke bitingly. "Dr. Crawford must have been leaving his practice, for he was coming from the direction of his office on Devonshire Place. If he is bound for home, we might overhaul him *en route.*"

Rapping out sharp orders to the driver through the trap, Holmes urged him to make all due haste in pursuit of the vanished cab.

"I say!" offered I. "That rude cabman wore a familiar face. He had been waiting outside my home the day I left to carry the first Thorson letter to you!"

"That, my dear Watson, was Thorson in the flesh," Holmes said bitingly. "The man works fast. He anticipated your impulse to carry the letter to me forthwith. He lay in wait, intending to abduct you upon the spot!"

"I did not like his glowering looks," I explained, "so I chose to walk instead."

"A choice that no doubt preserved your life."

We swiftly reached the Kensington home of Dr. Crawford, but no sign of him or his cab stood in view.

Dismounting, Holmes rushed to the door and pulled the doorbell. A maid answered.

"I am Sherlock Holmes, of whom you have no doubt heard. Has Dr. Crawford arrived in the last few minutes?"

"No, sir. But he is expected."

"Thank you," said Holmes briskly, leaping back into the waiting cab.

And once again we were off amid a clattering of hooves and the creaking and groaning of springs.

Our search ranged far and wide though the thoroughfares of London, but to no avail. We stopped at Shipley's Yard to inquire after the cab-owner, but no bewhiskered driver such as we described worked for him. It was the same story at other hackney head offices. The man was unknown to all.

"A gypsy driver, I imagine," I suggested to Holmes.

"If that," was his succinct reply. "The man's crabbed handwriting suggested to me one unaccustomed to penning letters, and their brevity supports that assumption. I daresay a cab driver would be more literate, if only by a degree or two. Mark me, Watson. The man in question plies a manual trade of some sort."

THE SUN BEGAN going down when Holmes ordered the cab back to Dr. Crawford's domicile.

Again conversing with the distressed maid, we discovered that he had never reached home, and was in fact late for a prepared dinner. The maid was beside herself with worry.

Sherlock Holmes wasted no time in consoling the poor creature. He was back in the cab and soon we pulled up before Scotland Yard.

Inspector Lestrade listened intently as Holmes implored him to undertake a search for the missing dentist.

"You have good reason to suspect foul play?" Lestrade demanded.

"I have excellent reason. Put your men to work. The doctor's life hangs in the balance!"

"Very well, Mr. Holmes. You have never steered Scotland Yard wrong yet."

Nothing came of this expanded search. We were forced to our uneasy beds—or should I say, I did so. I cannot speak for Sherlock Holmes, who prowled the city like an errant wraith long after I left him.

BUT ON THE morn, a body was discovered in a field in Lower Brixton. It was quickly identified as the missing dentist.

Holmes was called to the scene. I accompanied him.

Examining the body, he noted scorch marks at the neck and temple. Lifting the inert wrists, Holmes brought two additional superficial burns to light.

"No natural lightning bolt did this!" he cried out, standing up. His voice shook as I have never before heard it shake.

"Why was Dr. Crawford killed in this horrible manner?" I wondered aloud.

Holmes shook a futile fist at nothing in particular. "Because he waved to me, Watson. Nothing more and scarcely less."

"And his motive?"

"That infernal cabman is our electrical murderer. Of that, I am resolutely certain. All masks have dropped. I now know his face and he knows that I know it. He will go underground now, like a human mole. At least for a time."

"None of this makes very much sense to me."

"I think, Watson, that you are safe for now. Small comfort in that realization. But mark me: Thorson will strike again. As the lightning strikes from the sky, leaving anything it touches smoking and riven."

As I pen these words, I confess that a shudder wracks my body even as it did when I first heard them from Sherlock Holmes's own lips. They left me shaken to my core, now as then.

A MONTH PASSED, during which nothing more was heard from the murderous Mr. Thorson, whomever he might be. The Thursday letters ceased to be posted as well.

During this time, Sherlock Holmes retreated to his preserves, and I often found him reading electrical journals and, to my surprise, certain periodicals imported from the United States.

"Are you still pondering the matter of Mr. Thorson?"

"Among other things," said Holmes distractedly, laying a magazine aside. His chin was buried in his chest and his eyebrows were thrown together with such force as to suggest a collision of caterpillars.

"I am still at sea regarding the nature of the contrivance with which Dr. Crawford was so grievously slain," I observed. "I cannot imagine how such a thing was engineered."

Holmes made a gesture as if to brush away my comment as if my remark was merely an annoying fly buzzing about.

"I sometimes imagine," he stated, "that future generations will look back upon our musings with amusement, if not ridicule."

"Why, whatever do you mean by that?"

"Imagine a man of 1820 learning of the invention of the incandescent lightbulb or the telephone. If credulous, he would be astounded. If skeptical, he would be dismissive. The scientific marvels of our time verge upon being beyond his comprehension. Take, for example, the electric carriages appearing on the streets of this great city of ours. Within a generation, they promise to replace all horse-drawn coaches and carriages. No doubt greater marvels await us in this new century. We should welcome them, as we have embraced the taming of electricity and the harnessing of artificial light."

"I imagine that you are saying just because we cannot conceive of the means by which Dr. Crawford was so cruelly removed from this earth, does not mean that such means is beyond the fashioning of mortal men of our time."

Holmes staggered me with his snappish rejoinder.

"The means is known to me, Watson. I have satisfied myself upon that score. What I do not yet understand is the devil's motive, and where the diabolical contraption is kept."

"The so-called 'throne of gilt?'"

"I doubt that this makeshift throne is gilded in any way. It is clear to me that the man misspelled the word 'guilt.' His motive is revenge. But for what? If I have that, perhaps I can locate this demon who wields electricity the way a coachman wields his whip."

"Well, I cannot help you there. I have racked my tired brains for a motive for the man's evident enmity towards myself. I can think of none."

"Nor can I," admitted Holmes.

"It is baffling," I confessed.

"More maddening than baffling, I daresay. The criminal mind, however devious, spins its webs in discernible patterns. I am troubled by the absence of such patterns."

"Could it be the man is merely mad? Could his enmity be a product of imagination, or the poisonous influence on the brain of alcohol?"

"I would not rule it out," said Holmes flatly. "I am ruling nothing out."

"Well," said I, "it appears that your prediction that he has gone underground has proven correct. Nothing has been heard of him in nearly thirty days. We have seen his face and doubtless he is fearful of showing it again in London."

"Doubtless, doubtless."

My friend fell into a deep silence, punctuated by clouds of black tobacco smoke, for he was at his briar again.

THURSDAY THE NEXT was eventful.

I received a message from Mr. Thorson, this time signing himself Donner Thorson. It had been posted from Thundersley.

The envelope was addressed thusly:

> *The Honorable John A. Watson, M.D.*
> *Did you think I had forgotten you? Well, I have not! I have been busy fashioning your hearse. Soon you will lie in it.*
> *Yours sincerely,*
> *Donner Thorson*

I took this letter at once to Sherlock Holmes, forgetting in my haste my previous precaution of not opening it beforehand.

Holmes was unperturbed by this slight negligence. Without a word, he read the note and made a strange sound deep in his throat. I imagine it was a grunt that did not quite escape his larynx.

"My bedeviler is as careless as ever," I remarked. "Thorson is giving me the wrong middle initial and the honorific usually accorded to solicitors."

"He has an elevated if not inflated view of you," remarked Holmes. "Such as would a lesser man casting scorn upon his superior. This brands him as one occupying a lower stratum among the classes. And I see that he is no longer fixated on setting you upon his fanciful throne of gilt. You are to go directly to a hearse, no doubt by which means to be conveyed to the graveyard without delay."

"I had rather hoped that we had seen the last of Thorson."

"I hardly thought so," commented Holmes. "The poor devil is obsessed with you."

"But for what reason? It confounds me."

"I should like to ask him myself, if only I could lay hands upon the wretch."

I found myself pacing the floor. "Have you turned up nothing?"

"Not the fellow's name, not even a scratch of his identity. Donner is a German word, signifying thunder, so I imagine this name to be entirely fictitious. Note also that this communication was posted from Thundersley, in Essex, a hamlet which in pagan times was held sacred to *Thunor*, otherwise *Thor*. Taken all together, it smacks of concoction."

"You have nothing to go on then?"

"There is the matter of the dead horse."

"What dead horse is that?"

"According to the afternoon newspaper, a horse was discovered in a Hackney meadow without a mark on him, but he was deceased."

"What of it?" I asked in undisguised exasperation.

"The poor animal showed signs of having been struck by lightning, according to witnesses. Watson," said Holmes, coming to his feet abruptly. "Let us go to the animal rendering plant and examine the poor beast."

I saw no reason not to comply, but I confess that I was frustrated in the extreme.

Producing the soft sound that had inspired Londoners to dub the horseless vehicles "hummingbirds," a Bersey electric cab soon conveyed us to the unpleasant establishment. All but holding our noses against the horrid odors that assailed us, we were escorted to the corpse. It was a handsome bay horse, lying on its side covered with a coarse blanket.

Holmes examined it from nose to tail, and found no outward injuries.

Lifting one of the rear hooves, he saw that the horse's shoes had been removed. The underside of the hoof in question was quite black and had split most grievously. If this happened when the horse was alive, the injury would no doubt have been very painful.

Turning to the plant manager, who was hovering nearby, Holmes inquired, "Where are the shoes of this poor creature?"

Cocking a greasy thumb over his shoulder, he grunted, "All shoes are disposed of in that big bin behind me."

Holmes hurried at once to the bin, and noisily picked through the horseshoes, finally lifting one into the light.

"Would you know if this was one of the shoes belonging to that animal?" he asked the plant manager.

The other shot back gruffly, "It was. I wondered why it was so black."

"Not black," mused Holmes. "Scorched. Fire did this. Fire also blackened the hoof and split it."

Dropping the shoe as if it was no longer of interest, Sherlock Holmes strode back and announced, "That horse was electrocuted, Watson."

"My word!" I cried. "Do you think this was an experiment gone awry?"

"No," replied Holmes thoughtfully. "I believe it to be an accident. But a very fortuitous one, as far as my investigation is concerned. I think I understand the significance of Mr. Thorson's most recent message. Watson, let us be off. The trail that was cold is now becoming warm. Soon it will be hot—I imagine quite hot. And we must step carefully if we are to avoid the fate of this unfortunate animal."

With that, we left the rendering plant and claimed a passing hansom cab, after first scrutinizing the features of the driver, which were non-descriptive and bland.

AS WE RATTLED along, Holmes remarked, "Our foe is attempting to keep one jump ahead of us. I reason that he has not abandoned his scheme to place you upon his 'throne of guilt.' But rather, he has modified this game. Knowing that we would be in search of the infernal throne, he has relocated it. And if my surmise is correct—and I believe it to be entirely correct—the fiendish plan has evolved in the most diabolical way."

After that pronouncement that smacked of doom, my friend Holmes fell into a deep silence, which he refused to break until we reached Baker Street.

There we parted company, but not before he asked me a question that took me aback.

"In your acquaintances in the medical profession, are you aware of another Dr. Watson? Specifically a John *A.* Watson?"

"Not in London, nor in any adjoining town. Why do you ask?"

"It may be that our careless antagonist is not always careless. Perhaps he has mistaken you for a colleague unknown to you."

"I can make inquiries, if you would like."

"Do so. At once. Ring me up if you discover such a name-sake physician. He may prove to be the key that unlocks a most obdurate door."

My inquiries bore substantial fruit the next day. A Dr. John A. Watson, now retired, had formerly had a practice in distant Blackpool.

Obtaining his residence address, I rung up Holmes and we agreed to meet at Euston Station. Soon, we were rattling towards the seaside town, celebrated for its curative waters.

Dr. John A. Watson was a generation my senior and cordial in his easy way. Emphysema I judged to be the cause of his difficulties in breathing. But he managed to answer our questions just the same in his thick Lancashire accent.

"This is a delicate matter," said Holmes after introductions. "And I pray that you take my questions in the spirit in which I pose them. That is, in the sense that this is an investigation into several mysterious deaths and not an inquiry into your medical competence."

Dr. Watson nodded faintly. "Well, please ask your questions. I am acquainted with your reputation, Mr. Holmes."

"Very good. Doubtless you have lost a patient or two in your many years of practice."

"I have lost several. What physician has not?"

Dr. Watson looked to me at that last, and I nodded in silent encouragement.

"Did you ever lose a female patient whose husband might have held a grudge against you?"

"It is conceivable, but I cannot call to mind any such specific case."

"How about a child?"

Dr. Watson hesitated only slightly before he spoke.

"There was a young boy. Rheumatic fever took him. I could do nothing. His mother was beside herself, for she was all alone, having divorced her husband, who was nowhere to be found."

"Do you recall the names involved?"

"The boy's name was Walter. Walter Smith. The mother was Anne Smith. The father's name I do not recall. I had no communication with him. It was said that he was a sailor, and his home port was Liverpool."

"Smith is a difficult name, of course," said Holmes. "But being a sailor from Liverpool does narrow the track. How long ago was this boy buried?"

"Seven, perhaps eight years ago."

"And where does the mother live?"

"I heard that she died in the interim. Broken heart and all of that. It was a double tragedy."

Rising from his chair, Holmes said, "I commend you for your earnest help, Dr. Watson. It may prove to be indispensable. Now let us bid you a good day, for we have much to do."

AS WE RODE a trap back to the station, Holmes said, "This is clearly a case of mistaken identity. The sailor returning home from the sea learning that his wife and only son had perished, vowed vengeance against the physician who failed to save his only son. Through some subterfuge, perhaps on the part of neighbors, this Smith was told a lie to throw him off the track of the poor retired Dr. Watson. Perhaps he searched far and wide for him and, discovering another Dr. Watson, leapt to an erroneous conclusion. Hence, the letters you have received."

"As a theory, it appears sound," I remarked. "As to circumstances, I find it appalling. I have been marked for death by a person I do not know for an imagined crime I never committed."

"And it would do no good to communicate the truth to Seaman Smith, for he would only turn upon the actual Dr. John A. Watson. No, that would not do. I am afraid, Watson, we must once again bait the trap using your name and reputation. I'm sorry, but this must be done."

"I agree that I will know no rest until this man has been brought to justice, if not for my sake then for the sake of those he has so callously slain."

Holmes suddenly made a noise in his throat. "Smith! I perceive the connection now. A blacksmith wields a hammer. The thunder god Thor possesses a hammer. His alias was a clue to his true name, but it was nothing that could have been arrived at by deduction, induction, or in the other rigorous means of reasoning. Yet it is good to know, along with his motive, for we may not be dealing with a demented soul, but a merely vengeful one. It is important to understand which one it is, if for no other reason than it will sharpen our wits for the struggle ahead."

"No doubt the fellow's habit of posting these taunts from places such as Hackney and Hammersmith are an equal part of his cruel game, I venture to say."

"Yes, yes. So oblique were these clues that I failed to perceive them as a species of sly mockery. Whatever we may think of

Thorson, he is a man of details. For like the lowly spider, he spins his web exceedingly fine."

Holmes paused. I noted an almost imperceptible tightening of his aquiline features, and a decided inward turning of his gaze. Knowing my friend as well as I did, I understood that I should hold my tongue while his mental machinery toiled in silence.

At length, Holmes roused from his reflective posture. A fresh energy revitalized him. Turning to me with something like a wry grin, he said, "It may not be necessary after all to bait the hook with your irreplaceable life, Watson. Suddenly, pieces of the puzzle I did not suspect existed have fallen into place. All that is left is to investigate them. Come! We have a train to catch."

"Back to London?"

"To Hammersmith, to be precise. To the lair of the modern thunderer, whose lightning bolts are, in fact, as silent as they are insidious."

THE TRAIN RIDE was swift, but passed slowly to my mind. From the station, a hummingbird cab whisked us directly to Hammersmith. Alighting there, Holmes went straight away to the first constable he could locate.

"Good afternoon, Constable. I am Sherlock Holmes, in the unlikely event that you do not recognize me."

"But I do recognize you, Mr. Holmes. It is good to make your acquaintance. Are you in need of official assistance?"

"I am, indeed. As a constable who patrols Hammersmith, you are no doubt acquainted with the various cabriolets who prowl these byways, are you not?"

"I am. Is there trouble?"

"There is always trouble. Trouble is a pestilence in greater London. But in this case, we are attempting to avert further trouble. I ask you to cast your memory back to the cabmen of your acquaintance. Is there one lately arrived to this area? One sporting side-whiskers, which may in fact have been recently shorn."

"I conjure up such a fellow," replied the officer. "But I do not know his name, nor where he hangs his hat and whip."

"No matter. When did you first notice him hereabouts?"

The constable rolled up his eyes as he searched his memory.

"No more than two months ago, and conceivably less."

"Ah. Good fellow! That narrows it down perfectly. Now if one were to purchase sulphuric acid in Hammersmith, who would be the likeliest purveyor?"

"Why, that would be old Burkholder, the chemist. He has a shop on the end of Black Lion Lane."

"Excellent, my man. When did you last notice the cabman?"

"Not two days ago."

"Was he driving his cab?"

"Not quite. He has traded up to a four-wheeled Clarence. A coachman, he is now."

"I see," mused Holmes. "Would you recall if either horse was the same?"

"They were not! The new ones are both dun mares."

"Was the former horse a bay?"

"You have it exactly right, Mr. Holmes. Exactly right. A handsome animal. I do not know what became of it, but I can make inquiries, if you wish."

"No need. I have it on good authority that the animal unexpectedly expired and was conveyed to a rendering plant. Thank you and good day, Constable. We must be on our way."

"If you need any further assistance," called the eager-voiced officer as we parted company, "I would only be too happy to pitch in, as it were."

"We may yet take you up on your kind offer," returned Holmes. Turning to me, he confided, "A four-wheeler coach, Watson. My suspicions are confirmed. Fearful of discovery, he has abandoned the stolen hansom cab and acquired an old growler. I think that this is a sinister development."

"How so?"

But Sherlock Holmes would not reply. Instead, he hurried to the chemist's shop and made swift inquiries, after first identifying himself.

"Sulphuric acid, you say? That could only be one man. Mr. Hammersmith."

Holmes frowned. "Hammersmith? Odd coincidence, that."

"No, not very odd at all. Common enough name around here."

"Is this Hammersmith clean-shaven, or does he sport whiskers?" pressed Holmes.

"The latter when he first called upon this shop, but more recently the fellow had removed all such facial adornment. Glowering gent, no matter how he presented himself."

"That fits him to a *T*," I remarked.

"Would you confide in me the address of the fellow?" pressed Holmes.

The chemist hesitated only briefly. "Normally, I would not reveal the address of a regular customer. But since you are Sherlock Holmes, I can hardly deny you this bit of data."

Consulting a ledger, the chemist swiftly wrote out an address and handed a slip of paper to Holmes, who read it.

"Hmm! Number five Hammersmith Mews. No doubt that is where he stables his horse and carriage."

"I beg your pardon?" grunted the chemist.

"Pay me no mind," murmured Holmes. "I was merely thinking aloud. Thank you for your time and trouble. We must be on our way."

Once we left the shop, Holmes resumed our conversation.

"When I remarked that our Mr. Hammersmith spun an exceedingly fine web, it occurred to me that he may have commenced his weaving immediately after leaving Liverpool. Hence, the selection of Hammersmith as his London headquarters."

"Is he Smith or Hammersmith?"

"The former, I would think. The latter alias relates to his fixation with the mythological Thor. It hardly matters, but he established his base of operations in Hammersmith for the same diabolical reason that has threaded throughout this affair. He saw himself as a righteous avenger of his shattered family."

I admitted, "I follow you only so far as this chameleon has laid his tracks. But what the devil does sulphuric acid have to do with the matter?"

Holmes was about to answer when he spied something up the way that brought him up short. Bringing up a sinewy arm, he forced me backwards. We withdrew into an alley, out of which Holmes peered carefully around the brick façade.

"What is it?" I whispered.

"It is Smith of the glowering countenance. And he is engaged in lively conversation with our friendly constable."

"A chance encounter?"

"A fortunate one, I fear," countered Holmes.

Distant voices escalated into an argument.

"I am placing you under arrest, pending further instructions from Sherlock Holmes himself!"

"I refuse!" raged the other. "I will hear no more about it!"

A moment later came a thud, followed by a sharp outcry.

Holmes sprang from the alley mouth like a hound after a fox. I pursued as best I could.

Holmes reached the constable first. The unfortunate one lay on the ground, blood seeping from his bare head, his helmet in the gutter. He groaned loudly. Of the elusive Smith, there was no sign—other than a braided blackjack of the type carried by sailors the world over lying athwart the cobbles.

"Watson! Attend to this man."

"Indeed! Will you pursue Smith?"

"Smith can await a kinder hour. Note that this man is grievously wounded. I must fetch medical help."

As I knelt down, tending to the insensate constable's head

wound, Sherlock Holmes disappeared. In short order, an ambulance pulled up, no doubt summoned by my friend.

"This man has a concussion," I told the arriving medical man. "We must convey him to the nearest infirmary."

Together, we finished binding his head and set him on the stretcher, placing the dazed fellow in the back of the ambulance. I climbed aboard, and continued my ministrations.

In the back of my mind, my thoughts were of the missing Sherlock Holmes, and the peril into which he was no doubt plunging.

I remained in the infirmary for over an hour, attending to my duty. The constable would recover, but it would be some time before he was again fit.

Sherlock Holmes turned up in due course, looking both fatigued and pale, but nevertheless no more the worse for wear than that.

"Wherever have you been?" I inquired in relief.

Instead of responding directly, my friend said flatly, "Smith is dead. He will trouble us no more."

"Dead, you say? My dear Holmes, I am relieved for both of our sakes. But whatever happened?"

"The trail led to his flat in Hammermith Mews. Wrongly suspecting that the constable he had felled had betrayed his address, Smith resorted to the only recourse a marked killer could be expected to do in such damning circumstances. He did away with himself."

"Suicide?"

Holmes nodded somberly. "One might say that he executed himself, and in a most abnormal manner."

My medical duties discharged, we went out into the night. As we strolled along in the deepening dusk, Holmes recounted the events of the evening.

"I did not go directly to Hammersmith Mews," he explained. "Rather, I collected another constable and we approached the flat together. Inasmuch as it was situated over a stable, we assumed that the coach was sequestered within. As we approached, there came a flash of blue light from the horse barn, followed by an unpleasant odor that I took to be burning flesh. The constable and I forced open the stable door and discovered that the horrid smell was emanating from the open door of the four-wheeler.

"Opening the door, we beheld a beastly sight, Watson. Therein sat sprawled the late Mr. Smith, upon what he termed his 'throne of gilt,' which he had lately installed into the capacious interior of the Clarence body. This coach was his means of concealing the diabolical device and transforming a commonplace growler into a murder machine. His scheme shattered and seeing no way out, Smith took his seat, attached a pair of electrodes to his head and ankle, then actuated an electrical switch. The blue flash resulted. He was quite deceased, as was evidenced by the fact that his hair was ablaze when we discovered him—yet he took no notice of the fact."

"My word!"

I did not fully understand Holmes's explanation. But he soon enlightened me.

"Are you familiar with the so-called 'electric chair?'" he asked.

"Only vaguely," I admitted.

"It is an invention of American origin. The death-dealing contraption was devised for the purpose of executing criminals by what is considered a more humane means than shooting or hanging. A simple wooden chair is fitted with solid metal electrodes to receive a charge of alternating current from a prison generator. Once the condemned man or woman is strapped firmly into the seat, the connections are set up to electrocute him via the temple, ankles, and other points of his anatomy, leaving scorch marks, but no other signs of galvanic activity. I understand that the living brain is destroyed by the first jolt of voltage, and the heart shocked into lifelessness with a second application, thus ensuring that the state's sentence has been carried out. Conceiving his plan to prosecute his grudge against the other Dr. Watson, Smith copied the idea, except that he devised accumulators for the storage of electricity which would then be discharged into the infernal throne, a generator being beyond his means."

"Hence the sulphuric acid purchases!" I cried.

Holmes nodded. "An essential ingredient to the required contrivance. The makeshift storage batteries were concealed inside the four wheeler. It was Smith's first idea to kidnap you via hansom cab, render you insensate with the braided black-jack he employed to such devastating effect upon our overea-ger constable friend, and convey you to the place where the so-called 'throne of gilt' lay waiting. But circumstances forced him to abandon that plan. He devised a variation in which the throne was installed into the carriage in place of the customary bench seat. He believed he could lure you into the cabin, and electrocute you at once before you realized that you sat upon no ordinary seat. This was the hearse referenced in his last posted communication to you. No doubt Smith would have swiftly disposed of your body in the most convenient meadow, as he did the others."

"Ghastly thought! But Holmes, why was the poor guiltless horse electrocuted?"

"His original cabriolet and horse having been discovered, Smith thought it best to dispose of the inconvenient animal. Selling it was out of the question. Such a horse could have been traced back to its owner. But I suspect there was another reason."

"Oh?"

"Seaman Smith needed to test the newly installed electric chair to ascertain that it would do a proper job in its enclosed environment. By electrical means, he contrived to do away with the horse, no doubt by attaching an electrode to his shod foot, thus quietly eliminating the animal, which was known to us by sight. His previous victims were no doubt in the nature of experiments as well. Methodical man, Smith selected victims who happened to be abroad during electrical storms in order to test the makeshift apparatus and supply cover to his operations, counting that no one would question bodies discovered under such elemental circumstances to be the products of foul play."

"Remarkable! But where did this ordinary sailor acquire the knowledge to bring about his electrical murder scheme?"

"Elementary, Watson. Seaman Smith was rated an electrician. His Majesty's fleet of ships, having been systematically electri-fied, require continual maintenance, as you full well know. No doubt he was kept very busy. Until his desertion."

"Desertion?"

"I recently inquired of the Royal Navy, and learned of an Able Seaman Donald Smith, who had deserted his ship earlier in the year upon her return to home port."

"An electrician?"

"Need I confirm the obvious to you?" sniffed Holmes.

"There is nothing left for us to do then?"

"On the contrary. There exists one more item."

"And that is?"

"To seek out our evening meal, for we have richly earned it. The only question before us is whether we should eat in Hammersmith, or return to our familiar Marylebone and repair to a restaurant whose worth is known to us both."

"I am weary of the very sound of the name Smith," I replied truthfully. "As I recall, my dear Holmes, you once remarked that our next started repast would be your treat—a generous offer, upon which I have yet to collect."

"So I did, Watson. So I did. In that case, you may select the restaurant of your preference. Price is no object, for this has been a most intriguing case which brought a more than satisfactory conclusion. The truly-named throne of guilt has claimed its rightful ruler."

THE UNSETTLING MATTER
OF THE GRAVEYARD GHOUL

W E WERE DISCUSSING coincidences, Sherlock Holmes and I, when a rather striking specimen of the topic knocked on the door of 221b Baker Street.

I was telling my dear friend, "You must admit that the long arm of coincidence often appears to be spectrally inclined."

"If you mean in a supernatural way," sniffed Holmes, "I reply with a pithy rejoinder. Namely, 'Humbug!' No offense intended, Watson."

"None taken," I returned graciously.

"As for the term itself," continued Holmes, "I should like to strike it from the dictionary and ban it from common use."

"Whatever for? It is a perfectly useful, if elastic, word."

"Bah! It is a crutch, a useless figment. As you well know, it is nothing concrete. Merely the point where two discrete lines happen to converge. That is all."

"Lines crossing on a globe indicate a specific point on the Mercator Grid," I reminded.

"*Imaginary* lines," stressed Holmes.

"Well, you will agree with me that reputable men of learning take refuge in coincidence to dismiss phenomena they cannot otherwise countenance."

Holmes blew out a plume of tobacco smoke. "Admitted. What of it?"

"An acquaintance of mine once observed that scientists

should not be allowed to invoke the term unless they can scientifically reproduce a coincidence under laboratory conditions."

This point struck home. "Well stated. My compliments to your acquaintance, whoever he is."

He resumed puffing industriously.

"May I inquire as to the cause of your rather foul mood, Holmes?"

In lieu of a spoken reply, my friend indicated the late edition of *The Times* with his pipestem, saying, "Page five, first column."

I opened the newspaper to page five.

The headline read:

Remarkable Story of Recovered Ring

I read the account with interest.

It seemed that a woman residing in Swansea had lost her wedding ring during a sailing excursion upon the Thames, near Richmond, two years previous. It had fallen into the water and was considered irrecoverable after a difficult search. A fortnight ago, she was dining in a restaurant in Cricklade and ordered carp. Cutting into the fish, she discovered her ring.

The article ended with the observation that there was no accounting for where the ring had been for these past two years, nor how the late fish had managed to carry the lost ring to the bereaved woman's dinner plate.

"This story strikes me as familiar," I mused.

"It should. A similar story was told eight years ago, but the scene was Scotland. The body of water a lake and the fish a brown trout."

"I seem to recall it," I allowed.

"There was an identical story told of a Chicago man who lost his college ring in Lake Superior. It was returned to him by a piece of whitefish served to him in a Boston hotel. Another version comes to us from faraway Brisbane. A different song, but with a monotonously familiar and dreary chorus."

"Astonishing!"

Holmes grunted disconsolately.

"Taken together," he fumed, "these are altogether too many parallel incidences to suit my view of this rather humdrum world."

Holmes puffed fretfully for some time. I could not help but notice his careful avoidance of the word *coincidence*.

At length, I offered, "Holmes, do you suppose that these are all tall tales spun by bored journalists?"

"I do not! They have all been verified. I performed some of that thankless duty myself." Holmes lifted his lowered head. His eyes harbored a deep and discontented glitter. My friend preferred to take the world on scientific terms, and contrary indications troubled him greatly until they could be properly dispelled.

"Watson, do you recall the story told by Herodotus of Polycrates, King of Samos?"

"Not immediately. I found Herodotus rather tedious in his lack of discipline. One never knows what to believe, or discount."

"He, too, lost a treasured ring. Polycrates, not the Greek historian. Rather, he cast it into the Aegean sea on the advice of a certain Amasis. It came back to Polycrates in the belly of a fish offered up as tribute. I daresay that was the first such fish story of its type ever recorded."

"Yet it continues to echo down to this very day and generation, you assert."

"I wish I could assert otherwise, but I cannot."

The doorbell rang, and our coincidence entered forthwith, escorted in by the page.

"Inspector Lestrade to see you, sir," said Billy, who swiftly withdrew.

"I am not surprised," snapped Holmes.

"You were expecting Lestrade?" I inquired.

"If not him, another of his breed," drawled Holmes, arising.

"For you see, Watson, I have been expecting a coincidence—if not on this night, then upon one belonging to the near future."

Lestrade said without preamble, "Mr. Holmes, there appears to be a cadaver on your doorstep."

Holmes appeared unfazed by this bit of intelligence. "As expected. Is this cadaver recent?"

"I took the liberty of unwrapping said corpse, and it appears to be rather advanced in its state of decomposition."

"My word!" I blurted out.

Regarding me, Sherlock Holmes said, "Calm yourself, Watson. This is the second specimen in less than a week."

"Specimen?"

"Perhaps 'remains' is a better term. I correct myself. There appears to be a grave robber at work. One with singular habits."

We stepped out into the evening light, and the cadaver lay athwart the stone step, swathed in his rather discolored funeral sheet. Fortunately, we were spared the sight of his or her dead countenance.

Studying the shrouded form from all angles, Holmes stooped and undid the linen at the top of the head, revealing a face that was black as bitumen but otherwise too unpleasant to describe.

"I do not recognize this face," remarked Holmes calmly. "Not that I expected to."

Unable to contain myself, I declared, "Holmes, did you say that this was the *second* corpse found on your doorstep?"

"Yes, yes, so it appears," he murmured, apparently deep in contemplation.

"Whatever would be the purpose of depositing such a grisly relic here?" I asked, aghast at the thought.

"That was exactly the question I put to myself after the first instance. You see, Watson, that body was hastily removed to the morgue, and traced to a certain open grave in the military section of Brompton Cemetery. The name on the stone meant nothing to me. In life, the man had been a colonel who had

earned the Victoria Cross. This occasioned considerable rumina-
tion. Since I could make nothing of the corpse itself, my attention actually went in the direction of the grave robber and his
recondite motivations."

"Of course. Did you form a conclusion?"

"A tentative one. But it could be supported only if a second
corpse materialized. And here we have one. This, Watson, I
submit to you, is *not* a coincidence."

"What do you make of this deviltry?" Lestrade prompted.

"Since the first corpse did not appear to be connected to me,
and I imagine the same will be true here, then the motivation
appears to be to draw our attention—in which case, we will
oblige. Once we have established certain facts, I might add."

Turning to Inspector Lestrade, Holmes said, "Kindly have
this charnel relic removed and give me your report once you
have determined the location which this poor fellow formerly
occupied."

"As you say, Mr. Holmes."

Turning to summon help, the inspector went off into the
night while Sherlock Holmes invited me back into his apartments.

We retreated to the sitting room, where Holmes returned
to his pipe and was soon puffing furiously, his sharp features
settling into its customary firm yet contemplative cast.

"What do you make of it?" I inquired.

"I think this outrage is in the form of an invitation, not an
accusation. If it were the latter, suspicion of myself as a conceivable grave robber would have made the newspapers, and the
perpetrator might not have felt compelled to deposit another
example of his grisly work."

"An invitation? To what?"

Ignoring my question, Holmes ploughed on. "However, I
think we will permit the newspapers to report on tonight's
misadventure, and see if a third corpse finds its way to my doorstep."

"What then, Holmes?"

"That, my dear Watson, depends upon whether we are dealing with a grave robber who is a specialist, or one who is a generalist."

"I fail to follow."

"If tonight's cadaver hails from the same burial ground as the unfortunate visitor of the other evening, we will have something to go on. A place to explore, if you will. For that could only be the conceivable invitation. To visit a certain graveyard in the hope of apprehending the perpetrator."

"And if these corpses were removed from different burial grounds?"

Frowning, Holmes remarked flatly, "Then I will require more tobacco. For I cannot presently conceive of a third alternative to the two already stated."

There, the peculiar matter rested.

THE NEXT DAY, *The Times* reported that a cadaver had been deposited upon the steps of the famous detective, Sherlock Holmes. Details given were scant, being limited to the essential facts in the case, shorn of all speculation.

The remains belonged to one George Cuniff, a laborer, and his disturbed grave and open coffin was discovered in Brompton Cemetery.

Curiously, no mention was made of the previous cadaver delivered to 221b Baker Street.

Inspector Lestrade was quoted as saying that Scotland Yard did not suspect Sherlock Holmes in the matter, if for no other reason than a man endeavoring to rob graves would not incriminate himself by depositing their contents upon his own doorstep.

That evening, I paid a call on Holmes, and we sat for over an hour discussing the matter.

"Nothing was said of the first corpse," I ventured.

"That was deliberate," snapped Holmes. "The general public need not know all of the details. Moreover, the story was planted purely for the edification of the grave robber himself. We have now broadcast to him that I am not a suspect, and await his next move."

I considered this. "If I were in the business of robbing graves and depositing bodies upon the same doorstep, I might forbear from doing so for quite some time, if indeed ever again."

Holmes said dismissively, "Our mysterious digger appears to be a supremely motivated individual. He might be reconsidering his next adventure, but I doubt he will be dissuaded from making another delivery. At this moment, he may be slightly confused as to whether Scotland Yard, and by inference, I myself, have put all the pieces together. To wit, that both bodies were removed from Brompton Cemetery."

"I take it that you expect him to repeat his provocation in exactly the same manner, and from precisely the same source?"

"On the contrary, Watson. I expect no such thing. He may be forced to change graveyards, in which case his motivations will remain obscure. However, if he resorts to the same stamping ground, we may have him."

"My puzzlement is no less cluttered for your words, I must confess."

Reaching over to a side table, Sherlock Holmes removed a small container, whose lid he lifted, revealing an unusual instrument. I did not immediately recognize it.

Extracting the thing from its receptacle, he placed it on his lap. It consisted of a steel tube terminating in an annular nozzle. A thin hose with a rubber bulb was attached to the other end, as on a sphygmomanometer.

Experimentally, Holmes squeezed the bulb several times, producing a low hiss from the instrument, but no other result.

Some distance away, a dog barked. I did not connect the two phenomena, considering them to be coincidental.

Holmes offered no explanation, and my thoughts were upon the conundrum before us.

"Holmes," I inquired, "why do you not simply investigate the graveyard for clues?"

"Because our adversary obviously expects us to. Otherwise he would not have left the plundered grave open as he did. And I do not care to make his plans any easier, but to frustrate them."

"Understandable. But how can you solve the case if you do not investigate?"

"By laying a trap, Watson. For the purpose of resolving the matter, it is not sufficient to work out all the facts to their logical conclusion, but to apprehend the culprit."

"Please excuse my directness if I remark that this sounds unlike the Sherlock Holmes I have come to know so well," I countered. "My good and canny friend would much prefer to work out the facts on his way to apprehending the culprit."

"In the end, it may turn out to resolve itself in exactly that order," replied Holmes. "But for the moment, I prefer my trap to that of my adversary's snare."

"That is the second time you've use that word. *Adversary.* It seems significant to me."

Holmes nodded, releasing a flight of tobacco smoke, which rose to the ceiling and pooled there.

"While I do not know who this individual might be, it is clear that he knows me. And is attempting to provoke me into action. I would prefer to provoke him into a blunder. Hence, I choose not to enter into his trap, but to set one of my own."

"I begin to see. Whatever is that device that you keep toying with?"

"It is called a *Galton's Whistle,* named after its inventor, Francis Galton."

"I do not believe I have ever heard of it," I admitted.

Holmes squeezed the rubber bulb again, and once more the dog answered from down the street.

"As you might surmise, Watson, if you are paying sufficient attention, this is what is commonly known as a 'silent dog whistle.' It emits a high-pitched sound well above the range of human hearing, but one which happens to impinge upon the canine ear with piercing sharpness, invariably eliciting a quarrelsome reaction."

"Ah, yes. Since neither you nor I can hear this sound, why are you toying with it?"

"Note the reaction of the neighborhood dog. The sound stirs him. I happen to know that a German shepherd dwells three doors up from this address. And it causes me to wonder why said canine neglected to bark when a stranger deposited a corpse upon my doorstep in the dead of night."

"Why? It is obvious. Because the dog failed to hear it."

"But why did he fail to hear it? That is the essential question, Watson."

I had no idea, and so I said nothing. We sat in silence for several minutes, while Holmes blew clouds of smoke against the ceiling and studied the shifting patterns created. I might have thought him then to be a sorcerer of old, indulging in a form of divination that involved patterns of smoke instead of the entrails of an ox.

We did not have long to wait for our third corpse.

THE NEXT EVENING, Sherlock Holmes rang me up quite late, saying excitedly, "Watson! Meet me at Brompton Cemetery. Bring your pistol. Our adversary has proven to be impatient. He has already struck!"

"Have you determined that the body was exhumed from that burial ground?"

"No, there is no time for that. But I will explain later. Hurry, if you would. The game is at last afoot!"

A hansom cab deposited me at the entrance to the old burying ground on Old Brompton Road, which was deserted except for a pair of gypsy wagons parked for the night some yards distant. Holmes had arrived ahead of me, as I expected.

There in the darkness, we conferred.

"Whatever do you expect to find?" I inquired.

"I do not know. But I wish to visit the scene of the crime ere my adversary could possibly expect it."

With that, we entered, carrying kerosene lanterns, shielded so as to emit limited but serviceable light.

Holmes was blessed with an acute sense of smell. Almost as soon as we were within the confines of the spacious cemetery, he began sniffing like a bloodhound.

He soon selected a direction, which was due north, and followed his nose. Before long I could smell freshly turned earth, and we were in sight of a yawning grave and an open casket—a beastly thing in the fitful light.

"Keep your distance as we approach, Watson," he whispered.

I obliged as my friend commenced a careful reconnoiter of the open mound of earth. He stooped often, lowering his glowing lantern, observing the ground, disdaining the casket.

Finally, he stood up and invited me to draw near.

"Behold, Watson—the footprints of the ghoul!"

Holmes's use of the antiquated term must have seeped into my mental machinery, for when my eyes fell upon his downward pointing finger, I struggled to suppress a cry of fear and outrage.

Impressed into the soft clods of earth created by digging were footprints such as I had never before beheld. Generally speaking, they were human. I would say they were of a size that suggested a man who might wear a shoe size larger than my own. But I could not imagine the owner wearing shoes at all. For both feet possessed only four toes! In both footprints, the center toe appeared to be wholly absent. I could not conceive of such a thing, and said so to Sherlock Holmes.

In response, he asked me, "In all of your medical reading, have you ever heard of such a natural deformity?"

"Never! Whilst the odd toe might be absent at birth, or lost through accident or amputation, I have never seen such symmetrically-deformed footprints. Can they be human?"

"I see certain signs of shovel work, so I would imagine so."

"How can you be sure?"

"Notice that dirty rock. See the shiny patch? It has been scraped by steel. A common spade did that, Watson."

He turned to examine the gravestone. The name cut into the granite was an odd one.

LONG WOLF

"A Sioux chief who died touring with the Buffalo Bill show when it visited the Earl's Court Exhibition Grounds," Holmes whispered to me before I could question him. "I doubt the decision to exhume the unfortunate fellow was anything other than capricious."

Holmes began throwing his lantern light around, seeking additional footprints. He soon found them.

Shushing me with a forefinger, he invited me to follow and we picked our way through the shadowy gravestones and dark brush, coming at last to a row of granite mausoleums that stood up on the outskirts of the graveyard.

With a start, Holmes brought himself up short and doused his lantern. Upon drawing close, he took hold of my sleeve and did the same to my own.

It was now quite dark, but upon a low hillock, a modest light was shining. It appeared to be coming from the iron door of a particular crypt, as if someone lurked within. The name upon the structure couldn't be read at this distance.

We studied this steady illumination for several moments in silence. I could feel my heart beating. Was the fiend already rummaging through another coffin?

The atmosphere of the place was heavy. Normally, I dislike graveyards, inasmuch as they represented to me a symbol of the inevitable and ultimate failure of my profession. This night I especially detested this one.

Finally, Holmes urged me to follow him via a tug on my coat. I obliged.

Stepping carefully, we came upon the crypt from its blind side. It became evident that the iron door was slightly ajar, and the light was coming from within. We could discern its shine, but not its source.

Holmes drew his pistol, and I did the same. We set ourselves.

Carefully laying our lanterns upon the ground, we waited. No sound came from within the crypt, but after a moment or so, there came a scratching, furtive and brief. At that, Sherlock Holmes sprang from his crouch, with I following close behind.

Rounding the blocky crypt, we found the ajar door. Throwing this open wide, Holmes plunged in, pointing his pistol at a stationary lantern that sat upon the stone sepulcher proper.

The lantern was shielded on all but one side, so the light was feeble.

My eyes were very wide when I followed Holmes in, and I pointed my pistol into the dark corners as Holmes stepped towards the light.

Holmes realized the truth before I did and suddenly whirled, crying, "Out, Watson! *Out before it is too late!*"

But it *was* already too late. The iron door suddenly creaked shut, locking with the sound of its mechanism groaning as it was turned.

Holmes reached the door too late, began pounding on it. It refused to budge.

Outside, the most cruel laughter I ever before heard rang out. It penetrated the granite walls of the tomb, and then seemed to trail away. I imagine that I heard soft footsteps. They were receding.

With a short cry, Sherlock Holmes turned and said, "Watson, please forgive me! I have been a fool. I suspected a trap and moved to evaluate it before it could be properly set. Instead, we have fallen into the very trap I thought to avoid. We are entombed!"

The shock of Holmes's words filled me with dread and horror. More so because I could hear in his tone a kind of self-disgust brought about because he had been outwitted at his own game.

"Is there no way out?" I cried.

Taking the lantern off the stone lid of the sepulcher, Holmes lifted the shield to cast illumination about. A rat scooted into a corner, revealing the origins of the sounds that helped to lure us within.

Carrying the light to the door, Holmes saw that there was no handle on the inside. In generations gone by, such crypts were sometimes fitted with handles for the benefit of those unfortunates who had been buried alive. But those incidents had grown infrequent, and the practice ended.

Holmes declared grimly, "We are immured, much as the unfortunate Fortunato was in Poe's celebrated 'Cask of Amontillado.'"

Memories of that horrid story came rushing back to me. They did not fill me with cheer. Quite the contrary, I shuddered the length of my body.

Holmes showed no such qualms. His features were as fixed and resolute as those of a Comanche chieftain.

I ventured to say, "This corner of the burial ground is rather far from the gate, and road traffic. If we set up a shouting, we might be heard, but not this late at night, I would think."

"I quite agree, Watson. We would be wasting our valuable breath in a futile exercise."

We searched the interior of the crypt, looking for we knew not what. We only knew that we could not simply stand there all night and contemplate our fate without endeavoring to discover a means of escape.

This occupied very little time and we were back where we started, both literally and figuratively.

"Tomorrow is Sunday," I pointed out. "There are bound to be mourners visiting their loved ones. If we conserve our strength until then, we might be able to attract rescue by strenuous vocal efforts."

"I dare say it is our best bet," said Holmes, "but I am impatient to get back on the trail of our adversary. I will not spend this night nor any part of tomorrow in his dank dungeon, if I have anything to say about it."

"Have you a scheme by which we might break free?"

Holmes emitted a sound that was dry and ironic. I would classify it as a chuckle, but it had a slightly macabre quality that dismissed the term.

Laughing self-mockingly, he said, "Coincidentally or not, I do."

In the light of the lantern, Holmes removed the Galton's Whistle that he had happened to pocket for no reason that I could imagine.

Taking this in hand, he squeezed the rubber bulb strenuously for some minutes. He was soon rewarded by the barking of a dog. It was not nearby, but neither was it far away. Moving about the spacious interior of the tomb, he continued this odd exercise.

Another dog piped up. Then a third joined in the chorus.

I now recalled noticing one upon my approach to the cemetery gate, in the vicinity of the gypsy wagons.

"Evidently, there are stray dogs about," I breathed.

"Evidently," said Holmes, continuing to squeeze the Galton's Whistle.

The barking continued, sometimes drawing near, but ofttimes moving farther away. Tirelessly, Holmes manipulated the bulb and produced what to our ears was a brief hissing each time, but to the canine inhabitants of the burial ground was a kind of aural agony.

Perhaps an hour passed. I could not be sure.

The sound of men talking amongst themselves came to our ears.

Leaving off his manipulations, Sherlock Holmes turned to me and said, "I hope you have conserved your strength, Watson. For you and I need all the lung power we possess."

With that, he began shouting. *"Halloooa!"*

I joined in. We set up a caterwauling that put the canine

chorus to shame. In surprisingly short order, voices could be heard beyond the obdurate walls of our confinement.

"Who is that? Who is making that confounded racket? Show yourself!"

Bidding me to be quiet, Sherlock Holmes lifted his voice alone and cried out, "We are trapped in a tomb within earshot of you. Kindly seek us out."

The voices drew closer, and Holmes shouted, "The crypt is situated upon a low hillock."

"What is the name engraved upon it?" a voice demanded.

"Regrettably," Holmes returned, "I failed to make it out."

It did not matter. Soon enough, there came a banging on the iron door and Holmes pounded back, adding, "You have found the correct address. Be good enough to fetch axes and iron crows to release us."

"Dear God! Is that you, Mr. Holmes?"

"Indeed it is I, along with Watson. Now please, Lestrade, provide us much-needed succor."

Crowbars were fetched and the men outside went to work, soon forcing the door open. Gallantly, or perhaps penitently, Holmes invited me to exit first. Which I did.

Assembled before us were Inspector Lestrade and two of his constables. All had upraised lanterns. They were a welcome sight, just as was the fresh night air filling our lungs with cleanliness and relief at the same time.

Lestrade looked at Holmes and remarked, "You beat us to the punch, I see?"

"We fell into a damnable trap," returned Holmes bitterly.

Holmes and Lestrade conferred for several minutes, and it developed that the inspector had brought a detachment of constables to the burying ground once the body left upon Holmes's doorstep had been consigned to the morgue.

"We thought it prudent to check this spot first," Lestrade concluded.

"And I am most pleased that you did so," replied Holmes. "We arrived before you, but fell prey to what I fear is my own eagerness."

"Well, you have been spared a night of involuntary entombment, if not accidental death."

"Not accidental, Lestrade. But premeditated murder. The grave robber was lying in wait. He knows me, Lestrade. He knows me well. But I do not as yet know him."

"Well, it is best that we take our departure, and start afresh in the morning. You men have had a disagreeable experience and there is no point in loitering. We have seen what we need to see."

As we turned to go, Holmes happened to look back at the face of the mausoleum and saw the name inscribed on the lintel:

CARFAX

Holmes stopped in his tracks, and regarded the name in sober silence.

"I still do not believe in coincidences," he murmured, then resumed walking.

"Whatever do you mean, Holmes?" I inquired.

But Sherlock Holmes would say nothing. He had out his pipe and was stuffing it with tobacco. Soon, it was blazing. From his expression, I could tell that his brain was also fulminating.

"He knows me, and now I know *him*...."

I DID NOT see Holmes for a full day after that terrible evening of dank imprisonment. When he did call, it was to make a strange request.

"Come around after supper, Watson. And if you would, bring your medical bag."

"Are you ill?"

"On the contrary, I am enervated, for I am well on the track of the ghoul. And make sure that you bring a tongue depressor."

"I shall," I assured him. I knew better than to ask why. It would do no good, and all would be revealed in due course.

When I came around, I set my valise down on the floor and took my seat.

"Would you be so kind as to indulge me, Watson? Observe what I do."

Taking the Galton's Whistle from its receptacle beside him, Holmes began to methodically squeeze the rubber bulb. The expected hissing was produced.

"Do you hear it, Watson?"

"Of course not. Is it not above the range of the human ear's ability to perceive its frequency?"

"You miss my point entirely," said Holmes dryly. "Allow me to continue by demonstration."

Holmes resumed. It dawned upon me latterly that the neighborhood dog had not barked in response to the silent irritant.

When I volunteered this observation, Holmes said, "The dog has never before failed to respond to the whistle."

"Perhaps the owner has taken him for a walk," I suggested.

"Perhaps. But if so, he has gone for a quite long promenade, for I have failed to gain the dog's attention during the course of the day. And believe me, Watson, I have been very industrious in my pursuit."

"But what does the dog have to do with anything?"

"Three times, a cadaver has been deposited upon my doorstep in the evening hours, by a person entirely unseen. Even an ancient and mouldering corpus possesses substance. Its weight may be negligible, but it must be conveyed by some human agency. Yet the dog failed to bark each time. This suggests that the cadaver was not brought by wagon or hansom cab, but that it was carried by hand by the perpetrator."

"How can you be sure?"

"Because I have become familiar with the dog's behavior over the course of the last month, when it first appeared in the neighborhood. It often barked, albeit briefly. But it did *not* bark when a stranger stole into the immediate neighborhood. What does that tell you?

"That it was sound asleep?"

"Oh, Watson! You exasperate me. Try again."

"That the perpetrator was not a stranger to the dog!"

"Very good. You redeem yourself, Watson. You are once more in my good graces. Not that you were ever far out of them. Yes, the depositor of the cadavers appears to be a neighbor."

"How can that be?"

"It is quite elementary. My adversary apparently moved into the neighborhood to put himself into a position both to observe me and to enact his scheme of revenge."

"Revenge! Whatever for?"

"For past wrongs—or at least imagined slights. I've been making inquiries of the neighborhood, and it appears that the owner of the dog returned last night to claim it and has not yet returned."

"Do you think he fled?"

"I'm not certain, but I think, since the hour is late, he is unlikely to do so. I have prevailed upon his landlady to let us into his apartment in his absence."

"Do you propose to do so now?"

Holmes threw on his coat, and took up a walking stick. "If you consider it unsavory, my dear fellow, you need not accompany me." He smiled tightly in my direction. "But your company is welcome, as always."

I didn't have to consider the proposition for very long. And so, we were soon walking not three houses up Baker Street, where Holmes rapped up on the door of a lodging house and the landlady appeared.

"Mrs. Malone, could we trouble you for the key?"

This was surrendered, along with an admonition, "Let there be no trouble, Mr. Holmes."

"Rest assured, Mrs. Malone, we will start none. However, I cannot guarantee that trouble will not be started upon us. But we will be hasty in our examination."

That settled, Holmes employed the key to let himself into the mouse-hole of an apartment, and we moved around in the vague light from the street lamps.

"The man appears to have been living alone, except for the dog," said Holmes. "This in itself is very suggestive."

"Of what?"

"Of a deeper reason for revenge beyond that of a prior altercation."

The place was meagerly furnished. Holmes came upon a solitary shelf stocked with books, some of a religious nature, but quite a few were sensational novels or collections of short stories. I noticed Edgar Allan Poe prominent among the latter, and I was reminded of our disagreeable experience not less than twenty-four hours ago.

Noting Poe, Holmes traced the spines of several books, tapping a thoughtful finger upon the names of de Maupassant, Baudelaire, and finally the thin digit came to rest upon a volume of Ambrose Bierce.

"Have you read Bierce?" asked Holmes.

"I have sampled him. Too morbid for my tastes."

"Have you ever read the ghost story entitled 'The Middle Toe of the Right Foot?'"

I began to reply in the affirmative, when my tongue became momentarily paralyzed.

"The footprints with the missing toes?" I exclaimed.

"Precisely."

"Whatever could it mean?"

"From the contents of this library," mused Holmes, "I would say that the owner is a man interested in religion, but who also takes his inspiration from some of the darker fiction writers of the past century. Also, that he does not have an imagination of his own, but must look to the works of others for inspiration."

"I deduce that you are certain now that the ghoul, as you call him, resides in this apartment."

Holmes nodded, replacing the book. "Under the alias of Mr. Arrowsmith. Come along, Watson. We are done here."

We had no sooner turned to go than there came a rattle of a key in the front door lock.

Taking me by the elbow, Holmes retreated into a closet, and there we waited.

The occupant stepped over the threshold, lit the lights, rushed to the bedroom and began to pack his things.

Holmes listened. "Fleeing. No doubt the dog has been disposed of and other quarters secured."

Abruptly, Sherlock Holmes stepped out of the bedroom and into the parlor, boldly and without concern for his safety or well-being.

"Welcome home!" he cried out.

The other was taken aback. He whirled. "What! Who the devil are you?"

I beheld a rather large man, florid of features, with intensely dark bushy beard and matching hair piled on his head, but did not otherwise recognize him.

"Tut, tut," remonstrated Holmes. "Such protestations are beneath you, Peters."

"Peters!" I cried, a flood of memories rushing back to my brain. "Not 'Holy' Peters of Adelaide, Australia?"

"The very same," exulted Holmes. Addressing the cornered man, he proclaimed, "The clues you left were numerous, I will have you know."

The other's lips twisted in a snarl that could be detected in his response. "Clues! There were none, damn you! None, I say!"

"On the contrary, there were many. They merely needed to be winnowed out. I tipped to your game early, saw that it was a bid for revenge. That certainly narrowed the field considerably. But it was the name on the tomb that gave you away."

My eyes went wide then. "Lady Frances Carfax! It was in the matter of her mysterious disappearance that brought us into contact with this dastard, who fled justice successfully before he could be hung for his past crimes."*

"Along with his wife," corrected Holmes. "But she appears to be absent."

"Perished!" exclaimed Peters, pulling the black hair off his head and revealing a completely bald pate. "After you run us out of Brixton, Holmes, she fell sick, and eventually died. Left me all alone in this dreary world. Before that, I saw you as merely an antagonist who had gotten the best of me. After that, I acquired a fresh thirst—a thirst for vengeance, one that could only be slaked by your demise."

"So you turned to Poe and Ambrose Bierce for inspiration. I must say you were cleverer than I would have imagined after our first scrimmage."

During this exchange, Henry Peters stepped back towards the door, beside which stood a standing coat tree. A walking stick leaned against it. Reaching back, he grasped this. Then with a cry that was a mixture of despair and desperation, he sprang in Holmes's direction, the stick raised high to dash out my friend's brains.

But Sherlock Holmes was ready for him. He stepped forward, meeting the attack with one of his own. Lifting one arm to block the downward-swinging stick with his own cane, he struck a blow with his free fist, rocking his assailant's head backwards. It was a magnificent blow, pugilistic and precise.

Henry Peters stumbled backwards, and during his momentary confusion, Holmes stepped forward and applied the knob of his own stick to the fallen man's left temple. It was a very scientific blow, and Peters did not rise after he fell.

His breathing continued, however, noisily and stentorian.

"Good show, Holmes!" I exclaimed. "You dropped him with one blow."

"Would that I could have given him a second one for your sake. Last night was one of the most horrific in my experience."

---

* "The Disappearance of Lady Frances Carfax" by Arthur Conan Doyle.

Kneeling, Holmes removed the fellow's shoes and stockings, and fell to examining his bare feet. They were intact, possessing the usual number of toes. After an examination of the large toe of the left foot, Holmes stood up and announced, "It is he. There is no doubt upon the matter."

"But he is in possession of all of his toes," I pointed out.

Instead of addressing that point, Holmes said, "Take note of his left ear, and its ragged state. You will recall that Peters' left ear had been bitten rather severely during a saloon fight in Adelaide back in '89."

Peering closely, I noted that this was unquestionably so. But it did not clarify my puzzlement over the unanswered question of the four-toed grave robber.

Inspector Lestrade was summoned, and "Holy" Peters was carted off to Scotland Yard, not regaining consciousness until he was firmly behind iron bars.

Repairing to Baker Street, Holmes and I sat comfortably in his sitting room, tying up the loose ends. Naturally, I plied him with further questions.

I began by commenting, "There is more to this than you have so far divulged to me, I am sure."

"Let us begin with the mysterious four-toed footprints. Kindly hand me your tongue depressor."

As I was digging it out, I was surprised to see Sherlock Holmes remove his right shoe and stocking. He accepted the tongue depressor, which was of steel, and inserted it between his toes in such a way that it elevated the middle toe at a painfully acute angle, resting upon the other four.

Standing up, Holmes walked about the room awkwardly, but somehow managing to navigate.

"Observing the strange footprints," he said as he sat down again and pried free the tongue depressor, "I saw that there was no stump as such, but that the root of the missing toe simply faded, as if the absent digit were elevated, and not amputated. I struggled for some time to imagine how this was done, when curiously I thought of your profession. You have proven my point and I thank you. No doubt you'll need to sterilize your instrument before you dare insert it into a patient's mouth again."

Returning to my seat, I asked, "But what was the purpose of that subterfuge?"

"To create a singular and irresistible trail—one he knew I would follow to the mausoleum, which Peters kindly left illuminated and ajar, the better to lure me inside. I imagine there was some consideration given to creating the impression that the mysterious grave robber truly lacked his middle toes. But there, Peters has only incriminated himself, for I discerned by lantern light that the large toe of the left foot bore a jagged scar. An examination of the blackguard's bare feet revealed an identical mark, thus sewing up the matter."

"It strikes me as a great leap from knowing the identity of your antagonist to deducing that he lived just a few doors up the street," I ventured.

Reaching for his pipe, Holmes nodded. As he loaded it, he continued speaking.

"I haven't been toying with my Galton's Whistle exclusively these past twenty-four hours, but intermittently. Once the mocking significance of the name Carfax became clear to me, I knew my foe. His ability to deposit cadavers upon my doorstep with impunity suggested proximity. So I set out to prove said proximity. It was as easy as a trip to the local bakery."

"How would the local baker help you?" I exclaimed.

"A man from Australia visiting London would naturally crave familiar food. Among them would be such traditional sweets as Lamingtons and Neenish Tarts. I merely asked the baker if anyone had put in a special order for such fare. I expected the baker to describe a woman, but instead a man was named: Arrowsmith. This suggested that the wife was not present in London and possibly was no longer among the living. The local baker noted that the man's hair was rather full and an unconvincing black. Since Henry Peters was known to be bald, this must be a hairpiece. And not a very cunning one, either. But it served to conceal his tell-tale ragged left ear. All of these particulars formed threads in a tapestry that became clearer and clearer as I collected them."

"Well done! Bravo! But Holmes, what motivated you to carry the Galton's Whistle to the graveyard?"

Holmes took his pipe out of his mouth and frowned rather distastefully, I thought.

"I must admit to you that I am not entirely able to account for that action. Absentmindedly, I imagine, I pocketed it whilst deep in thought. I can assure you it was not a conscious decision on my part. If it were my unconscious acting up on the matter, conceivably it saved our lives, or at least truncated our involuntary entombment. And for that, I am profoundly grateful. No doubt, Holy Peters intended to decamp from London as rapidly as possible, once the blackguard had achieved his diabolical ends."

I eyed Holmes rather skeptically at this point.

"May I venture to suggest that coincidence, if not Providence, played a role in your absent-minded decision?"

"You may suggest either alternative, or, if you please, both," snapped Holmes. "But I reject them out of hand. Coincidence is utter humbug!"

"So you declaim. But what was the purpose of the dog?"

Subsiding, Holmes clipped, "Companionship, I'll wager. The man had lost his wife and was lonely. Nothing more."

"I see. Yes, that is perfectly sound reasoning. But one unresolved issue still vexes me. How did Peters convey the corpses from Brompton Cemetery to your doorstep unobserved?"

"Ah. He did not. At least, not directly. Do you recall the gypsy wagons arrayed along Old Brompton Road?"

"I noticed several."

"This is mere conjecture, but I believe it to be sound. I imagine that crossing a gypsy's palm with sufficient silver will purchase many an unsavory chore. Peters carried the remains to a waiting wagon and arranged for delivery to his own address in the dead of night. Later that night, or possibly the next, he personally carried the shrouded dead three doors along, and made his deposit. He had a perfect vantage point to watch for passersby, and the dog served as a secondary sentry. Peters quietly slipped back into his own mouse hole before discovery could possibly be made."

"Plausible. Yes, it conceivably might have been accomplished as you outline."

We lapsed into silence. A final objection came to me.

"Holmes, how could you not be certain that the name on the mausoleum was not, after all, a … coincidence, if you will pardon the expression?"

"Really, Watson. You can be rather dense at times. Cast your mind back to the matter of Lady Carfax, and summon up your memories of the fate Holy Peters had intended to be hers."

"My word! She was to be buried alive in a coffin she shared with a dead woman, never to be discovered!"

"The very fate Peters engineered for you and me, Watson. The detestable ghoul had gone to considerable pains to visit upon me the doom from which I had rescued Lady Carfax—and to apply his signature to the deed in a manner both cunning and cryptic, if I may be forgiven the use of that latter adjective."

"I see now why you chose that antiquated term to describe him," I allowed. " 'Ghoul,' I mean."

Holmes relit his faltering pipe, his tone slightly annoyed. "You should know by now, Watson, that I chose my words with utmost care. Holy Peters was indeed a ghoul of the first order. Unwilling to kill by direct means, he was perfectly willing to consign others to premature burial."

"Was? He is still among the living."

"Not for very long, Watson. Not for very long…."

WILL MURRAY IS the originator of the Wild Adventures line of pulp fiction novels, which commenced in 2011 and continues to this day as a vehicle for resurrecting iconic heroes of Twentieth Century popular fiction.

The author of approximately 75 novels and numerous short stories, Murray has revived or brought to life an amazing number of classic character franchises, including Doc Savage, The Shadow, King Kong, Tarzan of the Apes, John Carter of Mars, Remo Williams, Mack Bolan, Nick Fury, The Spider, James Christopher, G-8, the Suicide Squad, Superman, Batman, Wonder Woman, Spider-Man, Ant-Man, the Hulk, Iron Man, the Spider, The Avenger, the Gray Seal, the Green Hornet, The Secret 6, Sherlock Holmes, John Silence, Honey West, Zorro, Sky Captain, Cthulhu, Dr. Herbert West, Mars Attacks, Planet of the Apes, Lee Falk's the Phantom and Sir Arthur Conan Doyle's immortal Sherlock Holmes, about whom he was written more than 20 new stories for various anthologies.

His non-fiction books include *Wordslingers: An Epitaph for the Western* and *Forever After: An Inspired Story.* With legendary artist Steve Ditko, he created The Unbeatable Squirrel Girl for Marvel Comics.

ABOUT THE ARTIST

JOE DeVITO

JOE DeVITO IS the founder of DeVito ArtWorks, LLC, an artist-driven transmedia studio dedicated to the creation and development of multi-faceted properties including Skull Island, War Eagles, and the Primordials. DeVito ArtWorks is exclusively represented by Festa Entertainment and Dimensional Branding Group.

DeVito has painted many of the most recognizable Pop Culture and Pulp icons, including King Kong, Tarzan, Doc Savage, Sherlock Holmes, Superman, Batman, Wonder Woman, Spider-man, *MAD* magazine's Alfred E. Neuman, with a decided emphasis on dinosaurs, Action Adventure, SF and Fantasy. He has illustrated hundreds of book and magazine covers, painted several notable posters and numerous trading cards for the major comic book and gaming houses, and created concept and character design for the film and television industries.

An avid writer, Joe is also the co-author (with Brad Strickland) of two novels, which he illustrated as well. The first, based in Joe's original *Skull Island* prequel/sequel, was *KONG: King of Skull Island* (DH Press) was published in 2004. The second book, *Merian C. Cooper's KING KONG,* was published by St. Martin's Griffin in 2005.

In 2016, Boom! Studios published a twelve-issue comic book series based in DeVito's Kong IP titled *Kong of Skull Island,* resulting in two Graphic novels. The success of *Kong of Skull Island* spawned further multi-issue Kong tales set in the history of Skull Island, including an entire crossover series with the 20th Century FOX *Planet of the Apes* franchise titled *Kong on the Planet of the Apes.*

The year 2020 will see the further development of DeVito's Kong prequel/sequel series in the coming books *King Kong of Skull Island: Exodus* and *King Kong of Skull Island: The Wall,* with the property also in full development as a TV series and movie.

DeVito continues painting covers for *The All New Wild Adventures* series, featuring Doc Savage, Tarzan, The Shadow, Pat Savage and King Kong—including *King Kong vs. Tarzan,* the first-ever authorized meeting of the two iconic jungle lords. Concurrently, he is developing the imagery for his newest creation, a faction world of truly epic proportions tentatively titled *The Primordials.*

www.jdevito.com
www.kongskullisland.com
FB: Kong of Skull Island
FB: DeVito ArtWorks

THE ALL-NEW *WILD* ADVENTURES OF
DOC SAVAGE

Doc Savage:
The Desert Demons

Doc Savage:
Horror in Gold

Doc Savage:
The Infernal Buddha

Doc Savage:
The Forgotten Realm

Doc Savage:
Death's Dark Domain

Doc Savage:
Skull Island

TARZAN®

Return to Pal~ul~don

"This first authorized Tarzan novel from the sure hand of pulpmeister Will Murray does a fantastic job of capturing the true spirit of Tarzan, not a grunting monosyllabic cartoonish strongman, but an evolved, brilliant, man of honor equally at home as Lord Greystoke and as the savage *Tarzan the Terrible*."

—*Paul Bishop*

$24.95 softcover
$39.95 hardcover
$5.99 ebook

The Wild Adventures of Edgar Rice Burroughs™

TARZAN®

Return to Pal~ul~don

by Will Murray

WORDSLINGERS

AN EPITAPH FOR THE WESTERN

☞ **WILL MURRAY** ☜

Will Murray's Wordslingers is not only the first in-depth history of the Western pulps, it's one of the best and most important books on the pulps ever written, perfectly capturing the era, the magazines, and the writers, editors, and agents who helped fill their pages. Pulp fans will be fascinated by the rich background provided by hundreds of quotes from the people involved in producing the Western pulps, while writers will benefit from the discussions of characterization and storytelling that prove to be both universal and timeless.

—James Reasoner

$29.95 softcover
$39.95 hardcover
$8.99 ebook

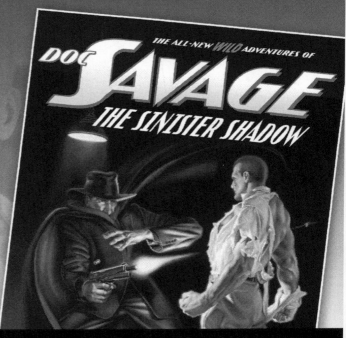

The Wild Adventures of Edgar Rice Burroughs™ Series 9

TARZAN®

CONQUEROR OF MARS
by Will Murray

Made in United States
Orlando, FL
10 January 2024

42319797R00181